THE
UNVACCINATED

Jean Grandbois

To Judith, my raison d'être – I am grateful for the love that you give your fop.
To my children, Pierre, Lisa, and Abigail – decades apart, but equally close to my heart.

1. MAURICE

"Please, I beg you, take him! He's only four, he won't survive on his own. You're the only one I know who isn't vaccinated!"

Maurice "Mo" Biggs listened to the woman's plea as her crying son gripped her leg. *What was her name again?* he wondered. *Jenny? Janet?* The supplicating look in her eyes, tinged with panic, was a sharp contrast to the judgemental glare she and the rest of his friendly neighbors had given him for the last five years. Not that he had missed their pasted smiles.

The early morning sun shone brightly. *Another beautiful spring morning*, he thought. Hungry birds chirped excitedly while searching for food. The row of single-family homes across the street cast long shadows, overlapping each other. One porch after the next, one ornate front door after the next. Each striving for uniqueness in Cobbs Hill, an upper middle-class neighborhood that thrived on sameness. SUVs and pickup trucks dotted each double driveway. The upstate New York scene was idyllic, except for the woman standing in front of him trying to give her child away.

The woman swayed to her left and took a step backward, dragging her little boy with her. She reached for the post on his front porch to steady herself.

"It's coming soon," she said. "He can't see it happen."

A look of primal fear overtook her face, like an animal realizing it had become prey. Fresh tears spilled over, obediently running along dried streaks. She took several deep breaths and seemed to steady herself.

"The dizzy spells are coming more often." She let go of the porch post. "I've already had two this morning."

She's right, Mo thought. He knew that if she already had two dizzy spells this morning, she probably wouldn't make it past the evening. The spells usually started two to three days before death. Once they were coming every hour or so, death was imminent. Complete and sudden heart failure: the victim simply fell over.

Mo looked down at the little boy. He knew nothing about children. Taking on a child while the world was crumbling around him was the worst idea he could imagine. Unfortunately, Mo wasn't very big on thinking before acting. Amy, his last girlfriend, used to playfully call him Rambo. She even made a verb out of it when he made a reckless move.

"You Rambo'ed it again," she would laugh as he stood over some Mo-made disaster in the house or yard. *A lifetime ago*, though it had only been two years. Amy was one more item on the bill he'd had to pay for refusing to get injected. Her media-brainwashed mind, plus the mounting pressure of so-called friends and neighbors, finally drove her away. He wondered if she was having dizzy spells yet. Mo banished the painful thought.

"Hey, kid, do you have a name?" He knelt down at the boy's level. *Rambo*, he thought.

The boy shook his head, still clutching his mother's leg.

"Really? No name? Well, that's so cool. I don't have a name either," he exclaimed with a surprised face. "When people call me, they just say, 'Hey you!'"

The boy's eyes seem to weigh his words.

"Yeah, well, that's going to be a real problem, isn't it? When someone yells, 'Hey you!', we're both going to say, 'What?'".

Now the boy smiled. "No, I have a name. You're being silly."

"Aww, you're luckier than me. What's your name, big guy?"

"Ben," the little boy murmured, lowering his eyes.

"Nice to meet you, Ben. Do you like dinosaurs?"

The boy nodded.

"Well, I've got the coolest dinosaur book in the whole world. Do you want to see it?"

Ben shook his head.

"No? Why not?" Mo asked.

"Mommy says you'll make me sick."

With a blank expression, Mo stared at the woman. It was the best he could muster after years of mistreatment. By now, he had trained himself to hide his anger at the injustice people had flung his way on a regular basis.

"He's all better now," she interjected, with a nervous glance towards Mo, not quite making eye contact. "He won't make you sick, honey, it's OK."

"Look, your mom has to go somewhere, and I've got a dinosaur book just waiting for a little boy to read it. What do you say?"

"I can't read."

Under any other circumstance, he would have found it funny how the boy's four-year-old brain took Mo's words verbatim. Instead, Mo became increasingly anxious, wondering how he would separate Ben from his mother's leg.

"OK, OK, I mean, I'll read the book to you, but you'll get to look at all the pictures. Deal?" Mo asked.

The boy seemed to hesitate. "Is there a T-rex in it?"

Mo feigned an indignant look. "Would it be a real dinosaur book if it didn't have a T-rex?" He prayed it did. He got the book from Amy as a joke when he had turned forty, but had never actually read it. "Of course it has a T-rex," he added.

Ben let go of his mother's leg. Mo reached out for his hand. The woman bent down and kissed her son ferociously on the cheek. His mouth squished up into a fishlike grimace.

"I have to go now, sweetie, but...", she hesitated a moment, "this man will take good care of you, OK?"

She doesn't remember my name either, Mo realized.

"I love you so much. Never forget that," she added.

"Mommy!" Ben cried, reaching out for her as she backed away.

Mo latched onto the boy's outstretched hand. "Come on, Ben, the T-rex is waiting for you."

"Thank you," the woman mouthed silently when Mo glanced her way. She ran off, her shoulders shaking, and her hand covering her mouth.

Mo escorted Ben into the house, shutting the door behind them. He loved the feel of the heavy door shutting off the otherworldly madness on the outside. His suburban oasis had a smooth white tiled entrance hall. An oak banister on the right snaked along the stairs leading to the second floor of the three-bedroom house. Mo didn't bother removing his or Ben's shoes. He led the boy into the living room at the end of the hall where a tall bookcase stood next to the TV.

"Have a seat, Ben." Mo pointed towards the black leather sofa. "Let's see." He crouched down to the bottom shelves of the bookcase. "Here it is." He pulled a tall, slender book out from the last shelf of the pine and white enamel Ikea bookcase. He brought it over to Ben, who had already taken a seat on the sofa.

Ben giggled. "Why is your face on it?"

Mo smiled, looking at the cover. A small picture of Mo's face covered a rather large brontosaurus's head. "My friend thought that would be funny when she gave it to me," Mo explained.

Ben giggled again, his small fingers passing over the taped photograph. He then turned the first pages of the book and looked at the various colorfully illustrated dinosaurs.

Looking for the T-rex, Mo thought. The shock that this boy was now his new charge started to sink in. *What have I done?*

It was ironic that people who had feared getting infected by Mo were now running to him, knowing that he would survive the current apocalyptic death rate. He had survived delta, omicron, the devastating theta, and the host of other variants that came along after them. He had fought for his right to remain unvaccinated, even in the face of the deadliest and most virulent variants. Some shunned him, some resented him, and more than a few expressed a visceral hatred that he couldn't understand.

Ben slipped off the sofa and slammed the dinosaur book onto the coffee table with all the grace of a four-year-old. He kneeled on the carpet and continued reading.

"Easy there, little buddy," Mo said, rescuing his laptop from under the book. *Not that it's much use anymore,* he thought. With the internet down, the chimes of new posts in his provocatively titled blog *You Never Know* had been silenced. His blog had attracted both ends of the extremists. Those who thought he was condemning people to death, and those who were convinced the vaccine was a government sponsored way to inject monitoring or controlling nanotechnology into their bloodstream. Mo had argued that there'd been insufficient time to study the long-term effects of the vaccine. He feared the FDA had recklessly approved its use and saw himself as a bit of a Frances Kelsey, fighting against thalidomide approval in the sixties.

But as the weeks and months of controversy turned into years, with no side effects coming to light, his blog's popularity waned. *Only the crazies left*, he had thought, despondently.

When the elderly started dying, there was a mad scramble to find the cause. Authorities suspected, but failed to identify, a new virus. It wasn't long after the health care workers started dying, the second category of people to be vaccinated, that the authorities laid the link between the COVID-19 vaccine and the mounting deaths. Though they could not explain the reason, they did establish a roughly five-year timeline. Like a ticking time bomb, the vaccinated were dying five years after having had their first shot. The number of boosters also seemed to play a role in the timing of the death. The Vax Plague, or VP, as the headline-hungry media had dubbed it, seemed inescapable.

Extremists still following his blog almost jumped for joy. They had urged him to write some "I told you so" type of entries. But Mo didn't feel any sense of vindication — only sadness and fear.

With most of the health care and virology workers dying in the first months after the VP discovery, research had ground to a halt. The world turned away from understanding the why, to coping with the new reality of their limited remaining time. Some turned to family, some to religion, and others to anarchic violence.

Despite the crumbling society, there were signs of humanity that impressed Mo. Overall, the rate of violence could have been a lot worse. It turned out that at the end of times, humans were not all bands of villains portrayed in shows like *The Walking Dead*. Compassion and a sense of togetherness fueled by trauma held the basic fabric of community together.

Mo seemed incapable of thinking about the future. He had retreated into his house, waiting for — what exactly? *The end of the VP*, he thought. When the dying finished, he would think about the future. For now, he preferred doing the ostrich thing, head in the sand, warming his cans of beans on the BBQ. His mind was incapable of handling anything else. Until Ben unexpectantly plopped into his life.

"Why don't you have a name?" Ben asked.

Ben's question startled Mo out of his reverie. After a month without TV, telephones, or internet, he was getting used to the utter silence in his house.

"A name?" he responded, confused.

"You said you didn't have a name," Ben reaffirmed.

Mo smiled at him. "Oh, I was just kidding," he replied. "My name is Maurice. But you can call me Mo."

"Why would I call you Mo if your name is Maurice?" Ben asked.

"Mo is just short for Maurice."

Ben frowned. "Your name is Maurice, not Mo," he concluded. "I'm hungry," he added.

"So am I. How about peanut butter on crackers?"

"I love peanut butter." Ben nodded emphatically.

Mo entered the adjoining kitchen and gradually opened the pantry door, being careful not to let the precariously stacked jars and cans tumble onto the floor again. Being a vaccine skeptic and a borderline conspiracy theorist had worked in his favor. He had stocked up on necessities before most of the incredulous population understood the significance of the early signs of the VP. Then the looting and hoarding began. People quickly emptied store shelves and supply chains ground to a halt. He still felt somewhat guilty about the six propane tanks for his BBQ, which were locked inside his garage.

Mo froze at the sudden sound of the doorbell chime. *What now?*

He ran back into the living room. "Stay here," he commanded, briefly putting his hand on Ben's shoulder.

2. DEBORAH

"**A**ll set for our adventure, Lucy?" Deborah Kearns asked. She smiled widely, trying to reassure the frightened child clinging to her hand.

Lucy looked up at her intently, saucer-eyed. She neither nodded nor shook her head. Lucy's big brown eyes simply stared at her.

Deb had found Lucy stumbling down the street four days ago. She guessed the child was about three. The girl hadn't been crying, but her dirty, tear-streaked face told a different story. Her clothes had reeked of urine. Her blonde hair had been a tangled, tousled mess. At first, she had shied away when Deb had approached her. But when Deb had offered her a water bottle, Lucy had grabbed it eagerly, put her mouth on it and tilted her head back sharply. A coughing fit had ensued.

"Take your time, sweetie," Deb had urged her.

Lucy still spoke little. Deb could not figure out where she'd come from, nor what had happened to her parents. She didn't understand how a three-year-old managed to get out of her parent's house where, presumably, they had died. Now she was eating and drinking well, beginning what was going to be a slow recovery from whatever trauma she had experienced. She would not let Deb out of her sight. Deb gladly indulged her, rapidly falling in love with the little girl.

There are more like her, Deb thought. *In fact, there will be a lot more like her,* she realized. She had horrible visions of children trapped in homes with well-meaning, but dead, parents. Saving the children had become a primordial drive within Deb.

Schools had mandated vaccines for children aged five and up. It broke Deb's heart that she couldn't save these kids. But she could, and she would, save newborn to four-year-old children who were becoming orphans in droves. Finding them in time was an urgent undertaking. How she would care for them was a problem for another day.

Deb caught a reflection of herself in the mirror above the living room sofa. She passed her fingers through her disheveled shoulder-length hair. Dyeing her hair was her one act of vanity. *Silver Fox* was her color of choice, with streaks of black. It made her feel sexy, despite her current drought of romantic relationships. Her blue eyes stared back at her in the mirror.

I look tired. She hadn't gone for a run in several weeks. The empty streets were creepy enough, but then she had spotted a body on a lawn. That was almost two months ago now, but it had ended her morning runs. Running had always energized her. Her slender body began to feel tired and sluggish when she didn't exercise. *But still, not bad for a sixty-two-year-old kindergarten teacher.* She allowed herself a half-smile. *Retired teacher,* she corrected.

Deb escorted Lucy to the front door, and they

stepped outside into a warm early afternoon. The May sun shone brightly on a near-cloudless day. Spring had always been Deb's favorite season. Summer was too hot, winter too cold, fall too dreary. A cool breeze swept in from Lake Ontario, a frail remnant of an unusually cold winter. Deb had spent her whole life in the Rochester area and appreciated the lake's moderating effect on the weather. Though it sometimes caused a big dump of snow, it took some of the chill off winter. And it cooled you in summer.

"OK, let's go for our walk," Deb announced to Lucy.

They made their way to Winton Road, the main road out of Cobbs Hill. Deb shifted Lucy to her left, to block her view of the United church on the right. Deb thought it was the ugliest building in Rochester. A sprawling, brown-bricked assortment of cubes stacked together in a seemingly haphazard way. But it wasn't the building that Deb was trying to hide. Normally it appeared deserted, except for Sunday service. But now there were scores of people wandering about, seeking comfort in their final moments. There were also bodies that had recently succumbed to the Vax Plague. Deb didn't know how long they'd been there. *Hours or days?* she wondered.

"We're almost there, little girl," Deb said brightly. They crossed the large overpass of the I-490. The interstate was eerily quiet. Abandoned cars dotted the wide ribbon of asphalt that cut through her city. Deb had never thought there'd be a day where she wished for traffic.

"That's the grocery store," Lucy said, perking up.

"Yes, sweetie, very good," Deb exclaimed. "That's where we're going. We're going to borrow a shopping cart and I'm going to give you a ride. Does that sound like fun?"

"A ride in the store?"

"No, that's boring. We're going to ride around the town, right on the sidewalks."

"But the shopping carts are not ours. That's stealing," Lucy said, her tone filled with certainty.

"No, no, I asked them first if I could borrow one," Deb lied.

"And they said yes?"

"That's right."

This seemed to satisfy the young girl.

The Wegmans loomed on their left, just past the empty intersection. The colossal supermarket took up an entire block. No one had bothered replacing the tattered tape that swayed lazily in front of the broken door. Lucy's grip tightened as they neared the dark, cavernous entrance. Deb reached down and lifted the frightened child into her arms. She hoped there were no bodies inside the store. She tried to snuggle Lucy's face into her shoulder, but the child wriggled free and bravely looked at her surroundings.

The floor was littered with discarded debris. Looters weren't interested in cleaning supplies and cosmetics. Deb doubted that there were any food items left in the store. Or toilet paper, for that matter. One large shelving unit had been toppled over. Every cash register was open or smashed. Money seemed rather pointless now. *A force of habit*, thought Deb. Fortunately, there were several shopping carts strewn about the chaotic wreckage.

"What happened?" Lucy asked.

"Looks like someone had a bit of an accident," Deb replied lamely. "Don't worry dear, they'll clean it up soon."

Deb put Lucy down next to the nearest shopping cart. It was lying on its side, inexplicably filled with paper towel packages. Deb scooped out the rolls and righted the cart. Her shoulders relaxed gratefully as she dumped her heavy backpack into the cart. She unzipped the side pocket, pulled out a water bottle, and offered Lucy a drink. The saucer eyes were back, gliding right and left as she shook her head.

"Up you go," Deb said, lifting Lucy into the cart. "First, we'll take a little ride in the store, then we'll go back outside, OK?"

Saucer eyes glided up and down.

Deb followed a familiar path through Wegmans, heading for the Home section. The tingling on the back of her neck increased as the daylight radiating from the entrance receded behind them. *A flashlight would have been nice*, Deb chastised herself. The shopping cart careened through the aisles, narrowly avoiding the bigger piles of debris.

"I'm scared," Lucy said.

"I know, honey, hang in there."

The zig-zagging cart decelerated as they entered

the Home section. Deb's heart rate slowed a few notches at the sight of the jumbled slew of towels and bedding. She smiled at Lucy.

"Now you're going to ride in comfort, little girl."

Deb had been thinking of the logistics of her orphan search. If she found babies, how would she bring them home? A shopping cart with plenty of padding was all she could think of. With a small comforter, she made a cozy corner in the cart for Lucy. Deb added two pillows, a half dozen large fluffy white towels, and a few packages of bedsheets.

"Why do we need all those?" Lucy asked. Her feet kicked at the piles of linens crowding her.

"Because we're going to see if we can find you some friends. And they'll want to be all cozy-comfy like you are."

"I don't want friends." A perfect, almost cartoonish pout emerged from her face.

"Well, if they are friends, then that means you like playing with them, right?"

"I won't like playing with them. They're not my friends!"

"Sweetie, you haven't even met them." Deb laughed.

The walk towards the sunlit entrance was far less frantic. Lucy's eyes were no longer saucers, and she began exploring her little nest in the cart. Deb slowed her pace even more, as the tension left her shoulders.

"They used to shoot looters, you know."

The gruff voice behind them startled Deb, and

the cart shook under her tightened grip. A tingling sensation slithered up her spine. She whipped her head around towards the voice, the cart swinging around with her. A man emerged from the shadow of a partially toppled display of seasonal products. He stood next to an incongruent poster of a smiling family sitting on a blanket with a picnic basket, the soon-to-be summer sun shining on them. His penetrating eyes scanned in turn Deb, Lucy, and their loaded shopping cart.

"Where are you ladies headed with all that stuff?" he asked. "Are you planning a little sleepover party?"

His cold, menacing smile rendered Deb speechless. A week's stubble formed a patchwork of gray over his round, immense face. Deb began stepping backwards. The man lumbered forward one step, two steps.

"Please," Deb pleaded, her eyes shifting to Lucy.

The man appeared confused and stumbled backwards. With a crash of sunblock bottles, the family of four, along with their picnic basket, lay face down on the floor.

"Heh, heh," the man chuckled. "That was the fourth one this morning. Don't think I'll be making it to your sleepover, ladies, sorry."

Deb stopped in her tracks. The man was clearly a danger and yet would die imminently.

"Is there anything—" she stammered.

"Get the fuck out of here."

Deb hesitated no longer. She whipped the cart around, Lucy leaning into the comforter.

"Your time will come," he shouted, as she broke into a run towards the entrance. "You wait till you get your first one, then see how you feel about your fucking blankets and shit."

Deb breathed deeply when they made it outside.

"Why was he angry?" Lucy asked. "Is it because we took the shopping cart?"

"No sweetie," Deb panted. "He's just having a bad day. He's grumpy is all."

"He said a bad word." Her little eyebrows curved into a frown.

"Yes, he did, and that wasn't very nice, honey."

She ran across the parking lot. A quick glance in either direction, by force of habit, for the streets were deserted. Then she bolted across the intersection, the cart's hard wheels bouncing Lucy around her nest. The cacophonous rattling of the cart on the sidewalk turned several heads as they passed the church. Fortunately, no one called out or followed. Deb's pounding pulse finally slowed when they turned the corner and re-entered her blissfully quiet block.

"OK, let's see if we can meet some new people," Deb said.

Lucy crossed her arms with her hands in tight little fists. "I don't want friends," she warned.

Now how, exactly, does one go about this? Deb thought. It felt surreal to knock on someone's door and ask if they wanted to give her their children. And yet that was precisely what she was about to do. She had pondered about this moment for several days and had come up with zero alternatives.

The first house on the corner was a tall, squarely built white and dark brown two-story home. Deb pushed the cart up to the pillared front porch. She lifted Lucy out of the cart and put her on the first step leading up to the porch.

"Let's see if anybody's home," Deb said. A sense of dread filled her, as her feet climbed the four stuccoed steps to the porch. With a deep breath, she pressed the doorbell.

After what seemed like an eternity, but was under a minute, Deb resorted to knocking hard on the door.

"I don't think anyone's home," Lucy said.

"You're probably right," Deb nodded. "But let's peek through the windows and see for sure."

The curtains were drawn behind the large window on the door's right. Deb picked up Lucy, descended the porch steps, and headed along the walkway on the right side of the house. There were no ground-floor windows on this side. Deb hesitated in front of the gate leading into the backyard. With a firm grip on the handle, she turned the lever down and pushed the gate open.

The small yard was empty, save for the shed at the rear. No one had cut the grass recently. Spring growth reached above her ankles as she made her way along the back wall of the house. A semi-circular paving stone patio spilled out underneath the sliding patio door. Keeping Lucy to the side, Deb leaned forward to peer through the glass door.

She examined the kitchen through the glass. Dirty dishes spilled out of the sink and onto the counter. The owners had piled more dishes onto the natural pine kitchen table. The digital clock on the oven blinked a steady rhythm. A half dozen pizza boxes on the floor leaned against an overflowing recycling bin.

Pizza? They haven't delivered pizza around here in at least a month, thought Deb.

The house was in disarray, but hadn't been looted or vandalized. Deb pressed her ear to the glass. There were no perceptible sounds from inside. She rapped the glass sharply.

"Hello?" she called out. She rapped again. Ear to the glass one more time.

"I was right," Lucy said proudly.

The next five houses were a repeat of the first. Deb had brought a notebook and pen in her backpack. She kept track of houses that she had visited. She assumed she would find symptom-free parents that would be understandably unwilling to hand over their children. These she would keep tabs on, ready to swoop in when the parents started having dizzy spells. Or died.

That's the plan, she thought, placing the pen back into her pocket. Pushing aside her doubts and growing discouragement, she moved on to the next house. The sand-colored vinyl siding gave way to brick midway down the A-frame structure. The curtains were drawn in all three windows: the double pane to the left of the door, the window on the second floor, and the window over the attached garage.

Lucy reached her arms out to Deb — she knew the routine. Up, out of the cart, and together they marched up the steps to the front door. Deb rang and waited. She was about to knock when she heard a tapping on the window a few feet away. With Lucy in tow, she went down the stairs and looked into the window.

A man had parted the curtains. He looked them over, then leaned right and left, scanning the front of the house. With a curt nod to Deb, he pointed to the door. By the time Deb and Lucy went up the stairs, the man stood in the open doorway. He was tall, around six feet, and thin. His closely cropped black hair had receded at the top. Gray patches creeped back along the temples. Deb estimated he was in his late 40s or early 50s. A day-old stubble covered his chin and the sides of his face. Piercing brown eyes studied Deb. A hand nervously ticked, fingers tapping on his hip.

"Can I help you?" he asked.

Deb spotted a little boy's face peering out from behind the wall of the entrance hallway. She cleared her throat.

"Um, hi," she began. "I'm not really sure how to say this, but do you need help with your child?"

"He's not" — the man hesitated — "we're fine," he finished.

"OK, you are now, but, um, what about dizzy spells? Have you had any yet?"

"No, I haven't. Like I said, we're fine, but thanks for your concern." He began to shut the door.

"Sir, wait!" Deb added, speaking more quickly now. "Look, I get it. It's hard to think about this, but you need to consider your little boy. What if you, well, what if the dizzy spells start coming?"

The man frowned. "And what about when the dizzy spells start coming with you? Then what?"

"They won't. I'm not vaccinated."

The man's eyes opened wide. He tried to speak, but his mouth comically remained half opened. After a moment, his shoulders sagged. He took a deep, slow breath.

"Neither am I."

Now it was Deb's turn to freeze. *Another unvaccinated!*

"Wow, I don't know what to say," she stammered. "You're the first one I've met since, well, since all this started."

"Same here," the man replied. "So yeah, I'm fine. We don't need help. Good luck to you."

He shut the door with a parting nod and a perfunctory smile. Deb stood in front of the door, trying to process the shock of finding another adult like her.

Someone who's not going to die, she thought. She pounced forward and beat her fist on the door.

"Sir, come back," she shouted, her face close to the door. He opened the door quickly, and they stood toe to toe. Confusion washed over his face.

"I need your help," Deb began. "They need your

help."

"Who?"

"The children! Lucy here was orphaned last week. There will be thousands of children getting orphaned." She lowered her voice to a whisper, "or have already lost their parents and are alone. We need to save them."

"So, what's your plan? Go around and fill your shopping cart with kids? And then what?"

"Well, yes, for the first part. That's urgent. We can figure out everything else later. But there's no time to plan, first we have to find the abandoned, um, little ones."

Deb was well aware of a three-year-old's ability to listen to every word that the adults said when the child sensed tension. She reached down and patted Lucy's head reassuringly.

"Please, will you help me?" Deb pleaded.

"I... I don't —"

"My name is Deborah Kearns," she pressed on, and grabbed his hand for a firm shake. She always surprised herself when her rare bouts of assertiveness came through.

"Maurice Biggs," he answered. "You can call me Mo. But I haven't agreed to anything yet, crazy lady."

He said 'yet'! Deb smiled, and stepped into Mo's house.

3. JESSICA

The bodies were stacked like cordwood. Hallways, offices, even their old lunch room had rows of piled up bodies. The crematorium's cold room had filled first, with bodies stacked up to Jessica's shoulder height. And at five feet ten, she was not a short woman. Fortunately, Mason, her director, had had the foresight to order a large shipment of body bags from the military base at Fort Drum. The influx of bodies had slowed to a trickle now that emergency services had ceased operations. Jessica was mostly dealing with the backlog. Some mornings there would be a body or two dumped near her work's entrance. And occasionally someone had the courage to haul in a loved one's body personally. They exchanged no money, only a few words of gratitude on one side and condolences on the other.

Mason had died almost three weeks ago. One day she caught him having a dizzy spell as he helped her move a body onto a gurney. The next day he didn't show up for work. He had always been kind to her and she missed him. He had known she was far overqualified for the job, and he had treated her with respect. Being a twenty-nine-year-old med school dropout was not exactly a recognized qualification. But Mason had handled her failure well and had never made her feel like a disappointment. She felt that way plenty of times because of her worst enemy, herself.

Her other colleague had stopped showing up for work a few days after Mason had died. Jessica didn't know if he had also died, or given up. She wasn't sure why she kept coming to work, nor how long she would continue to do so. It felt respectful to deal with the dead as long as she could. But her self-imposed, and isolated, twelve-hour shifts were taking their toll on both her physical and mental states.

Jessica checked the timer on the electric furnace. Forty-two minutes to go before the current cremation was complete. Mason had been proud to be a driving force in converting their crematorium from gas to electric furnaces. She recalled how he had argued from a renewable energy point of view, despite an increase in the cost of cremation. Jessica had patiently listened to his calculations of kilowatt hours per body, with a burn temperature of sixteen-hundred degrees Fahrenheit. Then he would zoom in on the key points of approximately thirty-five dollars of energy per body, and a sixty-to-ninety-minute burn time. Mason's dark sense of humor manifested itself when he quipped that if they could drum up more business, the cost per body would decrease, since the furnaces would not have to be cooled and reheated each time. *Probably cut our costs in half at this point*, Jessica thought, smiling sadly, wishing that she could joke with Mason just one last time.

She glanced at the wall clock — 1:35. She had been at work since seven that morning. *Halfway*, she thought, smiling to herself. Wearily, she stood, and started rolling the empty gurney towards the door.

The room plunged into darkness.

Jessica froze, waiting for the power to come back on. Other than the tick-tick-ticking of the cooling furnace, there was utter silence. She waited for her eyes to adjust, but the unrelenting cloak of absolute blackness persisted. When it became apparent that the power was not coming back anytime soon, if at all, Jessica pushed the gurney aside. Hands outstretched, she made her way in the general direction of the door. Soon her hands touched the wall.

Right or left, she wondered. She edged right and found the door jamb. She had walked through this building thousands of times, and thought she knew her way around without hesitation. But the total darkness disoriented her far more than she could have imagined. With a grimace, she felt her way along the bagged bodies stacked in the corridor. Feet, legs, chests, heads — all felt uncomfortably familiar under her probing hands. The crinkling of the vinyl seemed impossibly loud in the darkness. When her left hand slipped off the last body's head, Jessica knew she had reached the end of the corridor.

Left, through the doors, up the stairs on the right, she instructed herself. She crossed the short empty space in the middle of the hallway until her hands met the next row of bags. Turning left, she followed these until her shoulder unexpectedly hit the doors leading to the stairwell. She reached down to the push bar and opened the door wide. With a heightened sense of caution, she gingerly searched for the first step with her foot. She found it and reached clumsily for the handrail. Confident now, she began climbing the first set of steps out of the basement. At the landing she turned and finally saw a glint of light flowing out from the bottom of the door above her. She climbed the next set of stairs and opened a door into the semi-gloom of the ground-floor interior offices. She rushed to the front office, and burst through the door into the bright sunshine.

Now what? she thought. She breathed deeply, enjoying the fresh spring air. The immediate answer was of course to head back to her basement apartment near the university campus. But longer term — she had buried herself in her work rather than deal with that all-important question.

She walked through the gates of the crematory, and headed south on Mt Hope Avenue. It was strange walking the fifteen-minute route in broad daylight. She both arrived and left work in the semi-darkness. The emptiness of the stores and restaurants seemed lonelier under the bright sun.

My kingdom for a Grande Pumpkin Spice Latte with Extra Chocolate Malt Powder, she thought, passing the abandoned Starbucks. It wasn't until she reached the liquor store that she saw another person on the street. She was too close to avoid him by crossing the road. That in itself was an invitation for trouble. He must have noticed the break in her stride before speaking.

"You don't need to worry about me, miss." Jessica detected a slight slur in his speech. An assortment of cans surrounded the man. His eyes followed her gaze, and he then sat up straighter.

"Those aren't all mine," he assured her. "There've been others before me, from what I can gather. All that's left now is these shitty fruity beers, pardon my French. 'Pardon my French'?" he chuckled. "OK well, they may taste shitty, but they work." He placed the can he had in his hand down on the sidewalk next to him.

"Dr Stephen Banster," he said gregariously, reaching a hand out to her without standing.

"Nice meeting you," Jessica replied, picking up her pace as she passed him. She gave him a wide berth, easily avoiding his outstretched hand.

"I've had five since this morning," he called out behind her. "The spells, I mean, not the fruity beers," he chuckled.

Jessica paused, then turned to him, trying to evaluate the veracity of his words.

"Should be any time now," he added softly. The sun sparkled on his watery eyes. His voice, shakier now, pleaded, "please, can you sit with me a minute?"

Jessica hesitated a few seconds more before heading back to him. She stood next to him, looking at his frightened face. He pushed some cans out of the way and patted the sidewalk next to him. She sat awkwardly, not too close to him, but not so far that he would ask her to come closer.

"Thank you," he said to her, smiling.

"You're welcome," she said automatically. "I'm so sorry about... about the spells."

He shrugged. "I don't want to talk about that. Tell me something about you. Who are you? Where are you going?"

"OK, well, to start, I'm Jessica Albert," she reached out her hand to him. He grabbed it with his right hand and placed his left over their joined hands.

"Very pleased to meet you, Jessica Albert," he said warmly.

"Let's see, I work, well, I worked as a crematory technician," she continued, pointing up the street with a nod of her head. "The power just went out, so I guess I'm not working anymore. And so, I'm heading back home now."

"Crematory technician? I've gotta ask, what on earth led you to that career? I mean did you just wake up one morning and decide 'I want to be a crematory technician'?"

His smile took the sting out of his words.

"No, that's not exactly how it happened. I started out in med school at RU. But, uh, things didn't work out." Unwanted images of her father flashed through her mind, as they so often did. "I needed a job, there was a posting at Mount Hope, and well, two years later, here I am still."

"I worked at the hospital. Did you intern there?

Would be strange if we had actually met before without realizing it."

Jessica shook her head. "No, never made it to an internship, dropped out before then."

"So what's the plan now?" he asked.

"I don't know. Work has kept me busy, I haven't had time to think about what's next. But now tell me something about you."

"Well, I went to med school in Boston, actually," he began.

"Stop," Jessica interrupted. "I don't want to know that stuff. Tell me something about the real you, not your career."

His eyes seem to appraise her anew.

"OK, well if you insist on taking advantage of a mildly drunk and dying man, we can go deeper then, Miss Jessica Albert."

"No, no, I'm sorry, tell me whatever you want."

The man laughed out loud this time.

"I'm pulling your leg, my dear. I'm actually flattered that you want to hear more personal details. You're very kind — to a mildly drunk and dying man," he added with a mischievous smile.

"Do you know what solipsism is?" he asked her suddenly.

Jessica shook her head.

"Well, in a nutshell, it's the belief that nothing exists except yourself. So anything I see or hear is something my own mind made up."

Jessica's eyebrows raised up. "And you believe this?"

"My mind put those words in your mouth." The mischievous smile again. It took decades off his age, allowing the little boy that once was, to shine through again in these last moments of life.

"OK, seriously, no," he answered. "But as a teenager, I do remember wondering about it. Because if it was true, then my brain could be inventing everything that happens around me. It was really quite mind-blowing as a concept."

He paused a moment. Jessica let him gather his thoughts in silence. If he chose this topic, it must be important to him, she reasoned.

"Now of course, with an adult, logical mind, I don't believe that concept. But if I really have to be honest, it still crossed my mind now and then, over the years. Kind of a remnant fascination from adolescence."

He absently scratched his gray stubble before continuing.

"So it wasn't until right now, when death is imminent, that I am fully, one hundred percent convinced of the fallacy of solipsism. In fact, it would be a huge egotistical leap to conclude that everything ends when I die. That you ceased to exist, Jessica Albert," he added, smiling at her once more.

"Thanks for sharing that," Jessica told him earnestly.

"Ha, now you're making me feel like I'm at an AA meeting."

Now it was Jessica's turn to laugh.

"Your turn, top that one for being up close

and personal with a no-longer-a-stranger," he challenged her.

Jessica thought of her father again. And of — the Other. She could not name him, for she never knew who he was. She shuddered. Dare she talk about them to this dying man? She never spoke to anyone about the violence, the shame, the pain. Nor about how, despite her best efforts, she knew that they had shaped her life. They had changed the course of what could have been.

The sound of clattering empty beer cans shook her out of her reverie. Stephen had slumped over into the pile of shitty fruity beer cans on his left. Jessica stared at his prone body in shock. She knew it was coming, but the suddenness of it still floored her. She reached over, touching his hip, and shook him gently.

"Stephen?" she called out.

Wiping a welling tear from her eye, she stood up shakily. She bent down and straightened his body, wanting to make his last resting place more comfortable. She placed her hand on his chest, saying goodbye without words. Then she stood straight up once again and resumed her walk towards her apartment.

In the early days of the VP she would have called Body Pickup to report his death. She could not remember the official name of the service. From almost day one it was known colloquially as Body Pickup. Then the phones had stopped working. Rag-tag groups of volunteers kept the streets mostly clear of bodies. Jessica met several of these altruistic people while working at the crematory. The flow of bodies had started to peter out at work, as the volunteers also succumbed to the VP. But the streets remained relatively body free. She thought that most people were hunkering down at home, waiting it out. Besides, where could they go with everything shut down? She hoped some of the volunteer groups were still working, and would pick up Stephen.

A police cruiser rolled up to the intersection one block ahead of Jessica. She froze, hardly believing her eyes. Emergency services were long gone, this was like a minor miracle. A symbol of safety, of civilization pre-VP. She shouted, and ran towards the vehicle, arms waving madly. The cruiser turned right and headed towards her, on the wrong side of the empty street.

Jessica's smile disappeared when she peered inside the cruiser as it pulled up next to her. Trash littered the inside of the car. Bags of chips, soda cans, and more that a few beer cans were strewn about the floor next to the officer. The trash heap continued in the rear seat as well. The officer's uniform was badly wrinkled and had an indeterminate number of strains on it. The officer himself blended well with the surrounding chaos. His face was pock-marked with healed blemishes. His almost shoulder length, disheveled black hair looked like it had not encountered any shampoo in quite some time. Cold, brown eyes studied Jessica briefly before he reached for his door and climbed out of his cruiser.

This isn't right, Jessica thought wildly. Jessica stumbled backwards two steps. Her heart was racing.

The officer stopped mid-stride when he saw her face. He absently wiped down his uniform, failing to make it look any neater. He held out his two hands, palms facing Jessica.

"It's OK ma'am, I'm sorry about how I look. Are you OK? You waved me down, do you need help?"

He slowly took a step forward, and Jessica took one backward.

"Look, I would be scared too if I saw myself," he chuckled. "Truth is, there aren't many of us left, so we're pretty much working all the time. Hell, for all I know I'm the last cop in Rochester. I haven't heard any radio chatter in at least a week."

He stopped advancing again.

"Look, if you don't need help, I can go right now. Do you want me to leave?"

Jessica hesitated before blurting out, "a man just died a few blocks back that way."

The officer followed her pointing finger and grunted.

"Guess we need to clean that up." He scratched the stubble on his right cheek. "I don't suppose you can help me with that, huh?"

"What are you going to do with him?" Jessica asked.

"We've been taking them to the morgue downtown," he answered.

"But the morgue is tiny, it was overrun months

33

ago," Jessica replied.

The man cleared his throat, bowed his head slightly, as his eyes shifted left and right. Jessica's eyes widened in surprise.

"Is it true then? I've heard the rumors, but thought it was just that, rumors."

"Rumors?" he asked.

"Come on, you know what I mean. Mass burials, even open pits for burning. So it's true then?"

The officer's eyes lit up briefly, and he gave a small nod. "I can't talk about that. Will you help me load the body?"

"Sure," Jessica replied, in mild shock at his confirmation.

He opened the back door of the cruiser and cleared a space for her to sit. Jessica slid into the seat. The officer shut the door and headed towards the front of the car. He had left his door open, and so slipped behind the wheel with one smooth motion.

As the cruiser advanced, Jessica regretted her choice. The car stank of garbage. *I should have walked*, she thought.

"He's right over there, in front of the liquor store."

The officer didn't acknowledge her directions. The cruiser picked up speed, passing the liquor store seconds later. Jessica's pulse quickened, as panic surged through her.

"Where are we going?" she demanded.

"Something I wanna show you first."

"I don't want to see anything. I just wanted to help you load that man's body, and that's it."

"Have you ever been on top of the water towers?" he asked.

Jessica's eyebrows furrowed. Had she heard him correctly?

"The view is beautiful," he continued. "You can see for miles on a day like this. Best view of the city, and of course there's the water reservoir. Like our own small private lake. Beautiful."

"I want to get out now. Please stop the car, now!" She heard her voice cracking from the strain as she shouted.

The man met her eyes in the rear-view mirror. When he flashed a wide-open grin at her, she noticed some missing teeth, and what looked like blackened teeth.

Never again! she screamed inside, with an internal voice that she hardly recognized. Animal instinct kicked in as she tried to open the door of the speeding cruiser. Locked. She searched frantically for handles or buttons to roll down the window. Nothing. She grabbed at the cage-like wire separating her from the front seat.

"What's your problem?" the driver asked. "Got a hot date you don't wanna miss?" He laughed wickedly.

Now she screamed out loud. Her fists pounded the cage wire, the doors, the seats. Rage coursed through her veins. She was unable to think past the fury of the all too familiar feeling of helplessness.

"Hey! Calm the fuck down," he shouted back at her. The cruiser swerved as he reached for his side arm. He waved it wildly in her general direction.

"I wasn't going to hurt you, but if you don't shut the fuck up right now, I'm going to kill you right fucking now."

Jessica forced herself to stop screaming. She frantically sought an escape from this madman.

"That's better," he said, lowering his voice. "I told you, I just want to show you the city from the top of the tower. No need to go all fucking ballistic on me. Jesus Christ," his voice trailed off.

The two abandoned water towers were in a wooded section near the north end of the Cobbs Hill reservoir. Almost the size of a man-made lake, the reservoir had been supplying drinking water to Rochester for over a century. Located in the middle of Cobbs Hill Park, it attracted the usual crowd of joggers, dog walkers, and sun bathers. Jessica had wandered over to the park several times, especially since moving into her apartment near the university. It was a twenty-minute bike ride — perfect for a Sunday afternoon getaway. Today's horrific drive up Reservoir Road was a sharp contrast to those idyllic excursions.

The cruiser came to a stop at the Monroe County Radio Center. The top of Cobbs Hill Park, aside from the water reservoir, also housed the police and emergency services communications facility. The radio tower that reached hundreds of feet towards the sky dominated the gray, two-story cinderblock building.

Jessica remembered being bored by the host of

training and safety videos that they had forced her to watch as a municipal employee. And yet the topic of workplace violence stuck with her. Run away if you can, hide if there's no chance to run, and the last resort: fight. She slackened the muscles of her face, doing her best to look calm.

"You promise you'll let me go after the water tower?" she asked in a shaky voice. She didn't have to fake the timid shakiness.

"Yup," he answered, stepping out of the car. "As long as you don't give me no trouble."

She positioned herself in the middle of the back seat. As soon as he started opening the rear door, she spun, whipping her legs up and kicking the door out with both feet. The door hit his body with a gratifying thump, knocking him to the ground. With a guttural scream she scrambled out of the car and turned to her would-be assailant. He was already getting up. She kicked violently. He blocked her first kick with his arm. Pain shot through her shinbone. She moved a step aside, took better aim and connected with the side of his face. With a howl of pain, he rolled over. Jessica ran towards the woods.

"You bitch! Stop," he screamed shrilly.

A shot rang out. Jessica continued to run. A second shot. This time, bits of gravel stung the back of her legs. She could hear his heavy footsteps pounding towards her.

"Stop now or the next one's in your back," he screamed at her.

Jessica hesitated. Keep running and likely get shot, or face him and try again later? Her brief hesitation was enough for him to catch up to her. Before she could turn to face him, she was airborne. A truck couldn't have done a better job than his flying tackle. He landed on top of her, knocking the breath out of her. Her ears were ringing from the impact of the side of her head hitting the pavement.

"No tower for you, we're doing it right here then!"

She was too stunned to fight back. Her mind was already withdrawing into her familiar protective space. She sensed him tugging at her pants. Then a sound like an explosion ripped through her ringing ears. Blood spattered her face. Half the man's head disappeared. His body went limp and fell onto her. She screamed, shoving him aside. Hysteria propelled her to her feet. Without a look behind her, she ran to the radio complex.

4. DARNELL

"**O**ne," Darnell "Dee" Tiggs murmured, his hand on the dead gang leader's chest. Marquis had been more than a leader. He'd been Dee's mentor since he was barely old enough to join a gang. Marquis had in fact recruited him after watching eleven-year-old Dee beat up a kid two years older than he was. Dee couldn't remember who the kid was, or what the fight was about. But it had changed his life, lifting him out of anonymity, and poverty. A one-word farewell seemed pitifully inadequate, despite being perfectly respectful.

"You're the boss now, Dee," Javon said behind him.

The boss of what? Dee thought. The Vax Plague had decimated the gang. Marquis had been the latest, and last, victim of the VP. Dee and Javon were the only ones who weren't vaccinated. Dee secretly did not trust the vaccine. He had an innate distrust of all medical procedures. Outwardly he projected a bravado about the pandemic. Nothing could take him down — he didn't need no vaccine. Marquis thought he was crazy, but he didn't push it.

Javon had followed Dee's lead. He'd mimicked his boasting and swaggered about, mocking those getting the vaccine. Dee was to Javon what Marquis had been to Dee. He had recruited Javon and strived to be as good a mentor as Marquis. But it was hard.

Javon simply wasn't very smart. And too much of a follower, in Dee's opinion. He'd tried to correct the latter, but could do nothing about the former. And now it was just the two of them. His wariness of injections had inadvertently saved Javon's life, which secured a lifelong loyalty from him.

"Grab your sawed-off, bro. Time to get a new place," Dee said.

Dee stood up and checked his guns. He had tucked the Glock, his weapon of choice, into his front waistband. Short, fast, and deadly. A .44 Magnum Desert Eagle rested uncomfortably in an oversized nylon ankle holster. It packed a bigger punch, when he needed it. And finally, he checked the smaller .22 pistol in his rear waistband. As the gang's enforcer, Dee had become used to being the most heavily armed. He had moved from two guns to three when he ran out of bullets in one particularly violent encounter. Never again, he'd told himself. Since moving to three guns, there had been a handful of occasions where he needed them all.

"Take Marquis' four-pounder too," he added.

"But," Javon hesitated, looking from the prone Marquis to Dee.

"He ain't gonna need it no more, Javon," Dee said impatiently.

"Don't feel right," Javon mumbled. But he bent down and took the 40-caliber pistol. His shoulder-length dreadlocks danced in mid-air as he bent and rose again. At five-foot-eleven, Javon topped Dee by a good two inches. Where Javon was tall and slim,

Dee was short and powerfully built, with more of a barrel-shaped upper body. In contrast to Javon, he had a short drop fade afro. In a fight, or a gun fight, the last thing Dee wanted was hair impairing his vision, or being a convenient handle for an opponent to pull. A close-cut goatee added to his fearsome look. Dee didn't style his hair for vanity. He styled it for functionality and intimidation.

It was uncommon for a gang member to be both an enforcer and the leader's lieutenant. Dee had twenty-three kills to his name. There might have been more, it was hard to count kills in gang wars. But the twenty-three were up close and personal. At first, he'd tried to remember each one, but with time they faded into a blur of faces. Fear, defiance, anger, even peace — he'd seen almost every human emotion on those he had eliminated.

"Why we moving, Boss? What's the deal?" Javon asked.

Dee's eyes scanned their surroundings. Union Heights had one of the highest crime rates in Rochester. They were in the back parking lot of their low-rise housing project. A thin, peeling, faux-brick veneer covered ugly rows of poured concrete units. Each unit was a two or three story narrow slice of the structures. The good people of Rochester avoided this area during the day. And the night— it belonged to Dee and his crew. The streets were deserted at night, except for gang members and the police. Both patrolling what they considered to be their streets. Until the VP of course; now the streets were simply deserted.

"We don't need to stay here no more. We're going house-shopping." Dee grinned at his friend.

"For real? I like that," Javon smiled. "Don't need no bank neither."

"Where would you like to live, bro? Strong? Cobbs Hill? Upper Monroe?"

Javon hesitated but for a moment.

"Cobbs Hill, then we can look down at our kingdom." Javon's wide, toothy grin amused Dee.

"Cobbs Hill, then." Dee nodded.

"I want a house near that fancy park," Javon added excitedly. "A bro can see for miles up there. That place is prime, B."

Dee wasn't sure if Javon had ever ventured that far out of their neighborhood. It was less than five miles from Union Heights, but it was a world away. He certainly wouldn't challenge Javon on that minor detail. Boasting was part of gang culture, and calling him on it wouldn't be cool.

They walked over to their car, which was blocking the entrance to the parking lot. *Old habits die hard*, Dee thought. Preventing surprise attacks when exposed had long ago become second nature to them. But with everyone gone now, these extra precautions were unnecessary. The men climbed into their black Range Rover. Javon always drove, while Dee scanned the streets ahead, and behind. They headed south towards the Ford Street bridge. The bridge was one of eight downtown bridges over the Genesee River. The river sliced Rochester in two, both geographically and demographically.

"Whoa, whoa, whoa, whoa," Dee said, waving his hand to tell Javon to slow down.

"What the?" Javon muttered, when he spotted what had attracted Dee's attention.

The Rover pulled up to a small boy standing in the middle of the road. He neither waved for help, nor tried to run away. He stared up at Dee as he got out of the car and stood in front of him. His tear-streaked face belied the frowning, angry look he gave Dee. A comical pout completed the picture of childlike defiance.

"What's going on here, Little Bro?" Dee asked.

"Nuthin'," the boy answered, his voice cracking.

Dee bent down to be at eye-level with the boy.

"What're you doing out here one your own, shorty? Where your parents at?"

"Sleeping," the boy muttered.

Dee hesitated, unsure how to clarify what he feared the boy meant.

"The big sleep? They not waking up no more?"

The boy nodded, fresh tears welling up in his eyes.

"You better come with us then," Dee said, standing up. "Come on, get in the car."

"What the fuck, Dee?" Javon interjected, lifting his hands up in the air.

"So, what, you want to leave him here?" asked Dee.

"Hells yeah! What are we supposed to do with a kid?"

"Then he's gonna die. Wanna off him yourself?"

Javon responded with an exasperated sigh and headed back into the driver's seat.

"Come on, Little Bro, get in the car," Dee said.

The boy shook his head emphatically.

"You can't stay here alone, we ain't gonna hurt you."

"My sister's sick."

"Your sister? So you do have someone taking care of you."

"She's little."

"OK, let's check this out, where she at?"

The boy pointed towards a small street.

"Don't just point, come on, show me."

Dee followed the boy off the main road and onto an adjoining residential street.

"Now what?" Javon called from the car. Dee waved him back. He didn't need Javon making the kid more nervous than he already was.

They crossed one intersection before the boy stopped in front of a small, mint-green dilapidated house. The front door was ajar. Dee could hear a faint baby's cry from where he stood.

"Shit," he muttered, as he stepped towards the door.

He was within a yard of the door when he first smelled the rotting corpses.

"Stay here," he told the boy, and entered the house. Stairs on the right led towards the wailing. On the left, a dead woman lay on the sofa. He didn't stop to assess the state of decay, but bounded up the stairs, two at a time. He followed the cries to the second room on the right. Several milk bottles were scattered on the floor, and an empty bottle lay in the crib next to the crying baby. A dirty diaper was on the floor. Several other unsoiled diapers were bunched and scattered in the crib. Dee guessed that the boy had tried to put them on his little sister, but failed. The naked child stank of feces and urine.

Dee had never taken care of a baby. He was the fourth of five children, and his little sister was only a year and a half younger. His two older brothers, and an older sister, were all within seven years of his own age. All were dead now.

OK, clean the kid, find some milk, and get out of here.

He delicately picked up the child, trying his best to maintain his cool while she screamed the unignorable shriek of a baby in need. He headed down the hall looking for a bathroom and found it on the left. The missing father was decomposing in a bath full of opaque water.

"Fuck!" he exclaimed. The stench was at its worst. He pivoted and headed back to the main floor. The boy had ignored his instructions and stood at the foot of the stairs.

"Is she sick?" he asked Dee.

"I don't know. I need to clean her. Can you find me a towel or something?"

The boy nodded and headed up the stairs.

"No, no, not up there." Dee knew the boy had already seen everything there was to see in the house. Even so, he couldn't let him go back upstairs just to fetch towels in the gruesome bathroom.

"Come with me to the kitchen," Dee instructed. He walked down the hallway looking for the kitchen. It was the last room on the right. Another disaster area. Dee thought the boy must have been rummaging for food for days. He headed for the sink, removed the dishes in it with one hand, and turned on the faucet. A dirty dishcloth lay in a bunched heap under some plates. He pulled it out, and rinsed it as best as he could with one hand. The water was frigid. He placed the baby on the cold countertop and wiped her down with the wet cloth. It surprised him that she could increase the volume of her cries a few more notches.

The boy tapped his hip. Dee looked at him, with an unfamiliar feeling of being overwhelmed. The boy offered him a small hand towel.

"Good man," he praised the boy. He wrapped the towel around her tiny body. It barely covered the shivering child.

"Does she have any food left?" he asked the boy.

"Milk is all gone," the boy answered.

"Fuck, fuck, fuck!" Dee said, his eyes scanning the kitchen. An empty milk bottle lay on the counter. He grabbed it and dropped it on the floor in his haste. He bent and picked it up off the floor, the baby flopping in his arm and screaming all the louder. A quick rinse of the bottle in the sink, then he filled it with cold water, and brought the nipple to the baby's mouth. She latched onto it immediately, sucking greedily. And then she coughed, spat out some of the water, her eyes open wide in shock. A brief second of silence followed, and then she wailed again.

"I know it ain't your mama's milk, but it's all I got," Dee told her soothingly.

The baby instinctively took in the nipple again and suckled. Loud protests followed, and more sucking.

Good enough, Dee thought, and hurried out the front door. The little boy obediently followed in tow.

"What the fuck?" Javon asked, stamping his foot on the pavement. He had climbed out of the car as Dee, the boy, and the wailing child crossed the intersection.

"She's cold, gimme your coat," Dee ordered.

Javon said nothing. His incredulous eyes studied Dee. He shook his head, peeled off his coat and handed it over. Dee wrapped the child in it, and sat in the back of the car, beckoning the little boy to hop in as well. The boy didn't hesitate.

"Now what, Dee? What you wanna do with your new family?"

"We need to find food for them. Head over the bridge, there'll be lots of stores on the other side."

Javon raced over the bridge. The baby quieted inside Javon's jacket. The warmth, and a soothed thirst, seemed to have temporarily knocked out the exhausted infant.

"Take a right here, should be something close by."

Dee scanned the area, looking for a grocery store or drugstore. He spotted a movement in the distance, moving fast from the right on the street up ahead.

"Pull over, now!"

He held the baby against the seat as Javon swerved to the side and came to a rapid stop. They watched a police cruiser tear through the intersection. Dee had seen no police presence for several weeks now.

"Thought the cops were all gone," Javon whispered.

"They can't hear you," Dee said at a normal volume. "Follow them, see what they're up to."

"You lookin' for trouble?" Javon asked, with a hint of anticipation.

"Dunno. Might be trouble, might be a way to unload these kids."

Javon twisted around to face Dee.

"You get all superhero and shit, save a couple of kids, and then hand them over to the cops? What do you think they gonna do for two little black kids?"

"I said I dunno, just follow and let's see what's happening. Go, Javon, before you lose them."

Javon accelerated, turned left at the intersection, and began following the cruiser at a distance. With no other cars on the road, they had to stay far behind. The empty roads also made it easy for them to follow the cruiser from far away, as long as it kept going straight. Once it turned, by the time they got to the same intersection, they could lose the cruiser.

Far ahead of them, the cruiser veered left at a Y intersection. Javon sped up once the cruiser was out of sight. As they went left on the Y, Dee saw a red traffic sign:

Reservoir Grounds Open 6:00am – 9:30pm

"I can't believe this," Dee said, "Cops going to your Cobbs Hill Park."

Javon slowed the car as they drove up the circular Reservoir Road. The tall radio tower at the top of the hill crept into view. Then Dee saw the parked cruiser.

"Stop!" he ordered Javon. They watched, as the officer climbed out of the driver's seat and headed to the back door of the cruiser. He spoke to someone in the back before reaching for the door handle. The door swung open violently, knocking the officer to the ground. A woman leapt out of the car, kicked the officer, and ran away.

"Damn," Javon exclaimed.

The officer sat up, holding his face. He screamed at the woman, telling her to stop. When he pulled out his firearm and shot towards her, both Dee and Javon swung open their doors at the same time.

"Stay in the car," Dee said to the boy, in a forceful tone. The boy nodded mutely.

They hugged the treeline, running towards the cruiser, guns drawn. They heard the woman scream. As they reached the vehicle, Dee saw the officer on top of the woman, tugging at her pants. Without hesitation he strode over to the pair, placed the barrel of his gun behind the officer's head and fired. The woman screamed again, pushing the officer's body to the side. She scrambled to her feet and ran towards the building at the base of the radio tower.

Javon whooped. He stomped around the fallen officer. "You toe-tagged that mofo but good, Dee!"

Dee studied the carnage.

"He ain't a cop, check out his ink," he said.

A curved, three-pronged trident stuck out from underneath the body's collar. The pitchfork tattoo symbolized gang membership or prison time. Either way, a police officer wouldn't have such a design. Javon's excitement subsided at the site of the tattoo.

"How'd you know he wasn't real?" Javon asked.

"I didn't," confessed Dee.

"Now where did that fine piece of New York cheesecake go?" Javon asked, looking at their surroundings.

"Chill a little there, B. She ain't gonna be your girlfriend, but we can ask her to help with the kids. She went over there," Dee added, pointing at the communications facility.

Dee and Javon entered through the gray metal doors. A small reception desk stood in the entrance. Posters of distant radio towers, and closeups of various pieces of communications equipment, covered the walls. A spiral polished-concrete staircase led to the second floor. Behind the desk was a row of six offices, three on either side of a short hallway. Windows in the front and the back of the main floor provided dim lighting inside the building.

"You check those," Dee pointed at the back offices, "I'll have a look upstairs."

Dee heard a faint scraping sound above him as he started climbing the stairs. He looked up and jumped back as a computer monitor crashed inches away from him. Glass and plastic shot in all directions. The deafening sound echoed in the stairwell.

"Goddamn," Dee shouted, stumbling back.

"You good, Dee?" Javon asked, rushing to his side.

"Yeah, no damage done," Dee answered. Part of the monitor's frame had hit his shin bone. He ignored the sharp pain.

Dee took his gun out of his waistband and peered up the staircase. It was darker on the second floor. He let his eyes adjust for a moment before bounding up the stairs to the landing. Javon followed suit. Dee couldn't see the woman, and he heard no sound. He ran up the second set of steps, two at a time, and took a defensive stance at the top of the stairs.

A large, glass enclosed control room dominated the second floor. Small windows provided just enough light to give the abandoned control room a movie-like eeriness. Large mounted screens covered an entire wall. Most of the equipment and chairs were untouched, having no value in a dying world. But Dee noticed one computer had fallen on its side, wires dangling from the back.

She ripped the monitor off that one, he thought.

"Watch the stairs," he instructed Javon.

Dee pushed open the glass door to the control room. He had a slight limp from the shin pain. He peered under the rows of desks loaded with monitoring equipment. By now his vision was better, and he could detect that she wasn't under any of the desks. A large refrigerator-sized electronic device stood near the back corner on the right. Dee edged towards it, keeping some distance between him and what might be on the other side of it.

The woman stood next to the device, out of sight from the doorway. Blood covered her face and upper body. She held a keyboard in her hands, raised behind as if it were a baseball bat. She had a wild look in her eyes. Her panting breath and trembling body added to the animal-like fear that seem to exude from her every pore.

Dee lifted his gun and pointed it at her, twisting it sideways.

"You alone with us in a dark building, my friend over there is blocking the stairs, and he got a sawed-off. There ain't no one for miles around. I've got a piece pointed at your skinny ass. It can't get worse than this, right? If we was going to hurt you, this would be the place, right here, right now. But we ain't no rapists like the fake pig outside, OK?"

The woman stared at Dee with a fierce look of defiance. Her eyes darted to the side, trying to spot Javon.

"I'm gonna put my gun away now, but you don't pull any more of that crazy shit, deal?"

He lowered his gun and the woman's body slackened.

"We got a deal?" he asked again, now tucking the gun back into his waistband.

She nodded mutely, lowering the keyboard.

"Name's Dee," he said.

"Jessica," she replied in a shaky voice.

"Alright, we're on a first name basis," he replied with a hint of a smile.

"What do you want with me?" Jessica asked.

"Well, we got ourselves a bit of a situation. We got a baby and a little boy in our car, and we ain't exactly the parenting types, if you know what I mean."

"He means we don't know shit about screaming babies," Javon added, walking into the control room.

"Where did you get the children?" she asked.

"The little boy was on the street. We picked him up, and he told us about his baby sister. Found her screaming in her crib, both parents dead in the house."

"The baby is screaming?" Jessica asked. "Did you feed it? Have you checked its diaper?"

"Picked them up like five minutes ago," Javon interjected. "Crazy move I told Dee. Then he spotted your cherry top, and we followed you here."

"Let's go," Jessica said, pushing her way past Dee and sidestepping around Javon. She ran down the stairs, with the two startled men following suit.

5. AMANDA

The governor of New York smiled broadly in the photo hanging from the wall. He was shaking hands with another man, whose infectious smile gave the governor's practiced smile a run for its money. It was the other man that Amanda Jones stared at. She fought back tears, remembering how proud her husband had been of that photo.

"Why didn't you tell me?" she asked the silent photo.

Ken had not let on that he'd started having dizzy spells. And Amanda was so immersed in her preservation project that she didn't notice. Until she found him dead late one night on the sofa.

Amanda shook her head, then reached under her desk and shut off the second generator to preserve fuel. She sat back in her heavily padded black leather chair — her throne, she called it — with a satisfied sigh. *A job well done*, she thought. She alternated between the two generators, making sure that both were in good working order. Her home office looked more like the control room of a nuclear submarine than a suburban bedroom. The window was darkened to reduce glare. The corrugated metal exhaust pipe from the generator sealed off the lower half of the window. Four laptops, two large LED monitors, three printers with stacked cartons of spare ink cartridges, and a large box of meticulously arranged and labeled five-terabyte drives completed her surroundings.

After completing her master's degree in computer science, Amanda had spent the next fourteen years building her career. She had a natural ability to work with both software and hardware, which was a rare talent. It had led her to be an expert in the field of oftentimes controversial embedded software development. This was the low-level code that interacted directly with hardware. The Internet Of Things, monitoring hardware/software combinations, recognition algorithms: these were her domain.

It was also these skills that had allowed her to hack her phone and install a fake vaccination QR code app. Since the app didn't "call home," it was a simple matter of de-scrambling existing codes, and generating the same information with her data. She knew all of Ken's personal information, and so reverse-engineering his phone's QR code had been trivial. The harder part was keeping her secret. Being a devout anti-vaxxer is rather problematic when your husband is the Assistant Deputy Commissioner of the New York State Department of Health. Even worse, her husband was instrumental in establishing and guiding the state's COVID-19 task force. Amanda considered herself a truth-seeker, not just an anti-vaxxer. Ken called her a functional conspiracy nut. Then he died from his beloved vaccine.

Amanda had been well tuned in to the Vax Plague from its early discovery, long before the mainstream, and Ken, had accepted it. He'd frowned when her computer supplies and generators started arriving. But again, out of respect, he had said nothing. And so, she got to work with her preservation mission, while the internet was operational.

The first thing she did was write a scraper that downloaded all the Wikipedia pages and images. If she omitted all the talk and history, there were just under forty terabytes of data. Wikipedia may have been full of errors, but it was still the best all-round everyday knowledge site. She considered it an accurate snapshot of current society, with all of its controversies, errors, misinformation, and theories. She also went after other general knowledge sites, like howstuffworks.com. Without enough time or knowledge, she chose not to download the more specialized sites. She would have loved to get engineering diagrams and manuals on power grids, drinking water supply, gas distribution – all the infrastructure needed for society to survive. For those, she had to trust the other members of the Knowledge Preservation Society, or KPS for short.

She was exceedingly proud that the KPS had been her brainchild. She had put a straw design together in the very early days of the VP. Her fellow anti-vaxxers jumped onto the idea and helped refine it. The idea was to download and retain as much of the internet content as possible. Getting all of it was neither achievable, nor desirable: ninety percent of it was useless. But they wanted to preserve whatever knowledge might prove useful for the survivors of the VP. Everything from farming, to construction, to power generation.

The natural location to store KPS data was in public libraries. Each KPS member would collect hard drives filled with all kinds of data. For critical information, they would also provide print-outs. Amanda thought this was a bit of an overkill. With generators, they could power laptops for years to access the stored data on an as-needed basis. But they outvoted her on that issue, the majority of the almost ten thousand members spread across the globe wanted print-outs. Amanda couldn't choose what to print from her general information pages. In the end, she decided to cheat: she would store the disks in the library, along with a spare laptop, a printer and ink. Let someone else do the printing if they wanted.

Amanda had just completed the third backup of all of her data. One copy would go into the Rochester central library. One copy she would leave in her house, should she ever need it. And the last copy she would take with her, along with one generator. And that's where her plans became murky.

Where would she go? It seemed absurd to remain isolated in her quiet suburban home, and yet she couldn't imagine a better place. It was a problem that she had deferred until now. And one that she could defer longer: first she would drop off her data at the library. Eventually, she would make her way to the New York City library to see what KPS data had been dropped off there. But after that, she had no clue what to do.

Amanda nearly jumped out of her chair when she heard a sharp rapping coming from downstairs. She froze, waiting to see if it would repeat. The rapping changed to four loud pounding noises a moment later. She ran to the bedroom overlooking the front entrance. A woman with two young children was taking notes in front of her door. The woman moved to the front window, peering inside the house. Amanda craned her neck, looking outside in all directions. She could see no one else, and so decided it was safe to open the door.

She hurried down the stairs and yanked open the front door. There was no sign of the woman and children.

"Hello?" she called out.

A few seconds later the woman popped out from the left side of the house, with the two kids in tow.

"Sorry for snooping out back," the woman said, with a sheepish grin. "I didn't think anyone was home."

"Can I help you?" Amanda asked.

"My name is Deb Kearns," she began, using the tone of a well-rehearsed speech. "Some of us have been rescuing orphaned children. We are all unvaccinated. So, we go door-to-door looking for orphaned children. And when the parents are still there, we give our contact information so that they can come see us as soon at the dizzy spells start. I know this sounds very matter-of-fact, but believe me, not a single day goes by without heart-wrenching stories. Anyway, um, sorry to ask bluntly, but do you have children living here?"

Amanda tried to take in Deb's introductory speech. She had been so wrapped up in her KPS work that she hadn't even thought of the fate of the unvaccinated children.

"I don't understand, who exactly are you people?"

"Well, we're just a group of ordinary, and unvaccinated, people. There's no one else that can care for the small unvaccinated children. I mean it's not like we'll take your children away from you or anything, we just want you to know that we exist, as a fallback plan for you…" Deb's voice trailed off.

"I don't have children," Amanda clarified. She hesitated a moment, before continuing. Who had she been gathering data for, if not for a group of survivors like this?

"What I do have, is data."

Deb frowned, shaking her head.

"Sorry, my name's Amanda. I'm in IT. I've spent the last months gathering all the information that I could off of the internet. And there are others like me. We tried to capture the essential human knowledge before the internet went out."

Amanda's heart was racing. This might be exactly what she needed: to join forces with a group of obviously well-meaning fellow unvaccinated.

"Ok, now that is interesting," Deb exclaimed. She

paused, before continuing.

"So how do normal people get access to this information?" she asked.

"Normal people?" Amanda laughed.

"Sorry, I mean non-IT people. How can we make use of all your hard work?"

"I can show you, that's not a problem. The important part is almost done. I've made backups, and now I just need to deliver a set of drives to our agreed drop-off point: the local public library."

Deb cleared her throat and lowered her eyes slightly.

"And, um, no dizzy spell yet?" she asked.

"I'm not vaccinated," Amanda replied. She couldn't help but smile. It was the first time that she had openly admitted to someone that she was unvaccinated. An enormous weight fell off her shoulders as she realized that she no longer needed to perpetuate her lie.

"Oh my God, another one," Deb exclaimed. She grabbed Amanda's forearm. "You have to join us! We need all the help we can get. And with all your data, my God, that's going to be crucial going forward."

Amanda laughed at Deb's desperate earnestness. She felt giddy herself at the thought of rejoining society.

"Yes, of course I want to join you. How many are you anyway?"

"Three adults at the moment. There's me, Maurice, and Titus. Then there are the children. We have two infants, and five toddlers. Ben and Lucy here are our oldest."

She nudged Ben and Lucy out from behind her. They looked up shyly at Amanda.

Amanda did her best not to look crestfallen. Three adults. Somehow, she had expected to be joining a thriving community of dozens or even hundreds of people. *Well, it's a start*, she thought, as she crouched to the children's level.

"Well, hello, you two. My name is Amanda. You must be Ben," she said, pointing to the girl, and then moving to the boy, "And you must be Lucy."

Both children giggled.

"I'm Lucy! That's Ben."

"Oh, I'm so sorry, my mistake," Amanda replied with a smile. "Lucy and Ben," she repeated, pointing to the boy and then the girl.

"No," they choroused.

"I don't have a girl name," Ben cried out above Lucy's own protests, "I'm Ben!"

"Oh gosh, this is so confusing. OK, I think I've got it, but you might need to help me again later, OK?"

Ben nodded.

"He's Ben, and I'm Lucy," Lucy reiterated, as if to ensure it had sunk in this time.

Amanda smiled at them and tousled their hair. She stood up and looked at Deb.

"OK, so how does this work, exactly? And how can I help?"

"Well, there is no 'exactly,' we're flying by the seat of our pants here," Deb chuckled. "But, in a nutshell, I go out knocking on doors with Ben and Lucy. It may be a little manipulative, but people are more willing to open a door to a woman with children."

"Worked with me," Amanda acknowledged.

"I keep track of which houses had no answer. Then Maurice covers those later. He breaks into them to make sure that there aren't children inside who are too scared to answer the door. And finally, Titus stays with the smaller children at the house. He's a carpenter, what a blessing. He's been converting bedrooms to hold several little people."

She pulled out a map from what looked like a brown leather laptop sleeve. Deb had highlighted several streets around Cobbs Hill. The enormity of their project began to sink in for Amanda. They had only covered a handful of streets, there was an entire city in dire need of searching.

"This is the area we've covered in the last week or so," Deb continued. "I've got a car parked right over here. Today I'm doing this sort of square route that will bring me back around to the car. If you cover the opposite side of the street, that'll cut my time in half. Then we can go meet the others, and do one extra run before the end of the day. And we have several spare strollers over there now, so you can take one too."

Out of habit, Amanda locked her front door. On the sidewalk, Deb let the two children pile into the stroller for a free ride to the next house. The stroller, designed for a baby, creaked under the weight of the two toddlers. With a sense of disbelief at how her situation had drastically changed, Amanda crossed the street and started knocking on doors.

For the rest of the street, neither Amanda nor Deb found anyone at home. Midway through the second street, Deb had met a man at one of the houses. He had refused to open the door and had said he had no children. Deb told Amanda that the man was vaccinated. In the end they had let him be, and had instead decided to focus their efforts on children that might be in other houses.

Amanda approached one of the last houses on the third street of their four-sided itinerary. It was a large, beautifully painted colonial home. The blue wood cladding covered both floors. White shutters surrounded the three windows on the second floor, as well as the pair of windows on either side of the front door. A wide brick chimney was attached to the side of the house. At the attic level, two small quarter-circle windows adorned each side of the chimney. It was like the house had eyes.

Amanda knocked on the door, but there was no answer – again. She moved to the window on the right, but the curtains were drawn shut. She went to the left window. Amanda peered through a small gap between these curtains. The room was quite dark with all the curtains drawn, but she could see that it was in complete disarray. As she tried to make out more details, the curtain moved ever so slightly, as if caught in the airflow of movement.

Her pulse quickened, and she pulled back from the window.

"Is someone there?" she called out in a quavering

voice.

She reached forward and tapped on the glass.

"We're here to help." She tapped the glass harder.

"Please, we just want to talk to you."

She was just starting to wonder if she had imagined the curtains moving when she heard a faint whimper.

"Hey, are you OK? I can hear you!"

She tapped hard on the window with an open palm. The noise came again. Now she couldn't be sure if it was whimpering or sobbing.

"I'm coming in to help you," she called out.

Amanda tried the doorknob hopefully, but it was locked. She needed to break the window. She looked around for something to use to shatter the glass. Halfway to the sidewalk was a small rock garden. She ran to it, kicked loose a softball-sized rock, and ran to the window opposite of the side where she had heard the whimpering. She tapped on the window.

"I'm about to break this window, OK? Don't be scared."

She tossed the rock at the lower half of the window. It bounced off the window, leaving a hairline crack. She picked up the rock and threw it harder this time. With a loud crash, it shattered the window and disappeared into the house. Amanda kicked at the loose shards until she could safely stick her head inside the window. The stench of rot assaulted her nostrils, forcing her to pull her head back out. She unzipped her jacket and used it to cover her nose and mouth before peering inside the window once more. The enclosed room had a doorless entry on the far left. The wall prevented her from seeing the front door, or the area beyond where she had heard the voice. She would have to climb through the window.

Feet first, she thought. She wanted to avoid putting her hands on the shattered glass below the inside of the window. She stuck one leg through, paused, then twisted, almost doing a comical handstand on the lawn before getting both legs through the opening. Her stomach rubbed painfully against the window ledge. Fortunately, she hadn't missed any stray shards in the bottom ledge that would have cut her skin. Her shoes crunched on glass as she stood inside the house.

A wave of nausea almost brought her to her knees. The smell inside the house was far worse than anything she had experienced before. She rushed out of the room, across the hall, and into the room where she'd heard a voice. In the far corner, next to the window, a small girl crouched on the floor. In the dim light, Amanda could see that she was trembling. The girl's long blond hair was a tangled nest of knots. She wore a coat and some rain boots. What appeared to be food stains covered the front of the purple coat. Her arms were crossed, with her hands tucked up under her armpits. Her dull eyes watched warily as Amanda approached her.

"Hey there sweetie, are you OK?" Amanda asked, crouching in front of the girl. The girl stared at

Amanda, her little body trembling. Amanda noticed the dark bags under the girl's eyes. The child looked to be three or four years old.

"Come on, let's get out of here, OK? I'll help you."

The girl nodded weakly, but didn't get up. Amanda gently reached around the girl's back, holding her in a hug, and stood.

"That's it, good girl, let's get some fresh air outside. Everything is going to be OK."

Amanda almost made it to the front door before Deb's booming voice came in from the broken window in the other room.

"Amanda? Are you OK? I heard the window breaking."

The girl's trembling body stiffened.

"Shh, it's OK, honey, that's my friend, she's going to take care of you too."

"Amanda?" called Deb again.

Amanda didn't want to scare the girl with a loud shout back at Deb. The front door had a deadbolt that was too high for the girl. The key was in the lock. Amanda turned it several times in different directions trying to open the lock before the bolt finally drew back. She opened the door gently, fighting the urge to run madly out of the horrible house behind her.

"Oh, you poor thing," Deb said when they emerged from the house.

Deb gently reached for the girl in Amanda's arms. The girl shrieked in a hoarse voice and wrapped her arms tightly around Amanda's neck. Amanda immediately turned away from Deb.

"Hey, hey, it's OK, I've got you. Shhhh, you can stay here, I'll hold you."

"I'm just going to run back to my stroller for supplies. She's probably dehydrated and starving," Deb said.

Amanda nodded, while cooing near the girl's ear. The fresh spring air mingled with the stench of death imbued in the girl's hair. Amanda tried to stop her voice from cracking as tears ran down her cheeks. The girl's arms locked around her neck barely slackened their grip as Amanda walked in a small circle with slow, bouncy steps.

Amanda noticed Deb had tears as well when the woman arrived with a child's water bottle that had a straw poking out of the lid. She went behind Amanda to offer the drink to the girl. The girl jerked her head away and buried it into Amanda's shoulder.

"You'd better do it," Deb said, handing the cup to Amanda. "Small sips only." Deb took a few steps back.

Amanda shifted the child into a sideways position in her arms.

"Are you thirsty sweetie? I've got some water here."

She placed the straw close to the girl's dry, cracked lips. The girl latched onto the straw and sucked greedily.

"Easy, easy," Amanda said, pulling the bottle away. "If you drink too fast, it'll give you a tummy ache."

The girl's head settled back on Amanda's shoulder without a protest.

"I've got some rice crackers here, she should be able to hold that in," Deb said, handing a small saucer-sized wafer to Amanda.

"Can I have one too?" Lucy asked, as her and Ben joined them.

"Of course," Deb said, handing each of them a cracker as well.

Amanda untangled one of the girl's arms and placed the cracker in her little hand.

"Look, this is Ben and Lucy. They have crackers just like you." Amanda bent down with the little girl to get at Ben and Lucy's level.

"Ewww, she stinks!" Ben said, wrinkling his nose.

The girl burst into tears and began to wail.

"Ben!" admonished Deb.

Amanda walked a few steps away and began her bouncy rhythm once again, as the pent-up grief and fear poured out of the child. Amanda hugged the child, rocking her as she walked. When the wailing subsided, she reminded the girl about the cracker.

"Come on, sweetie, have a little bite."

The girl looked at the cracker in her hand and took a bite. She coughed and searched for the water bottle. Amanda let her have another sip.

"My name's Amanda, what's yours?"

"Sophia," came a reply just above a whisper.

Amanda smiled at her. "Nice to meet you, Sophia." Sophia took another bite of the cracker. Amanda felt a tapping on her leg. She looked at Ben, who had lowered his gaze.

"I'm sorry," he mumbled. He looked back hopefully at Deb, who nodded her approval.

"Did you hear that, Sophia? Ben said he was sorry." Amanda turned so that Sophia could see Ben. She glanced at Ben before reaching for the water bottle once more.

Deb approached Amanda. "Are you OK?" she whispered, placing her hand on Amanda's arm.

"I wish I had time to process this, but we have to keep going. How many more are waiting for us? We need to move faster." Amanda's voice quickened as she spoke, feeling overwhelmed with the urgency of the situation.

"I know, I know. Believe me, I know. We're pounding the pavement every day. But still, at night I can barely sleep thinking about the children who are trying to sleep alone in empty houses."

Except the houses aren't empty, thought Amanda, *they're filled with dead parents.*

"Sammy," Sophia whispered into Amanda's ear.

Amanda froze. "What's that, sweetie?"

"Get Sammy too."

Oh God, Amanda thought, heading back towards the house. "Who's Sammy?" she asked in a quavering voice.

"My brother, he's hungry."

Deb grabbed Amanda's arm. "I'll go, don't bring her back in there."

Amanda nodded, grateful not to have to re-enter the house.

"Stay with me, Lucy," Amanda ordered, as the little girl started following Deb. Lucy hesitated, looking back and forth between Amanda and Deb's retreating body before coming to rejoin Amanda and Ben.

After what seemed like an eternity later, Deb emerged from the house, cradling a small, limp boy in her arms. The boy seemed a little bigger than Sophia. Amanda's jaw clenched as she noticed his listless arms swinging along with Deb's hurried steps.

Deb's grim expression didn't change as she spoke. "Water bottle," she commanded, as she placed the boy on the grass.

"Sammy," Sophia called softly.

Amanda bent towards Deb, passing Sophia's water bottle. Her neck strained with the weight of the girl clenched to it. She watched Deb carefully pry open the boy's lips. They seemed stuck together at first. She placed the water bottle between his lips and tipped it upside down. The boy coughed weakly, water dripping down his cheek. Deb removed the bottle as he coughed again. He never opened his eyes, nor moved his limbs.

"I don't know if any went in," Deb said, looking up at Amanda with wide eyes. The grim and determined look had been replaced with that of a frightened woman.

"Try again, only let a few drops fall on his lips."

Deb obeyed, but the boy didn't respond to the wetness on his lips. Deb parted his lips again and let a tiny amount of water fall into his open mouth. This time they stayed in his mouth, though Amanda didn't see him swallow. Deb kept at it, a few drops at a time, until suddenly the boy coughed again. A small amount of water trickled down his cheek once more.

"Maybe if I sit him up," Deb said. She propped the boy into a sitting position, his back tucked against her stomach. She tilted his head slightly and tried giving him water again. Most of it poured straight out of his mouth. Then he coughed once more.

"We need to get him home," Amanda said. She felt helpless with Sophia locked around her neck.

Deb nodded in agreement. "We need help, let's go." With that, she picked up the limp boy once again. This time she placed him in the stroller. His head lolled sideways against the padded frame.

"Is Sammy OK?" Sophia whispered to Amanda.

I have no idea, Amanda thought. "We'll bring him home and take care of him, sweetie."

6. NEW ARRIVALS

Mo dropped his remaining flyers on top of the pile in the open box by the front door. His legs, and especially his feet, ached. He carefully set the heavy sports bag on the floor. The bagged tools, his B&E kit as he called it, clinked softly against the ceramic tiles. *Getting my money's worth out of these shoes*, he thought.

"Hi, Mo," Amanda greeted him, her head popping out of the kitchen doorway. Just below her, Sophia popped her head out in a perfect imitation of Amanda. The girl rarely left Amanda's side and cried when Amanda had to leave on a child-finding excursion. Sophia was still too unstable and weak to spend the day out searching from house to house. But she was getting stronger every day and was talking more. Mo thought Amanda would soon let her join the day trips.

Mo knew it wasn't only Sophia's physical weakness that made her unstable. It was also the trauma of losing her brother Sammy eight days ago. Deb had stayed up all night on the day the boy had arrived at the house. She had refused to let anyone else take over her shift. Painstakingly, she had tried putting small amounts of water into the boy the entire night. Mo had helped as well. Amanda wanted to help, but she couldn't leave Sophia's side, and they didn't want to expose the girl to such a distressing scene. Mid-morning the next day, the little boy had passed away. Poor Deb had wailed in a way Mo had never seen her do before. Mo had held her tightly, his own tears pouring onto Deb's shoulders.

But of course he knew that their pain was nothing compared to the agony that Sophia must have undergone. *Must still be undergoing*, he corrected himself. And yet, in her state of shock, she had barely reacted. She seemed to withdraw deeper into herself. Her only lifeline was Amanda. Mo admired how the woman cared for the girl with boundless patience, tenderness, and compassion.

Amanda had certainly added energy to their project. With her generator and printers, she had insisted on printing stacks of flyers to tell people about their operation. She argued that they could reach far more people that way than by systematically knocking on doors. So everywhere they went, they put up flyers on lamp posts, corner buildings, and any abandoned stores that survivors might wander into. And it was working. *Almost too well*, Mo thought. Despite Titus's heroic efforts at making rooms accommodate several children, the house was bursting at the seams with children. Most of the adults slept in the neighboring house at night, leaving two adults in the children's house for the night-shift.

"Hey Amanda. Any new arrivals today?"

"Maurice!" Ben cried before Amanda could answer. He ran to Mo and jumped into his arms.

"Hey hey, how's my Benny-Boo today?" Mo

hugged the child and kissed his cheek. He was surprised by how much he'd become attached to the little boy. And even more surprised by the reciprocated affection.

"Me and Lucy took care of the little kids today," Ben answered, with an earnest face. "Uncle Titus says that we were as good as grown-ups."

"They certainly were," Titus added, his deep voice punctuated by his heavy lumbering steps up the basement stairs. At six-foot-two, and built like a refrigerator, Titus made his presence known. His bald, dark-skinned head gleamed with sweat from his renovation work in the basement. His ever-present smile took the edge off what would have been a very intimidating man. Though in his fifties, he looked like his high school football days were not far behind him.

"How are things going down there?" Mo asked.

"Making progress. I've got some framing in place, I'll add the drywall tomorrow. The little ones sleep better when they don't see all their friends rolling around in their cribs. Speaking of which, I need to go do another crib run with my truck tomorrow."

Titus had been raiding all the nearby furniture and baby stores for cribs, bedding, strollers, and other baby necessities.

"You're a workhorse, my friend," Mo said, tapping him on the back as the man headed into the kitchen. Mo wondered how they would ever have made it without the man's skill and strong work ethic.

"I guess I'm a new arrival," came a male voice

from behind Mo.

Mo turned to face a man who appeared to be in his late thirties or early forties. His long black hair was neatly bound in a pony tail, and showed no signs of graying yet. He was approximately the same height as Mo, and was neither fat nor thin. He wore round, gold-rimmed glasses. *Bit of a John Lennon*, was Mo's first impression.

"Joshua Beauclair," the man said, extending his hand. "I saw your posters and came to see if you folks could use a hand. From what I gather, you could use several hands."

"Maurice Biggs, you can call me Mo. Nice to meet you, Joshua. Do you have any children with you?"

"Nope, just me," he paused before continuing. "My wife passed away, but we had no children. We did plan to have some one day, but somehow that day never came."

"I'm sorry to hear about your wife. So, are you vaccinated? Sorry to ask such a personal question right away."

"No, I'm not. I'm here for the long term, if that's what you mean. Trypanophobia."

"What?"

"Fear of needles. It cost me my job."

"What do you do for a living? Or did, I should say," Mo added with an ironic grin.

"I taught chemistry at RU, and conducted research, of course."

"So it's Dr. Beauclair then," Mo said.

Joshua laughed. "Yes, it is, in theory, but I would

rather drop titles at this point. And Beauclair comes courtesy of my great-grandfather, who settled here from France."

"Did you research anything to do with the virus or vaccines?" Mo had an innate distrust of academics in the field of science.

"No, unfortunately I can't help you there. My field is inorganic chemistry. I was researching solid state batteries. Trying to build a better battery, in essence."

Well, that seems pretty safe, thought Mo. "Welcome aboard, Joshua, thanks for coming to help us."

"Thanks Mo. I hear you and Deb started this thing, very impressive."

"No, no, it was all Deb. I was just her first employee."

"And I don't pay you to gab all day," Deb said with a smile, coming next to Mo. She was bouncing a small infant in her arm. Mo had found him in one of his house break-ins. The baby boy's father had been slumped in a rocking chair next to the crib. There were no signs of decomposition, and the infant was fine, so Mo assumed he'd been lucky to arrive not long after the father had passed. Mo had grabbed the man's wallet on the side table near the door. He thought the baby might want to know about his family some day. They named the boy after the father, Walter, according to his driver's license.

"Hi, Deb, wow it's busy here today. How's Walter?" Mo gave his little finger to the baby, who happily grabbed it in a fist and tried to suck on it.

"He's a little fussy, but nothing a bit of walking around can't take care of. Did you find more formula?"

"Yes, three cans of powder in one house. They're in my tool bag, let me get them for you."

"No that's OK, you've had a long day, take a break. But we do need to talk about food, and not just for the babies."

"Sure, we can do that. Where's Lucy by the way?" Lucy normally spent her time with either Deb or Ben.

"She's helping our other three new arrivals, bless her little heart," Amanda said, joining the group in the hallway.

"A father dropped off his boy and two little girls," Deb explained. "There's Emily, she's four-and-a-half, and Mia, who's three. And then there's Caleb, he's six."

"Six?" Mo asked, as the implication sunk in.

"Vaccinated a year ago," Deb confirmed.

Mo put Ben down. "Hey, Ben, why don't you go help Lucy show Caleb and the girls around." Ben trotted off towards the living room.

"Does the boy understand?" Mo asked. *More trauma coming.* Mo worried there might never be a day where people can live happily once more. He realized it wasn't the conveniences of the pre-VP world that he missed most. It was the sense of stability and security. The irony of this thought coming from a borderline conspiracy theorist didn't escape Mo.

"I don't know, he seems to act normally. Well, as normal as a kid can act in this madness," Deb answered.

"Is the dad still around?"

"No, he'd started getting dizzy spells, so he went out looking for help and saw our posters. He only stayed a few minutes, I'm not sure how much longer he had."

Titus joined the group. "So we only have him for four years, and then he's gone, just like that?"

"I heard that kids are hit by the VP much sooner than adults, so he might not even have that long," Amanda said.

"I heard that too," Mo chimed in.

"How can they know that? The VP just started months ago, they couldn't have studied the effect on recently vaccinated children," Joshua said.

"You can extrapolate based on the various ages of youths, and—" Amanda began.

"No, no, there isn't any way that a proper scientific study could have been conducted in that time," Joshua insisted.

"Do you really want to talk about proper scientific studies?" Mo asked incredulously. "Like the one conducted on the vaccine that's wiping out most of the planet?"

"Stop! Timeout. This is not the time for anti-vaxxers and scientists to start having debates," Deb interrupted. Walter started fidgeting in her arms. Deb bounced and rocked to sooth him.

The blood rose to the top of his head as Mo's pulse

quickened. But Deb was right, this was no time for conflict. Then he noticed that he'd stepped closer to Amanda, his ally. Right away the two of them had clicked. He was absurdly proud that she had followed his *You Never Know* blog. It only took days for him to develop a high school-type crush on her. The humor in that thought alone returned a sense of calm in him.

"Sorry, Deb, you're right," Mo admitted. "And now I see why you want to talk about food, with four new people today."

Mo's considerable stores were depleting at an alarming rate. They had raided a few supermarkets and found a fair amount of canned food, bottles and boxes of juice, and other food items with a long shelf life. Despite this, his personal stores were running short.

"I had an idea about that," Titus said. "Mo, you can't be the only one that stocked up on food. I know I did too, to a lesser degree. I suspect most folks did. Have you looked for food in the houses you broke into?"

A shiver ran up Mo's spine. He had witnessed so much death and decay with his grim search for survivors. It often kept him up at night. He wondered if he would ever sleep peacefully again.

"No, pretty much get in and out as fast as I can. Other than looking for baby formula I mean."

"Right, which makes sense," Titus said, in a reassuring tone. "But with Deb's maps, I could take the truck and start emptying the food from all the houses you searched. I think we'll be surprised by how much we have available right around us."

"It's a good idea, Titus," Deb said. "But we really need you here, you're a godsend for fixing up this place, and taking care of the little ones."

"OK, I just found my job," Joshua interjected. "How about I be the food gatherer?"

"That would be great," Deb replied. "OK, this is going to work out."

Mo wondered if Joshua understood what he was getting into. "You're going to need a respirator, it gets really bad in a lot of those places. People stayed home until the end. It's not pretty, I hope you understand that. I've seen a lot of things. The worst horror movies don't come close to what you're gonna see."

Joshua paled at Mo's words, his Adam's apple bobbing up and down. "I understand," he replied carefully. "But, someone has to do it, and you've all got your roles already."

The man just earned a few credits, thought Mo. "I've got a spare respirator in the car. You shouldn't need a B&E kit like I do, since you'll be hitting the same houses I already broke into. Respirator, rubber gloves, and bags for the food you find, that should do it."

"Thanks," Joshua nodded. "But we also need to start thinking about fresh food. I used to go up towards Heuvelton on some weekends. Lots of Amish there, with organic farms. I'm betting they're still operational. I don't think many of them would have gotten vaccinated."

"Oh my God, I never thought of that, you're a genius," Deb said.

"How far is that?" Amanda asked.

"About a three-hour drive," Joshua replied.

"That would be great, but how will you pay for food? I don't think cash is much use to them anymore," Mo asked.

Joshua's mouth opened to speak, then shut. He frowned as he thought about Mo's question. *Not so genius now*, Mo thought, with a tinge of guilt at his own pettiness.

"Yeah, that's a good point," Joshua conceded. "I can't answer that. But I do know a few of the farmers there. I'll go see them and find out what I can arrange."

"We can also go fishing in the lake," Titus said, with a grin, "not that I'm saying I want to slack off to go fishing." Fishing in Lake Ontario was an on-again, off-again proposition in terms of pollution and safety. But it was a far better alternative than running out of food.

"If anyone deserves a break, it's you, Titus," Deb said with a smile. "And that's a fine idea too at some point. Barbecue-grilled fresh fish sounds amazing."

"I know, I know, finish accommodations for the little ones first," Titus said.

"And I'll gather food locally before running off to my Amish friends," Joshua added.

"Please keep a lookout for baby food especially: infant formula, baby crackers, stuff like that," Deb said.

"Add toilet paper to that priority list please," Titus said.

"Amen to that," Deb said with a chuckle.

"OK, sounds like we have a plan," Mo said. The rest nodded in agreement, all except Amanda. She was biting her lower lip and had a worried look.

"Amanda?" he asked.

"Yeah, yeah, it's a good plan. For the short term. But it's not sustainable, what do we do about food in the long run?"

The thought had flashed in Mo's head several times, only to be quickly banished. He didn't have an answer and was struggling to cope with the present, let alone the future.

Deb eventually broke the lingering silence. "We should all give that some thought, but not right now. Our immediate needs are more than enough to keep our brains and our bodies fully occupied."

"OK," Amanda replied, hesitantly, almost like a question.

"Knock, knock," said a voice from the front entrance. A man stood by the open door. His wide smile seemed at odds with his high, inwardly arched eyebrows. He had well-groomed, medium length black hair. His large blue eyes jittered as his focus jumped from one person to the next. He was slightly overweight, with a somewhat round, puffy face. Mo guessed he was in his mid-thirties.

"Door was open." The man had a sheepish grin.

"Hi there, come in," Deb said, walking towards the

man.

"Brandon Jameson," he said, reaching for her hand.

After brief introductions, Mo asked, "So what's your situation, Brandon?"

"Well, I'm not vaccinated, for starters. And I don't have children. But if you'll take me, I'd be happy to join you folks and help any way I can."

The man's clammy handshake had left Mo feeling uneasy. He of course knew that it could be nerve-wracking meeting several people in such extreme circumstances. Nevertheless, there was something about the man that rubbed Mo the wrong way.

"What did you do for a living?"

"Insurance. Some sales, but most of my time was in claims. How about you?"

"Kind of a jack of all trades," Mo said. "Some bartending, restaurant waiting, house painting, deliveries — you name it." Mo had never really found his calling, when it came to established professions. His passion had been his blog, but it hadn't paid the bills.

"Bartender? You've been holding out on us Mo," Amanda said. "We've got to get you some supplies so that you can show us your stuff."

"Personally, I will be nothing short of disappointed if we don't see the Tom Cruise *Cocktail* scene," Deb added.

Mo had to laugh. "I make a decent mojito, but I do not, and will not, dance."

"How many children do you have here?" Brandon

asked. His left eye twitched when he looked at Mo.

Mo turned to Deb. "Three more than yesterday," he said, referring to Emily, Mia, and Caleb. "Deb?"

"That brings us to sixteen now," she replied after a brief mental calculation.

Sixteen! Mo thought. Their plan was going surprisingly well. He hoped they would be able to keep up caring for that many children. It helped put any discomfort aside that he had about Brandon, they obviously needed all the help they could get.

"Welcome aboard, Brandon, I hope you like kids," Mo said.

"I don't have my own, but I think I'm a pretty good uncle," Brandon replied with a smile.

"Well then, come meet your nephews and nieces," Deb said. "Oh, here's one now in fact. This is Lucy."

Lucy skipped into the room and stood next to Deb. Brandon kneeled down on both knees in front of her.

"Well aren't you just the cutest little princess," he said, stroking her cheek.

Lucy reached out and grabbed Deb's leg, burying her face in the woman's hip.

Brandon chuckled and stood. "And a shy princess, I see."

"Most of the kids here have been traumatized to varying degrees. Don't be surprised if they're closed to strangers at first," Deb said.

"Of course. Poor little darlings," Brandon added, tousling Lucy's hair.

Deb used her free hand to untangle Lucy from her

leg and hip. "Let's go show Uncle Brandon around, Lucy." She then led Brandon towards the living room where many small excited voices could be heard.

A loud clattering noise behind Mo made him turn around.

"Oops, sorry. I didn't do it on purpose," Ben said with an anxious look. He was standing over Mo's B&E kit, hammer in hand. The crowbar was lying on the tile floor where Ben had dropped it.

"Ben, what are you doing?"

"I'm going to look for kids too."

"Ah, Ben." Mo walked over and gathered up the child in his arms. "You let me worry about that OK? Besides, you still have a job to do: helping to take care of the younger kids."

"But I want to go with you."

"I know you do, and that's sweet. I miss you during the day, but it's not safe. You can hurt yourself with those big tools. And Uncle Titus needs you here, right?"

"I guess," Ben acknowledged with a disappointed face. Mo hugged him, rocking the boy in his arms.

7. THE BLINDING LIGHT SHOW

J avon slammed the door on the way in. Water poured off of his jacket, and his shoes squelched when he stomped into the living room. "Where's the wife?" he asked Dee.

"She's putting the kids to bed," Dee replied, seated comfortably on the sofa and sipping a beer. The thunderstorm showed no signs of abating. He grabbed a can of beer from the case they had found in a house this morning, and tossed it to Javon.

"Putting the kids to bed?" Javon asked incredulously, setting aside the unopened beer can. "Dee, do you even hear yourself talking anymore? You're living in a white suburban house, you have a white girlfriend, and you're playing daddy to three kids – one of them is even white! This ain't you Bro, and it ain't me. I didn't sign up to run no daycare."

Dee knew Javon resented how close he and Jessica had become in the last two weeks. And finding three-year-old Ethan hadn't helped the situation.

"You wanted to come live here, remember?" Dee replied.

"Not to raise a family, Bro."

"So, what do you want to do, throw them out on the street? Or just walk away?"

"No, this is what I want to do," he said, pulling a folded sheet of paper out of his pocket. "Let's bring the kids to these people." He handed the flyer to Dee.

Dee read about a group of unvaccinated taking in children. It seemed like a perfect solution. He was surprised to find himself getting attached to his young charges, and wasn't sure if he wanted to hand them off to this group. There were clear advantages of course. He and Javon could live a good life wandering around neighborhoods, grabbing food from any house they wanted. But still.

"Don't think Jess would go for it," he said, his voice trailing off.

"Oh it's 'Jess' now, is it? Well maybe you and 'Jess' can talk about it when your little family's asleep. I'm gonna get dry and eat." With that, Javon squelched up the stairs, leaving wet prints behind.

A bolt of lightning lit the room, followed by a loud thunderclap that seemed to rock the house. It matched both Javon's mood and Dee's discomfort. Dee felt uncertain and out of place, which was foreign to him. Life in the crew with Marquis had been hard and brutal, but he had had a role and he had known his place. But now, life was far more uncertain. Jessica and the three kids had at least provided him with something to focus on.

Four large red candles flickered in the living room. They had raided a Walmart and emptied the candle shelf earlier in the week. *Warm Apple Pie* was written on the large sticker of the nearest scented candle. *Javon might have a point*, Dee thought, with a rueful smile.

"Believe it or not, they're asleep," Jessica said in a hushed tone, tip-toeing down the stairs. "I'm not sure which is worst, the thunderstorm or Javon."

"Javon's not too happy about being a Daddy. He needs some action, you know?"

"Breaking into houses for food and surviving the end of the world isn't enough action?"

"Come on Jess, give him a break. He sees us, that's gotta make him feel like he's on the outs."

Jessica settled down next to Dee. They tried to hide their affection when Javon was around. But Dee loved it when she would sit right up next to him, touching his arm or his leg. *Damn she smells good*, he thought. Two successive bolts of lightning illuminated the room, followed by heavy rolling thunder.

"The blinding light show," Dee sang softly.

"What song's that?" Jessica asked.

"Blinding Light Show." He smiled at her. "Probably the most underrated song by the most underrated band in history: Triumph. Man, that song gives Stairway To Heaven a run for its money. Rik Emmett on a twelve-string, I tell you, he's like both Plant and Page rolled into one skinny white dude."

Jessica chuckled.

"What?" he asked.

"I just never pictured you as a classic rock expert."

"Oh, so I can only listen to rap? Don't put me in no box, girl!" He shoved her aside, turning her chuckle into laughter.

Javon's heavy footsteps sounding down the stairs cut her laughter short. Dee and Jessica both shifted in opposite directions, creating a space between themselves.

"You show her the poster?" Javon asked.

"Hi Javon," Jessica said.

"Hi," came the curt reply.

"What poster?" she asked Dee. He reached on the side table next to him and handed it to her.

Jessica leaned close to the Warm Apple Pie candle to read the flyer. "We should go," she said immediately.

"See?" said Javon.

"We could use their help, and they probably need our help. OK this is great," she exclaimed.

"Help?" asked Javon. "No, no, we handing off the kids to these people, that's it."

"No, we're not just making them someone else's problem," Jessica retorted.

Javon gave Dee an exasperated look. "Talk some sense into her, Dee."

"Chill, B. We gonna go check it out, see what the deal is."

"This is so messed up. If goddam Mother Teresa here wants to go care for all the kids in the world, let her. And you too, Bro. But I ain't having any of that, no sir."

Dee stood up and pushed Javon's right shoulder backwards. "I said chill, B! I didn't say we were joining up with that crew, and I didn't say we were dumping the kids either. We just gonna evaluate the situation. Alright?"

Javon exhaled loudly, shaking his head.

"You and me tight, Javon. That ain't gonna change. We cool?"

Javon nodded, then added, "I don't care how teeny tiny them little asses are, I ain't wiping shit off no one."

By next morning, the clouds were breaking up, revealing patches of blue sky once again. The rain-darkened concrete driveway glistened when the sun broke through. Fat drops of water clung to the leaves of the blooming rose bushes lining the left side of the driveway. The thick overgrown lawn was soaked, with blades of grass flattened by the heavy rain.

Dee climbed into the front passenger seat of the Rover, leaving Jessica in the back dealing with Nolan, his baby sister Thema, and Ethan. Javon resumed his position behind the steering wheel. Dee pulled the Glock out of the glove compartment. Its familiar grip soothed his nerves. He'd faced many life-threatening situations, but somehow this new experience of dealing with children and becoming their caretakers made him tense. He fidgeted with the pistol, pulling the magazine in and out.

"Is that really necessary?" Jessica asked, looking at the gun.

"Good thing we was strapped when we met you," Javon replied. Jessica rolled her eyes and sat back with Thema in her arms. She had strategically sat between Nolan and Ethan. The boys played roughly, which wasn't a good thing inside a car.

Dee hated the friction between Javon and Jessica. He decided it was wiser to say nothing, as he slipped the gun back into the glove compartment. Javon started the engine and Dee pulled out the map they had marked earlier that morning. It would be a short five-to-ten-minute drive to the address on the flyer.

"Stop!" ordered Dee, as they rounded the last corner onto the street listed in the flyer. Two blocks ahead there was a large commotion on the front lawn. A distant child's scream made its way faintly into the car. Dee opened the glove compartment and gripped the pistol, keeping it out of sight.

"Sawed-off's in the back," Javon said grimly.

"Hold up on that. Move up slowly," Dee said.

The car rolled forward one block. Dee could see several adults in a circle, looking at someone, or something, on the grass. There were several small children as well. Some were holding hands with an adult, and some with other kids. Many of them were crying.

"Someone's hurt," Jessica blurted out, before Dee had time to assess the situation. He clumsily released his grip on the Glock, dropping it back into the glove compartment, as Jessica handed Thema to him from the back seat.

"You two stay with Uncle Dee and Uncle Javon," she told the two boys, before leaping out of the back seat and running towards the group of people.

"Damn," Javon said, hurrying out of the car. Dee made his way out more slowly, awkwardly holding onto the baby. "Leave the sawed-off but grab your gun," he ordered Javon.

"Can I have a gun too?" Nolan asked, taking Dee's free hand.

"Not until you're older," he answered absently.

"I'm scared, Uncle Javon," Ethan said, taking Javon's hand. The look of surprise and discomfort on Javon's face as he held the little white boy's hand made Dee chuckle. Javon threw him a dark scowling glare.

"Nothing to be scared of," Dee said to Ethan. "Uncle Javon here won't let anything happen to you. Will you Javon?" Dee couldn't help himself: the situation was too priceless.

"Course not," Javon muttered to Ethan.

By the time they reached the group, the circle had already parted to let Jessica in. She was kneeling on the grass, examining a crying girl's arm.

"I think the ulna's broken," Dee heard Jessica say to an older woman who was stroking the girl's forehead and hair. "What happened?"

"They were horsing around in that tree and she fell off. Luckily, she wasn't high up there," the woman answered.

"Do you have any pain killers?" Jessica asked.

"We have some baby Tylenol,"

"How old is she?"

"Three."

"OK, give her the minimum dose for a five-year-old, that should be fine."

"Can you get that Maurice?" the woman asked another man. He was holding the hand of a small boy.

"You stay here, Ben," the man said, letting go of the boy's hand and running to the house.

"Dee!" Jessica said with relief when she saw him arrive. "I'm going to have to splint her arm, find me a thick branch as straight as possible."

"I can do better than that," a large black man answered. "I've got some lumber that will do the trick. Come with me young man," he told Dee.

"Stay with Javon," he told Nolan. Another woman reached for Thema, and Dee hesitantly let the baby go. He ran after the large man who'd already entered the house.

"Name's Titus," the man said, thundering down the steps into the basement.

"Dee," he answered, wishing he had the Glock as he descended into the semi-gloom of Titus' workshop.

"I've got some one-by that should do the trick," Titus said, rummaging through a pile of discarded lumber. The aromatic smell of freshly cut pine permeated the room.

"What do you think?" Titus asked, holding up a two-foot-long piece of lumber.

"Looks too long," Dee answered.

"I know that," Titus said, "but thick enough, right?"

"I ain't no doctor," Dee said, annoyed with Titus' questions. He found himself longing for his crew days again. This out-of-place feeling was getting to him, and chipping away at his normally solid self-confidence.

Titus chuckled. "We need common sense, not a doctor. This should be fine. Just need to cut them to size for Sophia's itty-bitty arm." He cut off two short sections with a handsaw in just a few seconds, to Dee's surprise.

By the time they got back to the lawn where Sophia was being attended to by Jessica, someone had also provided strips of cloth to wrap the arm. Dee could hardly recognize Jessica's assertive manner as she splinted Sophia's arm.

"This will do for now, but we will need to make a cast," Jessica told the older woman.

"I've got some drywall compound, that's pretty much the same as plaster," Titus said.

Jessica seemed hesitant. "That's a good backup plan, but I think we can find plaster bandages at the university." She turned to Dee, "Can you take me there now?"

"'Course," Dee nodded.

"Well, I can't believe how lucky we are to have a doctor drop right into our laps just in time," said the woman.

Jessica blushed, for the first time since Dee had met her. "I'm not a doctor. I've had a bit of training, that's all. And you," — she looked down at Sophia's tear streaked face — "have been an absolute superstar. I'm Jessica, what's your name?"

After introductions, they decided Dee would stay at the house with the three kids, while Javon took Jessica to the university. *Might do them some good to talk alone without me or the kids,* thought Dee. Though he felt uncomfortable with the situation, he had to admire what these people were doing. They seemed well organized, despite the chaos of having more kids running around than Dee had ever seen since grade school.

"You got yourself a real Children Hilton here," he told Deb.

She laughed. "Oh, I like that one Darnell." He thought of her as the group's mom. Calling him by his full name instead of 'Dee' reinforced the motherly role he'd pegged on her. Not that he had much experience with what a mother should be like. His biological mother, a crackhead who had disappeared when he was six, was hardly a role model for a nurturing mother.

"You are going to stay with us, right?" Mo asked.

"Uh, I dunno yet. I need to talk to Javon and Jessica first. I mean we're interested, we saw your posters and we're here. But —" he stopped, noticing Joshua and Brandon glancing nervously at each other. Joshua cleared his throat, looking at Mo and Deb. Brandon shifted from one leg to another.

"Maybe you folks need to talk about it too. Not sure everybody's too happy having gangs move in you know?" Dee added. He recognized the fear and instant mistrust all too well.

"Gangs?" Titus shouted. He stared at his all-white friends. "Just because they're young and black, you assume they're part of some gang?"

"I didn't say a thing," Joshua said, lifting his hands up.

"But you gotta admit they look the part," Brandon added.

Titus moved towards Brandon and was about to speak before Dee interrupted.

"Well, it's true. We were part of a gang. Ain't no gang left no more though. But I get it, and we'll be outta here as soon as Jessica and Javon get back. She might stay though, that's up to her."

"No, you are all staying," Deb said firmly. "There's no room for gangs here, and there's no room for racist crap either." She stared hard at Joshua and Brandon for the last part of that sentence. "Wake up, all of you." Her finger swept the room from Joshua all the way back to Dee. "We are just a few adult survivors, with a whole lot of children that need us. There's no time for the old fears and hate."

The woman has guts and class, Dee admitted to himself. "I'll talk to Javon, like I said. Maybe we can stay for a day or two and see how it goes there, Mama-Deb."

"I ain't your Mama," Deb replied with a smile.

"OK well that's settled then," Titus said with a defiant look towards Joshua and Brandon. "But we do have a problem. We're going to have to split some of the kids off to the adult house. With the two that

Amanda and Deb found yesterday, plus these three, there's just no room left in the children's house."

Deb nodded in agreement. "We knew we'd have to expand eventually. I'm sorry Titus, but it seems your work will never end."

"Perhaps these two young strapping men can help me out," he said, nodding to Dee.

"I ain't exactly a handyman," Dee said. "But why are you building all of this stuff up? Why not move somewhere bigger? Like one of them big-ass hotels?"

"That's a bad word," Ben said.

"Yes, you're right, Ben. Darnell won't say those words anymore, right Darnell?" Deb said.

"Sorry there, little man," Dee said sheepishly.

"Uncle Javon says 'fuck' a lot," Nolan added matter-of-factly.

"Both uncle Javon and Darnell are going to stop using those words," Deb admonished.

"I can't believe I didn't think of that before," Mo said. "A hotel! It's already divided into rooms, it's big, well, it's perfect. What do you say Titus?"

Titus nodded. "Makes a lot of sense. I could take the doors off the rooms and we could make an entire floor be the kids' rooms. Not a bad idea for a dumb-ass gang member, wouldn't you say?" Titus smiled at Joshua and Brandon.

"Uncle Titus said 'ass'," Ben said.

"Oh!" Titus exclaimed, slapping his own forehead. "You are right Mr. Ben, and I'm sorry." He picked up the boy and tickled his side. "Do you forgive me? Huh? Do you forgive me?"

Ben howled with laughter, screaming "yes" several times before Titus put him back down.

Brandon then repeated Titus' action with Ben. He lifted the boy up and tickled him, grinning broadly with his face an inch away from the boy. Dee frowned at the strange scene. He noticed Mo taking a hesitant step towards Brandon and Ben.

"I want to go down," Ben complained.

Brandon chuckled. "You want to go down? You really think I should put you down? What if Uncle Brandon doesn't want to?" He shook his head comically in front of the visibly uncomfortable boy.

"Now go see what your girlfriend Lucy is up to," Titus said, pulling the boy out of Brandon's arms. Brandon let go, still sporting a clownish grin.

"Lucy and me are getting married when we're grown-ups," Ben informed Dee, before dashing inside.

"Why don't you two go and see how Sophia's doing?" Dee said to Nolan and Ethan. Ethan ran off first. Nolan hesitated a few seconds more before letting go of Dee's hand and joining Ethan and Ben inside.

"There's a huge DoubleTree not too far from here," Deb said. "I mean it's overkill, it's really big. But, well, why not?" She smiled. "What do you think, Darnell, it's your idea?"

"Go big or go home," Dee said, smiling back at her.

"I'll do the babysitting while you go off looking for a place," Brandon volunteered, looking at Deb.

Jessica and Javon's plaster cast shopping trip had been successful. Dee watched Jessica set the poor girl's arm, getting help from Amanda to calm the child. He was so proud of her, he wanted to kiss her.

"It'll take a day to fully dry," she told Sophia. "You have to be extra careful, OK?"

Sophia nodded. Amanda cradled the girl in her arms.

"When does it come off?" Deb asked.

"Kids heal faster than adults. A month, no, a month and a half to be safe. That should do it."

"Are you sure you're not a doctor? What kind of medical training did you get, anyway?" Deb asked.

"I did two years of med school a while ago."

"Well, that's a lot closer to being a doctor than any of us. Congratulations, you are now officially our doctor."

"Ha, right."

"Seriously though, especially with all these little ones, we really need someone who has some medical knowledge. Will you stay with us?"

"I —" Jessica hesitated, looking at Dee.

"Javon and me are gonna stick around for a while, see how things go. But you belong here," Dee said. He forced his voice and facial expression to remain neutral.

"Yeah. Yes. I do want to stay and help out if I can," Jessica replied to Deb. "Emphasis on the 'if I can' part, OK? It felt great to help Sophia, but there are some serious limitations to my knowledge."

Despite having encouraged her to stay, Dee was crestfallen by her answer.

"I've downloaded all of Wikipedia," Amanda interjected. "Lots of medical articles there, if you're stuck."

"The university must have a medical library, you could get whatever books you need there too," Mo added.

"Slow down, slow down," Jessica laughed, "you make it sound like I'm going back to med school."

"Maybe you are," Deb said.

"Did you say that you downloaded all of Wikipedia? How is that possible?" Brandon asked Amanda.

"Oh it's not that big, if you throw out all the discussion chatter. Maybe forty terabytes with images. I then created a full-text index in a database. And partitioned it over several drives for performance."

Dee was glad to notice that his was not the only blank face staring at Amanda.

"Come again?" Deb asked, chuckling.

Amanda laughed in return. "Sorry, pitfall of being a nerd. I made it searchable. Kind of like Google."

"So you can just search for topics, names, anything?" Brandon asked.

"Yeah, for sure. If it's in Wikipedia, I'll find it. The bigger problem is filtering out results. If you search for too common a string, you'll have a huge rowset to iterate through."

"Nerd," Mo said, and even Dee had to laugh at that.

"So bottom line, anything in Wikipedia, you can find it," Brandon said.

"Sure can," Amanda said proudly.

"Impressive," Brandon said, before walking out of the room.

Dee had been exposed to a lot of liars in his neighborhood, and had done more than his fair share of lying. Lying was part of the game, part of the hustle of street survival.

"He's hiding something," Javon muttered to Dee, as if reading his mind.

"Let's walk," Dee muttered back.

They left the others, who were rightfully fussing over Sophia.

"What are you thinking?" Dee asked in a normal tone when they had distanced themselves from the group. Dee noticed evidence of Mo's crude break-ins as they walked down the street. Several houses had broken doorknobs. Some were ajar, while one looked like Mo had taken an ax to the deadbolt. *Note to self, give Mo a few tips on breaking locks more cleanly.*

"I'm thinking we need to keep an eye on that guy. Not just cause he's racist, he ain't the only one. But he's hiding something, and that makes me nervous," Javon replied.

"Same here. All those questions about that woman's computer—"

"Amanda Jones," Javon interrupted. Dee had grown accustomed to this quirk of Javon. He had an uncanny memory: for names only. His memory was average for everything else, but he only had to hear a person's name once to remember it for good.

"Amanda's computer," Dee repeated dutifully. "Anyway, like there's something he doesn't want her to find. No idea what, but like you, it makes me nervous."

"We should talk to her, see what she can find."

"Nah, we've got nothing to base it on but a hunch. And we've got no idea what to look for. Besides, I don't think we want to start showing our distrust when we just got here, you know? If we're even thinking of settling in with these folks, let's try to ease in a little more."

"I dunno about settling in with them," Javon admitted. "Don't feel like we belong. But either way, I'm gonna watch this Brandon guy."

"Me too, Bro, me too. Hey, thanks for driving Jessica to the hospital. How did it go?" Dee did his best to ask with a neutral tone, he didn't want to let on his nervousness. But the situation between Jessica and Javon was stressing him out.

"It was alright," Javon said. Dee detected some hesitation in his reply.

"Alright how?"

Javon sighed. "We had some words, I ain't gonna lie. But we kind of have a truce now."

Dee waited, giving time for Javon to sort out his thoughts.

"OK, look, she ain't that bad," Javon continued. "She called me out for, well, for not exactly treating her with respect. And I admit she's right on that. And I did tell her I'm sorry. And she apologized too.

So we got a truce, like I said. But Dee, how's this gonna work? I'm the third wheel here."

"What did she apologize for?" Dee asked.

"See?" Javon blurted out. "Right away you jump on her side."

"I'm not jumping on anyone's side, I'm trying to get the story is all."

"She said sorry for, well, you know, getting between us."

Dee stopped abruptly. "What are you on about Javon? Ain't nobody between us, now or ever. I like Jess, no big surprise there. But it has nothing to do with you and me."

"But things aren't the same, Dee. You and me, we were going to roam the streets, be kings wherever we wanted to go. Now, she's in the picture, and all of a sudden we're cozying up to a bunch of people taking care of a big-ass bunch of kids."

"Situation's changed, no doubt," Dee admitted. "But that's got a hell of a lot more to do with Nolan, Thema, and Ethan than with Jessica. Look at me in the eye and tell me you'd rather fuck around empty streets than save more kids like that."

Javon seemed to study with great intent the patch of asphalt directly in front of his feet.

"Goddammit, Dee," Javon finally said, looking up at Dee.

"What?"

"You're gonna drag it out of me, aren't you? Sadistic mofo. OK, you're right. There, happy?"

"It ain't about being right, B. I need you around.

No matter what we end up doing, it's gonna be about 'we' doing. Not me, not you, but we. If I can get that through that rock-hard head of yours, then I'll be happy."

He shoved Javon hard, almost toppling him over.

"What the fuck Dee?" Then Javon smiled, seeing Dee's grin. "Fucker," he said before launching a counter attack on Dee. The two of them struggled before eventually tumbling to the ground and wrestling.

"Oh my God Dee, Javon, stop!" Jessica yelled, running towards them. Javon had managed to get Dee into a headlock. They stopped struggling as Jessica approached. Dee thought about the ridiculous position they were in. But it was the look of horror on Jessica's face that made him burst out laughing. Javon joined in a second later, releasing his headlock on Dee. Jessica's confused look only added to the hilarity of the moment.

8. THE CHILDREN HILTON

"So, it's settled then, you'll help us out for a while?" Deb asked Dee and Javon. She sensed the unease in her friends around these two new arrivals. She felt it herself. But she fought against it, knowing that she, and they, were victims of stereotyping.

"Like I said, we'll see how things go. What do you want us to do?" Dee asked.

"The most urgent thing is rescuing more children. Parents are still dying off, so there's new kids needing help every day. Far more than we'll ever get to, so whatever you can do will be literally life-saving."

"You ain't got exactly all the colors of the rainbow here, why is that?" Javon asked.

"What do you mean?" Deb asked.

"We added two ink spots on your sheet of paper, that's what I mean."

"We're busy saving children's lives, and you are seriously playing the race card?" Mo asked incredulously.

"Busy saving white kids from what I can see," Javon replied, stepping closer to Mo.

Dee put a hand on Javon's shoulder, pulling him

back.

"Stop it, all of you," Deb said.

"Race is a big deal, it's not a 'card'," Titus said. "We're the ones who made it a big deal. And our parents, and their parents. Our ancestors may have started it, but we keep it alive and well. But" — he pointed back to the children in the living room — "they don't have to deal with it. There's only a handful of us, we have the power to bury this thing for good. Treat them all the same, don't bring up the color of their skin, ever, and they can finally be free of our past. First step is to treat ourselves as equals. So you lose your attitude," he said, pointing to Javon. "And if either of you get disrespected, you come talk to me, then we'll have this little talk again." With a parting glance at Mo, he lumbered back into the house.

Deb's jaw slackened. Titus had been a quiet, friendly, giant of a man. This was the first time she'd heard him speak so passionately, and eloquently.

"I'm not a racist —" Mo insisted.

"That's what every racist says when they're about to say something racist," Javon interrupted.

"Oh my God! Stop it! Both of you," Deb said. "Do you hear yourselves? Titus was absolutely spot on. For the first time in history, we can bury this damn thing. We've been given the chance to start over, don't screw it up."

"Me and Javon will go collecting kids for you. But back in our hood, not here," Dee said.

"That's perfect, please do. We've been focussed

on house-to-house searches in the immediate neighborhood. I swear to you that the convenience of working nearby was the only motivation for that. So yes, go back to the area you're familiar with, and find us children from there," Deb said.

"We'll find you some more kids, Mama-Deb. Come on Javon." He smiled at Deb, and tapped Javon on the shoulder.

"I'm not your mama, Darnell," she called after him.

"Deb, I swear," Mo began when Dee and Javon were out of earshot. Deb shook her head and put up her hand to interrupt him.

"Don't. I know you pretty well by now, Maurice. You're a good man. And it will take effort for all of us to become truly color blind. Fake it 'till you make it, OK? For the sake of the kids."

Mo nodded. "You're a good leader, Deb."

"Leader?" Deb gasped. "I am not the leader at all." She laughed at the thought. But then stopped short when she saw the intense look on Mo's face.

"Of course you are, everyone knows it. Well, everyone but you, it seems." Mo reached forward and hugged her. The tension in her body drained, starting from the top of her head and pouring out down through her shoulders and back. After several seconds, Mo stepped back again.

"Thanks for that," she said.

"Human touch, nothing like it." He smiled warmly at her. "Besides, I need it just as much as you." His face became somber. "Deb, the things I've seen in those houses," his voiced trailed off.

"I know, I've seen a lot too. Back at you," she said reaching out and pulling him close to her.

The hugs had certainly felt comforting, but not his words. A leader? Other than in the familiar surroundings of her classrooms, Deb had never considered herself to be a leader. And if these people, survivors of a veritable apocalypse, looked to her for leadership, well, she wasn't sure if she could deal with that. She'd been so focussed on saving children, that she'd missed the fact that people saw her in a leadership role.

Let's keep it that way, she thought. She decided she would ignore the leadership issue. Not only did it sound overwhelming, but it would also distract her from her primary goal: saving the children.

"OK, well, I'm going to go talk to Titus. He and I will go check out some hotels, see if we can find ourselves a new home," Deb said.

"Good idea, Boss."

"Oh cut it out," she laughed. Then she noticed Mo's glistening eyes. "Hey, are you OK?" She put her hand on his arm.

Mo didn't speak, he only shook his head as tears spilled down his cheeks. He looked like a little boy to Deb. In retrospect, she should have known that his job of entering houses would have taken a bigger toll than he'd let on. She pulled him back into a tight hug. His shoulders shook as he sagged against her.

"Aw, Maurice. I'm so sorry for not clueing in earlier to your pain. I know how awful it is, what you're having to do."

She waited for his sobbing to subside. It broke her heart to see someone in such misery.

"Maybe you should take a break from the searches. There's plenty of work to be done here, with the children."

Mo brusquely pulled away from her. "Absolutely not. I can't un-see what I've seen with the kids I saved. There's plenty more out there, waiting for me. More Sammys too, if we had just gotten to him one day earlier, maybe Sophia would still have her brother. Oh God, I feel like an idiot for breaking down like that, I'm so sorry."

Deb flinched at the mention of Sammy. She thought of him every time she saw Sophia. She repeatedly replayed the scenes of his tiny body in her arms. What could she have done differently? She was convinced that she could have saved him had she only been able to have him swallow some water. It haunted her dreams. *Maybe Maurice is right*, she thought, *perhaps it just had to do with timing.* She wished that she truly believed that Sammy had been beyond saving on the day that they'd found him. But she suspected she would never stop second guessing how he had died under her care.

"Maurice, don't you ever, ever apologize for having a hard time coping with the horror that you see every day. I can't say that I'm sorry I pulled you into this. Because you're literally saving lives, and that's bigger than the both of us. But I really am so sorry for the suffering you're enduring on their behalf."

"No need to be sorry for anything, Deb. I'm just tired, it got to me for a moment. But I'm fine. I am."

He brushed her arm affectionately. Deb wished she could see inside his head, to understand how far from 'fine' he really was.

"Go do your hotel shopping," he urged her.

"Promise you'll talk to me whenever it gets bad?"

"Promise."

"OK then. I'll hold you to that, Maurice."

"Maybe you're right, too small," Deb said. She and Titus had set off first thing in the morning, after helping with the Breakfast Challenge, as they called that special time of trying to feed some twenty-five children. They weren't the only ones on the road today. Joshua and Amanda had left to visit the Amish communities near Heuvelton that Joshua knew about. Deb hoped those two would come back with fresh produce for the children.

The Country Inn that she and Titus were currently looking at was the most promising hotel yet. It had plenty of space to accommodate everyone, with room to spare. But Titus had rightly pointed out some of its flaws. First, the rooms were too spread out among several attached buildings. Second, while there was considerable room to grow, there wasn't quite enough room, if their current intake of children, and adults, kept growing at the pace it was.

As Titus drove his truck in search of the next

hotel, Deb's thoughts turned to Darnell. He'd seemed quite discouraged the night before when he and Javon arrived late at night, empty handed. She had tried to assure him that it was quite normal. Mo, herself, and the others who went searching didn't find people every day. She wondered how he and Javon were doing today, and hoped they went about it methodically like she'd explained. She sensed a stubbornness in Darnell. He frequently looked away and shuffled his feet impatiently when she gave him instructions. *I need to turn off always being in teacher mode.* She sent silent good vibes to him and Javon now, wishing them success.

"OK, OK, OK, now we're talking," Titus said, interrupting her thoughts. The man's smile was even wider than usual. Deb followed his gaze to the top of a building jutting above a low-rise sprawling Victorian brick house. Titus turned right at the next street, which led to the hotel.

"It's huge," Deb laughed. The hotel was very wide. Deb counted eight floors, all of them taking the full width of the structure.

"I wonder if they have valet parking," Titus said, parking the truck under the overhang above the front door. He reached into the back of the truck and grabbed the spare B&E kit that Mo had prepared for them. The tools clinked against each other as he swung the sports bag over his shoulder.

"Um, Titus?" Deb said, as he started pulling a crow bar out of the bag. She had pushed open the unlocked door. Titus laughed and dropped the bag outside the door.

They entered into the semi-darkness of the hotel lobby. Straight ahead, a long reception desk sat in front of a curved wall adorned with glass blocks. To the left, a seating area was centered around a stone wall with an embedded gas fireplace. On the right, several bar stools lay in disarray on the floor of the lobby bar. Glass from the liquor cabinet doors littered the long marble-top bar. Most of the bottles were gone from the shelves.

"I'd say it's a five-star," Titus said.

Deb nodded in agreement. "I'll bet there's a pool too."

"Don't think I'd want to swim in it."

"Can I help you folks?" Deb and Titus spun around to face the man who spoke. He stood near the elevators. He wore an unbuttoned red and black flannel shirt, with a white t-shirt underneath. His tight-fitting jeans emphasized his slim build. His black, well-worn work boots hardly made a sound as he took a few steps towards them. A rifle hung loosely in his arms, pointed at the floor a few feet ahead of him.

"The door was open," Deb said, her voice trailing off.

"Not sure what you've got in that bag outside, but somehow I don't think you were going to let a locked door stop you. That's why I don't lock it, no sense in having it broken first time someone wants to get in here."

"Look Mister, we're not looking for any trouble

here. We'll be on our way," Titus said, smoothly positioning himself in front of Deb. She was grateful for his protective instinct, but wouldn't let him take all the risks. She gently put a hand on his arm and moved next to him.

"He's right, we're sorry for barging in. I must admit were getting used to most places being empty. We'll leave right away."

"I don't have much food, if that's what you're after," the man said.

Deb detected a hint of remorse in the man's voice. "No, actually we're looking for a place to live. We have about twenty-five children, and we're finding more almost every day."

"Twenty-five children? Where did they come from?"

"Some, literally on the street. Others were brought to us from dying parents. And others we found in house-to-house searches."

"How many adults are looking after all these kids?" the man asked, lowering his rifle until it was pointing straight down.

"Well, there's about ten of us right now. Which makes things a little crazy back at the houses. We started at my house, then moved in next door as well, and now we're bursting at the seams. Titus here has been working hard to make space for all the kids, but, well we're just outgrowing houses. We thought a hotel would be good, since it's already divided into a lot of rooms."

"So, what are you going to do with all these kids?"

"I haven't thought too far ahead, I'm afraid. Right now, we only have one goal: find orphaned children."

"What we're going to do," Titus chimed in, "is make sure that they get a chance to grow up."

The man looked them over for a moment. "Follow me please, I want to show you something."

Deb glanced at Titus, who shrugged his shoulders and started after the man. *Well, if he wanted to kill us, he would have done it by now*, Deb thought, as she followed along.

The man led them up a short flight of stairs, and down a long corridor of hotel rooms. He stopped in front of room 108 and pulled a plastic key card from his pocket. He placed it near the door handle, and they heard the bolt slip back. Even though she knew it was battery operated, Deb still found it odd, and yet comforting, to see something electrical working.

"Come on out, we've got visitors," the man called as he opened the door. An icy chill ran down Deb's spine as she realized they had too easily trusted this stranger. She wondered if they were walking into a trap as the man entered the room and held the door open. Titus stepped forward and peered inside. She could see the muscles in his arms had bunched up. *He's as tense as I am.*

Suddenly Titus' body relaxed, and his familiar smile returned. "Well hello there, what's your name?" he said.

"Liam," a small voice replied.

Deb made her way around Titus to see inside the room as well. A small boy stood a few feet away.

Behind him, stood a slightly smaller girl. Three other children cautiously crept out of a side room to see the strangers at the door. All of them, except for Liam, looked at Deb and Titus wearily. Liam seemed more curious about Titus than worried about strangers.

"You're big," Liam said to the giant in front of him.

"So are you," Titus replied with a chuckle.

"Are these yours?" Deb asked the man with the gun.

"Nope. Liam and his little sister Olivia drifted in first, about three weeks ago now. Liam's a brave boy, he and his sister walked a long time before arriving here." He tousled Liam's hair. Liam stood a little taller, still staring at Titus. "Noah and Levi arrived a week later. And Luna here came in all by herself just three days ago."

"I saw the other kids playing outside," Luna informed Deb.

"Wow, you're a brave, and smart, little girl," Deb said, smiling at the girl approvingly. She never ceased to be amazed at children's resiliency.

"How have you been coping?" she asked the man.

He shrugged. "Just face each day, one at a time, like everybody else. Name's Chris," he said extending his free hand.

"Hi Chris, I'm Deb, and this is Titus."

"Pleased to meet you," Titus said, shaking Chris' hand.

"How did you end up in this hotel?" Deb asked.

"You stole our idea," Titus added with a chuckle.

"Actually, I work here. Well, worked here, I guess. I was in maintenance here for the last six years."

"What's your plan? Have you thought about what you're going to do next?" Deb asked.

"Not really, no. But I can't care for these kids by myself. If something were to happen to me, well, you know." He nodded towards the children. "So, at some point I knew I had to connect with other survivors. And then the Lord delivered you to my front door."

Deb contained her laughter to a brief burst, more like a loud chuckle. She had never been very religious, and had trouble understanding people who were.

"Did I say something funny?" Chris asked.

"No, no, I just never considered myself as someone the Lord would want to deliver to anyone."

This made Titus laugh, which made Deb lose control of her own suppressed laughter.

"Anyone who's taking care of twenty-five children is worthy in the Lord's eyes, Deb," Chris said earnestly.

OK, this one's missing the humor gene, Deb thought. "Look, I do appreciate the sentiment, and I don't mean any disrespect. But I'm not exactly the religious type."

"Well don't worry about me, I'm not the missionary type out to convert you."

"And with that out of the way, are you saying that you'd like to join us?" Deb asked.

"Yes, absolutely, you folks should move into this hotel. I assume you've given some thought to how it would work when you found a suitable place?"

Titus cleared his throat. "That's my job, I suppose. I could use a hand, especially from someone who already knows the place. What I was thinking about is that we could have an entire floor be for the children. On that floor I was going to remove all the doors so there's no chance of getting locked out of one of their rooms."

"And a lot less scary for the kids," Deb added.

Chris was nodding. "And an adult sleeping in each of the rooms on the ends, sort of the night crew, if you like."

Deb chuckled. "Well, yes on the night crew, but with a mix of twenty-five babies and traumatized toddlers, there isn't a whole lot of sleeping going on at night."

"Fair enough," Chris agreed.

"We've experimented with taking shifts, and with alternative nights. We're finding shift-work is better. Even if you only have to get the night-shift every couple of days, an entire night without sleep was just too hard. And not very helpful for comforting children – tired adults are cranky adults."

"Of course, I don't have any babies, and a lot less than twenty-five kids, but I certainly have had to work on the tired and cranky part, being all on my own."

"Chris, you will be the first to get a night off when we're all together," Deb said, smiling warmly at their new companion. *This is a good man, despite the religious thing*, she thought.

"But, I have to warn you, you're underestimating the amount of work. For example," he turned towards Titus, "your idea of removing the doors won't work. They're far too heavy to lug around. We could simply prop them open."

"I'm not afraid of work. And what can be propped can become unpropped and hurt a little kid," Titus replied.

"I'm not afraid of work either, that's not what I meant. But you have to pick your battles, and removing doors is a waste of effort."

"Making sure that the kids stay safe is not a waste of effort in my book, ever."

Deb detected a slight rise in Titus' normally calm voice. She intervened before the discussion turned into an argument.

"Why don't you come back with us and meet everyone," she suggested.

"Yeah, I would love to. Can't say I get out much lately," Chris said.

There's hope yet for the humorless one, thought Deb.

"Who wants to ride with us?" Titus asked the children, turning away from Chris and crouching down to their level.

"I do!" Liam said, raising his hand.

His sister Olivia hesitated a moment before joining in with a "me too" and a raised hand.

"OK you three ride with me," Chris said, pointing to the rest of the children.

"I'll hop in too, if you don't mind. Then you're

sure not to get lost," Deb said.

"True, it's not like we can exchange cell phone numbers, is it?" Chris replied.

Titus chuckled. "Right, cause it's really hard to follow the only other truck on the road."

"Not sure about you, but I don't like to drive fast with a car load of children."

"It ain't about speed, the roads are deserted."

"Again, if you roar off, it doesn't matter if they're deserted or not."

Deb had to interrupt again. "We're not going to speed, now let's go, these kids want to move, right?"

The children looked on with a mixture of puzzlement and tentative smiles. Liam nodded.

I hope I don't have a two-alpha-male problem brewing here, Deb thought.

There were several unfamiliar faces when Deb, Titus, and Chris arrived at the house. A chaotic chorus of introductions and questions ensued. In Deb's absence, Dee and Javon had brought in a family of six. Dee beamed as he walked over to Deb with the new arrivals.

"Looks like we both brought in some new ones, Mama," Dee said. Deb had to admit that the young man was growing on her.

"Deb, is it? A pleasure to meet you, I'm Antoine," the newcomer said, extending his hand. The couple appeared to be in their forties. The children surprised Deb the most. *Teenagers!*

"This is my wife Vanessa," Antoine continued.

"Pleased to meet you both," Deb said, shaking hands.

"And these lovely young ladies are our daughters Alexis and Kalisha, and these young men are Jayden and Malik."

"Welcome. And how old are you?" Deb asked the children.

"Seventeen, I'm the eldest," Alexis said. Kalisha was fifteen, Jayden twelve, and the youngest, Malik, was ten. All were so much older than their current group of children.

"Are any of you, um, vaccinated?" Deb asked. She found it strange how 'vaccinated' had almost become a curse word.

"No, we trust the Lord will take us when our time is due. Putting man's potions in our veins does not sit well with our belief in the Savior," Antoine declared.

"Amen to that," Chris chimed in.

Oh no, more of them, Deb thought.

"Oh, I'm sorry, this is Chris. We found him in what might become our new home, a large hotel not far from here. He brought in five children as well, that he's been caring for on his own."

"The hotel is perfect," Titus added excitedly. "It's huge, all the children can probably fit on one floor, maybe two. And Chris here was part of the maintenance staff, he'll be able to help me out."

"When are you all gonna move into your new digs?" Dee asked.

"'Our' new digs, Darnell," Deb corrected.

"We ain't there yet Mama, you know that."

"Well, I should do some prep work on the place before we all move in," Titus said, ignoring Dee and Deb's side conversation. "What do you say, Chris, two, maybe three days to get the children's floor ready?"

"Yeah, that should be plenty. Kid-proof the rooms, take out breakables and dangerous things, that's about it," Chris replied.

"And get beds and cribs setup," Titus corrected. Deb could almost see the wheels spinning inside his head as he planned their new residence. "Plus remove the doors."

Deb winced, hoping that Chris wouldn't chime in.

"Well we still have to negotiate that, I don't think that's a smart move," Chris said, right on cue.

"Man, you can't mess with safety. If one of those —"

"Woah, that's a lot of new faces," Amanda declared, cutting off Titus as she, Mo, and Jessica came to greet Deb and the new arrivals. Their sudden arrival eased the tension.

"We growin' every day, Miss Amanda Jones," Dee said. Deb found it utterly charming how proud he was at having brought in a group of people.

Amanda stopped short. "What did you call me?"

"Jones is your last name, isn't it?" Dee asked, looking confused.

"It is, but Miss Amanda Jones? Why that?"

"Oh, it's an old song, that's all,"

"I know, it's a Rolling Stones song. Not many

people know it, so I'm surprised to hear you say that."

"Believe it or not, Dee is our local classic rock historian," Jessica said, poking Dee in the ribs. Deb noticed the way they looked at each other. *Something going on between those two?* she wondered.

"I told you, don't put me in a little box, woman."

Deb's smile disappeared when she saw tears welling in Amanda's eyes. "You OK, Amanda?" she asked.

Amanda nodded, wiping her eyes. Dee looked bewildered. "Sorry, I didn't mean no disrespect," he said.

"No, no, it's alright," Amanda replied. "The official story is that the song Amanda by Boston was a big hit when my parents were dating. That's why they named me Amanda. But my father, Darren Jones, told me in confidence that when he was a teenager, and a big Stones fan, he thought that if he ever had a daughter, he would call her Amanda after the Stones song. Anyway, I haven't heard anyone mention that song in a very long time, and so you reminded me of my father. And I miss my husband so much. And now I'm blubbering like an idiot." She laughed with embarrassment, wiping her eyes once more.

"Aw, sweetheart," Jessica said, pulling Amanda into a hug. "We all have loved ones that we miss, so we can certainly relate."

Deb understood the difficulty everyone had coping with their enormous losses. Saving the children and caring for them seemed to consume so much of people's minds that they didn't have the luxury of grieving. Though it saddened her to see Amanda cry, at the same time she couldn't help but feel that it was a good thing. *All of us will need to process this eventually.*

"Joshua is going to visit the Amish tomorrow, why don't you go with him?" Deb said to Amanda.

"No, no I'll be fine. There's more work to do around here than there are people to do it."

"No, seriously, go with him. We all need a break now and then. Besides, it's probably not a good idea to take any long road trips alone. If he gets injured, there's no way to communicate with us. If you're two, you can look out for each other."

Amanda seemed to weigh Deb's words.

"Road trip! You'd be crazy not to go," Mo added.

"Road trip, road trip," Jessica chanted.

"Fine, fine, I'll go," Amanda laughed.

9. MED SCHOOL

Jessica smirked when she drove the SUV over the sidewalk and parked next to the glass doors of the university medical center. *Parking a stolen car right up on the sidewalk, who's a badass now?* she thought. Jessica had mentioned the need for more vehicles to run errands, like she was today. Mo and Brandon had then brought back four vehicles during their house searching, swiping keys and cars from deceased occupants. With Amanda and Joshua on their road trip to Heuvelton, it seemed like a good time for Jessica to get away as well.

Treating Sophia's broken arm had been a wake-up call. Jessica needed to set up some sort of emergency care clinic in the house. And she needed to study more about emergency care. *Just like being back in med school, but without professors or other students*, she thought, smiling to herself. And so today was the day. She would load up the SUV with medical supplies and spend a considerable amount of time in the library gathering medical texts.

The library was in fact her first stop. Built in the nineteen-twenties, it was an over-the-top architectural monument, by today's standards. The entrance to the library reminded Jessica of a small version of the Arc de Triomphe in Paris, with the upper end of the arch filled in with a stained glass window. Topping off the impressive building was a glass dome-covered rotunda. A winding staircase inside of the rotunda led to a large round room with plush occasional chairs along the circular wall. Jessica had never understood the purpose of this arrangement. She, for one, couldn't read or study while sitting in a circle with some twenty other students, half of which were facing her.

The rotunda was not her destination today. Jessica scanned the You-Are-Here map to get her bearings straight. She would skip the sections on medical history, anatomy, pharmacy, nursing, and a host of other broad topics in the massive library. She took out her notepad and wrote down the floor and section numbers for surgery and anesthesiology. The latter, especially, was an area she had barely touched in her studies. *Alternative and Natural Medicine*, she read. That too might warrant a visit, she realized. As man-made drugs expired, she may have to turn to natural alternatives. Jessica realized she should later try to find a school of herbalism, if there were any nearby. *Time for me to bug Amanda and her search engine.*

The acrid smell of a dead fire infiltrated her nostrils when she was halfway up the stairs to the fourth floor. *Oh no!* She ran up the rest of the way to her destination. The smell became overpowering when she opened the door to the Surgery & Anatomy section. Jessica pressed her sleeve to her nose and mouth as she studied the devastation before her. Every single bookstack had been tumbled over. On the left side, they looked liked neatly fallen oversized dominos. The right side, and the middle section, formed two large piles of bent metal carcasses at either end of the room. In the clearing between them, a mountain of half-burnt books rose six feet up towards the blackened ceiling. A few wisps of smoke drifted from the ash-covered collection of lost knowledge. *Why? Why? Why?* her brain screamed repeatedly.

She spent the next three hours sorting through the undamaged pile of books beneath the toppled bookstacks on the left. The shelves were too heavy to lift by herself. She had to climb onto the metal racks, and reach through the gaps to pull out books. It was dangerous work. The metal frames would shift under her weight, and settle more as she pulled books out. She had visions of her hand getting pinched between two shelves. Or getting stuck if her entire arm got trapped in the unstable metal racks. *No one even knows I'm here*, she realized. She skipped any books that offered the smallest amount of resistance when she tugged at them. If they were supporting some weight, removing them might be exactly what would bring on her nightmare scenario of getting trapped in the library.

After she had rescued all the books that she could extract from the giant dominos, Jessica sorted through them. To her disappointment, they were almost all about anatomy. A few books from the bottom of the very last stack, the hardest ones to reach, touched on surgery. Which meant that the bulk of the books she wanted were in the smoldering pile of rubbish in the middle. She sighed, and started filling her two large and sturdy shopping bags with carefully selected books from her triaged rescue pile. She dumped the contents of the bags into the car when they got too heavy, and came back for more.

Fortunately, whoever had unleashed destruction on the fourth floor had not repeated their fury on the fifth floor, where the alternative medicine section was stored. Jessica filled her bags once more with books that covered topics from home remedies for minor injuries to herbal teas for various ailments.

It was past lunch time when she was done with the library. On a whim, she took her lunch up to the famously useless rotunda. For once she wouldn't be facing other students. She thought that perhaps this was her last chance to try to enjoy the strange round room.

Jessica began to regret her decision as she started up the pitch-black spiral staircase that led to the rotunda's inner chamber. *Useless room in normal times, useless room in an apocalypse*, she thought, as she struggled up the stairs with a death grip on the banister. It was only much later that the irony of finding a person sitting in one of the rotunda's chairs would register with Jessica. She froze after entering the room.

The woman sat in a chair facing the door Jessica had emerged from. The woman's eyes widened, but she remained seated. Jessica remained frozen at the door. The two of them could have been part of an odd photo. The woman was the first to speak.

"I thought I'd have it to myself for once," she said, chuckling. A small smile formed on her slightly wrinkled face. She had blue eyes and shoulder-length black hair mixed with streaks of gray.

"So did I," Jessica acknowledged. "You were here first, I'll go."

"Don't be ridiculous, come in. Maybe it's the room's will, it cannot accept solitude."

Jessica hesitated. Her crazy-radar was on full alert after such a strange statement. The woman laughed softly after a moment of watching Jessica remain in place.

"I'm just messing with you, I haven't lost my mind. My name's Nancy Walkman, I used to work here."

"You worked in the library?" Jessica asked, taking a tentative step forward.

"No, I mean at this medical center," Nancy replied.

"Oh good, so you won't be upset that I just stole a car load of books."

"Help yourself," Nancy said with a smile, and gesturing towards a chair. "Will you join me or not?"

"Are you a doctor?"

"Nope, dentist. I teach dentistry at the school. Taught, I mean," she corrected herself.

"But you have almost as much training in medicine as doctors do, right?"

"Sure, but we don't practice most of it. That's the biggest difference, and why you probably shouldn't rely on your dentist for general medicine."

"OK, maybe this was fate, meeting you up here. I have two years of med school, but now I'm with a group of survivors caring for a ton of children. And they expect me to be their doctor. I could really use your help, is there any way you would consider joining us? Or at least come meet the others and decide later?"

"I don't even know your name, and you're inviting me to come live with you? That's pretty bold."

"Sorry, I know I'm coming on strong. Desperation will do that. My name's Jessica Albert, if that helps."

"It helps Jessica, but no I won't be joining you. I don't have much longer, and honestly, I prefer to face the end alone. Strange as that may seem."

Jessica was taken aback. She had surmised that Nancy was another unvaccinated survivor.

"I'm so sorry, I didn't realize. I mean, I assumed you were unvaccinated. Have the dizzy spells started?"

"Not yet. Should be soon I imagine. It's a ticking time bomb, without the annoying ticking sounds, fortunately. I was a little late in getting my shots, but still. I don't know why I've been given more time than most. I always thought that if ever I knew I was going to die, that I would travel the world. I never imagined this scenario: knowing about my coming death but not having a transportation system to travel with. What a bummer."

"You don't have to be alone. Forget about helping

us, but you should at least be with people in your last days. We're all social animals, after all."

"Well, if I may be totally honest with you, I was sitting in this room contemplating whether I'll wait for the dizzy spells. Or take an early exit, so to speak."

Jessica paused, her mind spinning. How could she help this poor woman?

"You do know, I'm sure, that sometimes it helps to talk to someone," Jessica began. Nancy's laughter caught her off guard.

"I'm not depressed, Jessica. I'm going to die soon, anyway. You have no idea what it's like waiting every day for that first goddamn dizzy spell. Sometimes just getting out of bed I imagine that I'm a little dizzy and wonder if this is my last day."

"I'm sorry," was all Jessica could think of saying.

"Forget it. Now what's this business of stealing books?" Nancy said, abruptly changing topics.

Jessica felt guilty about her relief moving away from such an uncomfortable discussion. "If I need to be their doctor, I need to learn a hell of a lot more. I'm getting myself a mini medical library, and some supplies from the hospital."

"You're going to put yourself through med school on your own?" Nancy blurted out. "Jesus, that's dedication and courage. I think I would have enjoyed getting to know you, Jessica Albert."

Heat rose to Jessica's face. "I'm not courageous, I'm terrified! This is the only way I can deal with it."

"No. Brave is accepting your role and trying to do

your best. If you weren't brave, you would simply refuse, or do a shoddy job until they stop counting on you."

Jessica shrugged, refusing to accept the compliment. She knew at a logical level that this was one of her many faults. Despite the knowledge, she couldn't help herself from discounting other people's praise.

"In a way, I'm being selfish. Since I was a little girl, I wanted to become a doctor. Now I get to work towards it without some professor, no offense, grading me and deciding if I can continue or not. So I can go at my own pace, which takes some of the pressure off."

Nancy frowned at her. "If you can twist what you're trying to do into sounding like a selfish act, you might want to work on yourself just a wee bit. Physician, heal thyself."

Jessica's cheeks turned red. She had no response to Nancy's piercing comment.

"Anyway, you'd better visit the Oral Health building, there's a good library there too."

"Um, I think I have all I need now. I'm sure it's good too, but I have more books than I can probably ever read already."

"So what are you going to do when your first toothache patient comes in?"

"Oh shit," Jessica said. *Really? I have to study dentistry as well?* It made perfect sense, but how could she possibly become well-versed in all fields of medicine? It was an impossible task.

"You should have some basic understanding of oral health. At least some reference material for the day you'll eventually need it. I can go over there with you if you like. I can pick out a half dozen must-read books for you."

Jessica hesitated.

"Or not," Nancy said. "I'm not pushing anything on you here."

"No, sorry, that's a kind offer. I'm just feeling a little overwhelmed by everything I need to learn."

"Nobody's going to expect you to be the all-knowing healer. This is for your own benefit, something you can lean on if you need it."

"You're right, and yes, I would love your help picking out reference material. I have no clue what to look for."

Jessica drove Nancy the few blocks over to the Oral Health building. They spent less than an hour browsing the shelves, with Nancy adroitly plucking out a selection of some fifteen books.

"If only the main library had been in a pristine condition like this. I really needed books on surgery, but someone torched the entire section on the fourth floor."

"I certainly smelled the smoke on the way upstairs, but didn't want to see the damage," Nancy said. "So pointless. But—" her eyes light up, and she put her hand on Jessica's left shoulder. "OK quiz time, Jessica. Who reads a lot of books on surgery?"

Jessica wondered where this was going. "Students, I guess."

"And in particular, which students?"

"Come on Nancy, what are you driving at?"

"Which students, think, Jessica."

"Students who want to be surgeons." She humored Nancy so that the woman would end the strange quiz.

"I.e. interns. And interns have offices."

"Oh my God, Nancy, you're brilliant!"

"I have my moments." She smiled. "Shall we go book hunting?"

They made their way back to the main building of the medical center. After a few false starts, they eventually found the offices of the interns. Nancy's intuition proved to be correct. While not an extensive collection, Jessica was able to bring home seven books on surgical procedures. After the last office, Jessica turned towards her new friend.

"Nancy, I would love to spend more time with you. Are you sure you won't join us, even for a little while? Please?"

Nancy smiled, and, to Jessica's surprise, leaned in and hugged her. "Thanks for the offer, but no. I need to be alone."

They walked together in silence towards Jessica's SUV. Jessica carried her partially filled bag of books, and added them to the moderately large pile of books in the back of the SUV.

"You know what I've always wanted to do? No, more than that. What I really planned to do some day?" Jessica asked.

Nancy shook her head.

"I've dreamed of taking a really long road trip along the coast. I wanted to drive north, through small towns and zigzagging roads through Maine. Then up into New Brunswick, dip down into Nova Scotia. And then go back up following the coast along Quebec and Labrador. See some moose, for God's sake. And take my time, spread it out over four to six weeks. Stop at almost every beach and just enjoy."

"That does sound great, I hope you get to do it some day. No reason you can't still do it, right?"

"That's right," Jessica said, smiling. "There's no reason I can't travel like I've always wanted to."

Nancy stepped back with a momentary burst of laughter. "Oh my God, you are one manipulative lady."

Jessica shrugged, smiling. The road trip idea was true, though not a lifelong dream by any stretch of the imagination. But it had served its purpose. She had lured Nancy into thinking about an alternative to cutting her short life even shorter, while fulfilling her dream to travel before death. Jessica was proud of herself: a rare and welcome treat. And far better than the darker moments that she struggled with most of her adult life. Jessica was no stranger to flirting with ideas surrounding an 'early exit', as Nancy had called it.

"I'll consider it, that much I can promise," Nancy said.

"Collect postcards, and bring them back to show me when you get back."

"Sure thing," Nancy said, smiling.

They hugged once more before Nancy walked away. The encounter left Jessica with a strange mixture of emptiness and satisfaction at having helped someone. At least she hoped it would help Nancy, it was up to the woman to decide now. And most likely, Jessica would never know the outcome. It was the latter reality that left her feeling empty, and lonely. She resisted the urge to drive back to her group immediately. Instead, she drove the short distance to the hospital, which was also on the sprawling medical campus.

Contrary to the esthetically pleasing library, the hospital was a functional, rectangular, bricked behemoth of a building. The hospital also dated back a hundred years. But a modern-day curved glass addition had been incongruously pasted at a ninety-degree angle on the right edge of the original structure. The result was a strange L-shape, with the long side being plain red brick, and the short side having a futuristic curved glass architecture.

Jessica once again drove the SUV over the sidewalk up to the glass entrance. It was far more practical to do so, given that she would load it up with supplies. But even without that advantage, she would still have done it just for the 'because I can' feeling. "Not sure if I'm mischievously funny or just immature," she said out loud as she shut off the engine.

She grabbed her shopping bags and notebook once more, and headed through the emergency doors. She had expected them to be unlocked. But what she didn't expect was that someone had smashed them in. She couldn't imagine why they would want to break the glass doors of the hospital. But then she never could understand the random acts of violence and vandalism that humans seemed unable to stop themselves from perpetrating.

"Let's see, emergency supply room, pharmacy, and general medical supplies," she said.

Jessica started with the supply room next to emergency. While the main supply room carried equipment needed for the entire hospital, it was too far away and too slow for the emergency care department. A much smaller supply room catered specifically to urgent care, and was near the operating and examination rooms. She had not taken a dozen steps before noticing an AED machine in its wall cabinet.

"Need one of those," she said, taking the defibrillator out of the cabinet.

Since medical staff had been among the first to be vaccinated, and hence the first to die, hospitals were not littered with decaying corpses. When the Vax Plague began, the fabric of society had been sufficiently intact to deal with the deaths in the medical facilities. As a result, it was a surreal experience to be walking through an empty, mostly pristine, hospital. There were a few signs of disarray, like an occasional overturned chair. But in contrast to what their group would find in houses that they broke into, this was unbelievably sterile.

There were no signs leading to the store room until Jessica was past the bold red lettered sign announcing 'No admittance - staff only'. Two of the walls of the large, classroom-sized room were wall-to-wall shelves. The other side of the room had the larger pieces of equipment: patient monitors, EKGs, anesthesia machines. Jessica ignored those, given their need for electricity. Instead, she put aside a large pile of items on the floor that she would haul to her vehicle: more compression bandages, boxes of gauze, intravenous solutions and tubings, scalpels, blood pressure monitors, surgical gloves, alcohol pads. By the time she was done, she had a hip-high pile of supplies to load into the car. The store room had been better stocked than she had imagined, so she didn't see a need to go explore the larger central store room. Jessica looked at her two, now appearing very small, shopping bags. The AED machine she had taken near the entrance had already partially filled one of them. *These won't do*, she thought.

Jessica rummaged around the store room looking for larger bags. She found garbage bags, but they were too flimsy to carry her supplies. She had visions of the sharp corners of the various package tearing through the thin plastic bags and leaving her no further ahead. Then she spotted the gurney. *Aha!* She dumped several boxes of supplies from the shelves, being careful not to leave the room looking like thieves had ransacked it. *Though technically I am a thief*, she realized. Nevertheless, she thought other survivors might one day come here, and she wanted to leave it with some semblance of order. She filled the emptied boxes with her stash and loaded them up on the gurney. With only two trips, she finished unloading them into the SUV.

In contrast to the relatively unscathed areas of the hospital that Jessica had seen thus far, the pharmacy was in shambles. Jessica's primary goal was to secure antibiotics and prescription-strength pain medication. She could find plenty of antibiotics as she sorted through the debris. But clearly others before her had pillaged the pharmacy in search of opioids and other analgesics. She suspected they weren't treating medical emergencies, but rather they were numbing the pain of civilization's collapse. Jessica sighed. Most of the common drugs like ibuprophen were still there, but she could get those at any pharmacy.

Jessica stood over her much smaller than expected pile of medicines. *I should have made a list*, she thought, racking her brains for any other medication that she should search for while she was there. That was when she heard the faint scratching noise. She frowned, cocking her head to locate the source of the noise. It sounded like it came from the door she had entered only moments ago. She went to the door and peered through the eye-level, small viewing window. *Anti face-flatteners*, as she used to call them when she worked in the hospital, and later in the crematorium. She saw nothing, but could now better hear the scratching below.

Thinking it was most likely a mouse, she kicked

the door loudly to scare it away. She peered through the glass once more and caught a glimpse of some orange-tinged fur disappearing around the corner and into the adjacent corridor. *A cat!* she realized. How on earth it had survived and ended up in the hospital was beyond her. She swung open the door and rushed to the corridor where the cat had disappeared. She saw it enter a room on the left, far down the hallway.

She ran down the corridor, slowing when she got near the room, so as not to scare the cat even further. Not a cat, but a kitten, Jessica realized, as she stepped into the small examination room. Under the physician's desk, the orange tabby kitten trembled against its dead mother's body. Jessica noticed three other kittens in the room, all dead.

"Oh, you poor thing," she murmured, getting on her knees to make herself appear smaller. Jessica blinked slowly at the cat. It was a case of a random bit of information that her brain had decided to permanently store. A few years ago, she had read an article that said a cat blinked slowly when it signaled that it felt safe and trusted you. The article claimed that if you did the same to your cat, you were essentially communicating and bonding with it. She had no idea if it was true, nor why she, who had never been a cat owner, would remember this bit of trivia. And yet here she was years later, on a hospital floor, blinking slowly at an emaciated kitten. If not for the sad state of the cats in the room, she would have found the scene hilarious.

Whether it was the blinking or sheer desperation, when Jessica reached out her hand, the surviving kitten tentatively walked a few steps towards her and sniffed her fingers. Jessica remained motionless, allowing the kitten to explore her slowly. When the kitten rubbed itself against her leg, Jessica took that as a signal that she could pick it up.

"You're just a cute little orange fur ball, aren't you," she cooed at the kitten as she stood up with it in her arms. Her medical mind kicked into gear. The kitten was starving and severely dehydrated. Rather than going back to the car and getting her water bottle, Jessica had a better idea. She brought the kitten back to the pharmacy where she remembered having seen jugs of distilled water on a lower shelf. She grabbed a syringe and awkwardly popped it out of its cellophane wrapper. She sucked some of the distilled water into the syringe and offered it to the kitten. It eagerly took it in after a quick sniff, and suckled. Jessica ever-so-gently pressed the syringe plunger, allowing a bit of water to flow into the kitten's mouth.

She didn't let the kitten drink too much, applying the same logic as she would to a dehydrated human. The kitten purred in her arms, looking up at her, and trying to nuzzle in comfortably.

"What should I call you? If I don't name you right away, they might call you something generic like 'Kitty' and we don't want that now do we? Not for such a special little kitten, no we don't." She put the cat down on the pharmacy's counter top. It meowed, protesting the loss of the warm, comfy arms. Jessica turned it over gently, lifted its tail and peered in the genital area.

"Hmm. Sorry for violating your privacy little one. Well, I don't see any little balls, but maybe they don't show up yet in someone as small as you. Still, I'm going to guess you're a girl."

She picked the kitten up again, cuddling it and giving it her finger to suckle on.

"I'm going to call you Nancy," she declared. "You can remind me of my new, hopefully road-tripping, friend. And I suspect you're going to make a lot of little people very happy. I promise not to let them rough you up. Toddlers can be pretty scary, can't they?" Jessica continued using her cooing voice while walking through the emergency room door towards the SUV.

Then she remembered her pile of medications on the floor of the pharmacy. She turned around and headed back in. By the time she arrived at the pharmacy, Nancy was asleep in the crook of her left arm.

Now what? she thought. It was time consuming work, but Jessica was able to kneel, and stuff the medications into her shopping bags with one hand. She could only carry one bag at a time, and so made two trips to get the meager supplies into her vehicle.

Ignoring all pre-VP safety rules, she put Nancy on her lap, ignored the seat belt warning beeps, drove off the sidewalk, and headed home.

10. HEUVELTON

They had driven less than ten minutes before Joshua pulled into a gas station. "Need to fill up," he said brightly.

"Um, pumps aren't working," Amanda replied.

"Those aren't, that's true." A mischievous smile appeared on his face.

"I'm not very good at riddles."

Joshua got out of the car and headed towards the rear. "Watch and learn."

She followed him to the back where he pulled a set of long rubber tubes, and a hand pump. "There's ten to twenty thousand gallons in the storage tanks. This long rubber hose goes into the access port in the ground. The other hose into our car's tank. And then we pump."

"Well look at you Mr. Scientist getting all MacGyver. I thought you scientists only worked in the theoretical world?"

"I'm a battery scientist. As far as research fields go, battery science has much higher testosterone content than say, theoretical physics."

"Real men study batteries, you mean."

"Exactly."

Amanda had liked Joshua from the start. She and Mo had a strong connection with their shared beliefs. She knew Mo mistrusted Joshua, but she also knew that it stemmed from a basic distrust of all people involved in science. Amanda could see that Joshua was a gentle, well-meaning person. And one with a good sense of humor, she was discovering. She was glad that the others had convinced her to go on this road trip. Being away from the chaos back home was a welcome respite. *Back home*, she thought, *it really is starting to feel like home with the others.*

"The premium is on sale today, same price as regular," Joshua announced, as he peered down at a short, round end of a pipe sticking out of the concrete. It was indeed labeled 'premium', as Amanda joined him. A padlocked cap blocked the pipe. Joshua hurried back to the car and returned with a long crowbar and hammer.

"Courtesy of my arch-enemy Mo."

Amanda slapped his shoulder. "Oh come on, Mo is nice."

Joshua stopped in front of her. "Sure, he is. But he hates me for two reasons. One, I am a man of science. Two, he's worried that I steal his girl."

His words surprised Amanda. She and Mo were becoming good friends, but she hadn't detected any romantic interest coming from him. Perhaps she was so wrapped up in her own grieving that she'd missed his signals?

"His girl? There are so many things wrong with that statement that I'm not even sure where to begin. First, I'm a woman, not a girl. Second, I am not anyone's property."

"Didn't peg you as a bra-burner."

"And I thought your species had died out somewhere in the Jurassic period. Anyway, don't be ridiculous, Mo and I are just friends."

"Well now I'm starting to feel bad for the guy. No one ever wants to be put into the 'friend' category." His eyes were smiling just as much as his mouth.

"Enough," Amanda said. "Release some of that testosterone on the lock."

The crowbar was too thick to help with the lock. Several hard blows with the hammer didn't break the sturdy lock either. Joshua rummaged through the tool boxes and parts inside the service station and came back with a sturdy metal rod that fit into the shackle of the lock and a short-handled five-pound hammer. The rod didn't help at all. Finally, Joshua resorted to some wild blows of the heavy hammer directly on the lock. Soon enough, it gave way, and he could unscrew the cap.

Joshua threaded the long rubber tube into the hole. Once the other tube was in the car's gas tank filler neck, he started operating the hand pump. It thrilled Amanda to hear liquid splashing into the tank.

"Woo-hoo, well done MacGyver," she exclaimed.

"Not as fast as the pre-apocalypse pumps, but we'll get there." Joshua had the grin of a small boy discovering a hidden box of cookies. They took turns using the hand pump until some gas spilled out of the car's tank.

"That'll get us to Heuvelton and back no problem," he said in a satisfied tone.

"OK, Navigator, map our route along one of the state highways. Usually I take the I-90, but that brings us through Syracuse. I'd rather avoid cities," Joshua said, handing Amanda a map once they got back into the car.

"I can do better than that." Amanda pulled a GPS and cable out of her backpack.

"Those things still work?" Joshua asked with a surprised voice.

"Yes and no. The satellites are still up there, but without ground station calibration, the readings are surely getting more and more inaccurate. We can still trust it for finding highways, but I wouldn't punch in a specific address – you're liable to end up a mile away."

"Suit yourself, but for my sake, please follow along with the paper map too, otherwise we may end up in Canada with that thing."

"Well, well, the technophobic scientist. You are a strange man, Joshua."

"I'm decaying-technology-phobic only."

"No wonder you like spending time with the Amish."

"One point for you," Joshua laughed.

"Beautiful country," Amanda remarked dreamily after they had left the outskirts of Rochester.

"No place like Upstate," Joshua agreed. "So, given all this time on empty highways, why don't you tell me about Amanda?"

"What do you want to know?"

"Everything. Your dreams, hopes, ambitions. What makes you laugh, what makes you cry."

Amanda chuckled. "Well those kinds of ultra-personal open questions make me laugh."

"OK, then let's pick one of them, the least personal. Ambitions?"

"Hmm, OK. Well I always wanted to be good at my job, and I was. So I fulfilled my ambitions, I guess."

"Boring."

"You asked."

"You didn't give me a real answer. Being 'good at your job' is not a real ambition. There must have been something bigger that you barely allowed yourself to dream of."

Amanda gave some serious thought to this. She liked spending time being introspective, and so didn't mind his questions at all. In fact it was a great way to enjoy the scenery while thinking about what she wanted.

"I suppose I have something for your overly inquisitive mind," she finally conceded. "It was never an actual ambition, but more like a wish that I couldn't do anything about. So my husband was a politician, right? And had moved up quite high. I wouldn't have been shocked if fifteen or twenty years from now he would have run for President. And I'm not just boasting, he was very smart, very likeable, and very ambitious."

"So you dreamed of being First Lady?"

"Oh God, no. Are you crazy? The point I'm trying to make is that I got a good closeup view of how government works. Anyone who reads the news knows how corrupt and broken the system is. Was. But from the inside, it's even worse than people realized."

"You wanted to expose it all?"

"Stop interrupting with your silly guesses. You asked me a question, at least have the courtesy of listening to my answer."

"Fine, fine, I'll be quiet. Just try to finish before we get to Heuvelton."

"OK, that's it, I'm done."

Joshua laughed. "No, no come on! You can't do that to me, I was just joking."

"OK, well to cut it short,"—she raised a finger towards his mouth to cut off his protest—"I wished that there was a way to change it. More accurately, I wished I could just step in there and fix it, top to bottom."

"Holy...", Joshua said, smiling at her before returning his eyes towards the road. "I figured you were the type to dream big, but this is on a whole different level of dreaming big."

"What do you mean I'm the *type* to dream big?"

"So in this wishful fantasy, how exactly would you fix it?" he asked, ignoring her question.

She thought a moment before answering. "Yeah, well, where to start? True equality at all levels for race, gender, orientation. An end to Satan's invention that we call 'lobbying'. Putting the billions spent on elections to good use instead of campaigning. Free higher education. Put an end to our shameful homelessness epidemic. Replace the current—"

Joshua's laughter interrupted her. "Thanks for listening," she said, her irritation dripping out of every word.

Joshua stopped laughing, but still smiled at her. "I'm not laughing at you. I'm just delighted to discover this new side of you. A successful tech-savvy woman in a marriage with a high-ranking politician, with a secret anti-vax thing going, and now a wish to save the country from all its ills. You just surprised me, that's all. In a good way."

"Hmph," Amanda replied. She resumed looking at the scenery, with mixed feelings about her revelations to Joshua. She knew she had a lot of conflicting sides to her, which generally meant that she kept her personal thoughts to herself. Getting laughter as a response didn't make her want to open up more, even though he said he wasn't laughing at her. She also knew that it was his happy-go-lucky personality, he was childlike in his enthusiasm. *This is your own insecurity showing through*, she chastised herself.

They drove through several small towns along state highway 104. There were no signs of life in the towns, which Amanda found disturbing, and depressing.

"It's like a zombie apocalypse," she said as they passed through the deserted main street of a quaint small town.

"Without the zombies, thankfully," Joshua said.

"Seriously? You wouldn't rather be putting an ax through zombie heads right now?"

"No thanks, I'm a pacifist."

"OK, so how does that work if there's a horde of zombies running after you?"

"Man, are you still mad about the 'his girl' thing?" Joshua laughed.

"No, of course not. Well maybe a tiny bit. But, while I don't consider myself a warmonger or anything, I do have trouble understanding true pacifism."

"Violence begets violence, what's so hard to understand about that?"

"I agree with that part, but I also think at times violence is justified. Like defending yourself if attacked. Or going to war to stop someone like Hitler."

"Look what Gandhi achieved in India, probably the most famous pacifist in history."

"So you really believe that violence is never justified? Ever?"

"I wouldn't say never, but very rarely. If someone is attacking me, I would back away and try to reason, if possible. But if they are about to hit me or shoot me, then I would agree that violence is necessary. But, my point is, violence is used incredibly often, when there are far, far more alternatives to consider."

"I think I'm somewhere between you and what I would call 'the norm'. I've changed over the last few years. All the polarizing hate, intolerance, and violence that has gripped our poor little country has really affected me. But the question of how to scale back the anger and violence, that's the part that has me stumped. A little sprinkling of pacifism would certainly help."

"Ah, the mythical pacifism fairy and her wand, where is she when we need her?"

"Exactly. I guess all we can really do is start treating those around us with more care, even if we disagree on fundamentals."

"Right, for example, when we get home and Mo attacks me after finding out that we kissed —"

Amanda burst out laughing. "Oh my God, give it a rest with the Mo thing."

"Hmm, interesting that you oppose the Mo comment, but the not part about us kissing."

"Stop the car," Amanda said urgently.

"Hey, sorry, I'm just kidding around."

"I mean it, stop the car, I saw something."

Joshua braked hard and brought the car to a stop. "What did you see?"

"Some movement, it looked like people, but it was too quick to be sure. Can you back up? Near that old church-type of building."

The building had boarded-up arched windows that looked like they had once held stained glass panes. A large clock had replaced the cross atop the spire, turning it into more of a clock tower than a place of worship. There was an air of decay about the place. *The conversion must have happened a long time ago*, thought Amanda. It was hard to tell if the structure was still used for anything at all.

"Pull into the parking lot."

"I'm backing in. If these people don't take kindly to strangers, we may have to hightail it out of here."

Amanda climbed out of the car as soon as it stopped.

"Wait," Joshua called out. "Damn it," she heard him curse as she walked along the broad side of the old church. There was a large mural painted on the brick wall. It was a composite of several scenes of Americana, from the war of independence to Main St USA. Incongruously, the word 'Mexico' was centered at the top of the mural.

"Where are we?" Amanda wondered out loud, as Joshua caught up to her.

"Mexico," he answered simply.

"I guess you don't know either."

"I do know. We're in Mexico, New York."

"Seriously? Why did I never hear of this place?"

"You've been living under a rock, I suppose."

Amanda shook her head and shrugged. "Let's look around the back."

"For the record, I think we should get back in the car and move on to Heuvelton."

A small wooden door, flecked with peeling white paint, served as a rear entrance to the building. The door was ajar.

"Hello?" Amanda called.

"You're going to insist that we look inside, aren't you?" Joshua asked.

Amanda nodded.

Joshua pushed the door to swing it wide open. The inside of the building was pitch black. As her eyes adjusted to the darkness, Amanda detected a hint of light coming down the stairs at the far end of the church, leading up towards the clock tower. The lower floor was cavernous.

"There's nobody here, and I don't want to risk my neck walking in there. Risk my ankles, I should say, I'm sure there's all kinds of crap on the floor to trip on."

"You stay here," Amanda replied. "I just want to take a quick peek."

A flash of movement caught her eye as she took one step through the door. She instinctively raised her arms, shielding her face and head. Something hit her forearm, hard. A flash of pain caused her to cry out and stumble backwards out of the doorway. Joshua brushed past her. Blinded by the sunlight, she couldn't see, but heard, a brief struggle inside the dark interior. Joshua came out, holding a rake in one hand, and tugging a young boy by the arm with his other hand.

"Are you OK?" Joshua asked Amanda.

"Hurts like hell," she replied, gently rubbing her stinging forearm, "but I'll live."

Amanda studied the boy that Joshua had dragged out. He'd stopped struggling, seemingly resigned to his capture. He had blond hair that looked like it hadn't seen shampoo in quite some time. His defiant blue eyes stared back at Amanda.

"How old are you?" she asked.

"Nine," the boy answered.

"Is that the rake you hit me with?"

The boy nodded.

"Why?" she asked.

The boy shrugged and looked away.

"Mason?" a small, high-pitched voice called from inside the church. Mason's eyes opened wide. He tried to yank his arm free, but Joshua clenched it.

"Run," Mason yelled, twisting his head towards the door.

"Mason? I'm scared!" replied the voice.

Amanda stepped back into the abandoned church without hesitation. She heard a soft whimper to her left.

"I'm not going to hurt you," Amanda said, while waiting for her eyes to adjust to the darkness. Soon she saw the vague outline of a small person. She took at step forward and knelt on one knee. She could make out the long hair framing a young girl's face.

"Hi there Sweety, I'm Amanda, what's your name?"

"Zoe. Where's Mason?"

"Mason is right outside with my friend Joshua. He's worried about you, why don't we go outside together?"

She reached for Zoe's hand and met no resistance. They walked outside, and the two stood blinking in the sunlight. Mason hung his head, defeated.

"Are you two on your own?" Joshua asked.

"Mommy and Daddy are sleeping," Zoe said

earnestly. Her matted brown hair and smudged face made a pitiful picture.

"They're dead," Mason said.

"No, they're sleeping," Zoe replied, brown eyes flashing. "You'll see, they'll wake up soon and come get us."

"Well, you can't be out here all by yourselves. We're living with a whole bunch of other kids, and we would love for you to come live with us," said Amanda.

"How will Mommy and Daddy find us?" asked Zoe.

"Don't worry, if they come looking, we'll be easy to find." Amanda bent down to talk to Mason. "You have been a brave boy taking care of your little sister like that. Will you let us help you now? Where we live there are lots of grown-ups and lots of kids. We can take care of you both."

Mason nodded hesitantly.

"OK good. But we're not going home right away, first we have to visit some farmers. Would you like to go see a farm?"

"Will there be sheep?" asked Zoe.

"Maybe, I don't know."

"I know they have horses," Joshua added.

"I like horses," Zoe said brightly.

"What about you Mason?" Joshua asked.

"They're OK," he said, shrugging his shoulders.

Poor little guy, thought Amanda. She couldn't imagine being nine years old and having to survive on the street with a little sister, having just lost your parents. Her arm still stung from the rake handle's blow. It was too soon to question them about their vaccination status. She hoped they had not received their shots. *That kid is tough as nails, we're going to need people like him in the coming years.*

Mason and Zoe sat in the back of the car, while Amanda resumed her map reading role.

"We'll hit the I-81 soon, then it's pretty much a straight shot north to Heuvelton," she said. "About an hour to go."

"Once we're on the interstate, I can find my way there. That's the route I always took," Joshua said.

"You kids hungry?" Amanda asked their new passengers.

After receiving enthusiastic affirmatives, Amanda dug through her backpack and pulled out crackers and peanut butter. "I assume you don't mind donating your lunch?" Amanda asked Joshua.

He smiled back at her, "It's for a good cause."

Fifty minutes later, Amanda saw the sign announcing their arrival in Heuvelton. A yellow warning sign soon followed, featuring a horse and buggy, to warn drivers of slow-moving Amish buggies in the area.

"I have such good memories of this place," Joshua said. "There's this little pub on the main street that I often stop at. Great pizza, cheap beer: a traveler's paradise. What a cozy place it was to just kick back with the locals."

His words reminded Amanda of all the places that she used to enjoy, which she could never again. It was a constant struggle to suppress the overwhelming despondency. *How did I go from upper middle-class professional to post-apocalyptic survivor?* She wished she could travel back in time, and enjoy the chaotic normalcy of pre-pandemic, pre-VP, life.

"There it is," Joshua called out excitedly.

Amanda couldn't contain her laughter. "You call this a cozy place?" she said. *Pete's Pub*, read the sign hanging over the front door of a huge square brick building. The upper floor windows were boarded up. Amanda thought it must have been a large warehouse in the distant past. Some of the bricks on the lower floor were painted, presumably to soften the industrial look of the structure.

"Didn't your mother ever tell you not to judge a book by its cover? The outside might not be much to look at, but the inside has an optimal coziness factor, I swear."

"Like, 'extreme coziness', then? Or are we talking about 'neo-industrial coziness'?"

"Well, well, look who's suddenly turned into a comedian."

"'Dark and dank' cozy?"

"That's it, I'm not even going to show you the general store. The Heuvelton tour is now officially over."

They passed several evenly spaced large white homes along the main street. *Advantage of small towns*, thought Amanda, *lots of space*. Her attention turned to a simple, yet beautiful, white church on the right. Large stained glass windows adorned the barn-sized church. It reminded her of the abandoned church in Mexico. *It must have looked like this back in its day*, she thought.

"I saw some people there," Mason said.

"Where?" Amanda asked. Joshua slowed the car.

"Next to the blue house. They had funny hats."

The blue house that Mason mentioned was now two blocks behind them, on the opposite side of the church.

"I know, I know, turn around," Joshua said, before Amanda could utter another sentence.

"It's going to be a long day," Joshua added, as Amanda stepped out of the car after he'd driven back to the blue house.

"Is anyone there?" Amanda called out. "We're here to help."

"No we're not, we're here to visit farmers," Joshua muttered behind her.

"Stop your grumbling," she admonished.

They circled the house and saw no one. Mason and Zoe had joined them, despite being told to stay in the car. Amanda was about to try the front door of the blue house when Mason cried out.

"There they are," he blurted, pointing to the next house down the street.

A man with a long reddish-brown beard stood in front of his family. Amanda could see a woman and two teenage girls behind him. The man wore a wide-brimmed straw hat, with a black ribbon around it. He had dark gray work pants, and a steel-gray flannel shirt. The woman and her daughters wore long dresses and bonnets, reminiscent of a scene from the pioneer days.

"There are your Amish," Amanda whispered.

"Abram?" Joshua called out, his head tilted. His eyes squinted in the sunlight. The man waved at them. Joshua ran to them. He took the man by the shoulders and kissed him on the lips. Amanda's jaw nearly dropped. He then shook hands with the woman, and the two girls. By the time the greetings were over, Amanda had caught up to the group.

"Amanda, these are the Ebersoles. I've visited with them often, and bought lots of their organic produce. This is Abram, his wife Mary, and their two daughters Miriam and Hannah."

Amanda exchanged greetings with the Ebersole family. Their appearance struck her once again. She had seen many Amish before. But up close, it was like they transported her back in time. Their Pennsylvania Dutch accent added an almost guttural quality to their tone of voice. Each of them gave her a polite smile, but she also saw a wariness in their eyes. She wondered if this was a common way for them to feel about outsiders. *How long did it take Joshua to get to the kissing stage?* She had to work hard to suppress a grin.

"We were actually on our way to visit the Plain People, you included of course. What are you doing in the middle of town?" Joshua asked.

"It's dangerous here, my friend. You need to leave," Abram said, clearing his throat. "A lot of English in the area, with guns," he said, using the Amish term for outsiders. "They took over all our farms. They've killed most of the elders. They hurt a lot of the Plain People, men, women, children." He shook his head, before adding, "Bad people, the devil's in them all."

Armed thugs taking over an Amish community? Amanda had never considered such a scenario.

"I don't get it," Joshua spluttered, "why?"

"Food. They want us to keep working the land and providing them with food."

"That's outrageous! Who are these people?" Joshua asked.

"They're not from around here, we never saw them before."

"Do you have guns? How many are they? Can you fight them off?" Amanda asked. Her blood pressure rose as the anger flushed through her entire body.

Abram looked at her, and then at Joshua. Joshua responded, without taking his eyes off Abram. "The Amish do not fight. Ever."

"So what are you going to do now?" he asked Abram.

"What our people have always done when there is conflict. Move away and start anew."

"Will you let us help you? We've got a group of people, and lots of children. You could stay with us, at least for a while."

"That's very kind of you Joshua, but we'll be fine on our own."

"What about the gunmen, are they out looking for you?" asked Amanda.

Abram shrugged, but Mary looked worried. She

squeezed his arm.

"They could help us move away faster, and avoid any more violence," Mary said.

"Absolutely," said Joshua. "Stay with us for an hour, a day, a year, however long you want. But let us get you out of here."

Abram still seemed hesitant.

"I'm sorry, but I don't understand why you don't want to come," Amanda said.

"He doesn't want to ride in a car," Joshua told her. "But there are exceptions, Abram. If this isn't an emergency, I don't know what is."

Amanda hadn't realized how profoundly the Amish held their beliefs in avoiding modern technology. Most of the adult population was gone, armed men might be searching for them at this moment, and they were hesitant to get into a car. It almost made her wish that she could have that strong a faith in something. *Just not something that would prevent me from escaping a dangerous situation at any cost.*

With one more meaningful exchange of looks between husband and wife, Abram finally agreed. They silently walked back to the car. Amanda scanned the surrounding area, looking for any movement or signs of danger. Some of the tension slipped away when they arrived at the car.

"You're all going to have to get cozy in there," Joshua said.

The car was not designed for four adults and four children. Despite being the biggest passenger,

Abram refused the front seat, as did Mary. Amanda didn't understand why, but she realized she had better get used to not understanding these people. *Go with the flow*, she thought. Zoe sat on Amanda's lap in the front. Mason sat between Abram and Mary, while their teenage daughters sat on their parents' laps.

Joshua drove faster than on the way to Heuvelton. Amanda noticed he spoke less, and his shoulders tensed as he clutched the steering wheel firmly. His clenched jaw moved frequently, as if he were chewing on something. Amanda wondered how his pacifist beliefs were dealing with the injustice of the Amish being attacked, killed, and made to work for other men.

Amanda stretched her legs and smiled when she got out of the car as soon as they arrived at the house. Even a five-year-old can get very heavy on one's lap after a three-hour drive. She noticed Abram and Mary limping as they exited the car. Their two girls were stretching their legs and backs.

Amanda took Zoe by the hand. "Welcome to your new home," she said to her and Mason. The late afternoon sun was low in the sky, its spring warmth fading for the day. It was almost summer. Amanda loved the longer days in the summer months. She could do without the high heat, but the daylight — bring it on.

"Well, who do we have here?" Deb said, arriving to greet the carload of people that had landed at her doorstep. Joshua and Amanda proceeded to get yet another round of introductions going. It had become an almost daily event, it seemed to Amanda. She watched Deb's face alternate from gleeful as she took Mason and Zoe into her arms for a welcoming hug, to a dark frown as she listened to the fate of the Heuvelton Amish.

"I do hope you'll stay with us," Deb said to Abram and Mary.

"Thank you," replied Abram. "We'll stay a few days, but then move on. Our people don't usually fit in well with the English."

"Keep an open mind, Abram," Joshua said, "a lot of our modern conveniences no longer work. We might be living more like the Amish than you think."

"For that matter, we'll have a lot to learn from you, if you'll teach us some basics of living without all the electronics," Deb added.

This made Abram smile. Amanda thought it must have been a rare moment indeed for the non-Amish community to be asking them for help.

Just then a half-dozen children ran out of the house, chasing each other and squealing with delight.

"I had better get back inside, before they tear the place down," Deb laughed.

"You're not here on your own, are you? Where's everybody else?" Amanda asked.

"Not quite alone, Brandon is inside helping. Though he doesn't exactly have a knack for dealing with children. I tried to explain to him that he can't force them to open up. It's like he expects instant hugs or something. The two teenage girls though, Alexis and Kalisha, now they are a godsend. They're just great with the kids. Their parents went with Darnell and Javon, all four are out looking for children downtown. And of course, Maurice is also out looking, but in this area. And Titus is at the hotel with Chris, preparing our new home, I hope."

Amanda couldn't help but laugh. "It's a happening place! How do you keep track of everyone?"

"Old teacher habits, comes with the territory."

"What did you mean by 'I hope'?" Joshua asked.

"There's a hint of friction between those two, they don't quite see eye to eye. I'm hoping that by leaving them alone they'll work out their differences."

"Or end up in a fist fight," Amanda quipped.

"Don't even joke about that," Deb said, frowning.

"What are they disagreeing on?" Amanda asked.

"Small stuff. Like do we remove the doors to the children's rooms or not? They just seem to butt heads on a variety of topics."

"Vying for position as top renovation dog," Joshua said, smiling.

"Maybe." Deb paused before changing topics. "So how are we going to help the Amish in Heuvelton?"

"That's something that we should probably talk about as a group, when the other are back," Joshua said.

Deb and Amanda nodded. But Abram spoke out. "There's nothing to be done, their fate is with God."

"God helps those who help themselves," Deb said.

Abram was about to counter her words when Joshua interrupted. "Let's not get into that kind of debate right away, please. Abram, there's nothing wrong with just discussing the situation. But for now, please make yourself at home, and come meet all of our children."

It wasn't until they had put the children to bed that the adults resumed their conversation about the situation in Heuvelton. Except for Jessica's run-in with a fake police officer, their group had managed to avoid any violence. Amanda wondered how they would deal with this new situation. She couldn't call it a threat, since the armed thugs were three hours away and presumably had no interest in the Rochester area. Even so, how could they sit back while an unarmed Amish community was virtually enslaved?

"I'll start. We have to help these people," Titus said.

"How many guns are we talking about?" Dee asked.

"Whoa, whoa, whoa! Slow down before we start talking about guns. First, we should talk about whether or not they even want our help," Joshua said.

"We also need to consider the children. If some of us get killed, or if they decide to come after our group, it's the children who will pay the price," Deb said.

"Right, just like they did during the pandemic, with the damned shots," Mo added.

"What?" cried Joshua.

"Well, we certainly didn't vaccinate them for their own protection, the virus barely affected them. We vaccinated them to protect the adults. The children paid the price for protecting the adults, which is wrong by any measure of morality."

"Before I can even begin to tear that argument apart, I have to ask how on earth this is relevant to —"

"Stop it, you two," Deb shouted. "Focus on the topic please, what do we do about the Amish being held at gunpoint?"

"If I may," Abram said, clearing his throat and waiting for the group to settle down. "Our people do not fight. Like my family, the others will leave when they can, and start anew somewhere else. I am not asking you to go fight the men with guns. If the other families could talk to you right now, they would say the same. It's also not our way to stop you from doing what you want. So, Mary and I will go to bed now, and leave you to your discussions. But please, don't engage in violence on our behalf."

And with that he took Mary's hand, and with muted good-nights, they left the group.

"For the record, I'm with Abram. Violence begets violence. Plus, they specifically asked us not to go help," Joshua said.

"Did they?" Titus asked. "I heard him say he can't stop us from doing what we want. That sounds to me like he wants us to, but can't ask us because of his beliefs."

"No, no, that's not what he meant. He's saying that he can't control the actions of the gunmen, and he can't control our actions either. That's all," Joshua replied.

Brandon chuckled.

"What is even remotely funny about this?" Amanda asked.

"Well, I know I'm still new here, but I'm sorry, you folks seem to be living in the past."

"Explain," Mo said, irritation in his voice.

"Food security. That's all that matters now. These people have guns, and have found a food supply. If anything, we should find out if we can join them."

"Are you fucking serious?" Mo asked.

"Think long term. All these children will grow up, and can run farms. They're our old age security. In fact, they can start helping pretty soon, with the lighter chores."

"I can't believe I'm hearing this," Mo said.

"Neither can I," Deb added. "These are our children now. They are not farm labor to keep you fat and happy in your old age."

"You be in the asshole category now," Dee said.

"Don't shoot the messenger," Brandon said, raising his hands in the air. "I'll shut up for now. Hate me if you want, but when your bellies are empty, you'll come around."

"Never," Deb said.

Brandon's words disgusted Amanda. But she also

felt a chill of fear. In just one day, their group's peaceful cohesion changed radically. Now they were discussing armed conflict and forced labor. It made their status quo seem like a thin veneer of civility.

At the same time, she felt a surge of emotions when Deb had spoken. *These are our children now.* Amanda had never thought of it in those terms. Until now, she thought she was helping other people's children. But Deb was right, they had in fact become their children. A confusing rush of love, fear of failure, and the need to protect overcame her.

"Not only will I not allow you to treat them as labor resources, I will not allow any of you to go risk your lives fighting armed men. These children need you even more than the Amish in Heuvelton. Do I make myself clear?" Deb said, in a firm voice Amanda had never heard her use before.

A silence fell over the group. Deb looked around at the group. Amanda couldn't help but nod when Deb's iron gaze landed upon her.

"I guess we can skip the show of hands," Mo said with a grin.

That seemed to break the tension. Amanda could see Deb's cheeks flush red, even in the candle light. *She's embarrassed by her display of Mama Bear strength.* She noticed the group had formed a bit of distance around Deb and guessed they were experiencing the same strange sense of intimidation that Amanda was feeling right now. *That's the last thing she needs.* She stepped forward and took Deb in her arms.

"Thank you," Amanda breathed.

Deb's body trembled, and Amanda squeezed a little harder.

11. BANISHMENT

Mo stood in the open doorway, listening for signs of life. A few moments earlier, as he had walked towards the house, the fresh spring morning scents had had a soothing effect on him. Now, the smell of rotting flesh penetrated his respirator. He wondered how many more times he could repeat this ritual of breaking into the homes of the dead. It seemed that every time he wanted to stop, he would find a live child. With the adults dying off over time, there was a steady stream of newly orphaned children to be found and brought home. And so, he kept going out, day after day, being confronted by more death than he had ever imagined.

The smell alone told him what he needed to know. With ninety percent certainty. Crowbar still in hand from the back door break-in, Mo entered further into the house for that remaining ten percent chance. The entrance led into a utility room where a washer and dryer stood on the right of the door. A long, ornate oak plank was fastened to the left wall. A set of coat hooks were screwed into the board. Several coats, scarves, and umbrellas were hanging from the hooks. Beneath it hung a smaller replica of the board and hooks. It had four children's coats hanging. The smallest one had a pink mitten dangling from a string threaded through the sleeve.

The confirmation that children once lived here prompted Mo to keep going through the house.

He found the family in the upstairs master bedroom. The children were lying in a straight row, each covered with a bloody sheet. A woman was next, also covered. And finally, the father, gun in hand, lying in a heap near them, with half his head blown off. Mo stumbled backwards out of the room. *Why?* He thought. *Why would you kill your children when they had a chance at survival?* He wondered if the father had gone mad, or if he had really thought this was a better idea than risking them starving to death.

The crowbar thudded down on the carpet as it slipped out of Mo's hand. He slid down to his knees, ripped off his respirator, and squeezed his head between his hands. A primal scream erupted from his throat. He screamed until his breath ran out, and then screamed again. His throat raw, Mo stared at his hands, now trembling uncontrollably.

Keep it together, Mo. Jesus Christ, keep it together.

He forced himself to pick up the discarded crowbar and respirator, and make his way to the top of the stairs. He steadied himself against the banister and put the respirator back on. After a few minutes, his breathing became regular. He wiped the beads of sweat from his forehead and headed back down the stairs.

Mo couldn't bring himself to look for immediate supplies in this house. He stepped outside and dutifully marked it on the map. *BB can deal with this one*, Mo thought. He had started calling Brandon BB in his head, short for Bizarre Brandon. There was a strangeness emanating from the man. *He's just plain creepy.* Mo had developed a habit of giving people alliterative nicknames way back as a teenager. Names he kept to himself, of course. Like Jerkoff Joshua, another of his least favorite people. And of course, Amazing Amanda. If there was such a thing as soulmates, she was definitely his. He shook his head, thinking *I'm freakin' forty-six going on sixteen.*

A barking dog in the distance broke his reverie. He had encountered a few starving, wild dogs in the last weeks. In most cases he had been able to wait them out inside a house. However, there was a time where a pair of dogs had charged at him while he was in the middle of a street. Fortunately, he'd still been holding his crowbar from the last break-in, and could defend himself. The pair of yelping dogs had run away, one with a new limp. Mo had never been very comfortable around dogs, and was now positively frightened of them. *Justifiably so*, he thought, trying to gage the distance and direction of the barks.

The dog's bark seemed urgent, and persistent. Mo judged it to be one street over. He looked over the back fence of the house he had entered. All he saw was the back yard of the house on the next street. He couldn't see the street itself, nor the dog. It was a strange bark. Not one of an angry or attacking stray. Just a persistent, booming bark. Mo wondered if the dog was signaling some sort of danger. Despite his newfound fear of dogs, he had to investigate. With his crowbar firmly in hand, he climbed over the fence and into the neighboring yard.

He edged towards the front of the house, trying to remain silent and unobserved. That's when he heard the sounds of a crying child intermixed with the barking. Mo abandoned all attempts at a stealthy approach and ran headlong around the house, crowbar raised to fight off the dog. What greeted his eyes was an unexpected site. The dog was standing over the prone body of a man, barking steadily. A small, crying boy was holding the man's hand. Another child, this one silent, was lying down, her head on the man's chest, and her arms around him. Mo quickly lowered his crowbar as the boy spotted him.

The dog, a black lab, stopped barking and trotted a few steps towards Mo. It seemed to study him, as if trying to determine if he was friend or foe. Despite his recent experiences with dogs, Mo knelt on one knee, and offered the dog a hand to sniff. Tentatively, it stepped forward and sniffed Mo's hand. Apparently having decided that Mo wasn't a threat, the dog began to run, bark, and jump between Mo and the man on the ground.

Both children were now sitting up. Their tear-streaked faces looked at Mo with a mixture of fear and desperate hope.

"Daddy won't wake up," the young boy said. "Can you wake him up?"

The girl said nothing. Her helpless look broke

Mo's heart.

"Hi kids, I'm Mo. Let me have a look at your dad."

Mo already knew the man was dead, but made a show of checking for a breath and a pulse. *What do I say now?*

"Listen, kids, I'm so sorry, but your dad isn't going to wake up. But he called me here, to come and take care of you, OK? Come here," he said, reaching out his arms for an embrace.

The sobbing boy shuffled over to Mo.

"What's you name, son?" Mo asked.

"Billy. Why won't Dad wake up?"

"Shh, it'll be OK," Mo lied. "What about you little girl, what's your name?"

"Charlotte. Dad's not sleeping, he died."

"I know, baby girl, I know. But I'll take care of you, don't worry. And where I live there are lots of grown-ups and kids just like you, OK?"

Charlotte nodded solemnly. *The big sister putting up a brave face*, thought Mo.

The dog licked Billy's sad face. "And who's this fella? Or is it a she?"

"That's Hoover, he's a boy like me," Billy said.

"Do you think Hoover would like to come with us to meet all the other kids?"

Billy nodded.

"And what about you, Charlotte, will you come?" Mo asked.

"What about Daddy? We can't just leave him there," she said.

"No, of course not. I'll bring him somewhere more

comfortable. How about in one of these houses?"

Charlotte examined the nearest houses. Mo had already done this street, and knew they could step inside. But he had to make sure she didn't pick one with dead bodies in it. She pointed to a blue house behind Mo.

"OK, you wait here, I'll go make sure it looks good inside."

Fortunately, the house she chose was abandoned. Mo dragged the father into the house, gently and respectfully under the watchful eye of the children. He laid the man on the sofa in the living room and let the children say their last goodbyes for several tear-filled minutes. Mo then coaxed them outside and started leading them back home. Hoover padded along beside them, tail wagging.

"Maurice!" Ben yelled when they were nearing the house. He ran into Mo's arms. With the little boy's arms wrapped around his neck, Mo felt a tinge of regret at never having had children of his own. The love that he received from the boy, and felt for the boy, was overpowering.

Before he could tell Ben about the two new children and the dog, Ben blabbered on excitedly, seemingly oblivious to the new arrivals. "Sophia broke Amanda's things, and now she's in big trouble."

"And who do we have here?" Deb asked, as she strode out of the house towards Mo. He always appreciated her enthusiastic welcome whenever he brought home new children. She noticed children couldn't help but respond to her energetic, motherly presence.

Mo introduced the children, and Deb grabbed each one into a warm hug, welcoming them to their new home.

"Now who is this big guy?" she asked the children, patting Hoover's head, and scratching behind his ears.

"That's our dog," Charlotte responded. "His name is Hoover."

"Well, we have no dogs here yet, so we really need Hoover, don't we? Welcome to you too, big guy. Now will you two follow me, I want you to meet some friends. Maurice, why don't you go inside and talk to Amanda."

"I thought his name was Mo?" Mo smiled as he overheard Billy asking this, as Deb led them away.

As Mo entered the house, he could hear a child crying.

"Come on Sophia, I saw you do it, don't lie," Brandon said.

"Hey, what's going on here?" Mo asked. Brandon, Amanda, and a crying Sophia turned to him.

"Sophia was jealous of all the time Amanda's been spending on her computer. So, she took it upon herself to go at all the disks with a hammer," Brandon explained.

"No! It's not true." Sophia cried. Mo had already heard Sophia complain any time Amanda worked on her electronics. The traumatized little girl had bonded with Amanda, and tried her best to grab all of her attention, all of the time. Even now, she had her arms curled around Amanda's neck.

A bag of broken plastic and metal pieces, remnants of external drives, Mo realized, sat on the table next to them. A hammer lay next to the bag of evidence. Mo approached them and stroked Sophia's hair. He had no idea that she'd be capable of that much anger, to the point of destroying Amanda's things. Fortunately, he knew Amanda had a full set of backups at her apartment. And possibly still the third set she had dropped off at the Rochester library.

"Well, the good news is," he began, but stopped short when Amanda pinched his back, hard.

"What good side can there be of all this precious data being destroyed forever?" Brandon asked.

"The good news is, no one was hurt," Mo said, recovering from Amanda painful plea for silence. "Swinging hammers, flying pieces of plastic and metal – all that could have so easily led to some serious owies, there sweety." Mo patted Sophia's back as he spoke.

"But I didn't do it!" she cried again.

"We're all very disappointed in you," Brandon said, patting the girl's bottom. "Now I'm going to go clean up your mess."

"Don't worry about that Brandon, I'll take care of it," Amanda said.

"No, no, it's fine. You've got your hands full disciplining our little juvie here."

"Come on, that's a bit much," Amanda said.

"Just kidding around, trying to lighten the mood. I'll go clean up." With a last lingering gaze at Sophia, Brandon left.

As soon as he was gone, Amanda rolled her eyes at Mo.

"I pinkie promise I didn't do it," Sophia said, looking up at Amanda with pleading eyes.

"You know what sweety? I believe you. But now you need to calm down, OK? Everything is fine."

"What about your computer?"

"Let me worry about that, you just take a deep breath and relax, OK?"

Sophia obediently breathed deeply, snuggling deeper into Amanda's embrace.

"Um, Sophia, there's someone new that you really ought to meet," Mo said.

Sophia shook her head vehemently. Right on cue, Hoover barked outside. Sophia cocked her head.

"That's Hoover, the friendliest dog ever. He's come to live with us, along with his owners Billy and Charlotte. I think Billy must be about the same age as you."

Sophia untangled herself from Amanda's arms.

"Can I go see?" she asked Amanda, wiping the tears from her face, and swiping at her leaky nose.

"Of course, sweetheart." With that, the girl's little legs carried her as fast as they could towards Hoover and the new arrivals.

"OK, talk. What was all that about? And thanks for the permanent pinch scar on my back," Mo said.

"Don't be such a wimp," she answered with a smile. Her face turned serious before continuing. "There's no way a three-year-old could swing a hammer that hard. The drive casings are just made of plastic, but still. It takes coordination and strength that Sophia simply does not have."

Mo considered her words for a moment. "Hmm, yeah, you might be right there. But Brandon said he saw her do it. Why would he lie about that?"

"You mean why, other than the obvious reason that he did it?"

"Sure, let's go down that path for a minute. Why on earth would he want to break your hard drives?"

"I don't have a clue. But I want to find out. Let's go to my house, I want to poke around on the backups and see if we can find anything about Mr. Brandon Jameson."

"Two conspiracy theorists together, that's a dangerous combination," Mo said, smiling. "But OK, I'm in."

They went downstairs, leaving the bag of broken disks on the table. Amanda tried to say goodbye to Sophia, but the girl turned out to be a major dog lover. She was too busy with Hoover to pay any attention to the fact that Amanda said she was going. Fortunately, Brandon had already moved to Amanda's makeshift office in the house next door.

They quietly slipped away from the group and took the pickup truck that Brandon normally used when foraging through the houses Mo had broken into. They drove the short distance in near silence.

Amanda was at the wheel, and less than ten minutes later they pulled up to her old house.

"So, this is where it all happens," Mo said, as they entered her home office.

"That's what you said the first time you came here, to help me move stuff out."

"At least I'm consistent."

Amanda didn't answer him. Turning on the generator and firing up her computer fully occupied Amanda's attention. He loved seeing her in her element like this. Her focus and quiet confidence made her all the more attractive to him. He hadn't felt this way since Amy. The big difference being that his beliefs had driven Amy away, while those same beliefs brought Amanda closer to him.

"A woman surrounded by electronics – sexy," Mo said, using his best sultry voice.

"If you're into geek-sex, then I imagine so," she replied in a distracted tone, as she continued to work keyboard, mouse, and a variety of cables.

"Seriously though, what you've done is fantastic. I mean, I've spent a lot of time behind my computer. But never doing anything concrete. Trying to spread the truth is not, you know, nothing. But it doesn't compare to saving the world's information before the collapse of society as we know it."

This made Amanda pause, and flash her jaw-dropping smile towards Mo.

"That's really sweet, thank you Mo."

"And thank you for doing this, Miss Jones. It's strange, this VP seems to have brought out the best in us. As odd as it may sound, these house break-ins that I'm doing have made me feel more useful than I ever have in my life. It seems like I've always been a drifter, never really having goals. But now I do. The work is horrifying, don't get me wrong. But my God, saving the lives of children – how do you top that?"

"Well, I certainly haven't done anywhere near as much searching as you have. But what little I have done gives me nightmares. I'm so impressed by your strength, Mo. And you're right, how can you top saving a child's life?"

Mo pulse was racing as he stepped towards her. "Can I kiss you?" he suddenly blurted out loudly, to be heard above the din of the generator's engine.

Amanda rolled her chair back, away from him. To Mo it sounded like the needle of a record player scratching its way across the vinyl.

"Mo, I really like you —" she began.

"Oh God, stop right there. I'm so sorry. I just, well —"

"Let me finish please. I really like you. I admire your strength. We click wonderfully as truth seekers. You're a good-looking guy. But, it's too soon Mo. I lost my husband just a short while ago. And a lot of other people that were close to me. I am grieving. So much. Romance is not anywhere on my radar. I'm not saying it will be, or will never be, I'm just saying I'm not capable of anything in that area right now."

The familiar 'you asshole' feeling washed over Mo like a bucket of ice water.

"I am beyond insensitive. I am so, so sorry Amanda."

She stood and took Mo into her arms. "Don't be sorry, you did nothing wrong. And I'm sorry that I'm simply not emotionally available right now, as cliché as that may sound."

God, she smells good, Mo thought, breathing in the scent of her hair and skin.

"So you think I'm hot, that's cool," he said, to divert from the awkward discussion.

"What?" she asked, pulling away.

"You said I was a good-looking guy." A devilish grin spread across his face.

"Oh my God, is that the only thing you got from my little speech?" She slapped his shoulder and returned to her chair.

"Well, it is the most important part of your speech, yes."

"Men. Egocentric little boys, all of you."

Mo decided to give her some time to concentrate on her task. He walked over to the window, next to the vibrating exhaust pipe of the generator. As he peered through the blinds, he realized how accustomed he'd become to the silent, empty streets. He had trouble imagining cars driving by, or a man mowing his lawn, or some children going by on their bicycles. *Some day again*, he thought. *Maybe.*

With that thought, he vowed to take Ben cycling on some of these streets. Mo missed the one-on-one time he'd had with Ben prior to joining Deb on her admirable quest. In fact, it would be good to start cycling with several children, as long as they didn't go too far from home. But still, he resolved to spend some alone-time with Ben. It was a hard choice. Mo's obsessive nature made him search houses compulsively. It had come to the point where any other activity was like choosing not to save another child's life. He knew it was an unhealthy approach, but he had spent his whole life dealing with compulsions. He always had to consciously force himself to step away from the obsession-of-the-day, knowing it was all that kept him sane in those times. A bike ride with his darling little boy Ben would be just the ticket to break the obsession cycle this time.

My little boy? Am I allowed to say that? he thought. Before he could process that new dilemma, Amanda's cursing interrupted his thoughts.

"Goddammit! What the hell?" She stood and began checking cables behind her laptop.

"What happened?"

"Laptop just died." She continued checking behind the computer, following cables towards the power source.

"Blue Screen of Death?"

"No, died. As in dead-dead."

Mo came around the desk and saw the darkened screen.

"That's weird. It just went off?"

"I wish. But look, there's no power indicator light, it's as if it's not even plugged in."

"Oh shit. Power surge? Do you have a surge protector?"

"I do. But *surge protector* is actually a misnomer. They're spike protectors."

Amanda stopped pulling at the cables. She stood, frowning, and passed her hand through her hair.

"I don't understand, how's that relevant?" Mo asked.

"Well they're meant for very short spikes of power. If this piece-of-shit generator throws a longer voltage fluctuation it would blow the spike protector and the laptop. And the damned light on the protector is not coming on either. I think that's what happened. Fuck!" She stomped her foot.

"So now what?"

"Well, the laptop's fried, that's for sure. Hopefully the current didn't go all the way to the external drive." She paused and seemed to survey the room. "OK, clearly this generator isn't reliable. I'm going to switch to the other one."

"But your laptop's dead. Do you have a spare one at the other house?"

"Mo, this woman is prepared." She opened the lower drawer of a lateral filing cabinet behind her desk. Winking at Mo, she pulled out a laptop. Mo could see another laptop remaining in the cabinet drawer.

"I stand in awe," he said.

"As you should, as you should. Now let's see if the hard drive survived."

Mo retreated to the window once more as she turned off the faulty generator, swapped the exhaust pipe to the new generator and resumed her work with the new laptop. Mo concluded that the hard drive was undamaged, based on the fast clickety-clack of the keyboard keys under her dancing fingers, and the lack of cursing. He was envious. How he missed having his computer, researching the internet, and writing in his blog. He had only started becoming used to being disconnected. But now, hearing Amanda on her laptop, the longing for the old world was strong. *This must be what an ex-smoker feels seeing someone light up a cigarette.*

"OK, here we go. First, I'll try a fast search, where I just scan hyperlink text," Amanda announced a few minutes later.

"What's your search term, exactly?"

"I'm searching for his full name, Brandon Jameson. Should just take a couple of minutes."

"Google returns results instantly." He knew Amanda was aware of how great her achievement was, and so his banter was safe.

"When I hire a hundred thousand employees, mine will be just as fast too."

"What will your search engine be called?"

She hesitated a moment before replying. "Amanda's Search Emporium."

"Nah, too long. How about Amandoogle?"

She laughed out loud. Mo's heart skipped a beat.

Amanda's fast search was only looking at the text used in links on websites. It was checking if any Wikipedia page had a link using Brandon's name. Five minutes later, they had their answer.

"No luck," she said. "Time for the full-text search. That might take an hour or two. One word about Google and you are no longer welcome in this house."

"My lips are sealed," he replied. Though her computer was silent, Mo knew it was frantically comparing millions of text strings every second. She had started searching for Brandon's name in the text body of all web pages now. If his name appeared anywhere at all, her program would find it.

"With all the hubbub of finding Billy and Charlotte this morning —" Mo began.

"Hubbub? Who uses 'hubbub' these days? Are you like eighty?"

"Why don't you search for 'hubbub' and find out? Oh wait, we don't have all day."

"Out of my house. Now."

"Ok, but I'm taking my lunch with me, which I was about to propose we share."

"Wait, wait! OK I forgive you."

Mo laughed. "Let's go outside anyway, better than in here with that generator's infernal racket."

Now it was Amanda's turn to giggle. "Too much racket and hubbub in here."

"Oh my God, what's wrong with 'racket'? Are you part of the cool language police or something?"

They sat on her front doorstep, and Mo reached into his backpack for his lunch. He normally ate alone, as he was out searching houses during the day. Billy and Charlotte's rescue had broken up his morning, which was a nice change for him. *A very nice change*, he thought, glancing over at Amanda.

"Stale crackers and peanut butter. You know how to treat a woman right."

"Play your cards right, you might score a can of beans tonight."

"My knight in shining armor."

"I get that all the time."

They made quick work of their meager lunch. The rays of the sun warmed Mo's face. As if reading his mind, Amanda said "Spring is my favorite season."

He looked at her. She had shut her eyes and lifted her face towards the sun. Mo did the same.

"I'm more of a summer guy, but this will do just fine."

"A perfect compromise, we're right on the line between spring and summer."

They sat in silence for a few moments, each absorbed in their own thoughts, while drinking in the sun's rays. It was Amanda who broke the silence.

"I was thinking about what you said, about doing something concrete. That struck a chord in me, I had just never put it in words like you did. I've done some admittedly pretty cool stuff in my career. But still, it was all, I don't know, superficial? That might be a bit too harsh. But that's the idea, compared to what we're doing now. It's hard to explain."

"I'm pretty sure I understand what you mean. Everything before seems rather trivial now. I mean I would give anything to go back to our lives of comfort and trivia. Even so, somehow this feels more real in an odd sort of way."

"Yes, exactly. More real. Everything before was so detached from basic life needs."

"Oh, I like that – 'detached'. You hit the nail on the head there. I feel so grounded in reality now, you simply cannot be 'detached' when your survival, when innocent children's survival, is at stake."

Amanda nodded in agreement. "Well, I suppose I should go inside and see if we have any search hits. Hard to leave this sunshine though."

"Let's go," Mo said, standing and taking her hand to help her up.

As Amanda settled into her leather chair, Mo headed towards the window to resume gazing through the blinds.

"Oh fuck," Amanda said, before he could even get to the window.

"What?" Mo asked, spinning around to face her.

"Oh fuck, oh fuck, oh fuck," was all she replied. Mo could see her eyes scanning the words on the screen.

"You got a hit?" He stepped around the desk.

"Yeah, on the American Sex Offenders page. Look." She pointed to the middle of the screen. "His real name isn't even Brandon, that's just an alias he's used in the past. That's why the hyperlink search failed."

Mo read the entry on the page. Brandon was really Troy Hampton, a convicted sex offender.

"Oh Christ, 'attempted rape'," he breathed. "Did you ever make the right call checking up on this bastard."

"That's not all, look here," she said, pointing to

the next search result.

"Fuck," he cried. "Child pornography? Jesus Christ, let's go, now!"

He watched impatiently as Amanda shut down her computer and turned off the generator. Mo worried he might throw up from the fear that engulfed him. Where was Brandon/Troy now? Was he hurting a child this very moment?

They drove home in silence. Amanda raced the car through the empty streets, while Mo repeatedly clenched and unclenched his fists. He wondered what would happen now. He had an urge to kill Troy, and he suspected so would some others. But he wasn't sure that was a good idea. Without a police presence and a court system, would their fledgling new society resort to vigilante justice? *But what's the alternative, just let him go?* Mo wondered.

"Where's Brandon?" Mo shouted as soon as the car came to a stop. Deb was outside playing with several of the children on the front lawn. She stood up and looked at Mo with a mixture of surprise and alarm.

"He's out searching houses for supplies. Why? What happened?" Deb asked.

He led Deb out of earshot from the children. "Amanda searched her backup drives. He's a rapist and pedophile. He's the one that broke her drives here, so she wouldn't find out about him."

"He didn't know I had backups, thank God," Amanda added.

Deb gritted her teeth as the reality of this discovery sank in. Joshua, Dee, and Javon came out of the house.

"What's all the shouting about, you two?" Joshua asked, smiling towards Amanda.

"Yo, we got thirteen new people coming from the hood," Javon interjected with obvious pride. "Nine kids, two teenagers, and two adults. Can you beat that haul, Mo?"

Javon's smile faded when he saw the intense looks on Mo, Amanda, and Deb's faces.

"That's a lot of serious ass faces. What's the deal here, break it down," Dee said.

Mo explained what they had found.

"That fucker's a dead man," Javon said.

"SOS, shoot on site," Dee agreed.

"Whoa, whoa, whoa, we can't just start murdering people," Joshua exclaimed.

"That ain't people," Dee said.

"He's a disgusting, vile, asshole. And he has to go. But he is a human being, and we don't just kill people," Joshua insisted.

"Say we send him away, then what?" Mo asked. "Won't he just find more women and children to harm?"

"Well, we can't jail him, and you're right, he will harm others," Deb said.

"You too? I can't believe I'm hearing this. I'll have no part of your lynching posse," Joshua said hotly. He strode away with clenched fists.

"What I was going to add is, but we can't just kill him either," Deb continued, ignoring Joshua's departure.

"Why not?" asked Javon.

"What do you think we should do?" Amanda asked Deb.

"If you don't want any killing, then you leave me and Javon out of it. Cause he ever in our sight, we gonna put a bullet in his sick ass," Dee said.

"For sure! It be clockin' time," Javon agreed.

Mo was feeling increasingly uncomfortable with the idea of Troy being let loose upon the world. *Is this what they call mob mentality?* he wondered.

"If we let him go, then aren't we just as guilty? We're sentencing the children he'll find on his own to great harm," Mo said.

"Oh crap, I don't know," Deb said. "I didn't sign up for this." She smiled weakly at the others.

"What about you, Amanda?" Mo asked.

She paused for several breaths before answering. "There are so many more Sophias out there. We can't intentionally let loose a predator on them. But sentencing a man to death? I don't know if I'm able to do that."

"You can leave the dirty work to us, that ain't a problem," Javon said.

"I appreciate that, but that's us just pretending we didn't pull the trigger," Amanda replied.

"That's right. It doesn't matter who pulls the trigger, his blood will be on all of our hands," Deb said.

"'Will' be, does that mean you're with us?" Mo asked.

Deb didn't answer him. She stared out into the

distance before lowering her head with a sigh. Then she looked at Mo briefly before turning to Dee and giving him an almost imperceptible nod.

"OK, that's settled then," Dee said. He turned to Javon. "Lock and load Ace, we got a job to do."

"Where we gonna off him?" Javon asked. "We don't want the young ones to see that."

"Right. Do any of you know where he might be?" Dee asked the others.

"No, he plans the route with Joshua. They follow Mo's map, but I don't know where they're at now. Can't be too far," Deb said.

"Well let's go ask Joshua then," Dee said.

"Um, let me go ask him," Amanda said. "You saw what he thinks. He probably wouldn't tell you, he'd know what you're going to do. He might not tell me, for that matter, but at least I have a chance."

"Fine, you go do your thing," Dee said.

Mo thought it best if he stayed away also, given his rocky relationship with Joshua. Deb returned to the children in the front yard. Mo watched Dee and Javon head to their Range Rover, and open the rear hatch. The vehicle blocked them from his view, but he could hear the distinct metallic clatter of guns being worked.

"I can't find Joshua," Amanda said several minutes later, as she approached Mo.

"Probably went off sulking," Mo said.

"I spoke to him about his pacifist beliefs on the way to Heuvelton. It must be hard when you're faced with a situation like this. No courts or jails to keep you safe while maintaining your belief to not harm others."

"I'm certainly not a proponent of violence, but I do believe in self defense, or in defending others who can't."

"We're in the same camp there."

"What did the mad scientist say?" Dee asked. He had a large bulge under his shirt, just above his waist. Mo was glad he was on their side.

"He's gone to blow off some steam," Amanda told him.

"OK, so we wait. See who turns up first, Mr. Science or Mr. Dead Man. If it's Brandon, don't nobody say nuthin to him. Me and Javon will lead him away from the kids before we do anything. But we don't want him tipped off that something ain't right."

Ever since he was a child, Mo hated waiting. Nothing infuriated him more than someone being late for an agreed meeting time. Logically he knew that no meeting had been setup with Joshua. Nevertheless, an hour later, he felt increasingly irritated by the man's absence. Which is why, when Joshua finally did return, Mo was gruff with his questions.

"Where's Brandon at?"

"I don't know," Joshua replied.

"You plan the route with him every day, where was he going today?"

"That doesn't really matter, he's not there

anymore."

"What do you mean? Stop talking in riddles," Mo had raised his voice, and now Dee and Javon, who had been lingering nearby, were making their way towards them.

"About an hour ago I warned him he was in danger. Now he's gone, and I have no idea which direction he's headed."

"Are you fucking crazy?" Mo asked incredulously. "You can't do that!"

"I did do that. We're here to save lives, not take them."

"Maybe I should put a bullet in your ass instead, mofo," Dee said, advancing and putting his face an inch away from Joshua's.

"What's going on here?" Deb called from a few yards away as she strode towards them.

"Dickhead here done warn off the dead man," Javon spat out.

Deb pulled Dee away. "Don't do anything to him Darnell. But you Joshua, what did you think gave you the right to do something like that?"

"The right to save a life? That's an obligation, not a right. And one that all people should have when they're thinking straight."

"Fuck 'em. Let's go find Brandon," Javon told Dee.

"Where are you going to look Javon? He's had an hour head start. He could be anywhere," Joshua said.

"Jesus Christ. He's right, there's no chance of finding him," Mo acknowledged. "Always knew you were an asshole," he added while aggressively pointing near Joshua's face.

"Everybody take it down a notch," Deb said. "Joshua, please go for a walk, I don't think any of us are wanting your presence right now. And later you and I are going to have a talk about unilateral decisions."

"Of course Deb, any time you want," Joshua said calmly.

"So that's it then? We ain't gonna do nothing?" Javon asked, frustration dripping from every word.

"What can we do, B? He fucked us over good," Dee said.

As infuriated as Mo was towards Joshua, he also felt a strange sense of relief. He had sanctioned the death of a man, and that would have sat with him for the rest of his life. There was no question that letting Brandon go, 'Troy' he corrected himself, was the wrong thing to do. But that was now on Joshua's conscience, not his. Mo felt guilty thinking about it in those terms. But he had essentially done the right thing, without having to pay the price of having a man's death on his hands. *What does that say about me?*

12. PLAY TIME

Deb smiled as she pulled up next to Titus's truck at the hotel. They would soon move in, and it already felt like home. They now occupied four houses back at her place, which was absolute chaos. It had taken Titus and Chris a lot longer to prepare the hotel than anticipated, but she didn't begrudge them that delay. She was aware of how hard they worked and how guilty they felt about the time it took. But, like everyone, she was finding the wait increasingly difficult to bear. *I want to move in now* her mind cried.

Deb paused when she entered the building, listening. She couldn't hear any noises to give away Titus and Chris's location. Though she wasn't surprised, given the size of the hotel. She walked over to the stairwell entrance and listened again. Then she heard it: the faint, satisfying sound of a hammer far away. She began climbing the carpeted stairs in the dark, feeling her way up and keeping a solid grip on the metal banister. The intermittent hammering sounds grew louder until she reached the fourth floor. A dim sliver of light seeped out from under the door marked with a large white '4'. A small square viewing window also threw some faint sunlight into the stairwell.

She peered through the window and saw Titus moving a dolly with two large doors on it. He paused in front of one of the rooms on the right and lifted another door onto the dolly. The bulging of his muscles told Deb how heavy the doors were. The hammering noises continued from inside one room, though Deb couldn't tell which it was.

"Would go a lot faster with a little help," he bellowed. Deb winced at his tone.

The hammering further down the hall stopped long enough for a brusque reply. "Busy here, you wanted the doors gone, not me."

Enough spying, she thought, and pulled the fire escape door open.

"Deb!" called Titus, without his usual smile. "Coming to check up on your workforce?"

"Of course I am. I half expected to find the two of you sharing a six pack."

"Hardly," he replied, with a grim look.

Chris popped his head out of the third room on the right.

"I was thinking that either Titus had started talking to himself, again, or we have a visitor. I'm glad to see it's the latter. How are you, Deb?"

"I'm fine, I'm fine, I thought it'd be nice to see how the place is shaping up. I haven't been here since that first day Titus and I found it."

"It's coming along, but we'd be done by now if I had decent help," Titus said.

"I'm not your helper, can't you get that through your head? And it's this stupid door idea of yours that made us late, not me. I'm not getting any help doing the important work."

"Gentlemen, please!" Deb held out her hands between them. "I wanted you to work out your differences on your own. Clearly it hasn't happened. But this really has to stop."

As if she hadn't spoken, Titus continued, sharply pointing his fingers towards Chris. "I've been taking care of these people since almost day one, so I know a bit more than you about what is and what isn't important work."

"Yeah well you're in my hotel now, so no, I don't think you have the best handle on what's important." Chris was waving his hammer in the air while speaking.

"Your hotel? Can I see the deed please?"

"Stop!" Deb raised her voice loudly. "What's gotten into you two? You're arguing like the toddlers whose rooms you're supposed to be preparing. Titus, Chris is not your helper, you two are a team. And Chris, I know you worked here, but it's clearly not your hotel, so please don't act like it is. It's our home, all of us. Now grow up, both of you."

The two men glared at each other. Titus spoke first, after clearing his throat. "I'm sorry you had to see that Deb, not cool, to say the least."

"You're certainly right it's not cool. And personally I think the delay has a lot more to do with you two not working together than any decision about the damned doors."

"That's exactly what I was trying to say," Titus said, a small victorious smile forming on his lips. "If he would just help—".

"You're not listening, Titus," Deb interrupted. "Stop it with the helping thing. Like I said, Chris is not here to help you. You two are here to work as a team to help prepare the children's home. Please try to change your attitude, starting now."

An awkward silence ensued. Deb was well accustomed to scolding naughty children in this way. But she'd never treated grown men like that. It made her somewhat uncomfortable, but figured that they must be feeling far more uncomfortable than she was. She would be downright embarrassed to be called out for such immature behavior.

"Care for a tour?" Chris finally broke the silence.

"I would love a tour, lead on sir."

"Ok, well you can see that the doors are all off now. Titus has been hauling them out of here."

"Bringing them down the stairs is a whole lot of fun," Titus grumbled.

"They look like they weigh a ton. There are so many rooms, can't you use one as storage?"

"I could, but it's not the space I'm worried about. If one of the kids managed to get in there, there could be a bad accident. Dangerous stuff on another floor, that's our guiding principle, if you will."

"Safety first, thanks Titus." She noticed the smug smile he threw Chris.

"Here, Madam, we have the toddler suite," Chris continued, with a fake British accent.

The room's transformation pleasantly surprised her. They had laid four beds out in each corner of the bedroom. A wooden bar wrapped in tied towels was bolted to the side away from the wall, to prevent the child from rolling off the bed. They had installed office partitions to separate the beds.

"Oh that's smart, the dividers. Otherwise, the kids would have a toddler party every night. But where did you get these partitions?" Deb asked.

"There's several offices in the management area, a bit of a partition hell down there. And also, the conference rooms have these things," Chris replied.

"Notice all the exposed outlets though," Titus said.

"Well, I'm sure we can easily find plugs at a Home Depot or something, right?" Deb asked.

She was confused for a moment when Titus and Chris burst into laughter.

"Oh, right, no power," she said with a hint of embarrassment.

"Sorry, had to play you on that one to make ourselves feel better. We actually started plugging some outlets before realizing it was pointless."

"Well shame on you both," Deb laughed. She was quite happy to be the butt of their jokes – anything to ease the tension between them.

"On the topic of child-proofing, we removed all the breakables, and heavy things that could fall on an overzealous toddler," Chris continued.

"Like all the fancy table lamps, which were just about as useful as those outlets," Titus added.

"Now over here I envision a small play area, for early in the morning when not every child is awake yet. Or after dinner, to calm them down. You've seen how wild they get in large groups," Chris said.

Deb looked at what was once a hotel living room. They had emptied it out except for the sofa and two easy chairs. She could see herself sitting on the sofa reading a story to the handful of children staying that room.

"Oh you guys, this is just so awesome. Thanks so much for all your hard work."

"A couple of trips to Toys 'R Us will fill out these mini play areas nicely," Titus said.

"We'll probably fill this floor in no time. Dee and Javon found another six people yesterday alone," Deb mused.

"But wait, there's more!" Chris added. "Follow me."

He led Deb out into the hallway. They walked past several rooms that were organized the same way, from what Deb could tell with a glance. Chris stopped in front of one of the rooms.

"A suite for le bébé," he said, switching to a French accent.

"Well, you have a very international staff at your establishment. I'm glad you believe in diversity," Deb acknowledged.

The baby room held four cribs, two in the bedroom and two in the living room. One challenge they had faced in the houses was babies keeping each other awake with their crying. Deb was glad that Chris and Titus had given the babies more space. Essentially two per room, given the heavy bedroom door.

"Not much play area, but then at that age you mostly service them, not play with them," Chris said, smiling.

"Yeah, this is great. A couple of comforters on the floor to have them crawl around on, that's all they need for now."

"And some baby toys, don't forget those. Gotta stimulate those tiny baby brains," Titus said.

"Awesome. OK you guys have been cooped up in here for way too long, which brings me to the main point of my visit."

"Wait!" Chris said. "We're not done with the tour. We have the teenage area and the adult area in the floor above."

"Oh, that can wait," Titus said. "I want to hear what really brought the big boss lady to our humble work area."

"'Big' boss lady? Are you calling me fat?" Deb asked, feigned horror on her face.

"Not at all! In fact, I've been meaning to say" — Titus stopped to take Deb into a dance position, placing her left hand on his shoulder, his left around her waist, and holding each other's right hand. "I can't get enough of your love, babe," he crooned, in a deep voice.

Deb stepped back from him and bent over double with laughter.

"I swear, that was the worst Barry White imitation I have ever heard in my life," Deb said.

"Barry White? I thought he was having indigestion," Chris said with a smile.

After all the drama and hardships that they had endured, Deb didn't think she would ever be capable of laughing so hard. But Titus doing Barry White? She couldn't remember the last time she saw something that funny. As the laughter subsided, all she felt was immense gratitude towards these two men. *Especially Titus*, she thought with a tinge of guilt towards Chris.

"So, as I was saying, before Barry interrupted, I came to get you two because we're having a massive play date today. Maurice and I went to check out the big play museum in the city, and it's safe for the children. He's in there now setting up one of the generators and some lights. We're going to surprise the kids and go spend the afternoon there."

"What a cool idea," Chris exclaimed.

"I know, isn't it? We'll get all the vehicles involved and pile the kids in any which way. It's not like we have to worry about seat belt laws, or crashing into other cars. We take it slow, like a parade. They'll go crazy in there."

"I am so in," Titus said, his grin wider than ever.

"I figured you two would be. And it's not just for the kids," she said, her smile fading. "With all the Brandon and Joshua drama two days ago, I suspect the adults are just as much in need for some R&R. And now I see that you two certainly are."

The two men nodded somberly. She knew the Brandon affair was an awkward topic. It had divided the group into two camps, those who applauded Joshua's actions, and those who preferred executing

Brandon/Troy. The latter group was far bigger. Deb wanted to urgently heal the rift because they simply could not afford strife. Cooperation was the only way to manage all the demands placed on their shoulders.

"So, when do you want us to come?" Chris finally asked.

"Now. Let's go."

"I would prefer to keep hauling these doors down the stairs, but I guess I'll make the ultimate sacrifice and come play with you all," Titus said glumly.

"A real team player," Deb said, tapping him on the shoulder.

Getting to the play museum was even more fun than Deb had expected. She had finally lost track of their exact numbers, but knew that they were now over fifty adults and children. And the number showed, when everyone packed into a convoy of eight cars and trucks. Every single child was excited about the mystery field trip. Most of the adults were equally excited, although they knew the destination. They packed the older kids in the open back of Titus's pickup truck. Darnell and Javon's SUV was also packed to the gills. Poor Darnell had three little ones stacked on his lap next to the driver's seat. Deb suspected Javon was quite relieved to be the driver.

She had grown quite fond of Darnell and Javon. Sure, they were rough around the edges and she knew their past was questionable. But they genuinely seemed to be happy to contribute to their new group. They took great pride in bringing in heaps of new faces into the fold. She recognized their behavior from some of the troubled youths she had encountered in her years of teaching. Though she generally taught very young children, the same lack of self esteem would manifest itself in unpleasant, often harmful ways. Harmful to themselves and to others. Equal status brought out the best in children, and in these two young adults.

Oddly enough, she was only now starting to see some friction towards Darnell and Javon. Strangely, it came from some of the newcomers they had brought into the group. She made a note to monitor that situation. She didn't want them to feel alienated by the very people they'd saved.

Honking horns and hoots of joy interrupted her thoughts. They had arrived at the museum. She spotted Mo next to the propped-open door to the museum, a huge grin on his face. And that's when they lost control of the children. They piled out and ran helter skelter into the building. Deb laughed, delighted with the unleashed madness of the moment.

After realizing the futility of trying to have an orderly visit, Deb gave in to the chaos and spent the next two hours enjoying herself. Gnomes, princes and princesses, fairy tale characters of all sorts and sizes, and even a giant Mr. Potato Head amused and delighted the senses.

"You've done an amazing job lighting up the

place, Maurice," she said, putting her arm around his waist. Lucy held her other hand.

"Thanks. Yeah, it was hard to choose which areas to light up. The place is huge. We could come back another time and spend the day in an entirely different part of the museum."

"Judging by the children's reaction, I would say another visit is definitely in the cards."

"It feels wonderfully strange seeing them so happy," he said, after a brief pause where they watched the children running around them.

"And are you having a good time, young lady?" Mo asked Lucy. Lucy nodded shyly. She spoke easily with Deb when they were alone, but was still somewhat reserved with the other adults.

"You bet she is, she's been running all over the place," Deb said. "Do you want to stay with us, Lucy, or do you want to go play some more?" Deb asked.

"I want to play," Lucy replied.

"Then off you go, have fun sweetie," Deb said, letting go of the child's hand. It warmed her heart to see Lucy smiling and playing. She had grown so incredibly fond of the little girl. *Sammy would have loved this place too.* Whenever she thought of the little boy she had failed to save, her mind recoiled.

"Sometimes it's hard to remember the simple joys in life, like kids playing. It's really quite wonderful to just stand here and watch them. I'm loving this," Mo said, sighing.

"You deserve it, Mo. Soak in all the peace and happiness." Deb remembered the sobbing man she had held. "How are you doing lately?"

"Thanks for asking, but I'm fine. And this," — he waved his arms towards the frenzied rush of children — "this is a stress antidote."

"Can't argue with that." She knew he wasn't fine, but she was glad that the playing children soothed his nerves. She cared deeply for Mo and felt such conflict regarding his house searches. For his safety, she wanted him to stop. But every time he brought in a child, she was thankful that he continued. There was nothing to be done about it this minute, so she forced herself to stay present in the moment, enjoying this amazing time with the children.

"You never told me, Deb. Why aren't you vaccinated?", Mo asked after a few moments of silence.

Mo's question took Deb by surprise. She swallowed hard and decided to follow her mantra that telling the truth was almost always the correct path.

"OK, you asked, so here goes. Two years ago, I was given the choice between early retirement and vaccination. I chose retirement. You see, young-onset Alzheimer's, that's the rare, hereditary type of Alzheimer's, runs in my family. My mother and her grandmother both suffered with that horrible disease in their mid fifties. I witnessed firsthand my mother's mental deterioration. Now death by COVID-19 is a terrible way to die. But it lasts weeks, not years, like dementia. So it felt like I was picking the lesser of two evils, you know? Of course

I couldn't have known that refusing the vaccine would save my life. And now I'll almost certainly get the disease I was trying to avoid."

"Deb, I'm so sorry. I wouldn't have asked if – well, you should have just told me that it was for private reasons."

"Why keep it a secret? At least now when I forget things you'll know why." She tried to make light of a thought that was absolute darkness in her terrified mind.

"But it's not a guarantee that you'll get it, right? Like you're predisposed to it or something?"

"Can't know for sure, but the odds are very high. If there is a God, or fate, or whatever, I like to believe that it turned out this way for a reason. Otherwise, it's a pretty cruel joke."

"Look around you. None of this would have happened if you'd chosen to get vaccinated. Isn't that the reason you were looking for?"

"Thank you Maurice, that is a nice thought." And she meant it. Deb had already tried rationalizing the outcome of her choices by thinking of the children that they were saving. But hearing it from someone else felt better than she had expected.

Titus approached at a rapid pace, his face flush with excitement. "You two need to see this," he said, beckoning them with his hand.

"Well, this could be interesting," Deb said, happy to leave the uncomfortable topic behind. She and Mo followed Titus.

"Sorry Mo, Chris and I stole one of your lamps,"

Titus said breathlessly as they left the well-lit section of the museum and entered a darkened room. *Chris and I*, Deb thought with a smile.

"Whoa, no so fast, it's hard to see here," Deb said. She slowed her pace, waiting for her eyes to adjust to the darkness.

Titus and Mo disappeared around the corner ahead of her. When she reached the corner, she could see a glimmer of light at the opposite end of the cavernous, warehouse-sized room that they had entered. She caught up and saw Mo, Titus, and Chris standing together, looking up. The one light that Chris and Titus had set up cast eerie shadows as it illuminated a dizzying array of overhead ropes, planks, and metal beams.

She spotted Mason and Malik first.

"Oh my God is that safe?"

"Yep, they're all clipped in, they can't fall," Chris assured her.

Deb's gaze followed the overhead walkway and obstacle course. Up in the lead, furthest away, she spotted the two older girls, Alexis and Kalisha, making their way across a plank bridge in midair.

"We figured the older kids might want something more than Big Bird and teddy bears," Titus explained.

"I want to join them," Mo said.

"Go ahead, we already did the course before letting the kids on. We made sure it was safe," Chris laughed.

"Deb, are you in?" Mo asked.

"I think I'll pass, I'm not a huge fan of heights."

"But you're clipped in, there's no danger of falling," Mo said.

"Go, go, have fun," she said, shoving him towards the ladder leading up to the overhead course.

Oftentimes Deb felt down on herself, but this was certainly not one of them. She was so pleased with her idea of coming here. *Major therapy for young and old.*

Deb thought they were doing well. Sure, they had encountered a rotten apple, but he was gone now. Soon a floor of the hotel would be ready to move into. Darnell and Javon were doing a great job of rescuing children, and adults. *Mo needs help*, she thought. She made a mental note to get more people searching their neighborhood and beyond. She didn't want them to get too comfortable with their current situation when there were still millions of children out there needing help.

That thought chilled her to the bone. On the one hand she was terribly proud of their accomplishments. On the other hand, it seemed like a tiny droplet in an enormous swimming pool of water. Without getting caught up in the logistics side of the issue, Deb often wondered how they could scale up their child saving operation. Clearly, increasing the number of adults was critical. They needed adults for both the search effort and caring for the kids they had already saved. She had to make the childcare part of the operation more efficient, in order to free more adults for the searching part.

The teacher in her balked at the idea. *'More efficient' means less individual attention*, she realized. And she knew what consequences that entailed for a child's mental and emotional development.

Still, it was worth the price to pay for saving more lives. *Besides, the search and rescue part won't last forever, then we can focus on better care for the ones we've saved,* she thought. Deb nodded to herself, having settled the pros and cons in her mind. She resolved to free up more of the adults' time for finding children, and to get new adults helping quickly. She noticed that it often took newcomers a few precious days before finding their place in the group. *Need more efficient integration,* she thought, adding the note to her mental 'to do' list that she constantly checked and rechecked in her busy brain.

"You done good, Mama, all of them are having a good time," Dee said from behind her. She jumped as his voice startled her out of her ruminations. "Sorry, didn't mean to scare you," he added.

"Darnell, where did you come from?" she chuckled.

"It ain't where I came from, it's where were you just now?"

"Oh, just going over stuff to do in my mind. Where's your right-hand man?" she asked, looking behind him.

"If you'd told me a week ago what I just saw, I would have said you be playing me," Dee said, shaking his head and grinning ear to ear.

"What?"

"Javon is sitting in front of one of them big books with all them gnomes and shit, reading a story to about half a dozen kiddies!" He burst into laughter.

"Oh my God, he's really turned around on all this children stuff, hasn't he?"

"Big time. He's Uncle Javon to half of those young ones now."

Deb marveled at how dramatically some people could change, given a chance to break the mold that they'd been cast in.

"Anyway, I wanted to tell you that me and Javon talked it over. We appreciate how you treat us like we normal folks, you know? Not like bad-ass criminals. So, we decided to stay with you all. If you'll still have us, I mean," he added, shuffling his feet.

More good news: Deb couldn't believe how wonderful the day had turned out. She cupped his face in her hands, leaned forward and kissed his forehead. "You're a good man, Darnell, don't let anyone tell you otherwise. I'm thrilled that you two will stay with us."

She let him go and stepped back before continuing. "But only on one condition: you stop calling me Mama!"

"Well, now that part is gonna need some more negotiations," Dee chuckled.

"Seriously though, there is one thing I want to pick your brain about later. In a very short time, you've almost doubled our group size. I want to make the other adults learn from you two. Any tips on how they can find people more quickly, that kind of thing."

"Sure thing. I'll sit down with Mo and compare notes on what we doing."

"Thank you, Darnell. Now, care for a little high-flying adventure?". She pointed to the others above their heads.

Dee shook his head. "Maybe next time, I'm gonna go check how Uncle Javon is doing. Gotta make sure all them kiddies don't take him out."

Deb laughed, and urged him to hurry on, just as Amanda and Jessica arrived. Amanda held Sophia in her arms. The girl's broken arm was healing well, but it was too early to let her loose in busy play areas with all the other children.

"There's Deb and Dee. Ah Deb, ah Deb, ah Dee Dee Dee," Amanda scatted.

"Ah Dee, Ah Deb, ah Dee, ah Deb, ah Debba Debba Dee Dee Dee," Jessica continued, snapping her fingers and swaying her hips.

"That some fine shit you all smokin'," Dee said dryly, while managing not to crack a smile. His eyes lingered on Jessica's swaying hips.

Definitely a good day, Deb thought, with satisfied contentment.

13. AN UNWANTED RETURN

*W*ho would have thought that it would take the end of the world to make me happy? Jessica thought. She lay naked in the crook of Dee's arm, having just experienced possibly the best orgasm of her life. They were under a thick peach-colored comforter on someone's California king mattress, with some kind of plush topper that felt so damned soft under her body. The entire room was decorated in soft pastels. Muted watercolors hung on the pale-yellow walls. The night tables and dresser were painted a dark cream hue. A mint-green carpet covered the floor. By contrast, the curtains were bright red with vivid paisley twirls throughout. *A bit of punch*, Jessica thought. She remembered that her interior designer roommate used to be fond of that saying, back when Jessica was in her first year of med school.

"What are you thinking about?" Dee murmured.

"Just looking at this room. Someone went through a lot of trouble decorating it. Not what I expected from the outside."

It had been two days since their group's play day at the museum. Now they were back to searching for survivors in the city center. The house was dilapidated on the outside. Like all homes by now, the front yard was overgrown with weeds. Additionally, the door and window frames were almost down to bare wood, with most of the paint having peeled off long ago. The lower half of the exterior walls were bricks covered with mildew stain. The house had been empty, thankfully. When they discovered the luxurious bedroom, well, things happened spontaneously from there.

"Nobody wants to show money on the outside around here," Dee explained. "It's like asking people to rob you, and asking the cops to pay you a visit. This money came from drugs or hooking, it wasn't legit, for sure."

"These people had a story. All these empty houses are like reminders of the billions of stories that just," she hesitated, searching for her words, "that just ended abruptly."

"I'm glad your story is still playing out," Dee said.

"Likewise," Jessica answered.

"So, have you thought about what you want to do with, well, sounds weird, but the rest of your life?"

"Whoa, you're asking big questions now. Where did that come from?" She looked at Dee curiously, shifting in the bed to better see his face.

"I dunno, exactly. It's like we're starting over, in a way. You and me, for example. Our paths would have never crossed, you know? So what else might change? Or what else can we change about ourselves?"

"OK, let me turn that around, since it's obviously

on your mind. If this is a new start, what does the new Dee want to become?"

Dee chuckled. "Set myself up for that one, didn't I?" He paused before continuing. "Where I grew up, I didn't have a whole lot of choices. Funny, because the world is falling to shit, but in some ways I feel freer. I don't want to become a new Dee. I just want a more peaceful life, I guess."

Jessica ran her hand through his hair and then caressed the contour of his face. "Feeling more peaceful now?"

"Not too stressed at the moment, no."

At that moment Nancy jumped onto the bed. She sniffed Jessica, rubbed against her arm, and started up her purr engine, as Jessica called it. Then she walked onto Dee's stomach and started kneading his belly through the comforter. Dee absently scratched the cat's chin and head. Jessica smiled. Dee and Nancy had clearly taken to each other.

"You're lucky it's a thick comforter, or you'd be in trouble now. Those are pretty sharp kitten claws," Jessica said.

Dee smiled distractedly in a way Jessica had noticed before, when he wasn't really listening. As annoying as it was, it also made her feel close to him. By starting to recognize all of his quirks, her affection for him grew and grew.

"Jess, why didn't you get vaccinated? I mean, that was a pretty important decision: it's the reason your story hasn't ended."

Jessica could feel her body tensing up. "You never

told me either, what's your reason?"

"No big reason, really. Just couldn't be bothered. You face danger all the time on the streets around here. This virus didn't seem like that big a threat, compared to everything else. Well, I guess I didn't really trust it either. No offense, but it was probably made by a bunch of white folks in suits, who didn't really have this black man's best interest at heart, if you know what I mean."

Jessica nodded. "Yeah, I remember there was a lot of mistrust all around. But the fear of the virus was bigger than the fear of the harm the vaccine might do."

"Your turn," Dee prompted.

"Can I get a pass on this one?" she asked.

"Uh, let me think about that. No," he said, smiling at her.

Jessica took a deep breath.

"I haven't actually told anyone about this before. It's weird, but then these are weird times, so here goes. OK, first, I need you to understand that I am not suicidal. I mean at low points, I may have fantasized about it, but never taken it seriously. I think that's pretty normal, right?"

"The 'not suicidal' part is, but not so sure about the second part, Jess."

"Regardless, the point is I'm not suicidal, so I don't want you to get all weird on me now. Because, for pretty much all of my teenage and adult life I've had"—she paused once more, screwing up her courage—"a death wish. There, I said it."

"A death wish? What are you talking about? You want to die?"

"Well, sort of, yeah. I mean I wasn't out there trying to find ways to die. It's more like, I don't know, I would welcome death. I get that fearing death is what's 'normal'. I don't fear it at all. I do fear the process of dying, it might be horribly painful. But death itself is, well, a way to end the pain."

"That's some heavy shit you laying on me, Jess. What am I supposed to say to that? And what pain are you talking about?"

"It's hard to explain. When you hate yourself, when things are just too much to bear for whatever reason, you can get comfort from thinking about death. It's like a release, a way out. So, when I'm not feeling good for whatever reason, I think of death. And then I get this beautiful wave of calm that washes over me. And I just can't help but smile, it feels so good."

"Sounds to me like you are suicidal, no offense."

"No, you see, I would never, ever, ever do that to my parents, my friends, and all the people who love me. It would mess up their lives so much. Or would have messed them up, I should say now. Anyway, suicide, to me, is the ultimate act of selfishness. But hey, if the plane I'm on happens to crash, or I get hit by a bus, well, I'm good with that." She laughed nervously, trying to make light of a topic that she knew was anything but light.

"That's a shitty way to live though. Did you ever try to, um, get help?"

"Yeah, but most docs just wanted me on meds, which I don't want. Smoking weed helped a lot, but that's just another drug dependency I wasn't interested in." She turned towards Dee. "Hey, am I freaking you out here? That's the last thing I want to do."

"No, don't worry about me, Jess. I just wish I knew how to help."

"Well, listening to me and not freaking out, or judging me, is a pretty big help."

"That's no problem, trust me."

"OK, well, anyway, back to your original question. Why no vaccination? Let COVID take me out, that simple. Talk about irony, eh? I skip the shot so that I might die from a pandemic, and instead it's the shot that kills everyone else. How fucked up is that?"

"Look at you getting all foul-mouthed," Dee said, smiling at her.

"There's one more thing I want to say," she began. The heat rising to her face told her she was probably as red as a tomato now.

"Go ahead," Dee said after a moment of silence.

"Again, I don't want to freak you out. But lying here in your arms, that death wish is gone. I want to live. Very badly in fact."

She shut her eyes, unable to look at his response to this confession. As he moved her out of the crook of his arm, panic flooded her entire being. Tears formed behind her closed lids. Then she felt the heat of his breath before his lips pressed gently against hers. A waterfall of emotions washed over her. He continued kissing her face as the tears flowed down the sides of her head.

"Oh God this is embarrassing, I don't even know why I'm crying," she said. She opened her eyes and saw his smiling face hovering above hers. Slowly his face disappeared from her view as he moved his way down her body.

Jessica's eyes blinked in the bright sunshine when they eventually made their way back outside.

"Ready for the big day tomorrow?" Dee asked, coming up behind her, and wrapping his arms around her waist.

"More than ready. That hotel looks so cool. And getting out of those cramped houses – can't wait."

"Yeah, same here. Hey, we need to find Javon, he'll be wondering why we aren't keeping up with his house search."

"Is it just me, or does he seem, I don't know, more accepting of me? Of us?"

"Man, I can't believe how he's softened up. It's got to be all them kids, 'Uncle Javon' seems to be his thing now. I never would have believed it a month ago."

"Whatever the reason, it's sure nice to see him be a little friendlier. I don't think he liked me much at first."

"Nah, Javon just didn't want things to change. We was the last of our crew you know? He was worried you might break that up. Pull a Yoko on us."

"So, what do you want to do? Catch up with him,

or just continue house searching from here? I think we should continue searching, seems easier than remembering where we were once we find him."

Before Dee could answer her, three shots, in quick succession, rang out in the distance.

"Fuck," Dee said, reaching out behind him and pulling a pistol out of his waistband. "Get back in the house and stay there until I come get you."

"No way, I'm not sitting there by myself not knowing what's happening."

"Stay back!" Dee cried, as he started running down the block towards where they had heard the shots.

Jessica had no intention of staying alone, defenseless. She made a mental note to have Dee show her how to shoot a gun, and to arm her. She ran, following Dee at a safe distance. Two more shots rang out, closer now. Dee became more cautious ahead of her, crouching next to cars, and along hedges. Jessica tried to follow the same path.

Suddenly Dee stopped behind a car. He turned towards her, and signaled her to stop, and get down. She was approximately fifty feet from where he was. She got behind a large SUV and peered around it. There was Javon, crouched behind a truck two houses past Dee.

"What's the deal, Javon?" Dee called out.

"Mofo trying to pop my ass before I even get to the door."

"D'you tell him we ain't out to cause no trouble?"

"He ain't exactly in a talking mood, Dee."

"Let's just get out of here then," Jessica called out.

"Ain't got no place to go," Javon answered. Then she understood the problem. Javon had no cover except for the truck that he was hiding behind.

Jessica moved up three vehicles that were parked one in front of the other along the street.

"Hey Mister!" she cried out towards the house where the shooter was in. "Why are you shooting at us?"

"Stay the fuck away from us!" a muffled voice replied.

"We can't, you keep shooting while we're trying to get away," Javon called out.

The voice called out again after a brief silence. "Hands in the air, then you can go back to your asshole friends."

Javon looked at Dee, who nodded, while pointing his pistol at the house. Jessica watched Javon tuck his gun into his waistband, raise his hands, and run in a half crouch towards Dee. He stopped behind the car next to Dee, looking anxiously towards the house with the shooter. The man in the house didn't fire.

"I'm going again, further away," Javon called. He used the same awkward half-crouched run to get next to Jessica.

"My turn," Dee called out, and did the same.

"OK, we're good from here, we've got cover until we're out of his sight," Javon said.

"Wait," Jessica said. "There might be children in the house. The guy did say 'stay away from us'."

"I don't give a fuck if there's children, we don't want that crazy-ass living with us," Javon spat out.

"He's right Jess, let it go," Dee added.

"Let me just try," she insisted. Before they could object, she cried out. "We rescue children who haven't been vaccinated. Do you need our help?"

A shot rang out, and she heard the bullet lodge itself somewhere in the car that they were hiding behind.

"Nice move," Javon said.

"Let's go," Dee said, and began walking in a crouch behind the cars. This time Jessica didn't argue.

It wasn't until they were at a safe distance that Jessica spoke again.

"I'm very sorry about that. I just don't get why he would shoot at us when we're just talking."

"A lot of folks don't trust strangers. This one's a little quick on the trigger, alright," Dee said.

"For sure," Javon added, and then stopped, studying Jessica.

"What?" she asked.

"Are you serious?" Javon asked, turning to Dee. "She got JBF written all over her face. I'm busting down doors and getting shot at while you two are banging?"

"Uhh," was all Dee managed to respond. Jessica thought it was the first time that she'd seen him speechless.

"Aw Bro, you need to start thinking how you gonna make this up to me," Javon finally said. He chuckled before roughly pushing Dee's shoulder.

They spent the next four hours searching houses. Jessica and Javon each took one side of the street, while Dee alternately leap-frogged each of them, criss-crossing from one side to the other. It was nerve-wracking work. Especially now, after Javon had been shot at. Jessica used even more caution when approaching a house. She called out from a distance and then knocked on the door and windows before breaking in. Once she entered, she had to brace herself each time, not knowing what horror she might find. Usually, the smell alone would tell her if the house was empty. When it wasn't empty, things got very ugly.

"I say we call it a day," Jessica said to the others when they met up at the end of a block. "No luck today, except for Crazy Shooter Guy."

"Yeah, let's head home, help with dinner," Dee agreed.

The meals were difficult with so many children, but dinner was especially challenging since the children were tired. Jessica's favorite analogy was that the kids had little batteries inside which needed recharging every night. Temper tantrums and sudden tears for no reason were the symptoms of batteries running low. There were plenty of those symptoms by dinner.

They drove in silence for the short ride home. Jessica used this time to process the images of death that she'd seen in the homes. She dealt with corpses for a living, so it wasn't the dead bodies that affected her. It was the loneliness and neglect of rotting bodies, of entire families, that she had the most trouble coping with. She wondered how others were dealing with it, not having been hardened with exposure to dead bodies like she'd been.

"Where is everybody?" Dee asked as they drove up to the neighboring houses where they lived. There were always some adults and children playing in the front yard. But now the outside was empty.

"Jessica!" she suddenly heard from her left. She turned to see a very anxious Mo running towards their car from one of the houses. Jessica rushed out to meet him.

"Jessica, we need you inside, Deb's been shot!"

Jessica froze in disbelief.

"Whoa, what?" Dee asked, climbing out of the car.

"Say again?" Javon asked simultaneously.

"Brandon. Troy, or whatever his name is. I'll explain later. Jessica, now! She's bleeding all over the place."

Jessica's heart raced as she ran after Mo towards the house. Except for a few crying infants upstairs, the house was strangely quiet. Mo led her into the living room where Deb was lying on a sofa. A blood-soaked towel covered the right side of her upper chest. A scarlet stain spread beneath her on the cream sofa fabric. Amanda was kneeling beside Deb, pressing on the towel. Deb's eyes were shut, unresponsive.

"Oh God, she needs a surgeon," Jessica said.

"You need to help her," Mo said, desperation cracking his voice.

"I'm a crematorium tech, I'm not a doctor," she cried.

Dee took her arms and spun her towards him. He leaned in close. "You got to do your best, Jess, and that's all these people can expect," he told her.

"Darnell," Deb whispered. Jessica and Dee turned towards her. Her left hand beckoned him nearer. Both he and Jessica leaned in.

"Save the children," Deb said.

"Save the children?" Dee said. "What does she mean by that?" he asked Mo.

"Those fuckers kidnapped most of the children."

"What?" Jessica cried out.

"Left just the babies, took the toddlers, the teenagers, and two women, Vanessa and Mary. They killed their husbands, Antoine and Abram."

"Save the children, promise me," Deb whispered again.

"Don't you worry Mama, I'll get the kids back here before Jess is done patching you up," Dee promised.

"I ain't your mama," she said, before her eyes fluttered briefly and shut again.

Jessica tried to block all thoughts about the missing people and the deaths. She studied Deb and tried to assess the situation. She took a deep breath, trying to remember the basics of emergency care from her days in med school and her more recent informal studies. Slowly, she peeled back the layers of towels over Deb's wound. The bullet had entered just below the clavicle. Fresh blood oozed from the bullet hole. She grabbed Deb's torso and gingerly turned her body to see her back. The exit hole seemed clean, though still bleeding.

"OK looks like the bullet went clean through. If it had broken up, there wouldn't be such a clean exit. What's important now is to stop the bleeding. I need you to press down here firmly," she told Dee.

Dee pressed on the towels that Jessica had replaced.

"Harder, Dee, don't be afraid to hurt her. She's already lost too much blood, and we're not setup for transfusions. I'm going to go get some compression bandages."

Once she was satisfied that he was putting adequate pressure on Deb's wound, Jessica ran to her room in the neighboring house. She rummaged through her stockpile of medical supplies, wishing that she had better organized them. After rifling through several boxes, she found the compression bandages and raced back to Deb. With some help from Dee, who propped Deb up, Jessica was able to apply the bandages.

"We don't want her lying flat, she has to be sitting a bit upright," she instructed. Mo, Dee, and Jessica worked to get Deb into a correct restful, but not flat, position.

"OK, that's all we can do for now," Jessica said, her voice shaking.

"Don't we need to clean it? What about infection?" Mo asked.

Jessica shook her head. "Cleaning it will just cause more bleeding. If there's dirt and bacteria, and there probably is, it's already inside the wound. I have to start her on a course of antibiotics as soon as she's awake and can take medicine."

"So that's it then?" Dee asked.

"That's all I can do for now, yes. She's very lucky, if there had been any complications, I don't think I would have been able to help her."

"You did great," Dee said, putting his hand on her lower back.

"Absolutely," Mo agreed.

"Thank guys, but really, I put a bandage on her, that's it. We really need a proper doctor in our little group. And she's not out of the woods, not by a long shot. She's lost so much blood," her voice trailed off as she bit her lip.

"Stop selling yourself short Jessica. You knew what to do, and you had the right bandages to treat her. A doctor couldn't have done better." Amanda added.

Before Jessica could rebut the compliment, Dee spoke to Mo. "How about the details now, what happened here?"

"None of us were here when it happened," Mo said, nodding to Amanda and Joshua. "I got here first, and Deb was able to talk more at that point. She said that Brandon came with several men. Like I said, they shot Abram and Antoine. Then ran off with most of the children and some women. That's all we know."

"Did she say how many men were with him?" Dee asked.

"And what kind of guns they strapped with?" Javon added.

"No, she seemed confused and in shock. She did say it was Brandon who shot her. And just that there were several others."

"Where did he find men that he was able to convince to come and raid us? And why?" Joshua asked.

"Heuvelton," Mo said darkly. "He said it several times, that we should team up with the men holding the Amish hostage. Remember? Food security? Future labor force?"

"Oh Christ, what have I done?" Joshua said.

"You didn't do anything, Brandon and his new friends did all this," Mo said.

"How can you be sure it's them?" Javon asked.

"I can't. But it's the only thing that makes sense. Where else would he find people to attack us?"

"He's right," Dee said, nodding. "It's the only explanation."

"Let's go get 'em Boss," Javon said.

"What do you mean, go get them? These men are all armed," Joshua exclaimed.

"You don't want to know the details Mr. Don't Hurt A Fly. In fact, I don't think you should be around while we talk about this, you might go warn them off." Javon stepped closer and closer to Joshua as he spoke.

"Don't worry, these are not humans as far as I'm concerned," Joshua said grimly, "they're animals."

"Animals don't pull that shit on themselves,

they're humans all right," Javon replied.

"Well, I've got this." Mo pulled a pistol out of his back waistband. His revelation shocked Jessica, and she could see the surprised look on everyone's face.

"And you two have plenty of guns," Mo continued, looking at Dee and Javon. "But, no offense, is it just for show? It's one thing to talk tough, but I imagine shooting at another human being is a whole different matter."

Javon laughed. "Dee was Marquis' number two, and our enforcer. How many did you off, B? Thirty? Forty? Man they see Dee coming and they run, for sure."

"Not that many Javon, quit making shit up."

"Got any more questions on our creds?" Javon asked Mo with a smug smile.

Mo still seemed uncertain.

"Point your piece at me," Dee told him.

"It's loaded. I'm not going to point it at you."

"Safety on then. And point it at me."

Mo looked at his pistol, and at that moment, faster than Jessica thought possible, Dee stepped forward, grabbed the barrel of the pistol and twisted it out of Mo's hand. He turned it sideways and pressed the end of the barrel to Mo's forehead.

"Got any more questions?" Dee asked.

"Dee, what are you doing?" Jessica cried out.

Dee glanced at Jessica before pulling the gun back, nimbly flipping it around mid-air, and handing it back to Mo, butt-first. Mo took it hesitantly, appearing somewhat shocked by the experience.

Jessica desperately tried to process what she had just seen and heard. She wasn't so naïve to think that Dee's past was squeaky clean. She knew that he and Javon had some ties to gangs. But she never imagined that Dee was a killer. *What did Javon call him? The Enforcer?* she thought. This didn't fit with the warm loving man she was so fond of. *Oh my God, I've been sleeping with a murderer!*

"You OK, Jess?" Dee asked her. She hadn't noticed that he'd been staring at her, likely reading the fear that was sweeping over her.

"I don't know," she answered, honestly.

"That shit's behind me, you know that."

"Is it? Sounds to me like it's in your immediate future as well," she said. "How else are you planning to rescue the children?"

"Jess, I,"—

"Can we not talk about this right now? You do what you have to do, and I'll do my part, trying to keep Deb alive."

"Oh wow, I think I've missed something here, I didn't know you two were, you know, a thing," Mo said.

"Seems there's lots you don't know," Javon said.

"Amanda, can you please keep an eye on Deb? Make sure she stays still, keep her comfortable. I need to find her some antibiotics, from the stash I got at the hospital," Jessica said.

"Sure thing," Amanda agreed.

Jessica was glad to have a reason to leave the group. She needed to reflect on how to deal with

Dee's past. She doubted that she would be able to, and was already mentally preparing to break up with him. But she knew that was a knee-jerk reaction and wanted to think things through before acting. Besides, the last thing she wanted was to distract Dee from what was really important: trying to rescue the children from that sonofabitch Troy. She hated the fact that they needed from Dee exactly what was driving her away from him.

14. A TERREL SITUATION

"Remember Terrel's crew?" Dee asked Javon. They'd been on the road for over two hours, giving Dee plenty of time to consider the coming gunfight.

"Wiped out half those mofos in the first second," Javon smiled.

"Exactly. I think we got ourselves another Terrel situation."

"Sounds good, Boss," Javon replied, never taking his eyes off the road ahead.

Terrel had been the leader of a crew that had been slowly encroaching on Marquis' territory. Marquis had sent Dee and Javon to 'correct the situation', as he liked to put it, when sending Dee on a job. The two of them were heavily outgunned when they approached Terrel and his crew. Dee held his hands up, in a show that he wanted to talk. A pistol was in his hand, easily visible. Both sides knew you didn't just show up unarmed: that would be so stupid that it would be considered a mercy killing if they wiped you out. As they got closer, Dee waited for the other crew to bunch up together for the supposed talk. As Dee lowered his arms, he quickly pointed and fired at the leader, Terrel, getting a perfect headshot. Which was the signal for Javon to pull out his sawed-off and fire point-blank at the rest of the crew. And as Javon had said a moment earlier, they had wiped half of the entire crew out in a few seconds.

The situation that they were heading into now had a similar feel to it. Dee hoped it would be even easier, depending on how well-trained the Heuvelton gunmen were. He expected a few seasoned fighters, but hoped that the rest were tagging along with no real fighting experience. He still had to work out what to do with Mo and Joshua, who had insisted in coming along. They would just get in the way of Dee and Javon's team work.

"I still say we should have gone to get Titus and Chris," Mo insisted, right on cue. "We have no idea how many people they really have, two more guns on our side could make all the difference."

"Told you before, G.I. Joe, come with a couple of cars loaded with armed men and we'll never even get close to them. Then we'll be outgunned, surrounded, and killed. Now we be small enough to get in close and have a real chance."

Dee looked in the rear-view. Mo seemed to ponder his words, but looked unconvinced. Dee looked to the other side and observed Joshua. The man seemed in shock, barely moving, and with a vacant stare outside the window. *Both of them gonna be a problem*, Dee thought. But he needed Joshua to show them the way to the right farm where the gunmen were headquartered. Dee knew Joshua had spoken at length with Abram about the occupation.

"Battery-man, you gonna be OK?" Dee asked Joshua.

Joshua turned his head towards Dee and nodded.

"That's good, cause you need to tell us where to go to find these mofos."

"They'll be at the Bontrager farm."

"Now you know that don't mean shit to me, right? You gotta tell us how to get there. And, fill me in on whatever you know about this Bont-whatever place."

"It's the biggest Amish farm in the area. That's where the elders meet. Well, used to meet, I should say. Abram told me they killed all the elders."

"What's the layout? What kind of buildings are there?"

Joshua paused for a moment before answering. Which was an encouraging sign for Dee, it meant that he was coming out of shock and thinking along.

"The lane connects directly with the highway and leads to the main house. It's a big old farm house, must be seven or eight bedrooms in there. I was only in it once. I remember a huge dining room, lots of heavy dark wooden furniture."

"OK, that sounds like where the top guy and his lieutenants will be staying," Dee said, nodding. "That's where we go then. What else is there?"

"The usual. A stable, a big red barn and grain silo. Chicken coops and the like. It's a farm, what do you expect?"

"I expect you to give me the details, not ask questions," Dee said.

Joshua didn't answer, and resumed staring out the window.

"After the take down, we gonna need to be careful with those barns 'n shit. Easy for guns to hide in there and pick us off," Javon said.

"For sure," Dee agreed.

For the next forty-five minutes they drove in silence. Dee played through his head every scenario he could imagine. Most of them didn't turn out well.

"It's coming up soon," Joshua said, interrupting Dee's contemplations.

Half a mile later, Joshua pointed out the laneway that led to the Bontrager farm.

"We ain't driving in, that's an invitation for them to shoot first, ask questions later," Dee said. "Park it at the end of the lane. Back it in, in case we need to get out of here fast."

Javon complied with Dee's instructions.

"OK Battery-man, you gonna stay in the car, with the engine running. If you see anyone coming towards the car, and it ain't us, then you gun it out of here and warn the others. You can bet your ass that if we're dead, and they know where we came from 'cause of Troy, then they're going to go back to Rochester and finish the job. Am I being clear here? You got to tell the others to move out the second you get back."

"Got it," Joshua said.

Dee suspected Joshua was relieved not to have to be part of the violence. Dee was certainly relieved to not have him around. The man was too unpredictable, he might even do something like hit Dee's arm while he's trying to shoot. *Got enough enemies, I don't want to be watching our side too.*

"Mo, you come with us. But you keep your mouth shut, got it? Me and Javon will do the talking."

Mo nodded grimly. His hand trembled, which normally Dee wouldn't even notice. But the fact that he was holding a loaded gun made Dee decidedly nervous.

"Man you shaking like you saw a ghost. Keep your finger off the trigger if you gonna be all trembling-like," he told Mo.

Mo looked at his shaking hand and seemed to try to will it to be still. "I'll be fine," he said.

The three of them began walking down the lane towards the large farmhouse. They didn't conceal their weapons. Dee had a pistol in one hand. A second in his waistband, and a third that was concealed, in an ankle holster. Javon carried the sawed-off shotgun, pointed straight down towards the ground, in an as non-threatening way as a sawed-off shotgun could be. Already Dee could see some men gathering on the front porch of the farmhouse.

"They know company's coming," Javon said.

Dee raised one hand in the air as they approached the group of men. There were eight of them. *Only way out of this is to get them to bunch up in front of Javon,* he thought. He tried not to show the anger on this face when he spotted Troy among the men. One man stood slightly in front of the others. He was Caucasian, with a long black pony tail falling below his shoulders. Dee wasn't sure if the man had groomed a short beard, or hadn't bothered shaving in a week. The man was heavyset, with wide square shoulders. A shoulder and neck tattoo started just below his left ear, and disappeared under his shirt. It was hard to see from a distance, but to Dee it looked like a dragon's head. The man pointed the menacing pistol in his right hand directly at Dee.

"That's close enough," the man called out.

It wasn't close enough at all for Dee's plan, but they stopped anyway.

"We just want to talk," Dee said, keeping his left hand in the air.

"That's a lot of guns for someone who just wants to talk," the man replied. "How about you put them down on the ground, then we can talk."

"If we were that stupid, then we'd deserve to die," Dee replied, pasting a fake smile on his face.

"They're with that Rochester group," Troy called out, taking a step closer to the leader.

"That's right, that's where we come from. Thing is, me and Javon here are like the wolves among the sheep. We'd rather ride with other wolves."

The leader laughed. "Now that isn't what I expected. You're saying you want to join us?"

"What the fuck are you doing, Dee?" Mo asked.

Dee didn't turn to look at him. "Javon, if he says one more word, shut him up."

"You heard the man," Javon told Mo.

"You bastards! Are you really" — the butt of

Javon's sawed-off cut off Mo's words as it slammed his head and knocked him to the ground.

"Got one farm hand for you here," Dee said, pointing to Mo's prone body. "And another in the car back there. But more importantly, we learned from the sheep, how to gather more sheep. We can help you in that department, or of course just be damned fine soldiers."

Dee advanced closer to the group as he spoke, a few steady steps at a time.

"And why I should trust you?" the leader asked.

"Well, you might need help there too, figuring out who to trust."

"So not only am I supposed to trust you, but then you tell me who to trust? I don't think so."

"For instance," Dee continued, "that one there is going to be a problem. What is he calling himself here, Brandon? Troy? Something else? Thing is, he likes young ones, if you know what I mean. He like a kid in a candy store now."

"He's a fucking liar," screamed Troy in a shrill voice. "It's a trick, kill them!"

"Uh, Boss, I gotta say I find it creepy how he's been touching some of the little girls' hair," a red-headed, heavily bearded man said. *He might have been a Viking in another time*, Dee thought. He could picture the man with a horned helmet on his head.

"Same here, and not just the girls," another man said.

Dee's pulse raced. The men were subconsciously grouping together facing against Troy. Dee's head entered another space, getting ready to execute a dangerous plan that might now just work.

"No, no, it's not true. I mean yes, I comfort the kids, just so they don't cry, I can't stand their crying. But this other shit they're implying, that's just not true," Troy pleaded to the leader.

The leader turned his eyes away from Dee and looked at Troy. To Dee it was like the sound of a lock's tumbler falling into place. One step closer.

"You sure something ain't right?" the leader asked the other men. Several nodded.

"No, no, it's not true! This is bullshit," Troy screamed again.

The leader looked at Troy straight in the eye, raised his pistol, and shot him point-blank in the forehead. For Dee, the last tumbler fell into place and the lock opened. Lightning-fast after years of practice, he pointed his pistol and fired twice at the leader. One head shot and one chest shot. The loud boom of Javon's shotgun sounded in between Dee's two shots. *A well-oiled machine*, flashed through Dee's brain, happy to see Javon had executed the other half of the plan to perfection.

Dee turned towards his left, where red-beard and the others were. The shotgun blast had knocked them all to the ground in a bloody pool. Javon was advancing on them, looking for survivors. Before he or Dee could react, one of the men on the ground raised a pistol and shot Javon. Dee fired two rounds into the man. He scanned the others for a sign of life, but then heard loud footsteps running from inside the house.

Dee spun, crouched, and aimed his gun towards the front door as two men with assault rifles emerged from the house. Before they could assess the situation, Dee took them both out with head shots. He spun around again, but the rest in the group remained prone. He scanned the windows of the house, as well as the general area around him. There was no movement. Then he went to Javon.

Javon's eyes were open. His hand was on a gaping wound on his chest. Blood pumped out through his fingers. Dee applied pressure to the wound.

"Stay with me, Javon, don't you fucking die on me," he commanded.

Javon tried to speak, but blood gurgled out of his mouth, sending him into a coughing fit. Then his eyes shut.

"Javon? Javon?" Dee screamed, shaking his body. "Fuck, fuck, fuck," he whispered under his breath.

A woman screamed. Dee looked up, scanning the area. The scream sounded like it came from the barn twenty-five yards away. Dee crouched, running towards the barn. He made it to the left of the open door. Examining the aged barn board walls, he concluded that they probably couldn't stop a bullet. He decided that a direct entry would be better than trying to take cover behind the wall. He swapped guns with the one in his waistband. Standing straight, gun extended, he swung around and into the open door.

Dee's gun became an extension of his body. As

his eyes scanned the gloom inside the barn, the gun followed the direction that his eyes scanned. It only took a second to spot the man holding Abram's widow Mary. He held her in front of him, one arm was around her throat. In his other hand he held a gun to her forehead.

"Drop the gun and back the fuck up, or I blow her brains out," he shouted at Dee. His hulking body was sweating, Dee could see wet stains under his arms. His shaggy black hair tumbled around his forehead as he swayed from side to side, dragging a terrified Mary along.

Dee hoped she didn't believe him when he spoke calmly to the gunman. "Think I give a shit about collateral damage? As soon as I'm close enough to get that beady little eye of yours I'm firing."

The nervous gunman made the mistake Dee was hoping for, and starting moving the gun away from Mary's head, towards Dee. Dee fired into the man's forehead, killing him instantly. Mary, covered in blood, screamed as the man fell, the arm around her throat dragging her down as well. She rolled away from him, turned towards Dee with wide eyes, and started backing away.

"It's OK now, your safe," Dee said. "We've come to get you and the children back. There's got to be more of these men, right? Do you know where they are?"

Mary trembled, shock settling in. "Most are in the farmhouse," she said, unaware of the carnage he and Javon had caused. "They killed my Abram," she added, fresh tears running down her cheeks. "They have Miriam and Hannah, please find them. They're not safe around these men."

Dee agreed silently. Two teenage girls were indeed not safe around this gang of thugs.

"Where they keeping your girls and the other kids?"

"Over in the stable. They put the horses out loose on the farm. Now the older kids like Miriam and Hannah have to watch the little ones. There are too many small children, you can't ask children to take care of children."

"Any shooters in the stable?"

"Shooters?"

"Guns. Guards," Dee said, frustration creeping into his voice.

"Yes," she said, hesitating before continuing with a steadier voice. "There are one or two guards at the stable. And there's always a few walking around different parts of the farm."

Dee wasn't too worried about the roaming guards, most of them probably gathered at the main house when Dee, Javon, and Mo had wandered up the lane. The stable was another matter. He wasn't sure how to safely get the guards that were near the children.

"OK, you stay here, and stay out of sight until I come back to get you. Understand?"

Mary nodded, before adding, "please don't let the children get hurt!"

"I won't," Dee replied. Walking to the barn door, he peered in all directions before heading towards the stable at the far end of the farm. He was still a hundred yards away when he heard the children's wailing coming from inside. He forced himself to keep a steady, careful pace instead of running headlong towards them.

There were two large shutters on each side of the stable's wide doors. They were shut, which hid his approach. More importantly, no one would fire at him from inside. He was within fifty feet of the doors when an engine roared to life. A large pickup truck raced around the side and headed straight for Dee. A man in the passenger seat leaned out the window and fired.

Dee dropped to one knee, both to make himself a smaller target, and to steady his arm as he fired six rapid shots into the windshield, on the driver's side. The truck careened to the left, pulling the passenger back into the cab. The truck hit a glancing blow against the stable wall before coming to a rest in front of the doors. Before Dee could approach the vehicle, the passenger side shooter slipped out the opposite side of the truck and took up a position behind the rear bumper. Dee realized he was fully exposed and did the best he could by flattening himself on the ground and firing repeatedly at the rear of the truck.

His pistol empty, he quickly reached for his third gun, in his ankle holster. Tufts of earth and grass spattered his face and hands as the gunman behind the truck returned fire. Dee fired blindly in the truck's general direction, forcing the gunman to take cover and stop firing at Dee. He had no clue how he was going to get out of this precarious situation. *I'm running out of ammo.* He took careful aim at the back of the truck, waiting for the gunman to show himself. *Gonna have to start carrying four fucking guns.*

"Back away and leave, and I'll let you live," the gunman called out from behind the truck.

Bullshit, thought Dee. He had psyched out enough opponents, and had enough would-be killers try to psych him out, that he didn't fall for the ploy. But it gave him crucial, and unfortunate, information: this was likely an experienced gunman he was facing. And therefore, not likely to make a stupid mistake like rushing at Dee. He probably knew that time was on his side, as Dee used up his last remaining bullets.

Dee flinched as another shot rang out. However, this time instead of being spattered with earth, he heard the gunman grunt loudly. The man fell on his side, out from behind the truck. He was looking towards the rear of the stable. As if he suddenly realized where he had fallen, he turned towards Dee, his eyes opening wide in fear. Dee took him out with a head shot before the man could react.

Dee ran to the truck, confirmed that the driver was dead, and then peered around the other side of the truck. The last thing he expected to see was Joshua, trembling with a gun in his hand. Joshua was staring at the prone gunman that he'd shot. He looked up at Dee as he approached him, then dropped to his knees and vomited.

"You done good Professor, he was gonna kill me, and probably take some of the kids as hostages."

Dee knew very well how difficult it was dealing with shooting a human being for the first time. He could only imagine what a pacifist like Joshua must be feeling. He put his hand on the retching man's shoulder.

"Besides, you didn't kill him, I did."

His words didn't seem to have much effect on Joshua, who began sobbing in broken bursts.

"Hey no time for crying Battery-man, we got to get these young ones out of here. You crying is not gonna help calm them down, you know?"

Joshua nodded, taking some deep breaths.

"In fact," Dee continued, "I need you to go in there and stay with the kids. There probably aren't any more guns, but I can't be sure. So, you guard the kids, I'll go get Mary in the barn, and we'll find whatever van or truck they used to move the kids here. Then you got to talk to the Amish, tell them they should get out of here in case there are a few more that are gone out somewhere."

"Guard the kids? Are you serious? You think I can shoot someone else?"

"That or handover the kids, your choice," Dee replied shortly. "Now go." He pulled Joshua to his feet and led him towards the door. Dee didn't want the children seeing him. Some would run up to him and cling, but Dee needed to move freely. So, he gave Joshua a gentle shove through the door, before running back to the fallen gunman. He took the man's weapon and went back to the barn to get Mary.

When he entered the barn, he couldn't see her. "Mary?" he called out. "It's OK, I think we got them all. I need your help with the kids."

"Were any of the children hurt? Are my two girls there?" said Mary, stepping out from behind a stacked wall of hay.

"Kids weren't hurt. Joshua's in the stable with them now, but I haven't seen if all the kids are in there. Can you go over there are help him calm them down? "

"Of course, I'll go now," she said immediately heading for the door.

"Wait one sec," Dee called out. "What kind of truck or van did they use to bring you here? And where is it now?"

"It was a big dark blue van, but I don't know where it is." She ran off towards the stable.

It didn't take long for Dee to find the van parked behind the main house. He drove it around to the site of the gunfight. He gathered the weapons of all the fallen men, and stuffed them behind the driver's seat of the van. Then he went to see Javon's body one last time.

"I'll make sure the Amish give you a decent burial, B, far away from the assholes you killed." He put his hand on Javon's chest. "One," he said, out of respect. He grabbed Javon's sawed-off and added it to the pile of weapons in the van.

Dee heard a moan and saw Mo coming to. "I was

about to come wake you up Bro," he said.

Mo seemed confused, then sprang to his feet, fists out towards Dee.

"Chill. The baddies are dead. Fuckers got my partner though," he said, nodding towards Javon's body. He forced his voice to remain neutral, the last thing he wanted to do was display emotions in front of Mo.

"But, you" — his voice trailed off as he looked at the surrounding carnage. "Javon knocking me out was part of some plan?"

"That part was improv, for sure. But it worked, they believed us until it was too late."

"The children," Mo cried, holding his hand to where a lump was already forming on his temple.

"They in the stable with Joshua and Mary. Come on we got to go, now!"

Dee raced the van over to the stable. When he opened the stable doors, a chaotic scene met his eyes. There were children scrambling all over the stable. Some that Dee didn't even recognize. *Must be the Amish children*, he thought. He spotted Mary near her two daughters. All three were comforting younger children. Joshua, rather than guarding the door as he'd been instructed, was sitting shell-shocked on a pile of hay, surrounded by laughing children throwing hay in every direction. Vanessa and her four older children were also there, helping with the toddlers.

"Darnell!" Ben called out, holding a pile of hay in his small hands.

"Uncle Dee!" Nolan cried out, running towards him. Dee had a special fondness for the little boy, the first boy he had rescued. He knelt on one knee as Nolan crashed into his arms.

"Where's Thema?" Nolan asked, a worried look on his face.

"She's fine, back at the house wondering where you are," Dee replied. Nolan's little sister had been too young for the kidnappers to bother with. They had left all the babies behind.

Nolan seemed confused. "But I'm right here."

"Yeah, you are, but she don't know that, right?" Dee laughed.

"Oh, right," Nolan admitted, his four-year-old brain catching up to the subtleties of the situation.

Young Ethan soon joined the hugging. Seeing the little white boy made Dee emotional. He recalled the early days when it was just himself, Jessica, Javon, and the three kids that they had rescued. Javon had been taken aback caring for a little white boy. But with Ethan's persistent calls of 'Uncle Javon', and refusing to hold back on giving Javon some affection, it wasn't long before he had melted tough Uncle Javon's heart.

"Where's Uncle Javon?" Ethan asked, as if reading Dee's mind.

"He ain't here right now," was all Dee could say. He stood up quickly, before Ethan could pursue the topic further. Half carrying, half dragging the two boys, Dee made his way over to Joshua.

"We got to go Professor. Wouldn't be surprised

if there's more of them coming from somewhere. I got the van parked outside. Let's load up all the kids in there. It'll be tight, I'm telling you now. Vanessa, Mary, and her girls can try to keep them calm back there. You drive the van, I've got to take care of a few things here," he said.

Joshua stood, shaking the hay off himself. "No, you take the van. I know these people, I can help them deal with what just happened."

"And if a couple of guns show up?" Dee asked.

Joshua hesitated a moment before replying. "The children will be safe, you'll be far gone by then."

"I ain't talking about the kids. Any of these people's crew still roaming around, they won't be none too happy seeing all their friends dead, and the children gone. Who do you think they're going to take out all that anger on?"

"He's right," a voice called out behind them, "there's been enough violence here today."

Dee spun around, trying to reach for his gun with the tangle of children around him. A group of four men, and two women, stood at the door. Dee's muscles relaxed at the sight of the Amish.

"Take your children, and go, now," one young man spoke. Dee remembered Abram telling them that the thugs had killed all the elders of the Amish community.

"You ain't safe here," Dee said. "You should come with us."

"This is our home," the young man replied.

"Dee, let me handle this, please," Joshua

interjected.

Dee could see he wouldn't get through to the Amish. They were in a completely different world from his. *Might as well try to talk sense to some Martians*, he thought.

"OK, you win," he said to Joshua. "Help me load up the kids." He leaned in close to Joshua's ear and muttered "you make sure Javon gets a proper burial. You can burn the rest of the bodies for all I care."

"Of course I will," Joshua promised.

After a brief discussion, Mary decided to stay with the Amish community, along with her daughters. She pleaded with Dee to give Abram a decent burial.

Vanessa approached Dee, despair in her eyes. "They took my Antoine from me," she said softly.

"I know, I know, I'm so sorry," Dee told her. He had seen many people lose their children, their husbands, or their wives, to gun violence. There wasn't much he could say to Vanessa about her husband's death. He knew she would need time to grieve the loss. But for now, keeping her mind occupied would help distract her from the pain.

"Can you and your kids handle all them little ones if we pile them into the van?"

"Of course, of course," she reassured him. She took a deep breath and went to talk to her children.

The young children seemed more than happy to hop into the crowded van. The promise of going home was all it took. Once the van was loaded, Dee approached Joshua one more time, and took him aside.

"There's a good chance that these people are going to die if they don't move out. You need to convince them to come with us."

"Oh I'll try, but you can't convince the Amish of anything that they don't want to do. But I will definitely invite them to our new hotel. I'll offer them their own floor, away from the rest of us, so that they can feel that they have their own community."

Dee had not thought of that idea. *OK, the man knows how to deal with these people.* With a quick tap on Joshua's arm, Dee returned to the cacophony inside the van.

"It's gonna be a long drive, you all better do what you can to quiet these young ones," Dee told Vanessa and her children, with a smile. He hopped into the driver's seat. A stab of pain coursed through his chest as he remembered Javon always being the driver when the two of them went somewhere. He looked over at Mo, in the passenger seat. To free up space in the back, and more pragmatically because he wouldn't have been able to unglue Ben from around his neck, Mo sat in the front passenger seat. He had Ben and Lucy on his lap, happily chattering to each other.

Four hours later, after several pee-stops, the van rolled into the driveway of one of their houses. By this time Dee had a headache and instantly jumped out of the van to get some peace. He heard the van's side door slide open, and the sound of happy screams filled the air as the children piled out and headed for the house. And they had quite the welcome committee: Amanda, Titus, and Chris all ran out of the house at once. They were soon on the ground, rolling around with the children, picking them up, and group hugging several at a time.

Jessica appeared in the doorway. Dee was unsure if he should go to her or give her some space. She resolved that question by glancing at him, and then joining the melee of reunited adults and children.

15. MOVING OUT, MOVING IN

"N ot much of a guard dog, are you?" Mo said. Hoover sat next to him, tongue lolling out. He cocked his head sideways when Mo spoke. "I mean seriously, what kind of dog just lets strangers waltz in and take whatever they want?" Hoover stared at Mo, tucked in his tail, put his head on Mo's lap, and let out a soft whine. Amanda stepped out of the house in front of them. "We'll continue this discussion later," Mo murmured to Hoover, scratching between the dog's ears. Hoover's tail wagged as Mo stood.

"Don't get up on my account," Amanda said, smiling.

"What kind of gentleman would stay seated when a lady approaches?"

"I doubt your credentials as a gentleman, and I sure as hell ain't a lady. How's the noggin?"

It had been three days since the raid and subsequent rescue. The baseball-sized lump on his head where Javon had hit him was finally getting smaller. While he was convinced there had to have been a better way than almost cracking his skull open, he had to grudgingly admit that Dee and Javon's plan had worked to perfection. He could hardly begrudge Javon's over-enthusiastic action towards Mo's head when the young man had died for the sake of the children. Despite that, he would have preferred a less painful plan, and to be in on it.

"Headaches are gone. Only hurts if I touch it," Mo said. Then he grinned, adding "perhaps you should kiss it better."

"Points for creativity, I must say," Amanda replied. And to his surprise, she leaned in and gave his lump a gentle kiss. He wished he could better feel her lips, imagining their softness.

"I know I've already said as much, but seriously, I think you were so brave for going over there," she told him, staring into his eyes.

Mo's pulse quickened as his heart threatened to pound its way out of his chest. He tried to laugh off her remark so that she wouldn't see how much effect she had on him. "I missed the whole thing, I hear it was quite exciting."

"Come on, I mean it," Amanda said, taking his two hands. "You were brave, and I'm so grateful that my little Sophia, and all the children, are back safe with us. So, thank you, Maurice Biggs."

Mo felt a curious mix of embarrassment and absurd pleasure. "Wow, that's really sweet of you, thank you too, Miss Amanda Jones."

"Ah, Dee would be proud of you for remembering my rock 'n roll name."

"Speaking of which, I'm so glad how much he's taken to his official role as head of security," Mo added.

"I know, that was a brilliant move on Deb's part. Giving him the respect he deserves, plus now he's so busy that it has to be helping him deal with the loss of Javon."

"I can see how he's struggling with Javon's death. He's certainly quieter, and he's lost his swagger when he walks around. Anyway, yes, good for him, but I'm not so sure how smart it is for Deb to be involved in anything but her recovery for now."

"I spoke with Jessica, it's still touch and go. If it's that bad, how did Deb manage to make any decisions?" Amanda asked.

"She's strong, and as I'm sure you know by now, headstrong too. Whenever she's awake she's asking questions about what's going on. But she didn't take the transportation to the hotel well at all. Did you see Jessica's face when Deb wouldn't wake up after the car ride?"

"I did, and it certainly didn't help the panic I was feeling."

"Yeah, no kidding. I can't imagine our group without Deb at the helm." To Mo at least, Deb was the heart and soul of their group, not just their leader. Seeing her lying on a bloody couch had been a heart-rending experience that he never wanted to face again.

Amanda opened her mouth as if to speak, and then shut it again, looking at Mo. "What? Spit it out," he urged her.

"Can I ask you something?"

"You just did."

"No, seriously. I…" her voice trailed off. Mo waited for her to gather her thoughts. "OK, well I haven't gone to as many houses as you have, not by a long shot." Mo's skin crawled at the mention of breaking into the houses of death.

"But I still wake up with nightmares," Amanda continued. "So many times when I hold Sophia, I get flashbacks of where I found her, what she went through, of Sammy, and I have to fight back tears. And that's just one house. There's all the other ones that didn't have any survivors, and—"

"Stop," Mo interrupted, putting his hand on her arm. "I know exactly what you mean. I get the same nightmares, the same awful thoughts when I see the children I rescued. It's bloody hard to deal with."

"But how? How do you deal with it?" He could see that she was fighting back tears, which made his own eyes start to water. *Great, not again.* He swallowed hard and cleared his throat.

"Honestly, I don't have any tips," he said, his voice cracking slightly. He hoped she didn't notice. "It's a living nightmare. Well, maybe one tip: take it one day at a time. If I try to think about the future, and how I can ever possibly get over this – well then I start to freak out. Sounds corny and Zen-like, but focus on the present."

She nodded, releasing one tear in her right eye, while the left eye held on to its welling tear. "Would it be OK to ask you to hold me, without, you know, it meaning anything bigger?"

"Oh God, of course," he said, bringing her into his

arms. While he knew it wasn't what she wanted, he breathed in the delicious scent of her. He couldn't stop himself, she was intoxicating. He held her tightly, feeling her shoulders trembling against him. How he wished he could find the right words of comfort to counteract the horrors that they'd seen. In truth, he was barely coping himself. So he remained silent, and relied on the warmth of their embrace to comfort her.

"Thank you Mo," she eventually said, her voice muffled against his chest.

"Anytime Amanda, anytime," he answered as she pulled away. He smiled at her, and she returned a muted smile.

"Well, we had better get over to the hotel soon, before Mr. Head of Security turns it into an impenetrable fortress," Amanda said.

She and Mo were the only people left at the four houses that their group had occupied. The silence and emptiness felt odd after the joyful chaos of too many children being looked after by too few adults. As much as he looked forward to having all the space that the hotel provided, Mo felt a tinge of loss at leaving the place where they had started their now-thriving little group of survivors.

"And you're sure we're not making a mistake with the note?" Amanda asked.

"Nope, can't be sure. But I would say the risk is worth the benefit."

"You never told me you were an insurance actuary in your pre-apocalypse life."

"Well, aren't you the wise cracking not-a-lady this morning."

After having peppered the neighborhoods with posters about taking in children of dying adults, it seemed wrong to move away with no notice. Instead, they posted a note on the doors of the four houses, telling prospective parents, or other adults, where they had moved to. The nagging fear in everyone's mind was that some remaining gunmen back in Heuvelton might come for revenge. But in the end, they gambled that it had been a rag-tag gang of disorganized hoodlums with no loyalty to each other, rather than a tight unit of comrades thirsty for revenge.

"Anyway, I still think any leftover baddies will just drift around over there until they find someone new to terrorize. I can't imagine them caring enough to come all the way out here to do what exactly? Kill the adults? They can't steal the children again, there aren't enough of them left to handle having a bunch of kids around."

"I know, we've been through it lots of times already. I guess I just needed to hear it one more time," Amanda said.

"Ready to go to our new home?"

"Definitely ready."

"Are you ready?" Mo asked Hoover. Hoover cocked his head and wagged his tail furiously.

"I think that means yes," Amanda said, smiling.

"Did you check the other houses for any leftover water bottles?" Mo asked, suddenly remembering the importance of water. The water supply had finally broken down, having lasted unattended for much longer than Mo would have expected. Now they were flying through bottled water at an alarming rate.

"I did, nothing left behind," Amanda replied.

The drive to the hotel seemed like an otherworldly family Sunday drive. Mo and Amanda in the front, windows rolled down. Hoover in the back, with his head out the window, tongue lolling, wet nose sniffing the thousand scents along the way.

The hotel was nowhere near as inviting as the first time Mo had seen it. Sheets of thick plywood over all the ground-floor windows had replaced Chris's "open door" policy. Dee had even convinced Chris and Titus to replace the glass door with a metal door, complete with spyglass. Mo could imagine himself asking in a booming voice: *halt, who goes there?* Apparently, the children had had to be kept away from the work area because of some intense cursing from Titus as he and Chris built a frame to hang the new security door. *Mild-mannered Titus cursing up a storm? Must have been quite a job*, Mo thought.

Ironically, the security door was ajar when Mo and Amanda arrived at the entrance.

"Looks like they took a page out of your security book, eh boy?" Mo said to Hoover, as the dog padded into the hotel.

As soon as Mo and Amanda entered the lobby, they could hear the din of several voices competing for volume. Closest to them were Jessica and Deb. It shocked Mo to see Deb out of bed.

"Damn it, Deb, you were shot three days ago, you need to stay in bed," Jessica admonished. "Or do you want the bleeding to start again, is that it? Because if that's your plan, then you're doing a fine job!"

"Stop fussing over me Jessica, I'm not a porcelain doll. I'm sitting down, it's not like I'm going to lift some boxes or go for a run."

"Who helped you get down here? Because I'm going to have a serious talk with that person, right after they help me bring you back to bed."

A dozen or more children were running around the lobby area, playing some form of tag. Though there seemed to be more than one child who was 'it' in the game, judging by the number of squealing chasers. Ben was among them and spotted Mo.

"Maurice! What took you so long?" The little boy ran to Mo and with outstretched arms leapt into an embrace. Mo swung him up, and Ben's arms encircled his neck. He was happy to avoid that particular doctor-patient discussion. Apparently Amanda felt the same way, since she followed him and Ben further into the melee of children.

"Looks like you crazy kids are running all over the place," Mo said.

"I was 'it' and I tagged three kids, now they're 'it'."

"But aren't you supposed to tag just one person?"

"It's more fun this way."

"It's true, more fun is better," Amanda agreed, smiling.

"She understands," Ben said, with a why-don't-you look towards Mo.

An exasperated Jessica joined them. "I'm on the verge on injecting her with a horse tranquilizer."

"Are you saying that our wallflower leader Deb can be hard-headed at times?" Amanda quipped.

"Hard-headed is the understatement of the year," Jessica replied.

"I have a hard head too," Ben said, demonstrating his skull's impressive durability by hammering it with his tiny fist. The three adults laughed, leaving Ben with a puzzled, and pleased, expression.

"Have you and Dee, um, had a talk yet?" Amanda asked Jessica.

"He's certainly tried, but I'm not quite ready for that. It's a lot to take in, you know? The dark past, the recent heroics. I have no clue how I'm supposed to deal with that. Or if I even want to, for that matter."

"OK, that's our cue to leave, Big Guy," Mo said to Ben. "Time for some girl talk".

"And off lumbers the dinosaur," Amanda said.

"'Girl talk', I do believe that was an expression in the 1970s wasn't it?" Jessica asked with mock-innocence.

"No, it predates the seventies, I think it was the fifties, in fact," Amanda said.

"Come on Ben, let's show 'em what real dinosaurs sound like." And with that, Mo and Ben roared, with Ben aggressively waving his claw-hands.

"That showed them. OK Ben, let's go. You haven't

seen my room yet." Mo carried a still-roaring Ben towards the stairwell, leaving behind the two grinning women.

"This is it," Mo proudly told Ben, swinging open the door to his hotel room.

"It's big," Ben said, as he walked in, eyes soaking in the details. It was actually a rather modest hotel room. But Mo could understand how big it would seem to the children who were sharing rooms.

"You have a bath tub," Ben added.

"Yeah, but it doesn't work, right? The water taps don't work anymore. I don't know what I'm going to do with this bathroom space, none of it really works."

Ben wandered into the bedroom. It had a small writing desk with a dead TV mounted on the wall above it. The queen-sized bed was across from the desk. The outside wall consisted primarily of a large window. Stock prints of New York City adorned the interior walls. Ben focused on the bed, hopping onto its thick tan colored duvet, which was peppered with a colorful fall leaf motif. Mo joined him, sitting on the edge of the bed.

"Wow we haven't had any quiet time since we left my house," Mo said. "How are things going for you Ben?"

"Liam is mean!" Ben blurted out, his face a picture of someone faced with a grave injustice. Mo struggled with the name, before remembering the cute little boy that had already been living at the hotel with Chris.

"Really? And what did Liam do?"

"He's so bossy, he says it's his hotel."

"Well, you know it's not his, right? He was just here before us, that's all."

"Can you tell him that? Please?"

Mo chuckled. "No, I think he knows already. This is something you two are going to have to work out." Mo promised himself to talk to Chris about it, so the two of them could guide the young ones towards a peace accord.

"Now tell me about your friends. Do you have a best friend?"

"Ethan and Nolan are my best friends. Ethan is a bit too little though, he can't do the things me and Nolan do."

Too little, Mo thought. They were less than a year a part, but to a four-year-old, three-year-olds were almost babies.

"How about Lucy and Sophia?"

"Yeah, Sophia is nice too. And me and Lucy are getting married."

At times like this, Mo struggled hard not to grin, or laugh out loud. *I never knew children could be so funny*, he thought. But Ben was being very serious, and it would hurt the boy's feelings and self-esteem if Mo gave in to the hilarity of a four-year-old's wedding plans.

"Oh, that's the second time I hear that. Does Lucy know?"

"Yeah, we talked about it. But when we're grown up, not now, silly."

"OK, that's good, it's better to wait until you're older."

"My mom's not coming back, is she?"

Mo was taken aback by the sudden topic change, and especially to one that was so weighty. He thought Ben must already know the truth by now, and was just looking for final confirmation. *Best to be upfront with the boy*, Mo thought.

"No, Ben, I'm sorry. She's not."

"She's asleep forever, like my Dad? And all the others?"

"That's right."

"What about you? Are you going to go to sleep forever?"

"No, Ben. That thing that's making so many people go to sleep, it doesn't affect me."

"Good. I'd miss you. I don't want to be alone."

"That's sweet little guy. Don't worry, I'm going to be around for a long time."

"Will you be my new dad?"

"Oh! Uh," Mo stammered. *What am I supposed to say to that?* Of course, he was honored that Ben would ask. Though he'd been acting as Ben's primary caretaker, the leap to 'my new dad' seemed gargantuan.

Tears welled up in Ben's eyes, as the boy studied Mo's face. *Why the fuck am I hesitating?* It was fear of failure, he realized. His own Dad hadn't been exactly stellar, and Mo never wanted to be that kind of father. Which might have been part of the reason that he never got into a relationship that led to having children. But now, looking at Ben, he realized that despite his fear, he would love to have a little boy like him.

"Of course I will, I would be proud to have you as my son."

Ben wiped his wet eyes with his sleeve, sniffling as he did so.

"Thanks... Dad," he said, a small smile appearing on his face. The boy's tentative use of 'Dad' warmed Mo's heart. He leaned forward, kissed Ben on the forehead, and hugged him.

"Where am I going to sleep?" Ben asked, untangling himself from Mo's embrace.

"Uh," Mo stammered once again. "Well, this is where I'm living, but you've got your room down one floor, right?"

"The other kids with parents live with them. Why can't I?"

Checkmate, thought Mo. How on earth had a four-year-old outplayed him? He was sure that it hadn't been some master plan on Ben's part to move in with him. Ben may have been wise for his age, but he was still just a sweet child, not a manipulative, calculating adult. In his world, it was simply a natural consequence of having a parent, you lived with them. And Mo realized the boy was right. If Mo was willing to sign up as his Dad, then it made perfect sense for them to live together.

"You're absolutely right," Mo said. "Sorry that I didn't see that right away, all of this is still pretty new to me."

"Yay!" He jumped into Mo's arms and put his arms around his neck. Then pulled back and asked "So where do I sleep?"

"Well that we'll have to figure out. I've got to find a small bed, and make space for you in here. So tonight, you'll sleep in your room, while we organize this room for you."

"Maybe I can sleep in the bathtub," Ben said, giggling at the thought. Mo laughed along, but then stopped. *It might actually be a good idea*, he thought. He could install a sheet of plywood over the tub, add a mattress, and presto, instant bed for Ben.

"Well not in the tub, but I might be able to build a bed on top of the tub."

"Really? I'm going to tell Lucy that I'm sleeping in the bathtub," Ben said, bursting into fresh giggles. "Can I go tell her now?"

"Do you know how to get back downstairs?"

Ben nodded, already heading out the door.

"It's dark in the stairwell, hold the banister the whole time."

"I will, Dad!" Ben cried, running out the door like a rocket.

"Dad," Mo murmured, still in somewhat of a shock from the events of the last five minutes. He looked around his room and soaked in the solitude. After living in cramped quarters for the last months, it was good to have personal space. Although with Ben moving in, it would soon become not-so-personal again. The thought made him smile. Of course, there had been extremely difficult moments when Ben had first been dropped off by his mother. But Mo had helped him as best as he could, and the two had bonded over the experience. For Mo, that time with just Ben and him was a wonderful memory. He didn't think it would be the same for Ben. For him, it must be all about the horror of being abandoned by his dying mother.

"OK, time to go, lots to do," Mo said. He grunted and smiled. "Talking to myself now. Maybe being alone isn't treating me well."

"Hey Mo," Jessica said, as he stepped out of his room.

"Hi Jessica, any luck getting your high-maintenance patient to get some rest?"

"Ha, yes. I found a compromise. She stays in her room, and her subjects are summoned to discuss whatever is troubling her at the moment."

"Smart, and funny, I have to admit. How about medically? Is she doing OK?"

"Yes, I think so. I can't be sure, but it looks like she was quite lucky. Well, as lucky as one can be, given that you were shot. But if there were bullet fragments in there, or some damage that I didn't see, she wouldn't be recovering this quickly. So, I think we're good. The next week will tell us for sure. But she's exhausted, you saw how she took the short car ride here. She has to rest more, I'm having trouble with that part."

"Well, good on you Dr. Albert, well done."

"You people still don't get how little I know about medicine. She was lucky, that's all. I just bandaged her up."

"And evaluated her condition, and got the right type of bandages, and scavenged the right antibiotics. Need I go on?"

"Whatever," Jessica said, smiling. "Hey the medical clinic, if you will, more like a first aid station really, is just down the hall. I was on my way there, want to see it?"

"For sure. Lead on, Doctor."

"Grrr," Jessica said, rolling her eyes. She walked away, and Mo followed.

Jessica had converted one of the hotel rooms into a pseudo-medical clinic. Mo admired her courage, and resourcefulness. The room's living area became the examination room. There was a bed, a wheeled office chair, and a sofa for anyone accompanying the patient. A set of battery-operated LED lights were lined up on a shelf above the bed, along with several packages of spare batteries. The bedroom was filled with emergency medical supplies that she had pilfered from the university.

"Wow, I am impressed, Jessica."

"Thank you," she said, beaming with pride.

"Just one thing missing though. You need a small table with a stack of two-year-old magazines for the patients that are waiting."

"You're right, I'll get on it ASAP."

"Ah, there you are," Chris said, popping his head in the door. "Her Majesty the Queen requests your presence," he told Mo.

Mo laughed. "I hope she doesn't get used to this.

See you Jessica, and again, super impressed with your work in here."

"Thanks Mo. Good luck with your royal visit."

"Where is Deb's room again?" Mo asked, looking right and left.

"Through the doors at the end, in the next wing. I'm going too, she wants to talk with me and Titus at the same time.

They passed through a set of fire doors and proceeded down the hall to the fourth room. Deb had propped herself up on the sofa in the middle of the living room. A set of five chairs formed a semi-circle facing the sofa. Titus occupied one chair, while the others were vacant.

"Hey Titus", Mo said, sitting next to him.

"Welcome to your new home," Titus said, smiling.

"Thanks Man. You and Chris have really done well preparing this place, thanks so much."

"Our pleasure, Mo. Feels great to see everyone settling in nicely."

"Maurice," Deb interrupted. "Guess who I just had a rather disturbing visit with?"

Mo shrugged. He had no clue who Deb meant, but her tone sure gave away that she was not pleased.

"Lucy. And guess what she wanted?"

Uh-oh, Mo thought. "I'm guessing that she had a talk with Ben?"

"Bingo. And now she wants to call me Mom and move in with me. I don't think that's such a good idea. Do you understand the precedent that you're proposing here?"

'Proposing?' Mo wondered what she meant by that. "I'm not proposing anything. I'm essentially adopting Ben. That's probably the closest analogy to what he and I just agreed on."

"And so what am I supposed to tell Lucy then?" Deb asked, irritation creeping into her voice. This was not the Deb that Mo was used to. He guessed the pain and frustration of being incapacitated must be making her edgy.

"That's up to you Deb. If you want to adopt, then do so. If not, then tell her gently that you're not adopting anyone."

"My God, Maurice, how do you think that will make her feel? And what about the other kids that try to get an adoptive parent? Don't you see you're creating a class system? The elite few living with parents and the masses in community living arrangements?"

"OK, I have to admit that I never thought of it in those terms. But at the same time, it seems a little over the top to me. We're talking about toddlers and preschoolers here, not teenagers in a juvenile detention center."

"These toddlers are going to grow up into teenagers and adults. As I said before, an elite few will have a loving home with parents. And the others will fight for attention from a handful of caretakers. What do you suppose those two classes will think of each other when they've grown up?"

"Again, you may have a point," Mo conceded. "But

you're thinking 'big picture'. Ben's mother entrusted her son to me, and as far as I'm concerned, that takes higher precedence than the bigger questions about future societies of haves and have-nots."

"I strongly disagree, but obviously I can't stop you," Deb replied hotly.

Mo liked Deb very much. But for the first time he was starting to wonder if everyone's constant referral to her as the leader was getting to her head. He vowed to keep an eye on her behavior. The thought of Deb becoming a small-time dictator was both comical and distressing at the same time. His biggest fear was that there would be more and more conflicts and character clashes. He didn't really believe that Deb would suddenly turn autocratic. *But how I hate conflicts!*

"Um, so, about the solar panels," Titus said, after an awkward moment of silence.

Deb shook her head.

"No?" Titus asked in a confused voice.

"Sorry, I was just clearing my head, I didn't mean no," Deb said, smiling at Titus, "please go ahead and fill in Maurice on what we already discussed."

Titus turned to Mo. "Right, so Chris and I were thinking that if we could install some solar panels on the roof, we might get a little bit of power. Like for a few lights in the hallway and stairwells for example."

"Oh my God, that would be awesome," Mo exclaimed. "And you guys know where to find these panels, and how to install them?"

"No, to both those questions," Chris admitted. "But we should be able to get general information from Amanda's Wikipedia backup. And then we need to find existing installations. See how they work, and then steal the components from there."

"That sounds like a plan to me. How can I help?" Mo asked.

"You've got your hands full with other things, Titus and I will handle this, but thanks."

"OK sure. If you change your mind, let me know. So, why did you want me here for that discussion?" Mo almost said 'why was I summoned to the throne room,' but made a conscious decision to stop feeding Deb any more leadership thoughts.

"Well," Titus began, "we have bigger issues to think about too. The main one that has me worried is keeping warm next winter. I know it's not the biggest thing on people's mind when we're just entering summer season, but still. It will need some thought, planning, and a lot of work."

"We were thinking of getting several wood stoves, and venting them out the windows," Chris said.

"But it would be safer to cut out holes through the walls," Titus argued.

"Yeah, maybe, but that's a lot more work. Regardless, getting stoves and firewood is going to be a huge job. To cut down on that, in the winter we'll have to sleep in common areas. We can't keep everyone's room warm," said Chris.

"So, you're thinking solar panels first, then right away start preparing for winter?" Mo asked, still confused as to why they wanted him here for that conversation.

"Probably, yes. But Deb has another idea that we need to discuss."

Ah, the plot thickens, Mo thought, turning to Deb.

Deb cleared her throat before responding. "We should move South."

Mo's head started to spin. "Move South? All of us? How? Some giant bus convoy? But we're just getting installed here!"

"It would take a lot of planning, I understand that. And that's why I'm thinking we spend our first winter here, tough it out, and then move in the spring. Think about it Maurice, we could grow food all year round in a warm climate."

"And, if we go near a coastal area, we can fish all year too," Titus added.

"Fish, whatever crops we want to grow, even citrus trees," Chris said.

"So we're talking Florida? California?" Mo asked.

"Again, it will take some serious planning and research," Deb repeated. "But yes, something like that, or even further south, like northern Mexico. They key is to find a warm place that's not arid, we don't want to build a massive irrigation system, when we have no power to pump the water."

"Back to the convoy for a sec. Gas is going to be a problem, we're talking almost a year from now," Mo said.

"Well, we thought about that too," Deb started, wincing as she sought a more comfortable position.

"We're going to find a tanker truck, and fill it now, while there's plenty of gas to be found. And Titus said we can add some sort of fuel stabilizer in it, to help it stay somewhat fresh. And then we take the tanker with us on the trip."

"Kind of like refueling airplanes mid-air," Titus chuckled.

Mo couldn't help but feel hurt that they'd left him out of the early planning sessions. He and Deb used to talk to each other first about any kind of plan. Had their relationship started to decay somehow?

"It sounds like the three of you have already talked through all the angles. So why am I here? Are you testing how bulletproof your plans are before announcing it to the others?"

"You and I started this thing, Maurice, have you forgotten that? I've always consulted with you on important decisions," Deb said.

Mo was caught off balance by her statement. On the one hand he was feeling excluded, and, in retrospect, had been thinking of her in rather harsh terms. On the other hand, she was now reminding him that they'd been close partners from the start. Could he really be that petty and jealous, that he was hurt when she talked to others first? Titus and Chris were the handymen of the group, it made perfect sense to discuss the feasibility of this proposed migration with them first, to see if it was even possible. And then she discussed it with him for consideration, now that she knew it was at least feasible.

It was clear to Mo that he had some thinking to do. He would have to watch both Deb's growing sense of entitlement to lead, and his own insecurities about being left out. Neither of those were good for him personally, nor for the group at large.

"Sorry Deb, I didn't mean anything by that," Mo lied. "OK, so migrating south, huh? Well, massive logistics issues aside, I think it makes sense. Why not go where food security is highest, and we don't have to spend so much energy towards keeping warm in winter."

"Good, I'm glad you're on board. Because we'll need your help, as well as several others, for the planning. We need to consider all that could go wrong, and how we can be prepared for those possibilities. To me, even though it's about nine months away, planning should start now," Deb said.

"We'll need to balance that with planning for our stay this winter," Chris said. "Food, water, heat – we have to figure those out ASAP."

"We could get overwhelmed with too many things at once," Mo warned. "Maybe we should consider division of labor. Like, Chris, you focus on this winter, and Deb and I will work with Titus for the long-range plan. Does that make sense?"

Titus and Deb nodded.

"Yeah, that makes sense. But can we be clear on decision-making then? If I'm responsible for winter preps, I want to be able to make decisions without someone second guessing everything I do," Chris said.

Mo could read between the lines that the 'someone' he was referring to was Titus. Deb had confided in him the troubles these two were having getting along. Though to Mo, it seemed like it had smoothed over.

"Within reason, Chris," Deb answered. "You're in charge, but it's not a dictatorship."

"But, if you make winter preparations be your priority, then the rest of us know we don't have to worry about it," Mo added.

"Good. Then I'm all in," Chris said.

"Titus?" Deb asked.

"Works for me," he said. Mo wasn't sure if he only imagined the hesitancy in Titus' reply.

Still, for the first time, Mo was cautiously optimistic about the long-term future. In fact, it was one of the rare times where he even dared to reflect on it. Ever since people had started dying en masse, he had retreated deep into himself, living day to day. Having Ben delivered to his doorstep had forced him to think and plan for the near term, rather than day to day. But he'd never stopped to ponder what would happen in the coming years. Now, with a tentative plan to move to somewhere warm near the sea, with some fertile land, well, that gave a whole new hope for the future.

If they were successful, the next generation would consist primarily of farmers and fishermen. *And what will their children's generation be like,* he wondered. To even consider multi-generational issues was an exciting and inspirational moment for Mo. A renewed energy made him want to start planning the migration that very minute. It also brought home how demoralizing the Troy affair had been. He realized it would not likely be the last tragedy that they'd face. Mo vowed to work on his own resiliency in the face of adversity. *At this rate, I'll need the whole damned self-help shelf at the library*, he thought ruefully.

16. PRESIDENT KEARNS

"How are things with Sophia?" Joshua asked.

"Truly fabulous, like it was meant to be," Amanda replied.

She smiled, remembering the moment two weeks earlier where Sophia had run into Amanda's room, her face flush with excitement.

"Can you be my mom?" she had asked breathlessly. At the time, Amanda hadn't been aware of Ben's talk with Mo. Sophia's question surprised her, and Amanda felt a curious thrill of fear mixed with honor at being asked such a powerful question. After an all-too-brief discussion, she'd accepted. Which led to Sophia's more burning question.

"Can I live with you now?"

"Kids are so smart," Amanda continued, looking at Joshua. "I don't mean in a conniving way, but just that I'm surprised by how much brain power they already have at a young age."

"I remember Sophia," said Hannah, Abram and Mary's eldest daughter. "She was very sweet-natured. How is her arm?"

"Much better, pretty much completely healed. Sometimes she complains that it feels stiff in the morning," Amanda replied. *And sometimes she wakes up crying because of the brother and actual parents that she lost.* The death of Sophia's brother Sammy continued to haunt Amanda as well.

The three of them were in the car, on their way back from a trip to Heuvelton. Amanda and Joshua had gone to visit the Amish to make a deal: fresh food in exchange for future labor during harvest season. The Amish had politely refused their offer of help. However, out of gratitude for freeing them from the clutches of the gunmen, they had loaded up their car with fresh fruits and vegetables. The trunk and half of the back seat were full of potatoes, carrots, lettuce, peppers, berries and other assorted farm produce. It was a lot of food. But with their growing numbers, it wouldn't last very long.

What they had not counted on was bringing back another passenger. Hannah wanted to become a school teacher in the Amish community. She convinced the new 'elders' that it would be beneficial for her, and hence for their community, if she went to live with the Rochester survivors for a time. She would gain teaching experience, and provide much needed help for the far outnumbered adults, by working with the children. It was an unusual request for the Amish, and an even more unusual decision to allow her to go. Joshua had told Amanda that the decision was likely a result of the now-youthful elders. Had the occupying gunmen not executed the older patriarchs, Hannah would not have been granted permission to come to Rochester.

Deb, a school teacher herself, had already expressed her concerns to Amanda about the children's education. While Amanda shared Deb's concern, she also saw it as a positive sign. If their group was worrying about educating the next generation, then they mustn't be in pure survival mode any longer. And that gave Amanda some much needed hope for the future. With Hannah's arrival, perhaps Deb could start some sort of organized classrooms for the children.

Amanda was proud to see their new home from several blocks away. Much as she had come up with the idea of flyers at their old house, she had also increased their visibility at the hotel. No less than twenty flags fluttered in the breeze on the roof of the hotel. Fastened outside the windows of the top floor, all the way around the building, were large block-lettered banners announcing 'All Children Welcome Here'. Additionally, she'd posted more flyers in the neighborhood, as well as an information sheet at the front of the hotel. If she were a dying parent, she'd want to know more about the place before blindly dropping off her children at the hotel. So, it seemed a good idea to inform hesitant parents about who they were. *I missed my calling, I should have gone into marketing.*

Several children were playing in front of the hotel. Deb was sitting in a chair, watching them. Amanda was certain that Jessica had insisted on the chair. Despite having to sit down, Deb seemed happy with a ring of children running around her, playing tag, or randomly chasing each other.

"Oh my God, I'm starting to not recognized some of them," Amanda said.

"Join the club," Joshua replied. "Chris and Titus are at it again, working full time to open up another floor for us."

The effect of the flags, banners, and flyers had been almost immediate. Within a week they had doubled their number of children. Fortunately, a few unvaccinated adults had joined them as well, making the current horde of little people almost manageable. Their growing numbers both thrilled and frightened Amanda. She'd never experienced such satisfaction in her life. She was literally saving lives with her efforts.

"How far can this thing go?" she asked with trepidation.

"It's a good thing they're so small, we wouldn't be able to feed this many adults," Joshua replied.

"Even so, it's not sustainable. Especially not the way new ones keep arriving."

"That's your fault," Joshua said, smiling.

"Should we take down the flyers and banners? Are we endangering the ones we have by getting more and more children?"

Joshua looked at her quizzically. "Are you being serious?"

Amanda nodded.

"Amanda, look around you. Most of these faces that you don't recognize yet would have died without you. You've done your part, let some of us others figure out the food situation. Never, ever, second guess your flyers and banners. This is our, I don't know, purpose? Destiny? I feel very strongly that we were put here on this planet for this very reason. Not to hold back and save fewer kids because we're worried about the future."

"I haven't heard you talk like that before. You don't seem the fate and destiny type at all."

"I'm like an onion, you need to keep peeling back the layers to find my core," Joshua replied, smiling mischievously.

"Will you make me cry the whole time too?" Amanda bantered in return.

"Of course, everyone around me will cry."

"About the food, don't forget that we can help too," Hannah chimed in. "Our farms can produce more, if we had more people to work the land."

"You heard the elders, they don't want our help," Joshua said.

"We are always careful about interacting with the English, but I think they'll change their minds when they understand what you have going on here. That's also part of the reason they let me come with you. They want to better understand the situation."

"You mean they sent you as a spy?" Joshua quipped.

"No, not at all, I don't mean it that way," Hannah replied, her eyes widening in alarm.

Joshua laughed. "I'm sorry Hannah, I was just joking, relax."

A flurry of tapping noises interrupted their

discussion as children surrounded the car. They called out to Amanda and Joshua, while slapping the car doors to be let in.

"Uh oh, we're surrounded. We'll continue this discussion later," Joshua cried out, while laughing some more.

They climbed out of the car, while more children came to see what the excitement was all about. Many surrounded Hannah. Some had met her earlier, but the new children were curious to see a teenager in their midst. Amanda heard an excited voice call out.

"That's my mom!" Sophia cried, pushing other kids out of the way.

"Sophia, don't push," Amanda rebuked her. She scooped up the child in her arms. Amanda lowered herself on one knee so that her free hand could hug and pat the other children. Sophia tried slapping a few of the children's hands away. Amanda looked crossly at her.

"Why are you doing that?"

"You're my mom, not theirs!"

"That doesn't mean I can't hug them and be nice to them."

Sophia fabricated her best pout before turning her head away. *Need to nip this in the bud*, Amanda thought. But now was not the time. She resolved to have a serious one-on-one conversation with Sophia later, when they were alone in their room. Amanda also reminded herself to be mindful that a three-year-old's brain didn't work the same as an adult. She would have to teach the child how to share, but while also making her feel safe. She suspected Sophia wasn't yet entirely convinced that her position as Amanda's adopted daughter was fully secure.

"Hey, how was the ambassador mission?" Mo asked, coming up to Amanda.

"Joshua will fill you in on the details, can you please help him unload the produce from the car?"

"That's it? Not one hint of what happened?"

"Well, in a nutshell they don't want our help, we have a consolation prize of a car load of veggies, and we have a new teacher for the kids," she answered, pointing to Hannah who was already surrounded by children.

"I thought Joshua was some sort of Amish-whisperer, and could secure us a deal?"

"Well, he knows them, but he can't work miracles. But Hannah thinks the deal might still happen. She says they let her come here for a while so that she could learn about our group and its problems. She'll report back to them that we're not all devil worshippers and we have a small town's worth of children to feed. Then she thinks they'll accept our offer, and increase production on the farm with our help."

"Deb is thinking of moving us south next year, so we don't have to deal with winter. Not sure how useful a long-term deal with the Amish will be. Unless we can convince them to move with us," Mo answered.

"What? Why didn't anyone tell us that before we

went to see them?" Amanda asked.

"I don't know what's going on, exactly. Nor do I understand why it's hush-hush. Or even if it is supposed to be a secret, for that matter. I just know that her and Titus are trying to make some sort of plan to move next year. I was supposed to be involved, but both of them keep brushing me off. Titus is too busy expanding our living quarters. Deb is busy doing whatever it is that Deb does. Talking, organizing, handling the children, whatever."

"OK, well I definitely need to have a talk with Deb then. This is ridiculous. I don't know about the idea itself being ridiculous, but that only a privileged few know about it? Absolutely in the 'ridiculous' category."

"Yeah, I'm with you there, I have to admit. I suspect our little group has ended its kumbaya stage," Mo said.

"You're more cynical than I am," Amanda replied. She knew that both she and Mo were on the same wavelength regarding government control and conspiracies. But she hadn't seen this defeatist side of him before. She couldn't help but feel disappointed.

Mo shrugged. "Not sure what I'm supposed to say to that. But you have to admit, things are not the same as in the beginning."

"Nor did I expect them to stay the same. We're no longer half a dozen people with a handful of children. This thing has grown a lot since then, and we're still growing faster than any of us imagined.

Things can't stay the same, Mo. We're almost the size of a small town now."

"Village, at least," Mo said, smiling.

Amanda smiled back at him. Perhaps Mo was just having a rough day, she had to cut him some slack.

"Sorry for being a downer," he said. "I'll go unload the groceries with the Non-Whisperer."

Hmm, might also be that jealousy thing, Amanda thought. Somehow, her and Joshua made a good pair for road trips. She knew that didn't go over well with Mo. She wasn't ready to be in some sort of romantic relationship with either of them. And she resolved not to play any of their teenage boy games. *Mo, Joshua: deal with it.*

"Why aren't you happy?" Sophia asked, staring into Amanda's eyes.

"Sweety, I'm happy. Why don't you think I'm happy?"

"You were frowning, like this." She furrowed her brow in an exaggerated manner. "That's what I do when I'm not happy."

"Well, I was just thinking about grown-up stuff, but I promise I'm happy."

"OK," Sophia said, resuming her unconcerned child's cheerful demeanor.

"I'm just going to go to our room for a bit. Want to go play with the others?"

"Yes," Sophia replied, wiggling out of Amanda's arms.

Amanda made her way through the gaggle of children, and into the hotel. It took her several seconds to figure out what was different as she went up the stairs. Then she gasped in surprise.

"Lights," she said out loud, laughing with delight. A few lights were installed in the stairwell, with long wires disappearing into the darkness far above her head. She marveled at the dim light now illuminating the previously pitch-black stairwell. Amanda would have to remember to congratulate and thank Titus and Chris on their solar panel success.

She passed Jessica's room on her way to her own room. Jessica's door was open, so Amanda popped her head in.

"We have lights," she cried out.

Jessica was sitting at her desk, reading one of the books from the tall stacks precariously perched around the edge of the desk. She looked up and smiled.

"I know, and it is simply, well, fucking awesome," she laughed. "Chris came by a few hours ago to show me. Those two guys are amazing."

"I couldn't believe it when I came up the stairs. And what's with the potty-mouth, there Jess?"

"Heh, heh, well sometimes you just need to really emphasize a feeling."

"What are you reading, anyway?"

"Well, this article is about the effect of nutrition on the endocrine system."

"Wow, and what else do you do for fun? I never knew you were this exciting."

Jessica laughed. "Look you guys want me to be a

doctor, so I need to put myself through the Jessica Albert School of Medicine. And, given that the endocrine system is responsible for growth, and we have like a million children to care for, and food is scarce: seems to me that this is a pretty relevant topic. So there."

"All joking aside, I have to say I'm really impressed with your dedication, Jessica. And thanks of course."

"No need to thank me. It actually feels good to be going back to my studies, even if it isn't for an actual medical degree. But it's still fulfilling my little girl dream of becoming a doctor."

"And where does Dee fit into all this? Or does he?"

Amanda had mostly dropped the topic of Dee over the last few weeks. But every time she saw Dee moping around with a sullen look, she hoped the two of them would work things out. Now she was wondering if part of the reason Jessica was burying herself in books was to avoid having to deal with the whole Dee issue.

"I don't know, Amanda. He was kind and gentle with me. He cared a lot for Javon and did his best to make him feel included even when Dee and I were,"—she hesitated a moment—"were becoming an item. And he was nothing short of a hero for the children and the Amish. But, the guy murdered people in other gangs. Bottom line, he's a murderer. You can't move past that. I can't move past that."

Jessica's eyes glistened as she spoke.

"I totally get what you're saying. And, to be honest, I wouldn't be able to handle it. But that's easy to say when you're not in love with the guy. And as an outside observer, I see the both of you miserable as can be since you found out about his past. The only question I want to throw out there for you to consider is: do we all get a second chance now? Whatever circumstances and/or bad decisions led us to the life we had before, those are gone. Now we have radically new circumstances, and a brand-new set of decisions that we could screw up. Or like the Great Reset everyone was talking about a few years ago, maybe this is our personal Great Reset. A chance to start anew, and apply what we've learned in our past to the new reality. Fix, or repeat, the wrongs we did. To then"—Amanda cut off her monologue.

"Oh my God I'm soap boxing to the max. Where did that come from?" she laughed.

Jessica laughed with her. "Clearly something your subconscious has been chewing on for a while."

Amanda could feel her cheeks flush red. Her words surprised her. She suspected it wasn't all about Jessica and Dee, but something about herself as well. What did she feel she had a second chance to get right? Jessica interrupted her thoughts before she could properly analyze this new revelation.

"Well at least you spoke from the heart while on your soapbox. And, frankly, you raise a very interesting point. I'm going to need to ponder that for a bit. Not just about Dee, but about myself. I know that things in my past have shaped me quite a bit. Like you said, is this a reset that I can use to shed all the baggage? I don't know. I hope so."

"Funny I was just thinking the same thing. How does the reset idea apply to me?"

"Too bad that it takes the end of the world for people to consider giving themselves a new start," Jessica added with a wry smile.

"Knock, knock," Chris said, his head popping around the door. "Sorry to interrupt, but can I have a word with you Jessica?"

"Of course," Jessica replied, "what's up?"

"I was just on my way out," Amanda said, not wanting to invade Chris' privacy on what was likely a medical issue. "But, one thing right now: a huge 'wow' for the lights, you are freakishly awesome."

"Ha ha, thanks. I've been called a freak before, but never freakishly awesome. Anyway, please stay," said Chris. "It would be good to do a little brain storming here. It's about drinking water."

Amanda appreciated Chris' enthusiasm and work ethic. Like Titus, he was an invaluable man to have around. She admired people who took charge of their responsibilities and gave willingly to others. But today for some reason, and possibly it was the snug fitting, damp t-shirt he was wearing, Amanda felt a tinge of attraction towards Chris. *Great, Mo, Joshua, and now Chris to think about.* It's Raining Men started playing in the background of her mind.

"We're running low on bottled water. We knew it wasn't sustainable of course. But, now is the time to figure out the long-term solution. Do we collect rainwater? Can we drink the lake water? Are there cleaner rivers around? But for all of those options, there's the question of how to sterilize the water. Do you know anything about that? I mean I've heard the common street-wisdom of boil it for a minute. Is that accurate? And is it even necessary for rain or lake water?"

"Well Mr. Banner, you've come to the right place," Jessica replied, a smug smile spreading across her face. She put her book aside and rummaged through a pile of journals to her right. She pulled one journal out and flipped through a notebook filled with her own handwriting.

"Have you ever considered becoming a librarian? You seem to have a gift for it," Amanda joked.

"Believe me, in recent times I wish I was," Jessica replied.

A large book under the journals slipped to the floor. *Mosby's Comprehensive Review of Dental Hygiene*, Amanda read.

"Dental Hygiene? Are you changing careers?" Amanda asked.

"What am I supposed to do when one of you walks in with a toothache? Ah, here it is," Jessica continued. "So, I knew this would come up as a topic eventually, and did my homework in advance. The closest water source to us is the Genesee River, but that's been a chemical dumping ground for over a century. The lake is of course nearby, but that would definitely need to be filtered and sterilized," she said, referring to Lake Ontario. Amanda had wondered about the lake as well. It would be a virtually endless supply of water if they could turn it into drinking water.

"But, our best bet, and I'm surprised you haven't mentioned it, given where we moved from, is the Cobbs Hill Reservoir. It'll be our cleanest water source. We can test it: Home Depot probably sells water testing kits. But I'm quite sure we'll want to sterilize it too. And yes, boiling for a minute or two should take care of that."

Amanda saw Jessica's eyes cloud over as she spoke about the reservoir. Dee had told Amanda about the attempted rape he had stopped.

Chris turned towards Amanda. "Did you know we had such a fountain of knowledge in our midst?"

"I did become aware of that recently, yes. Have you noticed that I don't speak much in front of Dr Albert? Her greatness intimidates me too much," Amanda replied.

To Amanda's relief, Jessica's face cleared up, and broke into a shy laugh.

"Seriously though, boiling water will take a lot of energy. We'll have to burn a lot of wood, or go through a lot of propane tanks. Is there no other way we can filter out impurities? Aren't UV rays supposed to kill bacteria too?" Chris asked.

"Right, I'm still thinking about the glory days when we had power," Jessica said. "But there is a far simpler solution: bleach. There should be plenty of that in grocery stores. As long as it's pure chlorine bleach, no additives or scents. All we need is a few drops per gallon. Amanda, next time you fire up your computer, please let me on. There's probably a page on using bleach to purify water."

Amanda nodded. "Sure thing."

"OK that sounds way better. Adding bleach to our water though, sounds scary," Chris said.

"It does, but in the end, that's what tap water contained, right? Chlorine for disinfection," Jessica replied.

"Yeah, OK. I think it's psychological. You tell me to add chlorine, that sounds right. But tell me to add bleach, then it sounds like I'm poisoning the water. But I get it, they're the same thing."

"Almost the same thing. Close enough, anyway," Jessica said.

"What about pure chlorine tablets from a pool store?" Amanda asked.

"Even better," Jessica replied.

"Awesome," Joshua exclaimed. "Thank you, ladies, you've just made a giant problem in my head shrink to a small hassle. This is huge, drinking water: check! Now we just need to solve the minor issues of food and winter heat."

"I'm sorry, but we only solve one survival problem per day," Amanda said, pointing to the door.

Chris laughed. "I'll be back tomorrow then." He ran out of the door, leaving some of his contagious excitement behind. Amanda felt very uplifted by the discussion, and relieved to have these friends working together and solving problems.

"We rock," Amanda said to Jessica.

"We do, we sure showed him where the brains are."

"No, I mean our group rocks. Well, us two especially of course," Amanda said, leaning in for a high five. "But just look at how well we're all cooperating and surviving, without any proper structure to our group. Somehow, it all just works."

"I know, it's been great. But I do worry about how we'll keep it together if we keep growing like this. The larger we get, the more we'll need structure, right?"

"Are you saying we should slow our growth?" Rapid growth had been largely Amanda's responsibility, and a source of pride.

"No, absolutely not. The more children we save, the better, obviously. But I just mean that we need to prepare for the growth. We can't stay like a close-knit family if we have a thousand children."

"Whoa, now you're throwing out crazy numbers, no one is talking about that kind of growth."

"Aren't we? Have you done a count lately? We're now over sixty children! And the bigger we get, the more the word will somehow spread, and people will travel from further away to join us."

Amanda reeled from those numbers. She could see a lot of children everywhere, but sixty? With more arriving almost every day. She realized Jessica was right, they needed to think bigger. Almost like a miniature government system.

"I'll need to discuss this with President Kearns," Amanda said.

"President Kearns? I thought Deb was our queen, not our president."

"Well, you say we need structure. I would rather we have a democratic government, not a monarchy, right?"

"Amanda! You want to run for President, don't you?" Jessica laughed.

"No way. But I'll take a cabinet post. Maybe we can create a Department of Archives. You know, for accessing the pre-apocalypse knowledge."

"Knowledge is power," Jessica agreed, smiling.

"Yes, Deb will just be my puppet." Amanda launched into her infamous evil laugh.

"What was that? You sounded like a cross between a rooster and a cow in distress," Jessica said.

It took several seconds before Amanda could recover from the laughter.

"My Evil Laugh has been mocked and called many things in my life, but never that," she finally sputtered out. "OK, with that, I'm outta here. I was on my way to my room, but I probably just needed a mental break. This chat with you did it, thanks Jess. I'll see if I can go make myself useful now."

"Come back any time, I'll see what other fascinating reads I can share with you."

Jessica was growing on Amanda more and more. She usually clashed with medical types, given her secret anti-vax stance. But somehow with Jessica, it just worked, and the two were becoming fast friends.

Amanda was both excited and intrigued by the idea of forming a pseudo-government. The irony wasn't lost on her. She had watched her husband's political rise with a mixture of pride for him, and disdain for the institution that he represented. Clearly, she wasn't alone. America's political landscape had more animosity and distrust than it had had since the civil war. *The Great Political Reset?* she thought. Maybe this was her calling. To start a new government that really was for the people, not for the politicians' careers and power grabs, and free of the cursed lobbyists. She had enough credentials to start the work, given how much she had learned about political systems through her husband's career. *From IT specialist, to apocalypse survivor, to the Mother of the New Constitution*, she thought with a smile. She needed to reflect on this some more, but vowed to approach Mo and Deb on the subject soon.

17. JIM AND MARY'S ORIGINAL ORGANICS

"**S**he's not responsive. We need to get some water into her or she'll die."

Jessica couldn't quite contain the rising panic in her voice. Mo had just brought in the emaciated, dehydrated little girl now thrust into Jessica's care. While his house searching efforts still occasionally brought in a survivor, the numbers had slowed down dramatically. And whenever he did find a child, they were usually quite sick by this point. But he persisted, where even Deb had stopped searching. Jessica was worried about Mo's mental wellbeing. She could only imagine the horrors he must encounter every day. But her concern for Mo was not on her mind at the moment. The dying child in front of her was very much the focus of her attention.

"Prop her up a little," she instructed Mo. Jessica went to the cabinet where she stored an assortment of supplies. She took a syringe out from one bag and unscrewed the needle from it. She dipped it into the cup of water she'd prepared and sucked some of the liquid into the syringe. She gently pried open the girl's mouth, and squirted a tiny amount into it.

"Damn it," she said, as the water flowed out of

the girl's mouth. "Tilt her head back a little, let's get gravity on our side."

Mo did as instructed, and Jessica tried again. This time the girl breathed in the water and started a coughing fit. Jessica grabbed her out of Mo's arms and tilted her forward again. She cradled the child until the coughing subsided.

"Jesus, now what do we do?" Mo asked. "This is like Sammy all over again, damn it!"

"She's more alert, the coughing woke her a little. Hold her again, head tilted like before."

"Are you sure?" Mo asked. Jessica didn't bother answering him, instead she released even less water than last time into the girl's mouth. She waited expectantly to see if another coughing fit would ensue. Instead, she was rewarded with the glorious site of the girl's Adam's apple bobbing up and down a single time.

"She just tried to swallow," Jessica exclaimed. She inserted the syringe again, and released another few droplets of water. It was on the ninth time that the girl's eyes fluttered open. She had a dull, unfocused gaze, but at least she was conscious.

"OK, hold her a bit straighter now, we want her to swallow properly." Jessica put the syringe in the girl's mouth. But before she could depress the plunger, the girl started sucking greedily at the syringe. Jessica could barely contain her excitement.

"Not too much at once baby girl, it'll make you sick," she whispered to her tiny patient. She refilled the syringe three more times before the girl's eyes shut again.

"OK, we'll let her sleep a bit." Jessica looked at the gradation marks on the syringe. "We got roughly 20mls into her. It's not enough to keep her alive, but it's a pretty good start."

"Well done, Jessica, I don't know what we would do without you," Mo said.

"Don't get your hopes up yet, she's not out of the woods," Jessica replied, shaking off the compliment.

"I need to talk to Deb," Mo said, shaking his head. "This could happen to all of us if we don't figure out how to get more food. I know the water situation seems under control, but food worries me. Right now, we're plowing through cans of food, but eventually those will run out too."

"And won't the remaining cans freeze during winter?" Jessica asked.

"Jesus, good point. I don't know. Do cans burst when they freeze? Might depend on the water content. Soup cans probably explode. But maybe beans and the like are OK?" Mo said.

"No idea," Jessica replied. "But then if we're planning to move south, maybe it's not an issue? We could keep a large store of cans with us here for this winter. I assume we'll find a way to heat the hotel enough so that we at least stay above freezing temperature, right?"

"Chris is our winter planner, let's talk to him about this," Mo replied.

Deb rushed into the room before Jessica could reply. "How is she?" Deb asked, taking in the scene in

Jessica's makeshift medical clinic.

"Bad. We managed to get a tiny bit of water in her. Honestly, I don't know if she'll make it. Severe dehydration and malnourishment."

"Is there anything you need?" Deb asked.

"A real doctor, with a backing medical team."

"We have a doctor, and there's your medical team," Deb replied, pointing towards Mo. "Seriously though, is there anything we can help you with?"

"Not for now. I'll babysit her for the next few days. The urgency is getting small amounts of water into her as often as possible. I'll worry about feeding her later, it's the dehydration that's life-threatening right now."

"Was there anyone else in the house?" Deb asked Mo.

Mo cleared his throat, visibly uncomfortable. "Two adults, one older child, and a baby. The adults and baby have been gone a long time. The older girl must have taken care of this one as long as she could."

"Are you OK?" Deb asked.

Mo's eyes glistened as he nodded.

"I'm so sorry Mo. But hey, you're a hero to this little one, right?"

"If she lives," he replied.

"Lives or dies, you rescued her from a nightmare situation. But don't you think it's time you stopped searching houses? I'm worried about you."

"Same here," Jessica echoed.

"I'm in far better shape than this little girl, and

better than the next child that I'll find." Mo stared at the floor.

"Ben and the other children also need you, right? If you burn yourself out, how will they, and us, cope?"

"Drop it Deb. I'm fine, Ben will be fine, and I'll keep searching as long as there are children alive out there."

Deb seemed about to argue her point again. Jessica interrupted, seeing the growing anger in Mo. "Mo, can you please promise me one thing? If it does get to be too much to handle, you'll stop? Or at least come talk to one of us?"

Mo nodded. "Sure, that I can agree to."

"Deb, we were just talking about food supplies," Jessica said, making the final break away from the contentious topic of Mo's house searching. "Canned food can only last so long, and we might lose most of it in winter if they freeze and burst."

"We need to become farmers," Deb said, nodding. "I've been thinking about that very same thing. And we don't have to start from scratch. If we can find some abandoned farms, there might be some crops growing, or some livestock still alive if the farmers had the foresight to let them loose for grazing."

A loud meow interrupted the conversation. Jessica bent down and picked Nancy up, who had disappeared the moment Mo had rushed in with the sick child. Nancy had adapted well to living mostly in Jessica's makeshift clinic, but usually ran out when visitors arrived.

"Or even better, if we find farms with the owners still alive," Jessica said, her mind whirling with the possibilities as she stroked the purring kitten. "Setup some sort of partnership like we tried to do with the Amish. We supply some labor, they feed us." As much as she loved being able to offer medical help, she also wanted to be involved in something with more long-term benefits. She was patching up problems, not providing long lasting security.

"Yes, of course, that would be better, but I'm just not sure how great the odds are of finding a working farm," Deb said.

"We could use Amanda's computers to see if we can find any specialty farms. You know, like natural, organic farms. Those owners would be less likely to have been vaccinated," Jessica added.

"Oh, I like your thinking," Mo said. "She said she'd downloaded Google Maps of the entire state. Specialty farms would probably be on there."

A knock at the door interrupted their discussion. Despite herself, Jessica's heart leapt when she saw Dee at the door. She forced her face to remain neutral as he entered the room.

"I heard we had a sick little one come in," he said. He spotted Jessica's tiny patient and walked over to her. "She gonna be OK?" he asked, not looking at Jessica.

"I don't know. I hope so, but she's very weak and super dehydrated."

"If anyone can bring her back, I'd guess it'd be you," he said, still not looking at her.

Why have I fallen in love with a killer? she asked herself for the thousandth time. She had never been one of those women who were drawn to so-called 'bad boys'. So then why Dee? Was it because he had rescued her from the fake cop back at the reservoir? That thought didn't ring true in her heart. No doubt it had allowed them to become close enough to know each other. But it was Dee's equal mix of strength and gentleness that attracted her the most. He could appear tough to others when he needed to, but he always treated her tenderly. She recalled getting annoyed with him, proclaiming not to be a porcelain doll when he was overprotective. Ironically, Deb had used the same expression with her when she was in her early recovery stage from her gunshot wound.

And he is wickedly handsome, she admitted. But getting involved with someone who could kill others without extenuating circumstances, like self-defense, or a war or something? That would be a huge mistake. And she had already made more than her share of mistakes in her life.

"Thanks, you have more confidence than I do," she replied.

"Why you all talking about farms?" he asked, looking at Deb and Mo.

Now Jessica found herself getting irritated by his inability to make eye contact with her.

"I'm going to see if I can find some farmers willing to work with us," Jessica replied, putting emphasis on the 'I'.

"That where Amanda's Google Maps come in?" he asked.

"Yup," she replied.

"You're not going alone. A lot of guns out there, you need some security."

A rush of feelings overwhelmed her. She felt nervous and thrilled at the thought of being alone with him. But she also had no intention of being told what to do.

"I don't recall asking your permission to go," she retorted.

"You all put me in charge of security. I ain't letting our only doctor go out by herself," he said, finally looking straight at Jessica.

"He's got a point," Deb said, before Jessica could argue against the idea. "What would happen if we lost you?"

"I second that. Or third that, I guess," Mo added.

"But, you're not going dressed like that Darnell. You'll scare the farmers before Jessica can even approach them," Deb said.

Dee looked down at his clothes. "What's wrong with what I'm wearing," he asked, a confused look on his face.

"It screams 'gangsta'," Mo said.

"Why? Cause it's loose clothes? I thought we were leaving all that racist shit behind? I need to hide my guns, and I'm not going to change how I dress to suit your taste."

"I'm disappointed, Maurice. 'Gansta'? Really?" Deb shook her head, before turning back to Dee. "You've got holes in the armpits of your shirt, the bottom of your pants are shredding, and look in the mirror at how many stains you have. That's what I was talking about. Look, we're dealing with a lot right now, and grooming is not exactly at the top of everyone's list. But at the same time, cleaning up a little wouldn't be a bad thing."

"Um, I didn't consider the guns, sorry about that," Mo said, looking somewhat red-faced.

"Even if I didn't have any guns, same thing: don't tell me how to dress."

"Enough about clothing styles. Maurice you need to give some thought to, well, your thoughts. But Darnell, not everyone is bad. Do you really need to walk around armed to the teeth?" Deb asked.

"Maybe not everyone. But some. And it's them I need to carry guns for."

"Hmm. Well, I leave that to you, that's your expertise. I'm just as tired of guns as I am of racism. Jessica, take him to a clothing store before you go."

"But" — Jessica began.

"But" — Dee started simultaneously.

"No buts," Deb interrupted firmly. "He's right that you need some protection out there. But we can't have him going around looking like he's starving and barely surviving. People will be scared that he'll shoot the farmer and ask questions later."

And so, three days later, Jessica found herself waiting in front of a dressing room, awkwardly holding a flashlight through the gap over the top of the door.

"Can you point it to the side, you're blinding me, it's right in my eyes," Dee complained from the other side of the thin metal door.

"You should have brought yourself a lantern, you could stand it next to you," Jessica replied dryly, as she swung the flashlight's beam to the right.

"That's too far, now I can't see."

"Oh, for Christ's sake, open the door. It's not like there's anything I haven't seen before."

Jessica heard the latch being withdrawn. She brought the flashlight down to her hip as the door swung inwards. A visibly uncomfortable Dee, clad only in socks and boxers, glanced at her before trying on the next pair of pants. They had spent the better part of an hour negotiating which clothes to even bring into the dressing room. At this point, she was willing for him to pick just about anything. *Why do I even care?* she chided herself.

"I would like to check in on Rose again today, if that's at all possible," she said. Rose was the name she had chosen for the girl she had been treating. She guessed Rose was a little under two years old. And now she thought Rose was going to see many more birthdays. The little girl was conscious, drinking, and eating small snacks. Her blooming towards health had inspired Jessica to name her after a flower.

Dee stopped what he was doing and tossed the pants aside. She stepped back, seeing his frustration.

"Why you riding me so hard? What did I ever do

to you?"

"Oh, I don't know, maybe not telling me you were a killer?" Jessica immediately regretted her words. She saw him physically recoil from her verbal attack.

"I did what I had to do to survive. I don't suppose you would understand that, on your way to med school and all," Dee replied angrily. He bunched up all the pants and shirts that they had gathered, and started walking away, towards the entrance.

"Are you planning to ride back in your underwear?" she called after him.

Dee stopped, looked down at himself, and muttered an obscenity. He dropped his armload of clothes to the floor, picked a pair of pants, and started hopping on one leg as he struggled to get them on as quickly as possible.

Jessica couldn't help but chuckle at the sight. Dee looked towards her as the sound of laughter echoed in the cavernous shop.

"I'm sorry," she said. "But really, you are a funny sight at this very moment."

Dee slowed down his frantic dressing attempts. He shook his head, letting out a small chuckle himself.

"And I'm sorry for what I said. I know I've been mistreating you. I'm just so hurt, and angry, I keep lashing out. Hurt, angry, and scared, actually."

"Scared? Jess, I would never hurt you." He looked wounded as he spoke.

"No, I don't mean that. I'm just scared of having had feelings for someone so, um, dangerous."

"'Having had' says it all. We don't need to talk no more about this. For what it's worth, I'm sorry that I didn't tell you everything about my life on the streets. You had a right to know."

"'Having', is actually more accurate." *Jessica, stop right now*, her mind screamed. "As much as I wish there was a 'had', well there isn't. I don't know if I can ever trust you again, but I certainly still have feelings for you Mr. Darnell Tiggs."

His wide, toothy smile made him look so much more innocent than he really was.

"Can I ask you somethin'?" Jessica remembered how his speech would be more like street-talk in two situations: while talking with Javon, and when he was nervous.

"Shoot," Jessica said, before realizing the terrible pun. "Sorry, poor choice of words."

"Did you trust me the first time we met?"

"No, of course not. You may recall that I was hiding in that radio tower or whatever it was."

"Right. And I guess you didn't have no feelings for me either then."

"Right again. Why are you asking these silly questions?"

"Well from where I'm standing, we're one step ahead of back then. You don't trust me, but you have feelings for me. So, just sayin' if it happened before, it could happen again."

"What, exactly, could happen again?" Her heart was pounding, and she hated that she couldn't control it.

"You know. Me and you. That might happen again."

"No Dee, it can never happen again. I don't trust you." Truthfully, she didn't trust her own words at the moment.

"But you just said, you didn't trust me then. And it happened. So, it could happen again. That there is an iron-clad case, as the lawyers say."

"You're making no sense at all. Zip up your pants, put a shirt on, and let's get out of here," she said.

"Yes Ma'am," he said, either unable or unwilling to remove that annoying grin from his face.

A full week went by before Jessica was comfortable enough to leave Rose. The child was still weak and frighteningly thin, but she was eating and drinking normally again. Her trauma manifested itself in seemingly random tantrums. Jessica empathized with the child. Rose's experience would be hard enough for an adult brain. But only equipped with a toddler's brain? She couldn't imagine how frightening it must be. So, she cuddled the child as much as possible. She stood back, but stayed near her, when the rage-filled tantrums overtook Rose. Once Rose's angry energy burned off, she would fall back into Jessica's arms, weeping uncontrollably. It was heartbreaking to watch. Jessica prayed that the age-old adage 'time heals all wounds' would hold true for Rose, even though it hadn't for Jessica.

"You seem far away," Dee commented, taking his

eyes off the empty rural road for a moment to look at Jessica. The folded-out map crinkled on her lap as she adjusted her position.

"Just thinking about Rose, I hope she's doing OK. She was pretty upset when she found out I was leaving."

"Are you kidding? With Amanda and Deb fussing over her? Man, you'll be lucky if she remembers your name when you get back."

"Ha, ha, Mr. Funny Man," Jessica replied.

"Seriously Jess," Dee continued in a more sober tone, "she'll be fine. You nursed her back to health and now she has a small village full of adults and children to hang with."

"Soon she'll be asking to live with me, like Ben and Sophia with Mo & Amanda."

"Yeah no kidding. I've already had three kids ask to live with me: Ethan, Nolan, on condition that his baby sister doesn't come along too, and Mason. I hardly know Mason, that's the boy Mo & Amanda found. But he been following me around, you know."

"Hey, that's no fair! Three asked you? Why hasn't anyone asked me?"

"If you took your nose out of your books and played with them, they might."

"Great, at twenty-nine I'm the reclusive spinster that children are afraid of. Soon they'll throw eggs at me when I'm not looking."

"Nah, eggs are too important. Maybe sand, or small pebbles."

"Thanks, that makes me feel a lot better."

Jessica turned back to the map to avoid seeing the grin on Dee's face.

"Ok, should be very soon now, possibly your next right," she said, a few moments later. Her gaze alternated between the map and the road, looking for cross roads or signs. "Jim and Mary's Original Organics is the name of the place. They have some u-pick stuff, berries looks like. Or maybe apples. So, there should be a sign."

"Now that is what we should look for this fall, apple orchards," Dee remarked.

"For sure, the trees are still producing even if the farmers aren't there."

"There it is," Dee said, slowing down as they passed a brightly painted sign announcing the organic farm in one quarter mile. A smiling couple, presumably Jim and Mary, were holding a basket filled with strawberries, and another basket with potatoes and carrots, their long, leafy tails hanging over the basket's sides.

The first thing Jessica noticed as they drove up the lane was the abundance of chickens running loose. They scattered as the vehicle pulled into the parking area, which was no more than a designated patch of dirt with a thin layer of gravel spread over it. Dee checked his guns before stepping out of the car. It made Jessica nervous, while reminding her of his past.

"Hello," Jessica called out as they approached the store front. A sign by the door said: 'Come In! The food is fresh, and the conversation is never stale!'. It was a large, two-story farmhouse, complete with a front porch running along the entire wall. Curtains were drawn in the second-floor windows. Jessica assumed that was where Jim and Mary lived. It sounded like a cozy life, having a farm, and living above your own store.

Dee rapped on the door. After a few seconds of silence, he opened the unlocked door. A cloud of fruit flies streamed out, causing Jessica and Dee to wave their arms wildly. The wine-smell of rotting fruit also greeted them.

"OK, ain't nobody in there," Dee said, stepping back.

Jessica agreed. Well, sort of. Someone might be in there, but they wouldn't be alive. She didn't need to know. They wandered around the farmhouse, looking for signs of life. There were two other structures nearby: a barn and a stable.

"Let's check those out," Jessica said.

Jessica stopped when they were within fifty feet of the stable. She already detected the stench of rotting meat.

"I'm not going in there," she said.

"Nope, me neither," Dee replied.

"Whatever died in there, it must have been horrible. Why wouldn't they free the animals before they died? If it was me, the minute I got a dizzy spell, I let them all free, right?"

"I dunno, Jess. Maybe knowing you're about to die messes with your head so much that you can't think straight."

"For sure, but still. You'd know those animals would starve or die of thirst. I just don't get it. The wholesome Jim and Mary thing feels pretty fake to me right now."

They continued exploring the farm. They passed an extensive field with rows upon rows of strawberry plants. Jessica had been on u-pick excursions before. She remembered tidy rows of evenly spaces plants, with walking paths between each row. This field was completely overgrown. She could make out where the walking paths were, but the spreading strawberry plants and weeds had obscured them. With the strawberry season over, the plants were mostly green. She saw a few dark, rotting berries here and there. But mostly, it just looked like a field of green.

"I see a fence up there," Dee remarked. Far past the strawberry field, the land rose gently. Near the top, a long wooden fence ran along a great distance, up to a stand of trees far away.

"Might as well go have a look," Jessica said. "Besides, we'll get a better view of the rest of the farm from up there."

Jessica expected to see more abandoned field crops at the top of the hill. She was mildly shocked, and pleasantly surprised, to find a large black and white Holstein cow grazing on a patch of weeds near the fence post.

"Oh my God, how did they survive?" she gasped.

More cows dotted the expansive field in the distance. Jessica noticed that the grass was very short. Many areas had no grass.

"They must have a stream or something," Dee said.

"Yes, but look at the ground. There's hardly anything left to eat. Farmers move their cattle around to different fields, don't they?"

"I certainly did, when I managed my herd," Dee remarked.

"We've got to help them," Jessica said, ignoring his wise-crack.

The cow near them lumbered off as Jessica climbed over the fence. She felt silly being afraid of a docile cow, but the animal was just so big. It was a relief to see it wander away.

"What are you doing Jess?"

"I don't know yet. Might be another field next to this one. We could break the fence and let them through."

A sudden urgency to save these cows overcame her. There had been so much death and suffering on this farm, she didn't want these cows to perish as well. Logically she knew it wasn't an urgent situation, but she couldn't repress the near panic-attack she was feeling for the cows. She ran across the field, to see what was beyond it.

"Jess!" she heard Dee call behind her.

"I'm going to go look on the other side," she yelled back, not slowing down. It felt good to run. At first. But the field was far bigger than she had imagined. She slowed to a walk, and then jogged for a while, after catching her breath. *No wonder they survived, this field is huge,* she thought. Finally seeing the fence at the opposite end of the field gave her a fresh burst of energy. She ran again, reaching the fence after a few minutes. She leaned against it, panting heavily. The grass had been cleared past the fence for about two feet. *That's how far they could reach through the fence,* she realized.

Another vast field spread out beyond the fence. The grass was as high as her hip.

"Lunch time," she called out to the cows, though none were within earshot. She tugged at the upper bar of the wooden fence. It moved a little, but was very solid. She looked to the right and left, examining the fence as far as she could see, looking for any weak or damaged section she could dismantle.

"Damn girl, when did you become a marathon runner," Dee gasped, finally catching up to her.

"Look at all that grass," she said to him. "It must be torture for them to see it and not be able to reach it." She gave the fence a kick, but it didn't move. Dee gave it several kicks, but the fence held.

"We need tools. There must be a saw or something back there," Jessica said.

"Hang on, I ain't going all the way back there to fetch a saw," Dee said, pulling out his pistol.

"What? Wait!" Jessica cried out, pulling his arm down. "Are you crazy? You're going to shoot the fence?"

Dee pulled his arm away, but kept the gun lowered. "What's wrong with that?"

"Well, first, you'll scare the shit out of the cows. Second, you're going to waste your precious bullets. Third, who knows what kind of trouble you'll attract, we don't know who might hear the shots. Fourth —"

"Ok, OK fine, you made your point," Dee said, putting the gun back into his rear waistband.

They hardly spoke on the way back to the farmhouse. Jessica tried not to read too much into everything, but Dee's rapid resort to guns back at the fence bothered her. The tension inside her reached a boiling point by the time they crossed the near-barren grazing field.

"Damn it, Dee, we need to talk," she said, coming to a sudden stop. Dee's eyes briefly opened wide before he took a defensive stance in front of her, crossing his arms.

"Say what's on your mind," Dee said.

"Amanda gave me a big speech about everyone needing a second chance. How this damned Vax Plague was like a big reset button for all of us. A chance to start over. Life 2.0, you know?"

"OK, I sort of get it. Not sure where you're headed with this. Is it about what you told me a while ago, your death wish, you called it?"

"No Dee, it's about you. She was basically telling me that I should forgive and forget your past, and consider you a new Dee. Judge you on what you are now, not what you were."

"That don't sit right with me, I'll tell you that. I haven't changed. I do my best in whatever situation

I'm in. The situation has changed one hundred percent, I get that. And so it might look like I've changed, but I'm still me. I don't regret what I done, I survived and thrived on the street. Now I'm surviving and thriving in the world after the damned Vax Plague. But I am still the same damned Darnell Tiggs as ever."

"She was trying to throw you a lifeline. I told her I can't keep loving a killer."

"So you wouldn't ever hook up with a soldier boy then?"

"That's different, those men are sent to war."

"What do you think life on the street is? That's a war, damn straight. Now that war is over, and I don't need to kill. Until some asshole kidnaps our young ones for child labor. Then there's a war again, and I kill. That's who I am Jess. I fight, I defend, I attack, I kill. If there ain't no war then I'm happy planting potatoes and babysitting kids with you all. But when the nasty stuff comes, and it always does, then I take care of that business."

"Ahhhhh!" Jessica screamed in frustration, tugging at her hair in exasperation. She realized she wouldn't get what she wanted. She was hoping for contrition, but he showed no signs of remorse. Part of her admired that he stayed true to himself. At least he was not faking it and trying to please her by saying what she wanted to hear. That made the situation even more complicated.

"Jess, I like you. You know that. And that ain't changed, and it ain't gonna change. But you need to figure out if you like me, or if you only like this imaginary man you made up in your head. So you think about it. I got time, I ain't going nowhere. But until you make up your mind, and least we can be friends, right? Like the shit we're doing today, I like that. Are you with me on that?"

Jessica nodded. It was a perfect deal for her. He was giving her all the time she needed to sort out her feelings. She could still enjoy his company for what it was, without worrying about the long term.

"OK, I like that. Because I was having a good time too, until you pulled out your damned gun for nothing and ruined it all." Jessica gave him a playful punch on the shoulder to emphasize her point.

"Oww!" Dee exclaimed exaggeratingly, rubbing his shoulder. "I thought you were against violence."

"No, I didn't say that I was —".

"Hold up, hold up, I'm just messing with you," Dee said, interrupting her mid-sentence. His near-goofy grin was at such odds with his character that she couldn't help but smile.

"You're on thin ice, might be a bit too soon for edgy jokes, my friend."

They resumed their walk across the field. Jessica felt Dee's hand reach for hers. Warning lights were flashing in her head even as the electric thrill of contact crept up from her palm, up her forearm, and well past her elbow. *This does not fall under the definition of friends*, she thought, equally disturbed by his advance and her utter lack of desire to untangle their intertwined fingers. She cleared her throat, and kept walking, avoiding eye contact. Dee was equally silent. How she wished she could see inside his head.

"I really hope we don't have to go inside," Jessica said, as the abandoned farmhouse loomed ahead of them. "There has to be a shed around, right?"

"Dunno, but I sure hope so too."

And there was. A walking path at the back of the parking area led to a narrow, tall shed. It reminded Jessica of an English garden shed. She half expected to see Wellingtons, pots, seeds, and a spade inside. When they opened the unlocked door, she saw she was right about the spade at least. There was in fact an entire array of gardening tools. Dee rummaged inside, sorting through various types of rakes, two hoes, short and long handled spades, and a few tools she couldn't even identify. Suddenly, he triumphantly pulled out a long bow saw. She had expected to find a regular handsaw, but the mean-looking teeth on this saw would certainly tear through the aging fence wood much faster.

She wasn't sure why, but on the way back across the field, she stayed just out of arm's reach from Dee. After a few awkward starts, Dee got the hang of the bow saw and cut through the top fence rail.

"Like a knife through butter," he proclaimed proudly.

"Awesome. Want me to do the next one?"

"Nope, this is kind of fun," Dee said, attacking the next rail.

"Chris and Titus would be proud," she said,

smiling at him.

It wasn't long after they had completed their handiwork that the first curious cow meandered over to the hole in the fence. They had removed an entire eight-foot section between two posts. The cow turned its head towards Jessica and Dee, who had withdrawn fifty feet away to give them space. It tentatively walked through the gap, bent its head and tore out a sizeable tuft of fresh grass. After chewing and swallowing it, the cow let out a long low moo. Then resumed eating. Two other cows looked up and wandered towards the first brave cow.

"Jessica Albert, savior of humans and cows," Dee said.

"Feels good, doesn't it" Jessica said, as the rest of the herd headed towards the first cows now feeding in the new field.

"Yeah, got to admit it does. But at the same time, I'm seeing steak on legs, so that's kind of messed up. Sorry, don't mean to disrespect you, you know, since you don't eat meat."

Jessica had been a vegetarian for almost a decade. It was a personal decision and she never lectured others about the topic. And yet, she frequently ran into unwarranted criticism from others. She found the most common rebuttal was also one of the most amusing: 'but you wear leather shoes'. To her, that was like saying it's hypocritical to recycle paper and plastic if you throw anything else out in the garbage. To Jessica it was about reducing the suffering and environmental impacts of the human abuse of farm animals for meat. It wasn't about being perfect. But she'd grown so used to the unprovoked defensiveness that she encountered from others that it was easy for her to smile disarmingly and move on to another topic. Dee's comment about a steak on legs was indeed very mild compared to many of the aggressive responses that she'd had to deflect.

"No worries, Dee. All that matters is that they aren't starving anymore."

"You get we need to tell the others about this though, right? It's a big source of food for this winter."

"I get it, I know," she acknowledged.

She watched until the last cow, a rather thin straggler, crossed over into the new field.

"What do you say? Shall we see if we can find a farm that still has a farmer on it?" she asked Dee.

"Yeah, that was the point, let's move on."

With a last content glance at the feeding cows, Jessica turned, and they headed back towards the car.

18. TEACH YOUR CHILDREN WELL

"Teach, your children well," Deb sang softly, as she arranged chairs and desks in the hotel's Idea Brunch conference room. Titus and Chris had pilfered work desks from several rooms in the unoccupied floors of the hotel. She favored her right arm, being careful not to overexert the torn muscles within her shoulder. But physical activity while preparing their makeshift classroom filled her with far more joy and exuberance than what a stiff shoulder could possibly take away.

"Don't you ever ask them, 'Why?' If they told you, you would cry. So just look at them and sigh, and know they love you," she continued, drawing out the word love for far too long. The Crosby, Stills, Nash, and Young song was her favorite. It spoke to her, as a teacher, and had always inspired her. And now, setting up a brand-new classroom, Deb had never been so inspired.

"You really shouldn't be moving those," Hannah said, walking into the conference room with three boxes of whiteboard markers. "Let me move things around."

"Don't fuss, I have enough of Jessica trying to

mother me. Besides, I'm mostly using my legs to push them around."

Deb appreciated Hannah's help in setting up a classroom and curriculum. The girl meant to become a school teacher in her Amish community, and so was eager to help. And much to Deb's pleasure, Hannah was also keen on learning from Deb. It felt good to pass on her decades of experience to the next generation's teachers. *Well, just one teacher for now*, she corrected herself.

As a group they were facing an education crisis that had never been dealt with before. She'd seen first hand how harmful neglectful and absent parents were to a child's development. Now this problem was being taken to the extreme. Almost all children had lost their parents and extended family. And if that wasn't bad enough, there weren't nearly enough substitute caregivers to care for them. The long-term effects of this trauma and neglect would be devastating for this generation. Try as they might to compensate for the lack of support, Deb knew they could never make up the attention-debt that the children would suffer. *But damned if I'll ever stop trying.*

Together, she and Hannah had decided to have a class size of up to twenty children. They would organize the various age groups in shifts, giving each of them a different time slot. For now, they could only offer part time schooling. But they planned to expand over time, once they trained or found new teachers.

"I had an idea I wanted to discuss with you," Hannah said.

"Sure, go ahead," Deb replied, plopping down heavily on one of the padded chairs. She hoped the rolling chairs wouldn't distract children excessively. But the adjustable height of the chairs was necessary for the large hotel desks, and the variety of student ages that they would seat. *Most comfortable classroom ever*, she reflected.

"We don't know the exact age of many, if not most, of the children. We should spend some time with each of them individually and estimate their age. And then, create a sort of birthday calendar. Otherwise, we'll never celebrate their birthdays."

"Wow, Hannah, that's a marvelous idea."

"I don't know if we should rank them by height, or how advanced they are with things like counting or reading. But somehow, we have to find a date for each one. We'll be wrong on all of them, but still."

"I couldn't agree with you more. Again, fantastic idea, I'm so happy you came to stay with us. Imagine celebrating birthdays again, won't that be wonderful?"

"Yes, but, with the number of children here, and the amount arriving all the time, we'll almost be celebrating every day," Hannah said, laughing.

"True, true," Deb said, laughing as well. "We don't want to put up balloons and make cake for each one. But we can certainly sing happy birthday, and have a mini celebration. Every child wants to feel special on their birthday."

"So how do you want to go about guessing their birthdays? You have a lot more experience than me in seeing the variety of childhood development stages."

"First thing we need to do is write down the ones we do know about. Those kids can then become our standards that we essentially calibrate against." Deb was already going through the battery of tests she had administered in her career, sorting out which ones would be best. She had not faced this interesting an educational challenge in a long time. The thrill of it filled her with energy.

"Maybe it's not a one-size-fits-all. Perhaps we should consider a combination of height and abilities," Hannah said.

"I agree. But keep in mind the vast majority aren't even at school age yet. Their abilities only reflect how much attention their parents gave them in terms of stimulation. So, we'll take a guess, but as you said, we'll be wrong on all of them."

"OK so limited lessons for the older kids then, and we know their ages. And then preschool for the rest and move them up a grade when ready?"

"Yes, something like that. I love the idea of giving them a birth date now. But where they fit in school can wait until we get to know the children better," Deb said.

"So maybe we need to concentrate on the preschool equipment," Hannah said, observing their efforts on desks and chairs.

"We still need the desks," Deb said. "But you're

right, we need more preschool toys, and crafting supplies. Paints, markers, glue sticks. Maybe even plastic aprons so that we can have them do hand painting. Sounds like a fun shopping trip to the neighborhood toy stores."

"Did I hear toy store? I'm in," Amanda said, walking into the conference room.

"We were talking about preschool supplies for all the younger kids," Hannah explained.

"Ah, shop-talk among the teachers," Amanda replied with a smile. "Well, this is a perfect time to show you this, then." She handed Deb a tablet.

Deb missed her old tablet. She recalled evenings of playing silly but addictive online games, curled up on the sofa with her fake fireplace's dancing flames casting a red glow in the room. Holding a tablet again was like smelling a freshly baked apple pie: it made her miss the old world dearly.

"What's this?" she asked, swiping the screen to wake up the tablet. '1 + 3 =' was printed in a large font taking up the entire screen. Deb stared at it, open-mouthed.

"Where did you get this?" she asked. She typed in a four, and a clapping and cheering sound rewarded her correct answer.

"I didn't get it. I wrote it." Amanda replied.

"Wrote it? You mean you made this app?" Deb asked, her eyes appraising Amanda.

Amanda seemed to beam with delight at Deb's surprise. "I told you, IT is my thing. I thought a bit of software might ease the burden, since you were short on teachers. We can get as many tablets as we need, install this app, and presto, you can have some self-learning going on in here. We just need to make sure that we have chargers set up near the generators. Whenever we fire one up for anything, use its spare capacity to add some charge to all the tablets."

"Amanda, this is fantastic," Deb breathed. '4 – 2 =' was now printed on the screen. Deb typed in five. "Not quite, try again," came Amanda's voice out of the tablet.

Deb chuckled in delight. "Wow, I'm speechless. Thank you Amanda, this is awesome."

"You're very welcome. Next I'd like to brainstorm with you on other apps that would be useful for these little ones' brains."

"Absolutely. OK, this changes things for sure. What do you think, Hannah?" She held the tablet towards her young apprentice.

"I'm sure the kids will love it," Hannah answered hesitantly. She didn't reach for the tablet. *Oh, right, technology*, Deb realized.

"Any word from Dee and Jessica?" Deb asked, turning back towards Amanda.

"No, they haven't come back yet," Amanda said.

"Where are they?" Hannah asked.

"Out looking for farmers that might feed us this winter," Deb said.

Hannah wrung her hands. "Don't give up on our community just yet. They won't let all these children go hungry."

"Maybe not, but at this point food supply is becoming our number one priority. If we can find multiple sources, that would be safest for us, and less demanding for our suppliers," Deb said.

"You have to understand how hard it is for us to deal with everything that's happened. We"— Hannah hesitated, searching for the right words —"don't deal with change very well. We like to keep the old ways. All of them. So it takes time to come to grips with changes that we have no choice but to adapt to. Do you understand?"

"I think it's a pretty known fact that the Amish are a conservative lot, Hannah," Deb said, laughing. "Again, we're just expanding our search for food. I really hope your community can help, but I don't want our survival to depend on it."

"I should go back soon, and talk to them."

"No, not yet. We haven't even started the lessons yet, I need your help as a teacher," Deb said, patting Hannah's shoulder. "Now enough talk about food, let's talk about this preschool setup."

"Actually, before you do, there is another idea I've been meaning to talk to you about," Amanda began. "I've been waiting for the right time, but there never seems to be a right time. So, if you two can spare a few minutes, I'd like to run this by you."

Deb nodded. "Go on." She worried when someone said they wanted to talk about something, rather than just talking about it.

"OK well, I'm not sure where to start. It all makes sense in my head, but saying the words out loud sounds strange." Amanda swallowed hard before continuing. "Everything we've done has been working well so far. But we're outgrowing ourselves, if you know what I mean. We're going to need more structure."

"What exactly do you mean by 'structure'?" Deb asked.

"Well people can't come to you for every little decision," Amanda said.

"I agree, and I certainly hope they're not doing that now."

"Right, but maybe we need to delegate areas of responsibility to individuals, or small groups. Like a mini-government."

"Government? Are you serious?"

"I was married to a politician, trust me, I know all the good and the bad about governments. But this is our chance to start over and learn from our mistakes. To write a new constitution, and new laws that protect everyone, not just the rich."

"Amanda, listen to yourself. We are under a hundred people. And what, a dozen adults? Talking about a government seems ludicrous to me at this point. Maybe if we ever join up with a group that has thousands of people, then it'll make sense."

Deb shrugged. She didn't understand where Amanda was coming from. Forming a government while all they wanted to do was survive and care for the children. *Why can't she put those brain cells to work on something more practical?* Then she remembered the tablet in her hand and tried to soften her thoughts towards Amanda.

"Is this something that you and Maurice cooked up?" Deb liked Mo a lot. But she didn't like his fear of organized authority, and distrust of anything linked to the old government. She knew that Amanda and Mo shared similar feelings, so this could very well be one of their paranoid schemes. She was worried that one of these days she would lose her cool and tell them to smarten up. Despite her respect for both of these intelligent individuals, she couldn't help but find that side of them rather juvenile.

"Mo? Absolutely not, why would you say that? Anyway, I agree it seems over the top now, but at the rate we're growing, it won't be long before you can't manage this thing alone."

"Is that what you're after? You want to help manage this 'thing' as you call it? Sure, I would love more help on the planning and decision making, Amanda."

"No, no, that's not what I was after. This isn't some power grab or whatever. I just feel we need to get more organized in terms of authority and decision making, that's all."

"I'll tell you what. I won't lie, I think dreaming up a new government structure is a complete waste of time. But, yes, we could use more organized decision making. So why don't you shadow me for a couple of days. Watch and listen to what people approach me with, and then make a plan to offload some of that. Really, I don't need to hear that Titus is going to pickup some new tools or Mason scraped his knee and Jessica put a bandage on it."

Amanda didn't reply right away. Her brow furrowed, and she crossed her arms.

"Actually, we may not be far apart on this," Amanda finally said. "I didn't mean that we start forming government agencies right away. But offloading from you, that to me sounds the same as what I was thinking. What are the needs of the people, even though there are very few of us now? That's what needs a supportive structure. Call it government or call it 'getting organized', that doesn't matter to me."

"What you just said now sounds like we aren't far apart. But earlier you were talking about writing a new constitution," Deb said with a smile.

Amanda smiled back. "Maybe, just maybe," she said, stretching the second 'maybe,' "I was getting a little ahead of myself."

"Maybe just a wee tad," Deb said, chuckling. "But I'm glad you talked to me about this. It shows you're thinking ahead, and I'm glad some people are. Most of the time I get so caught up in the day's tasks that I don't have the time or energy to plan ahead."

"Hannah, you've been quiet, what do you think of all this?" Deb asked.

Hannah paused before answering. "I'm sixteen, I'm not exactly a good source for you to be asking. I can tell you that we don't have a central government. We have the Ordnung, which we all follow. And each settlement has its elders."

"Sorry, the 'Ordnung'?" Deb asked.

"It's our rule book, if you like," Hannah answered shyly.

"The Amish constitution," Amanda said, smiling.

Hannah shook her head. "No, your constitution is about the rights of people. The Ordnung is about our way of life, our code of conduct."

"Nice try Amanda, still no takers for your new constitution," Deb joked.

"Damn it," Amanda said, snapping her fingers in mock frustration.

"So, how about that preschool shopping trip?" Deb asked.

"How far is it?" Hannah asked. She was wringing her hands again, visibly uncomfortable.

"What's wrong?" Deb asked.

"You can stay here," Amanda cut in, "Deb and I can take the truck to pick up some things. Maybe you can sort through our haul and organize the toys when we get back?"

Shit, Deb thought, chastising herself for forgetting about the Amish's reluctance to use cars and trucks.

"That's a good idea," Deb added quickly. "Take a break Hannah, I'm going to need your help to organize our stolen goods when we come back."

"I'll just finish setting up these desks then," Hannah said, busying herself with moving desks into place.

"Feels good to get out of the compound," Deb said, climbing into the passenger side of the SUV that she and Amanda commandeered for the toy shopping trip.

"Compound?" Amanda laughed, "that's a little harsh."

"Not when the whole world is telling you to watch out for your arm, to get rest, etc."

"Are you sure you don't want to rest instead of this little side trip?" Amanda asked playfully.

Deb couldn't help but smile, despite trying to sound stern. "Keep that up and I'll have your arm in a sling in no time."

Fortunately, Deb was able to stop using a sling almost two weeks ago now. The liberty was so refreshing, to be able to move her arm freely, if a little cautiously. Combining that with a drive out to a mall, well, life was just divine, as far as Deb was concerned. At least, until Mo ran outside, shouting at them.

"Get back inside, now!" Mo cried.

Amanda and Deb looked at each other. Amanda's obvious puzzlement matched Deb's.

"What's going on?" Amanda asked, stepping out of the car. Deb, moving more slowly, also got out of the car.

"Some kind of military column headed our way, Titus spotted it from the sixth-floor window."

"Military?" Deb asked, her mind racing through the possibilities. She didn't know if these were friendly military personnel, the last vestiges of their dying central government. Or they could be the same caliber of rogues that had terrorized the Amish in Heuvelton.

"Yeah, a bunch of jeeps, and some heavier, armored vehicles of some sort. Titus didn't stop to get binoculars, he just raced down to tell us all."

"Damn, and with Darnell away," Deb muttered, headed for the front door.

"Not sure Dee could help us much against a small army," Mo said.

"Good point, but still, he's thought about security more than any of us. I wish he was here," Deb said.

"It might actually be a good thing," Amanda added, "who knows, he might have provoked them."

"Good point again," Deb acknowledged. Though inside, she still would have felt safer with Darnell helping to organize their response to the coming military convoy.

Titus shut the heavy metal door behind them and secured the multiple locks he had added to the door. Chris and Joshua were herding the children upstairs, away from the ground floor where any violence would most likely occur.

"Now wait a minute," Deb said. "If this is an armed convoy, then why are we locking the door. Can't they just blast through?"

"Maybe," Titus said. "Probably," he corrected. "But we don't know how much they know about us. No need to invite them in."

"Well, our posters and banners have already told them all they need to know about us," Deb replied.

"So what do you recommend, Deb? That we just leave the door open and wave them in?"

The exasperation in Titus' voice left no room for interpretation of exactly what he thought of that idea.

"It seems nerve-wracking, I admit," Deb said. "But it beats them sending a rocket or grenade at our door, doesn't it?"

"We don't even know if they have those kinds of weapons," Titus replied.

"They probably do," Mo said. "But I agree it makes more sense to lock them out initially. We'll get to study them a bit when they come face to face with the locked door. Will they try to talk to us, or just blast through? That will tell us something about what their intentions are."

"OK, fine," Deb agreed. There wasn't much point of disagreeing, she realized. The door was already secured shut, and she didn't think anyone was about to let her open it. Nor did she even know what the right move should be. "But we watch, and we listen. If they want to talk, I want to make sure that we open up a dialog."

Titus and Mo nodded their agreement. Amanda and Chris then came racing down the stairs after having helped settle the children upstairs.

"What's happening?" Amanda asked.

"We've locked down, and now we wait," Titus said. "But Chris, can you go up a few floors and be our lookout? And Amanda can you run back and forth between us and Chris, to let us know what you two can see from up there?"

"Sure thing," Chris said, turning and running to

the stairs. Amanda followed close behind.

"If you're going to want to talk to them, you should head up one floor, get to a balcony," Mo said.

Deb nodded and headed towards the same stairwell that Chris and Amanda had run to. *Talk to them? What am I supposed to say?* She wondered how she had gone from retired school teacher to spokesperson addressing a possibly hostile army.

Deb squeezed by stacks of doors that Titus and Chris had stored in the first room she found facing the front of the hotel. She slipped open the lock on the sliding door handle and stepped out onto the balcony. Though it was a pleasantly warm day, Deb shivered as she leaned over the balcony railing. The knuckles on her hands turned white as she gripped the railing. From her low vantage point, she couldn't see any sign of the approaching soldiers.

Mo joined her a few minutes later. "I thought you might want a bit of company," he said, stepping out onto the balcony.

"I think I'll need advice more than company," Deb remarked.

"President Kearns needing advice? I don't think so," Mo said, smiling.

"President Kearns, eh?" she scoffed. "I know who you've been talking with."

"She may have a point. It sounds crazy when you consider how all this started, but really, the way we're growing?"

"All that may end in the next hour, so how about we put yet another pause on the government idea?"

"Sure, I was just trying to lighten the mood."

Amanda made both Mo and Deb jump when she burst onto the small balcony.

"OK," she started, trying to catch her breath.

"Spit it out," Mo urged.

"We're looking at a long convoy, could even be a mile long. There are several trucks. Chris thinks they could be personnel carriers. So, we could be looking at several hundred soldiers, if he's right."

"Did you see any weapons?" Mo asked.

Amanda shook her head. "Nothing like tanks, if that's what you mean. They're still too far away to see any small arms."

"Thanks for the update, please tell us when they get close," Mo said.

"We'll see them when they get close," Deb said staring out into the distance.

They didn't have to wait long. Amanda ran back to them three times in the forty-five minutes before Deb spotted the front of the column. It took another fifteen minutes for the column to arrive in front of the hotel. Deb knew it had been just a fantasy, but she was still bitterly disappointed that they didn't simply ignore the hotel and keep moving wherever they were headed. Instead, three of the trucks rolled into the entrance area and dozens of armed men spilled out of them. They carried machine guns and crouched low, running in several directions at once.

"It's like watching a bad movie," Mo observed, echoing the thoughts in Deb's head.

One of the soldiers spotted Deb and Mo up on the

balcony. A bright red dot immediately lit up on Mo's chest. The soldier had signaled his comrades, and several red dots now appeared on both Deb and Mo. Both raised their hands.

There had better be a Hollywood ending to this crappy movie, Deb thought. She cleared her throat to speak.

19. MARTIN'S FARM

"How many more of these do you want to do today?" Dee asked.

"Not sure. It's pretty discouraging, I'll admit. One or two more?" Jessica answered.

"I vote for one," Dee muttered.

It had been a long day. After their first success with the rescued cows in the morning, they had hit nothing but abandoned, lifeless farms. A few had overgrown gardens that might have salvageable vegetables. Dee had watched Jessica take note of each, for someone to follow up in the coming weeks.

"This one isn't too far away," Jessica said, her finger on the map. "It doesn't have a name, just the little produce symbol."

"Doesn't sound too promising, but let's give it a try," Dee said. His stomach growled. They had packed a lunch, but now it was almost dinner time. He'd be happy to turn around, but knew it was important to Jessica that they try longer.

Dee was finally making some inroads with Jessica, and regaining her trust. He knew now how much she hated violence. But he couldn't change who he was. Their group needed to be protected, and being the muscle was what he knew best. He wasn't sure how he and Jessica would navigate that challenge, but he knew they would, somehow.

He certainly loved her enough to keep trying. The feelings he had for Jessica were so foreign to him that he had trouble understanding and coping with them. At times it seemed harder to cope with than the end of civilization that they were dealing with. At least there he had a place, a role. But with this love minefield, he was out of his depth.

"I think we missed it," Jessica announced a few minutes later. "That scenic lookout point we just passed is after this farm."

"No name on the map, no sign on the road. Are you sure there's even a farm there?" Dee asked. His stomach growled again.

"Turn around. If we don't see it on the second pass, let's go home. Deal?"

"Deal," Dee answered, pulling over to the side of the road and turning the car around.

He drove slowly, as they both scanned the roadside more closely. He spotted a small dirt lane ahead.

"Let's give this one a try," he said, veering into the lane. Though he had never needed it before, he knew he could always engage the Range Rover's four-wheel drive if the lane got too rough.

Though it was narrow, the lane ended up being quite smooth to drive over. The trees were trimmed back and there were no major ruts. But after five minutes, it was Jessica who was ready to turn around.

"OK, this isn't going anywhere," she said. "If it was a farm, we would have arrived by now."

"Well, it has to lead somewhere. Is there a rule that the farm has to be near the road? Help me out here, I'm just a city boy."

Jessica laughed. "Well OK, I'm a city girl so I actually don't know what I'm talking about. Maybe I'm just looking for an excuse to turn around and go home."

"You hungry? I'm starving. Just a couple more minutes, then let's call it – whoa what's happening here?"

The lane ended abruptly, giving way to a large flat area, with a few pieces of farm machinery which Dee couldn't name scattered over it. A rusted, dented pickup truck was parked a little further, in front of a large garage. The garage was attached to a small, well-maintained house. It had neatly painted white shutters, and pale-yellow clapboard siding.

"I see farm equipment, but no animals," Jessica remarked. "Either it's a crop farm or the animals are all dead in a barn somewhere."

As if they had heard her, a pair of chickens strutted out from around the far corner of the house.

"Let's check out the inside, then we can go home and have dinner," Dee said, turning off the engine. He stepped out of the car and discretely checked his guns, hoping that the car blocked Jessica's view from his habitual check. Being tired and hungry was no excuse to let his guard down. He had seen enough people die when they cut corners at the wrong time.

If Jessica had seen him, she did not let on. She

joined him, and they walked to the front door. As per their routine, she initiated the greeting for anyone that might be inside.

"Hello, is anyone home?" she called out, rapping softly on the door. No answer. She tried again, with a louder voice and a louder knock. Still no answer.

"Over to you," she said, stepping aside.

Dee first tried the knob. It twisted easily, and he swung open the door. Barely noticing his own movement, the Glock was now in his right hand. He took a step inside the house, and let his eyes adjust to the dim light of the evening sun filtering through the windows.

The entrance led to a bigger kitchen than he had imagined for such a small house. It was remarkably tidy, very much unlike the mess they usually found in abandoned houses.

"Someone might still be living here," Dee said.

"Then where are they?" Jessica asked.

"Might have run when they saw us coming. Might just be out for a bit, who knows. Might have died recently." He shrugged his shoulders.

They walked to the other side of the kitchen where a small hallway led to a pair of rooms in the back. Dee thought one was likely to be the person's bedroom. Dee walked towards the first room, gun-hand outstretched, with Jessica following close behind. They had almost reached the room's door when a voice spoke behind them.

"Put the gun down son, nice and easy."

Dee froze. *Damn it, where did he come from?* Had he

made a mistake? He quickly replayed their entrance, and couldn't figure out where the man might have hid. Now with Jessica behind him, Dee couldn't spin around and fire, even if he had a chance.

"I see you hesitating. Thing is, I've got a twelve-gauge that I think can blow off both you and your girlfriend's heads off. That's a mess I surely do not want to be cleaning up. Please, son, put the gun down."

With no other choice, Dee bent down and placed the gun on the floor.

"Now the one sticking out the back of your pants, nice and slow," the man said.

Dee obeyed.

"And now your last one. Which ankle you got one strapped to?"

"That's all I got," Dee lied.

"You've been doing great, don't disappoint me now. I ain't got a little itty-bitty gun to wing you. If I have to get your third gun myself, you'll be a dead man by then."

The man knows his business, Dee thought grimly. He reached down to his right ankle and removed his last gun.

"That's much better. So, as you can see, I didn't run, I wasn't out for a bit and I most certainly did not die recently. You and your lady friend please walk to the end of the hall now."

Dee stepped over the guns and walked down the hall. He peered inside the bedroom as he walked by. He saw a single bed, a chest of drawers, and a small pile of books on a night table next to the bed. A closed door hid the second room's interior.

"You can turn around now," the man said when Dee and Jessica reached the end of the hallway.

Standing in front of Dee's guns was an old man. He had short, white curly hair. His ebony skin had more creases than Dee could count. Despite the tense conditions, the man's crinkly eyes and open-mouth smile were disarming. *He looks like the grandpa I never had*, Dee thought wryly.

"Name's Martin," the man said, as he shoved Dee's guns further away with his foot, towards the opposite side of the hallway. "Who might I have the pleasure of hosting in my home?"

Jessica cleared her throat. "I'm Jessica, and this is Dee. I'm sorry that we just walked in, we knocked first but there was no answer. We don't mean you any harm."

"Well now, coming into a man's home uninvited and armed to the teeth doesn't exactly scream 'I come in peace', if you know what I mean," Martin said, still smiling.

"I know how it looks," Jessica continued, "but you have to believe me, we weren't coming here to rob you or hurt you."

"You'd be a fool going anywhere without some chrome these days," Dee said sullenly.

"Ah, the young man speaks. Well, why don't you tell me — Dee was it? — why you came here then."

"We're looking for food," Dee replied.

"So, then you were here to steal," Martin chuckled.

"No, that's not true," Jessica said, squeezing Dee's arm to silence him. Dee complied. He could feel his anger rising. Martin made him feel, well, like a fool. He realized he was angrier at himself than at Martin. Dee couldn't believe how he'd let the old man surprise them. He vowed to be more vigilant, he was slipping. *It wouldn't have happened back in the hood.*

"We're not just looking for food to steal. We're looking for a working farm that might be able to provide food for the children during winter," Jessica said.

"How many children do you have? And who's watching them while you hunt around for food?"

"Honestly, I've lost count now. Maybe a hundred kids in all. A dozen adults. We're in a hotel in Rochester."

Martin laughed. "I thought you were talking about you and this young man's children. A hundred: you've been busy." He laughed again.

Jessica smiled at the man. Dee forced himself to remove the angry scowl from his face. Jessica was charming the old man, and Dee didn't want to blow her game.

"It's a long story how we got started. But the bottom line is, we are a few adults who are trying to care for a large number of unvaccinated and orphaned toddlers, and even a few babies. Food is becoming an issue, especially this coming winter."

"I surely do like long stories," Martin declared. He winced as he bent down to pick up Dee's three pistols, while keeping the shotgun aimed in their general direction.

He may be old, but he knows his way with guns, Dee thought. Martin had kept a large enough distance between them so that Dee wouldn't be able to rush him when he bent down.

"These old bones don't like to bend," Martin said, straightening back up with a grunt. "Now if you don't mind, I'll put all this firepower outside for now, just in case your young man here feels a bit of temptation to turn things around a little."

By then Martin had reached the kitchen. He walked to the door after turning his back on them. Dee tensed. Was this the right time to run and jump him?

"Don't," Jessica whispered, pulling on his arm. "He's not going to hurt us, you know that."

"No, I don't know that, and neither do you," Dee said, not quite believing his own words. Martin did indeed seem quite friendly and harmless. But Dee was still angry at his own sloppiness.

"Dee, he's a farmer, and he's alive. This is exactly what we were hoping to find."

Dee nodded, relaxing his body. She was right. He had to let go of his injured pride and see what could come of this. Though he doubted such an old man could really have a working farm.

"Come on in the kitchen folks, have a seat," Martin called to them. Dee and Jessica obeyed, and sat in two of the sturdy wooden chairs around the small kitchen table. Martin remained standing, in front of the door.

"Now Dee, before I can relax, I need to know you, in particular, a little better. You have gangbanger written all over you. Am I right?"

Dee nodded. There wasn't any point in trying to deny it, given the three pieces he was carrying.

"Why don't you tell me a bit about your crew?"

Dee shrugged. "Not much to tell, they all dead now."

"So they were all vaccinated?" Martin asked

"Most. Me and Javon were the only two holdouts."

"What happened to Javon?"

"Shot by some mofos who stole some of our young ones." The painful memory of Javon's loss washed over Dee once more, as it had so many times since his death.

"Sounds like your little group has had its share of adventures then. I'm sorry about Javon, son. Now tell me more about the old crew."

Dee sighed. He hated talking about this in front of Jessica. "Marquis was the boss. We was thirteen all together. The Lucky Thirteen. Union Heights was our hood."

"And your role in this fine organization?"

Dee shrugged again. "Just a soldier."

"I don't think so," Martin said, still smiling. "Show me your ink."

"Ain't got no ink," Dee lied. Jessica whipped her head up at him. *She ain't any good at keeping secrets.* Martin chuckled, and said nothing, waiting. Seconds passed like minutes before Dee sighed, turned his body sideways, so that Martin could see his back.

He lowered the back collar of his shirt, revealing the head of a coiled cobra.

"Dee the enforcer then," Martin exclaimed. "Now we're making progress. Honesty is the first step towards trust, wouldn't you agree?"

Both Dee and Jessica shifted in their seats. Dee wondered where this was heading. Martin recognized his tattoo immediately. Was he a former cop? If so, they were in deep trouble, he would never trust Dee. And Dee would never trust Martin.

"How did you like being the enforcer? You got respect, I'll bet."

"I did what I had to do."

"Now I get being forced to be in a gang for survival. I'm not blind to the hardships of living in the inner city. But nobody told you to become an enforcer, Dee. You could have been, like you tried to lie earlier: just a soldier. But you decided to go up a level or two. Why?"

"I dunno, it just happened."

Martin sat back, his smile fading. "That's disappointing. Here we were, building up trust at an astonishing speed. And now you're not being honest. I'm not quite sure if you're lying to me, lying to yourself, or lying to Jessica over here," Martin said, pointing to Jessica.

Dee felt increasingly uncomfortable. Why was Martin probing like this? And why was he picking such damn personal questions? Dee himself had never really thought about why he became an enforcer.

"I ain't lying to you. I... I guess it was to impress Marquis. I wanted his respect most of all."

"Because he was the boss," Martin said.

Dee hesitated a moment before shaking his head. "No, because he the only one who saw something in me. He picked me off the street and made me a somebody. Someone throws you lifeline like that, you don't forget you owe them. And you spend your days making sure they don't decide they made a mistake on you."

Dee emphasized his point by stabbing the table with his finger multiple times while talking. He was angry at Martin for bringing up old shit.

"That's good, son," Martin said, smiling and nodding. "Very good. We're almost done with the questions, I know this is hard on you. Now how are you running your new 'crew', so to speak. A bunch of children in a hotel: not exactly an enforcer's paradise, right?"

"It's a lot closer to paradise than living in the streets. We peaceful, get it? I ain't running nothing. We got Deb, she's the top dog. Her lieutenant Mo. They good people. They put me in charge of security, trying to keep them all safe. We're holed up in a big hotel, it's like our fortress. Not too hard to defend, if we had more adults. And the kids, well, are kids, you know. Sometimes a pain in the ass but mostly just fun to play with."

Martin sat back in his chair, staring at Dee. It made him uncomfortable, as if the man could see inside his soul. Finally, Martin broke his stare with laughter.

"I have to say, you surprise me, son." He chuckled some more. "In a good way though, in a good way. So, if you're supposed to keep them safe, why are you all the way out here with this young lady?"

"Jessica wanted to go look for farms. She's our only doc, I wasn't going to let her go alone."

Martin's eyes widened in surprise. "So it's Doctor Jessica then," he exclaimed, turning his attention to Jessica.

"I'm not an actual doctor, I just have some medical training. As I keep saying over and over again." She elbowed Dee for emphasis, while smiling at Martin.

Well, she trusts him, Dee realized.

"It seems you've earned everyone's respect for your limited training. Don't fight it, embrace it. I'll bet you give hope to a lot of your fellow survivors," Martin said.

Jessica swallowed, and nodded. "Thank you, I'll try."

"Now how do you see this farm thing working out? Money doesn't mean anything anymore. What are you going to offer this lonely old farmer in exchange for food?"

Dee tensed. Martin was addressing Jessica now.

Martin laughed out loud. "Good Lord, Dee, you are one high-strung young man. I didn't mean anything disrespectful. I'm trying to understand your proposal is all."

Martin chuckled some more before turning his

attention back to Jessica. Dee was surprised and annoyed at how little Martin missed.

Jessica cleared her throat. "Well, we can't offer anything of value, that's true. What we're hoping for is that altruism becomes the norm, now that we're essentially trying to save our civilization. The children are going to have an enormous task ahead of them as adults. So really, we're looking for volunteer farmers. We can help with some of the farm labor, or hunting for supplies, that kind of thing."

"I lost most of my crops, truth be told. I need an irrigation system of sorts," Martin said, shaking his head in dismay.

"I've got some guys that can help with that," Jessica exclaimed. "Joshua is brilliant with science and engineering, and Chris and Titus are like the MacGyvers of the post-apocalypse!"

"Don't forget Amanda and her computers, Jess. She can probably find out all kinds of shit about irrigation in the old days," Dee added.

"Brilliant! Of course," Jessica added, twisting in her seat.

"Well now, this is almost sounding like a workable plan, I have to say," Martin said, nodding.

"So you're in? You'll help us?" Jessica asked.

"No, I didn't say that. Yet. Don't get ahead of yourself young lady. We're still just getting to know each other. But, I think I can put this away, now." Martin swiveled the shotgun so that it pointed at the ceiling. "Am I right son?"

He stared hard at Dee. Dee nodded, clearing his throat. He couldn't help but trust and respect the old man. Martin nodded and passed the shotgun over to Dee. Dee's eyes widened in surprise.

"Can you put that down over in the corner by the door, please?"

Dee took the shotgun from Martin. He had expected to feel a sense of power and safety to flush through him, now that he held the gun. But oddly enough, he felt nothing. Just like a friend was passing him a coat to hang. Dee nodded at Martin, stood, and propped the shotgun up next to the front door. Martin nodded back at him with a small smile when Dee sat back down. Dee looked over at Jessica. She was smiling at him too.

"I'm hungry," Martin declared. "It's dinner time, and I would like you to stay for dinner. We can chat some more, I sorely miss company. Will you?"

"Love to, I'm starving," Dee said.

"That's very kind of you, Martin," Jessica said.

For the next hour they exchanged stories about how they had survived in the dying days of the Vax Plague. Jessica and Dee had a lot more stories to tell than Martin. His life hadn't changed as dramatically as theirs, whereas they had stories to tell about all the people at the hotel. Martin had killed a chicken, and was preparing a large soup over a small propane stove. Dee was almost salivating from the delicious smell. Martin added potatoes, carrots, and cabbage to the soup.

As Martin began to serve the soup, Jessica

declined a bowl. "I'm vegetarian," she explained.

Damn, thought Dee, *I should have said something when he went to get a chicken.* The truth was, he'd forgotten about her vegetarian diet. He felt guilty, like he had let her down.

Martin seemed confused. "Didn't you say you wanted to get some meat supply?"

"Yes, for the children, and other adults. Being vegetarian is my choice, I don't impose it on others."

"May I ask why you are a vegetarian?" Martin asked.

"Lots of reasons. Cruelty to animals is the first. I really do believe our generation will go down in history as barbarians for the way we treat animals in the food factories. And for ecological reasons, greenhouse gases, and the like. I also believe that a balanced vegetarian diet is healthier for humans than a meat-based diet."

Martin passed the bowl he had intended for Jessica over to Dee. He sat down, seeming to consider Jessica's words. Meanwhile, Dee's stomach continued its rumbling protest. How he wanted to dig into his soup.

"You make some interesting points, Doctor Jessica," Martin began. "And I might even have considered following you before the VP. But, I don't think any of your reasons are still valid. Factory farms are all gone, and I don't see them coming back for a few generations at least. Look at my chickens, they're running free. Greenhouse gases? Global warming? Not a problem anymore with most of the human population gone. And what was your last point? Healthy eating? That was fine when you could go into the supermarket and get every variety of bean and vegetables that you wanted. But when food is scarce, you'll be hard pressed to get a better meal than meat and a few veggies."

Jessica sat back, looking at Martin. Then she laughed, shaking her head. "Oh my God how things have changed. I don't know how long it's going to take for everything to really sink in."

Martin tenderly put his hand on hers. "I think you're coping amazingly well. Give yourself time, Jessica. We all need to give ourselves time. If nothing else, humans have proven to be remarkably adaptable."

Jessica nodded. "Yeah, I agree, it's just, well, so bloody hard."

"Know what would help?" Martin asked.

"Tell me," she said, smiling up at him.

"Chicken soup." They all had a good laugh. Dee felt a warmth inside him, everything about this was good.

"Come on Jess, have some soup," Dee urged.

"No, I can't change overnight. But I do need to reflect on what you said, Martin. You're a wise man."

"Ha, you clearly don't know me well," Martin replied. "How about just the vegetables and a bit of broth? You need to eat something."

Jessica hesitated, then nodded. "Sure, thank you, that sounds wonderful."

They ate mostly in silence. Dee eagerly accepted

a second bowl of soup. It was the best tasting meal he could remember. He also enjoyed the unfamiliar normalcy of three peaceful adults sharing a meal around the dinner table.

"A pretty homey meal, eh Mr. Enforcer?" Martin said, as if reading Dee's mind.

"Please don't call me that. That was a lifetime ago."

"I'm sorry, Dee, I meant no disrespect," Martin replied. He paused a moment before continuing. "But life in a crew was very exciting, right? Adrenaline on the go all the time. Don't you miss it, or parts of it at least?"

Dee thought about the question before answering. "No," he finally said. "Well, I do miss my friends, no doubt. But that life compared to what I've got now? Nothing to miss there."

Martin nodded thoughtfully. "We're not born violent. We're born innocent and pure. It's what we're surrounded with that makes us violent, or makes some people turn bad. I truly believe that," he finished, his gaze alternating between Dee and Jessica.

After they had hand-pumped some water from Martin's well, and finished cleaning up the dinner dishes, Jessica returned to the subject of food supply.

"I hate to press you on this again Martin, but will you help us and the children with food?"

Martin paused, as he was putting away the now empty and cleaned cooking pot. "One thing I've learned over the years is to never rush big decisions.

I need to sleep on this one, and I'll give you an answer tomorrow. Now it's getting late for me, I need my beauty sleep you see," he smiled at Jessica, his eyes twinkling in the candlelight.

Martin carefully placed the cooking pot in a low cupboard, and stood back up, placing both of his hands on his lower back. He couldn't quite hide a small grimace of pain.

"I've got a spare bedroom in the back. Sheets might be a little dusty, I can't remember the last time I had guests over. Dee, why don't you grab the top sheet and give it a shake outside."

"Um, we're staying overnight?" Dee asked, looking back and forth between Martin and Jessica. Jessica looked as puzzled and uncertain as he was.

"It's getting late, it's dark out, no need for you to find your way home tonight. And like I said, I'll give you an answer in the morning. Now if you'll excuse me, I'm done for the day." Martin took one of the two candles and walked towards his bedroom. "Have a good night you two, don't light the place on fire with the other candle."

And with that, he shut his bedroom door, leaving Dee and Jessica alone in the kitchen.

"Interesting man," Jessica whispered.

Dee nodded. "Sure ain't how I imagined it would go down," he whispered back.

"Do you think he'll agree to help us?"

"Hard to say, he's not an easy one to read. If I had to guess, I would say yes."

"Fingers crossed, I hope you're right."

They made their way into the spare bedroom and stood over the double bed.

"This isn't awkward," Jessica remarked.

"Don't sweat it, I'll sleep on the floor. Wouldn't be the first time," Dee said.

Jessica touched his arm. "No, don't."

Dee woke up to the delicious smell of frying eggs.

"Good morning," Jessica murmured, her head on his chest.

"Is that butter-fried eggs I smell?" he asked, sniffing the air.

"'Good morning Jessica, how wonderful to wake up with you in my arms.' That would be a better response than 'is that butter-fried eggs my stupid man-brain is registering'," Jessica replied.

Dee chuckled. "I'm sorry Jess, you're right. But damn... butter!"

Jessica pinched his side, hard.

"Oww!" he whispered, squirming away from her hand.

"When you two are done your morning coo-coo'ing, come and have some breakfast," Martin called out from the kitchen.

"I don't have any wheat crop yet, so I can't offer you any toast," Martin said as they arrived into the kitchen. "I'm going to have to find some wheat seeds and plant them next year though. Never grown wheat before, not sure how it'll turn out."

"Where did you get butter?" Dee asked.

"I didn't get any, I made some. Butter churn," he

said pointing to a small device on the far counter. Dee had always imagined butter churns as large wooden contraptions from the eighteen-hundreds. This looked like a Mason jar with a metal gear on top.

"You make your own butter? Unbelievable," Dee said.

"Where are your cows, we didn't see anything but a few chickens," asked Jessica.

"Back field, I'll give you a tour after breakfast."

Dee saw Jessica wringing her hands, shifting her weight from one foot to another. He knew she wanted to ask Martin about his support, but didn't want to push him.

"Go ahead, say what's on your mind. Or ask what's on your mind, I guess," Martin said, smiling at Jessica.

He really don't miss much.

"OK – have you decided to help us?" Jessica asked.

Martin placed a plate of eggs on the table. He stood and shifted his gaze from Jessica to Dee, and back to Jessica.

"Running a farm is a lot of work. A lot more than you probably think," he said.

"We can help. We don't have a lot of adults, I'll admit. But we'll help as much as we can," Jessica said in a pleading voice.

"I will help you," Martin began, before being interrupted by a joyous whoop from Jessica. "But on one condition," he added loudly, to be heard about Jessica's cry of joy. "And this is non-negotiable, so think about it carefully."

"Anything," Jessica said more calmly. "If it's in our power, we'll do it."

"It isn't 'we' in this case," Martin said, turning towards Dee. "It's 'he'".

Dee shifted uncomfortably. "Bring it on Bro, what you need?"

"First, I am not your 'Bro' young man, have a bit more respect for your elders."

The sudden change in Martin's easygoing demeanor startled Dee.

"Sorry Martin, I didn't mean no disrespect."

"Second, I won't be able to run this farm for much longer. I'm seventy-two years old. Farming is a young man's game. And this farm will need to expand if it's supposed to feed a village full of children. So I will agree to help if you take over this farm. You'll work with me for as many years as I've got left, and then you continue without me."

Dee laughed out loud at the absurdity of the idea. Him? Never mind even helping on a farm, but running it?

"I'm sorry Martin, but haven't you heard anything about where I come from? I don't know shit about farming."

"Third, you're going to clean up your language."

"Bro, what did you smoke this morning?" The situation was losing its humor, as Dee realized Martin was serious.

"I said stop it with the 'Bro'. You've got a good head on your shoulders, you'll learn. And you have the gift of a healthy young man's body, something you can't really appreciate until you're old and gray."

"Martin, seriously, I will not be any good at this, you've got the wrong man for the job."

"I don't think so. And for the record, I knew nothing about farming when I got started, some forty years ago."

Martin turned sideways and leaned towards Dee. He tugged at the back collar of his own shirt, revealing the top of a faded coiled cobra tattoo.

20. NEGOTIATIONS

"**S**outh is not an option," said Captain Tiago Fernandez. "There are far too many crazies with guns down there. They're fighting among themselves for control. You and the children wouldn't survive."

Amanda watched Deb to see her reaction. Migrating south had been Deb's plan, almost an obsession, and she had grown increasingly annoyed with any opposition to the idea.

"We've had our share of violence here as well, Captain Fernandez," Deb said. "We take our security very seriously, and will of course be extremely cautious."

"And how did that help you when we arrived at your doorstep?" he asked.

The truth was, it hadn't helped one bit, Amanda realized. Despite all of their preparations and guidance from Dee, Fernandez and his men proved they were hopelessly vulnerable. Dee had prepared defenses against roaming bandits, not an army. When Deb had failed to turn them away from up on the balcony, they'd had to let them in. Captain Fernandez had correctly pointed out that they could blast their way in, causing tremendous fear and trauma in the children. And so, without a shot being fired, the soldiers had entered their hotel. Their home.

What Amanda wanted to know was Captain Fernandez' intentions. However malevolent or benign, she intended to use her negotiation skills to secure their wellbeing. She didn't want Deb to get into a head-butting contest.

"Is that why you left the south? To get away from the violence?" Amanda asked, before Deb could argue further about migration plans.

"Partially," the captain admitted. "There is this dominant player right now, and they're too powerful to take on by ourselves. We headed to D.C., hoping there might be some vestiges of government and defense there, but we found nothing substantial. So now we're heading up towards Vermont, or maybe across the border into Ontario or Quebec. Somewhere we can regroup and grow."

"You're going to invade Canada?" Mo asked, smiling.

"Borders don't mean much anymore," the captain replied, without a hint of a smile.

"Who is this 'dominant player', that you mentioned?" Deb asked.

"They call themselves the New Libertarians. Which is ironic, because what they are really about is taking away liberties from the people that fall into their territory. They don't tolerate any difference of opinion from their dogmatic beliefs. They're power-hungry expansionists, and pose the biggest threat to our future, in my opinion. They already control large swaths of the south, from Florida to the Carolinas."

"Closer to home, can I ask what your intentions are regarding our community?" Amanda finally asked.

Fernandez cleared his throat. "Well first, let me assure you that we mean you no harm. What you've built here is impressive and demonstrates a level of kind-heartedness that's getting harder and harder to find. But I've been answering a lot of your questions, and it's time that you answer some of mine."

His avoidance of her question put Amanda on alert. What did he want with them? What was he planning? She wasn't the only one who was worried by his deflection. Deb frowned, and Mo backed up his chair an inch or two as he shifted in his seat. Amanda was glad Deb had agreed to have just the three of them be present in their talks with Fernandez. She didn't think Joshua, or Titus for that matter, would have been able to stay calm in this situation.

"What do you want to know?" Deb asked.

"In a nutshell: your story. How did you get started, how did you end up here, where do you see your community ending up? What's the end game here?"

Deb told them a brief history of their group, starting from a small group of stragglers to the operation they had going at the hotel today. Fernandez raised an eyebrow when she retold the events around the children's kidnapping and the rescue at the Amish farm. But other than that, he listened quietly, rarely interrupting to ask a question.

"And now you've shown up at our door, so you are the one deciding the end game," Deb finished.

Fernandez shook his head. "No, we're just passing through, Deb. We won't change your plans."

Amanda felt an immediate sense of relief, mixed with disbelief. Could it be that easy? This small army would just walk away?

"I am aware that I'm being forceful about your proposed migration south. But that's because it's suicide, and you don't seem to understand that," Fernandez added.

Before Deb could answer, Amanda jumped into the conversation. "We hear you Captain, but give us some time to absorb the news. We've been planning and working towards our move south for a long time. It's hard to suddenly have to drop it."

"But now back to Amanda's question," Mo said. "Are your intentions really that you're just going to move on? You're leaving us alone?"

Fernandez took a deep breath. His hand started tapping his knee, alternating between his thumb and pinky. Amanda found it amusing, almost like his hand was a butterfly. Nervous ticks were a dead giveaway when there was something bigger on someone's mind. She had learned that first hand in the many government functions she'd attended in the evenings with her husband.

"Captain Fernandez?" Deb prodded.

"We've actually met people like you on our

way here. Small clusters of adults who took it on themselves to care for some orphaned children. Never anything this size, or this well organized," Fernandez said, waving his arms in a circle, trying to encompass their hotel. "We've also encountered groups this size, but they were intent on their own survival and wellbeing. And they used violence to achieve their goals. What we haven't encountered yet is a group this size that is peaceful. That's what makes your community so unique."

"Credit to Deb for that, she's a master at nipping in the bud, when it comes to conflicts," Amanda acknowledged.

"And reminding us constantly that as long as we put the children first, then we're doing the right thing," Mo added.

"Those are just words," Deb said. "If I wasn't surrounded by good and sane people, the words would fall on deaf ears."

Fernandez nodded thoughtfully. "You're still having trouble accepting credit for your leadership, it seems."

Deb seemed flustered. "It's a team effort is all I'm trying to say."

"Deb, think about it. None of this, absolutely none of it, would have happened without you," Amanda said.

"It's true, but let the good Captain continue. He still hasn't said if he's really just going to walk away with all of his soldiers," Mo said.

"OK, well, we tried to stamp out the violent

groups when we could," Fernandez continued. "But the small bands of Child Savers, as we called them, more often than not, they would pack up and follow us, hoping for some protection."

"What happened to them? You don't have any children with you now," Deb asked.

"I've divided my men into two companies. We're the advanced company. I've got another one hundred and fifty men in the rear company, escorting the Child Savers. They're about a day behind us."

"This is only half your men?" Mo said, looking at the two-armed guards behind the captain. Amanda knew he was considering them as representatives of the two hundred men spread around inside and outside the hotel.

"How many Child Savers are they escorting?" Deb asked, before Fernandez could answer Mo's somewhat rhetorical question.

"I, uh, don't know the exact number. Several hundred, maybe close to a thousand."

Amanda gasped.

"A thousand?" Deb cried out.

"Less than, but close to. Call it eight or nine hundred," Fernandez replied.

"So you're migrating them north, while we were planning to migrate south. Ironic," Mo said, shaking his head in wonder.

"We're not migrating them anywhere. Like I said we're looking to set up our base somewhere around the Vermont area, and they're choosing to follow us.

We don't turn good people away, and we don't force any civilians to come with us."

"Sir?" one of the men behind Fernandez interrupted.

"Harper?" Fernandez replied, turning towards the man.

"Guzo, err, I mean Corporal Gonzales, told me the other day that the Savers are grumbling about all the distance they've come. When they see this place, they might want to stay."

Mo and Amanda's voices blended as they loudly protested in unison. Nine hundred refugees? *We can't accommodate those people*, Amanda thought. It was physically impossible to hold that many in their hotel. But even if they expanded to other sites, managing that many would be a staggering feat.

"We've never turned away good people either," Deb said calmly.

Amanda stared open-mouthed at Deb. A thousand questions threatened to spill out, but she held her tongue. Where was Deb going with this?

"For the sake of argument, let's say that they would want to stay with us," Deb continued. "We would need a lot of things from you in order to take them off your hands."

Fernandez shifted in his seat. "Go on."

"I can talk to Titus and Chris, they're the ones who maintain the hotel. I doubt we can fit all those people in this hotel, but they might have a different opinion. I doubt it, but maybe. But even if they could squeeze them in, we would soon need to expand to either a bigger location, or to several adjoining locations. We can't split into two totally separate places. So, we need to find a suitable place, and some help to set it up. Titus and Chris worked miracles with this hotel, but I can't expect them to do it for a group almost ten times our size."

"Done," Fernandez replied. "We can stay behind while you setup. I've got a hundred men who would be happy to stay put for a while and help out."

"Deb, you can't be serious. How —" Mo began.

"There's more," Deb continued, overriding Mo's objections. "A group that size needs some sort of governance. They outnumber us, so we can't force them to think our way. But we do need to work out a common vision forward before we accept to merge with them. Amanda can lead that effort. She's got a government background, and has already proposed a new constitution."

"Wait a sec, a new constitution? How did that come up?" Fernandez asked.

Deb paused, looking over at Amanda. *Yeah, and you made fun of me at the time*, Amanda thought. "Well, I just thought, even at our small size, we had different skills, different viewpoints. It was all manageable now, but it seems we keep growing. So, to prepare for when we had a lot people, in the future, not tomorrow," she emphasized, "I thought it might be good to start thinking about how to run ourselves. Without all the failings of today's government system."

Amanda braced herself for the captain's ridicule,

but he didn't even crack a smile. *He's taking me seriously.*

"She means an open government. No more keeping secrets from the people, no more corrupt lobbying, but a real government for the people," Mo said.

"You mean like our forefathers intended," Fernandez said.

"Partly. They got a lot of it right, but not all. We can learn from their mistakes, and from the tendency of power-hungry people to pervert a good idea," Amanda replied. She still enjoyed how well she and Mo connected on these issues.

"OK, I can help with that," Fernandez said.

"We're not interested in a military based constitution," Mo said, raising his voice.

"Hell no, I want nothing to do with your constitution. I'm a soldier, not a politician. But I can give your group the credibility it needs, and deserves, for the Savers to agree to work with you. With Amanda, in this case," he said, nodding towards Amanda.

"I need Mo as well, we're on the same page in this regard. And Deb of course, we need her leadership," Amanda said.

"No, I'm the shepherd, not a politician either," Deb laughed.

"You organize yourselves however you like, I'll just make sure that they recognize your authority," Fernandez said.

"And the last thing," Deb said. "You need to leave

half your men behind, to protect us."

Fernandez sat back, staring at Deb. Then he leaned forward, towards her. "Out of the question. We need to regroup and prepare for eventual battle with the New Libertarians. I can't cut my force in half. I can leave you fifty men on a temporary basis. They'll help prepare your defenses, provide some training. But that's it."

"Then no deal. I will not be responsible for a thousand people without any protection," Deb said adamantly.

Fernandez took a deep breath. "Like I said, I don't control them, they are deciding to follow us. When they see your hotel, they'll be inspired, shall we say, to put roots down here. I can't stop them. How will you?"

Deb crossed her arms. Amanda recognized that stubborn look of hers.

"I didn't say I would stop them. But I certainly don't have to let them inside our home," Deb said.

"So you'll start competing with them for food, water, shelter. That sounds like a smart way to go," Fernandez replied, his voice rising.

"Deb, Captain Fernandez, stop. Butting heads gets us nowhere," Amanda interrupted. "Let's go back to this topic in a few minutes, cool down a bit." She turned towards Fernandez. "I get that you want to regroup, but you never told us what's in Vermont. Why there?"

With reluctance, it seemed, Fernandez turned his angry stare away from Deb. "Not sure why that's relevant, but there are several reasons. First, an abundance of natural resources to build with. Lots of forests for cover and defense. Plus, a fairly high proportion of isolated population. We're hoping to find recruits essentially, there should be more unvaccinated in those areas. Not to mention the small militias in the remote north east. And finally, like I mentioned, we'll have some incursions north into Canada. We plan to scope out the Native American reserves in those areas. Again, looking for unvaccinated people that want to join our unit."

Amanda looked at Deb and Mo. She was unsure if she should proceed with her thoughts before consulting them. Deb simply had a sour expression, likely still upset with not getting what she wanted from Fernandez. Mo returned Amanda's gaze, cocking his head slightly in curiosity. Amanda pressed forward.

"Well, if you're interested in militias, you're going the wrong way. Head straight west from here, through the southern tip of Canada, and you'll reach our Michigan friends nearby. It's probably closer than Vermont, and a lot more militia for you to pick from. First Nations? There you're right, head north east into Ontario and especially Quebec."

"Tell me something I don't know," Fernandez interrupted. "Why the geography lesson?"

"You're in upstate New York right now," Amanda continued undeterred. "Surely you've seen how much forest we have here. Plenty of fresh water, game, foresty defenses, whatever you need if those badass New Libertarians try to make their way north." She paused looking around. All eyes were on her now. "There are things you want to the east, and things you want to the west. This area has all the requirements for setting up your base. So why don't you? Set up here, send some men east and west to recruit, but settle here."

"Uh, Amanda, are you sure?" Mo asked anxiously.

"I trust what the captain said, Mo. He has no ambitions to set up a military dictatorship, right Captain?"

Fernandez nodded, studying her.

"This is our chance, Mo. We can create the type of government we always wished for, while benefitting from excellent protection right at our doorstep. It's like karma or something, everything coming together." Amanda shot to her feet with the growing excitement, as she began pacing around the room. "Deb, you would be our new George Washington, our first president in this new world. Mo and I will work in the background to prepare the new constitution. The captain and his men and women will setup whatever defenses they need, with our support. Don't you all see? This is it! This is the new beginning."

"A government that's really for the people, this time," Mo said dreamily. "I'm in, Amanda, you're right. This is not only the chance of a lifetime, but the chance of … of a nation."

"The south though, remember why we chose to migrate? The amount of energy we will waste just trying to keep warm," Deb said.

"Honestly Deb, a lot of people were unhappy with that plan," Amanda admitted. "Several came to me saying that this was their home, they didn't want to move. Mo and Titus told me the same thing, people approached them as well."

"What? Are you serious? Why am I hearing about this now?" Deb said, her cheeks turning red.

"Because we love you, and you led us this far. We want to continue following your lead," Mo said. "But Deb, you heard what's waiting for us in the south. It's just not an option."

Amanda loved the way Mo could disarm people with his genuine warmth. She knew the two of them would work wonderfully together if this opportunity came through.

"He's right, you need to get south out of your head," Fernandez reiterated.

Deb seemed deflated. Amanda racked her brain trying to find ways to pump her back up. They needed Deb on their side.

"Truth is, I never really wanted to go south either," Deb said with a small smile. "It was best for the group, I truly believed that. But it felt like leaving home."

"So you're in then?" Amanda asked.

"I'm in, as far as not going south. But before you get into your constitution talks, we need to understand what will happen with these thousand people arriving in a day or so. I already mentioned defense, and the captain here doesn't seem to want to help. But there's also the logistics. They could eat through our meager food stores in a couple of days."

"'An army marches on its stomach', if I may quote Napoleon," Fernandez said. "The US Army is obsessed with logistics. We've been gathering food as we go. There are trucks full of food with the Savers. And stocked warehouses that we registered and mapped, to go back to. We're not dumping a starving horde on you."

"Hopefully you're not dumping anyone on us. I want you to be included in 'us'. Will you stay, Captain Fernandez?" asked Amanda.

"I won't deny that you make a compelling argument. And I pity the poor soul who will choose to argue against your ideas. But I'm not going to upend my strategy on one carefully crafted, and I don't mean this meanly, but a carefully crafted and self-serving speech."

Amanda knew better than to bite on the self-serving jab. And besides, he was correct. It was self-serving in the sense that she wanted to protect their community, and extend that protection to a much larger group of like-minded people she had not met yet.

"Can you please explain to me why my proposal is a worse plan than your current strategy?" Amanda asked.

Fernandez laughed out loud. It surprised Amanda on several fronts. First, she hadn't said anything funny. Second, she hadn't even seen him crack a smile until now. Third, and most surprising, he had an unexpectedly jolly laugh, similar to a child. Amanda couldn't help but smile and chuckle herself.

"What's so funny?" she asked, bewildered.

"Your persistence. Or stubbornness? Whichever, it's both irritating and charming," Fernandez replied.

"It's persistence, definitely persistence. I own the stubbornness around here," Deb said, smiling as well.

"I've listened to your arguments. I don't intend to change my mind, but I do want to think about it carefully. I'm tired. My men are tired. We're going to move out of your hotel and find a place to hole up for the night. We'll talk again in the morning."

"Nothing is more difficult, and therefore more precious, than to be able to decide," Mo said.

"Excuse me?" Fernandez asked.

"Napoleon," Mo said, smiling smugly.

Fernandez chuckled, shaking his head. "You people are something else." He stood to leave.

"Captain, the top floors are unoccupied. You and your men are welcome to stay the night. It'll be crowded, but it's better than roaming around looking for a place to crash," Deb announced.

Amanda was profoundly grateful to Deb for extending the invitation. An olive branch from Deb meant as much as any cajoling on Amanda's part. Not to mention that it might give her the opportunity to talk some more with the captain tonight and argue her case further.

"That could have gone a lot worse," Deb said, after

Fernandez and his two guards had left the room. She stood and paced back and forth from the door to the window.

"A lot worse," Mo agreed.

"So now what? How do we prepare for almost one thousand people coming our way?" Amanda asked.

"Honestly, we don't have time to prepare at all. What we do depends on Captain Fernandez," Deb said.

"Does it really, Deb? What if he packs up and buggers off? Are you really going to lock up the hotel and not deal with these people?" Amanda asked.

"What choice do I have? Without protection, how can I, how can we, be responsible for their safety?"

"In the same way we're responsible for our own safety now," Mo said. "We'll figure it out, and do what we can. Do you remember what you told me the first day we met, when you showed up at my door with Lucy in a shopping cart?"

"No, but I suspect you're about to tell me, and it will make my refusal to help these people look bad," Deb replied with a wry smile.

"It will," Mo admitted, also smiling. "You said that there were going to be thousands of orphaned children that needed saving. Thousands. I thought you were crazy trying to take that on, with one child and a shopping cart. But I was wrong. One step at a time, one child at a time, you kept at it, and got us where we are today. Now a thousand people are arriving tomorrow. We say 'people' like they're all adults. But in reality, we can probably expect the same adult-child ratio as here. Which means maybe seven or eight hundred children. And they need saving, just as much as Lucy, Ben, Sophia, and all the others we know and love dearly."

"Damn you, and your memory," Deb said, slumping back down into her chair.

"I sense where this is going," Amanda said. "But Captain Fernandez is not to know any of this. We need to keep the thumbscrews on him. Let him believe that we'll abandon those folks without his protection. That is, I'm assuming we all agree that we want him to stay, right?"

Deb nodded, her position was already clear.

Mo hesitated before finally answering. "Yeah, I agree. You of all people understand my innate distrust of institutions. But I believe him when he says he wants nothing to do with running a government. We lucked out big time with him, he's not a wannabe dictator. So yes, we want and need him and his small army."

"Either way, it looks like you're going to get to play out your crazy constitution fantasy, Amanda," Deb said, shaking her head.

"So that's what you really thought about it all this time? A crazy fantasy?" Amanda asked. She put her hands on her hips in mock anger.

"Hatched by two crazy conspiracy theorists, yep," Deb replied laughing.

"We finally get to stick it to the man," Mo whooped.

They all chuckled, after which Amanda said "Ok,

let me see if I can find the good captain and work on him a little more tonight."

"Are you sure it's not better to give him some space? Sometimes pushing too hard makes a person push back," Deb warned.

"I'll be careful. Remember that I've watched these sorts of negotiations countless times. If I sense he's digging in his heels out of defensiveness, I'll back off right away. But it's important to press the point, and try to understand what his resistance is."

Deb and Mo agreed. Amanda's pulse was racing. As much as she despised the politics of the old world, in this new world it was exhilarating.

21. INFLUX

Mo kept pacing as they waited for Fernandez to come join them for breakfast. 'Funny Fernandez', as Mo had started calling the man, due to his complete absence of humor. It wasn't because he was nervous that Mo paced, but more to stay awake. He and Amanda had been up most of the night. They had intended to talk about ways to convince Fernandez to stay, should this morning's decision not be favorable. But instead, they had spent most of the time bouncing ideas off of each other regarding the new government that they would help establish, along with a newly drafted constitution.

Amanda seemed perfectly composed as she sat patiently. Deb fidgeted with her gray cotton blouse, twirling one button one way and then the other. They had opened up some canned peaches, and two granola bars each. Glasses of water completed the meager breakfast spread. He was hungry and couldn't wait to have some of the sweetened, syrupy peaches.

"Sit down Maurice, you're making me nervous," Deb said.

"Maybe it's not my pacing Deb. Maybe it's something else, like, oh, I don't know, the birth of a new nation?" Mo replied.

"I guess you and Amanda have been at it already,

right?"

He wished that the innuendo was true. But the conversations had been almost as good. What they were about to embark on was exciting, with or without Captain Fernandez.

Hoover padded silently into the carpeted room. He went over to Mo first, for a sniff and a quick lick.

"Worst guard dog ever," Mo chided him.

"Not true, licking the first soldier's gun muzzle was pretty disarming in a Gandhi sort of way," Amanda said.

Mo chuckled, petting Hoover's head and doing his best to avoid the wet licks.

"At least he wasn't like Nancy, nowhere to be found," Deb remarked.

"Cats suck, eh boy?" Mo said, ruffling the lab's big ears.

Fernandez finally arrived and knocked on the open door before stepping inside the room. *No escorts this time, he's starting to trust us*, Mo thought. Hoover quickly retreated from the room.

"Good morning, everyone," Fernandez said.

"Have a seat, Captain." Deb gestured at the seat across from her.

"We can skip the small talk during breakfast, let me jump right to it," he began, as he sat down.

The man's words easily brushed aside Mo's yearning for the peaches. He appreciated a straight shooter, and was pleased that Fernandez didn't stretch out the moment, toying with them.

"I am not committing to a permanent base here,"

Fernandez said. He met everyone's gaze in turn.

Mo heard Deb exhale audibly, deflated. Amanda straightened in her chair and cleared her throat. Before she could speak, Fernandez held up his hand.

"But, you do make a good point about us needing to look both west and north-east. So, I am committing to spending the winter here. I'll send out scouting parties in both directions and keep a strong presence here for your protection. Both from outside forces that may come, and, hopefully not, but also keeping the peace within your new, much larger community."

"That's good news Captain," Deb said, visibly relieved. "That buys us a lot of time."

"What happens after the winter?" Mo asked.

"I don't know," Fernandez replied. "It depends what happens here, what happens south, and what the scouting parties find. I can't predict any of those things at this point."

He's just being non-committal, Mo realized. This was great news. If everything worked out as they hoped, then Fernandez wouldn't have any reason to move out in the spring.

"Who knows, you might get some recruits from the adults in the Savers coming our way," Amanda said.

"If the adults are spread as thinly among the children as we are, then we can't afford any of them joining the army," Deb said. "But training several of our adults in fighting might be a great help to us."

"I was thinking the same thing," said Fernandez,

381

nodding. "Use the winter to train you in self defense, and to help set up a more defensible position."

A loud rap at the door interrupted their conversation.

"Sorry Sir, but we found these two trying to sneak up on one of our positions. They were armed," the soldier at the door explained. He walked into the room, followed by Dee and Jessica, their arms zip-tied behind their backs. Two more soldiers followed close behind.

"Jesus! Let them go," Deb cried out, leaping to her feet.

Mo and Amanda also stood. Dee tried to move past the soldier who had spoken, but one of the soldiers grabbed his arm from behind. Dee shoved him backwards with his shoulder. Dee continued to struggle as the other soldiers held him.

"Get your fucking hands off me," Dee shouted.

"Stop! All of you," Fernandez commanded.

His men loosened their grip on Dee, who quickly shook them off and faced Fernandez defiantly.

"I take it they're with you?" Fernandez asked Deb.

"They are. They were out searching for food supplies before you arrived."

"Let them go," Mo said, relieved that Deb didn't expose Dee as their security chief. Somehow Mo was worried that might raise questions. *The less you say, the better*, was his adage for dealing with anyone in authority. "You can't blame them for not trusting you when they arrive to an occupying force in their home."

Fernandez stood and nodded to one of his soldiers. "Cut 'em loose."

"Who are these people?" Jessica asked, rubbing her wrists and moving to Deb's side. Dee ambled over, glaring at each soldier and bumping the nearest one's shoulder as he passed by.

"I'll let you do the explaining," Fernandez said. "Thanks for the breakfast, but I've got a lot to do." He grabbed his two granola bars, but left the peaches behind.

"Shut the door," Amanda said when the soldiers were gone.

"Where have you two been? I was so worried when you didn't show up last night," Deb said.

"Long story, first tell us what's happening with all these soldiers," said Dee.

They told Dee and Jessica about Fernandez and his men, as well as the coming horde of Child Savers.

"It's a lot to take in, we're still trying to get our heads around it," Mo said.

"Do they have a physician? They must have some sort of medic," Jessica asked.

"Sorry, we didn't think of asking that," Amanda admitted.

"Why aren't they dead? Didn't Uncle Sam force soldiers to get vaxxed?" Dee asked.

"They tried, and got most of them. But some delayed with medical exemption claims and various other refusal reasons. Most who refused were thrown out of the army. Who knows what the story is with Captain Fernandez and his men, maybe they're mostly ex-army for all we know," Mo said.

"That wasn't discussed, how do you know this stuff?" Deb asked.

"That's my thing, I followed everything about vaxxing, even blogged about it," Mo admitted.

"How do you know we can trust them?" Dee asked. "They don't seem like the friendly types to me," he added, rubbing his wrists.

"No, I can see why they wouldn't come across as neighborly to you, given your first encounter," Deb said. "But the truth is they would much rather move on and do their soldiering than stay here and babysit a civilian population."

"What about you two, did you have any luck contacting farmers?" Amanda asked.

Mo and the others listened as Dee and Jessica told them about the abandoned herd of cows, Martin's farm, and his condition for helping them out.

"What did you say, Darnell?" Deb asked.

"I said no. Like I said, I don't know shit about farming. And I'm needed here, I know about security. Well, I thought I was needed here, maybe not anymore with GI Joe moving in. We gonna have to find another way to get Martin to help us."

"Dee, don't you see? This is your chance to reinvent yourself," Jessica said.

Mo noticed how she took his hand. *I guess those two patched things up last night.*

"It's like fate. Meeting Martin, the soldiers taking over security. You said it yourself, you did what you had to do. Well now you don't have to do that anymore."

Dee appeared confused by her words. "I'm not a farmer, Jess."

"Neither was Martin. Forty years ago, he was you. And now he wants to help you find your peace. You can do this babe. You have to do this. Oh my God, it's the chance of a lifetime, let someone else handle the guns for a change," Jessica pleaded.

"She's right Darnell. If you've got a chance to get away from the violence you were forced to live with all of your life, take it. And frankly, getting us a food supply is a hell of a lot more valuable right now than any extra security," Deb said.

"A farmer? Damn," Dee said, sitting down heavily in a chair.

"I can picture it, rake in one hand, chewing on a long strand of hay hanging from your mouth," Mo quipped.

"Please, say you'll think about it?" Jessica asked, crouching in front of Dee and taking both his hands.

"Yeah, I'll think about it," Dee said in a bewildered voice.

"Thank you," Jessica said, reaching forward and hugging him.

"Um, guys?" Amanda said. She was standing in front of the window, her back to them.

Mo and the others joined her. In the distance, a long column of trucks was approaching. There was a mix of army vehicles, cube vans, and open pickup trucks. Mo could make out groups of children the size of ants sitting in the back of the pickups. The line of trucks went on forever.

"Oh my God," Mo breathed, "here they come."

"This will be good," Deb said. Mo turned away from the astonishing view to look at Deb. Her serene smile calmed him.

This will be good, he repeated to himself. He returned his gaze to the oncoming group of new arrivals to their community. He reached for Amanda's hand next to him.

ACKNOWLEDGEMENT

I would like to thank my wife, Judith, for putting up with the writing process for over a year. I suspect she had sometimes wished she had "The Unvaccinated" tattooed on her forehead in order to get my attention. Your patience, support, and feedback have contributed to this book's creation just as much as my fingers tapping on the keyboard.

I would also like to thank A.R.W. for her wonderful insights into the plot and characters. It's simply a better book because of her.

Thank you Marianne, my favorite vaccine skeptic. About 18 months after the pandemic broke out, I questioned why she was still unsure about getting vaccinated. Then my overactive imagination asked: what if she's right to be worried? And so, taking it to the extreme as I am prone to do, the seeds of The Unvaccinated were sown. Without her, the story wouldn't exist.

ABOUT THE AUTHOR

Jean Grandbois

Jean has refused to set roots, having lived everywhere from the frozen winters of Alberta, to the scorching heat of Southern California, to the wet and windy Netherlands. He is a firm believer that pizza is the  perfect food (unless you put pineapple on it, that's just wrong). When not writing software, he is writing prose, renovating his house, or making herbal soap with his six-year-old daughter.

Jean has had two shots and a booster, but no dizzy spells. Yet...

Manufactured by Amazon.ca
Acheson, AB

10204169R00216